All My Tomorrows

Donevy Westphal

Cover by Diane Turpin Designs • Diane Turpin—. DianeTurpinDesigns.com

This is a work of fiction. Names, characters, places, and incidents are products of the author's imagination or are used fictitiously. Any reference to actual persons, living or dead, is entirely fictional. All scripture references are from the King James Version.

.

All My Tomorrows
Copyright © 2022 by Donevy L. Westphal

.

Published by Westerness Enterprises LTD Box 52 Casey, Iowa 50048

.

All My Tomorrows / Donevy L. Westphal
ISBN 978-1-7349256-5-4 (first printing)
ISBN 978-1-7349256-6-1 (second printing)
ISBN 978-1-7349256-4-7 (eBook).

Printed in the United States of America

Books by Donevy Westphal

Ebenezer: My Stone of Help Series

If I Should Die
As A Lovely Song
All My Tomorrows

Ebenezer Prequel

Songs in the Night[†]

Other Books

Gene's Story[†]

[†]Coming Soon

Then Samuel took a stone, and set it between Mizpeh and Shen, and called the name of it Ebenezer, saying, Hitherto hath the LORD helped us. (1 Samuel 7:12 KJV)

AND, LO, THOU ART UNTO them as a very lovely song of one that hath a pleasant voice, and can play well on an instrument: for they hear thy words, but they do them not. (Ezekiel 33:32)

TAKE THEREFORE NO THOUGHT for the morrow: for the morrow shall take thought for the things of itself. Sufficient unto the day is the evil thereof. (Matthew 6:34)

DEDICATION

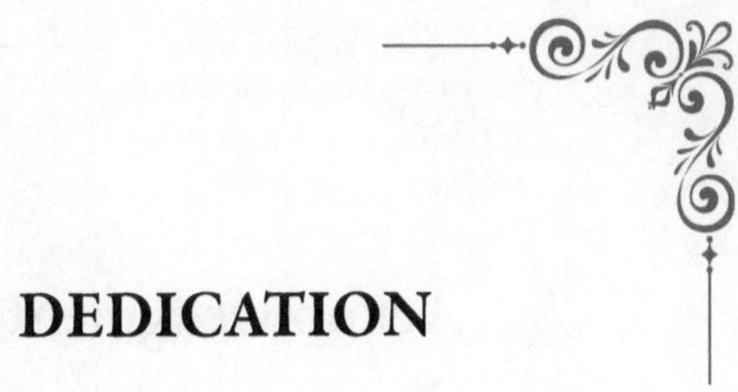

Dedication—This book is dedicated to Cora. Cora is what most writers want. A dedicated reader who anxiously awaits the next book and wants to purchase it immediately—if not sooner. I need at least two million more like Cora.

Just getting to the point of publication is a mile stone, but at this point in the manuscript, the hard work of the task is done. Because of the tireless encouragement of the chosen few who have not flagged in their reinforcement for the project we have accomplished this goal. From long-time personal friends, family members, and newly added recent friends and readers this book is dedicated to that inspiration to finish this step in our journey... and Cora. Thank you, all of you, may you all read and enjoy this installment in the series.

Acknowledgments

Many belong here on the acknowledgment page. Those who have poked, prodded and commiserated with me as I struggled with writing, not just the first book, but the next books in this series—Those who have read the first book and encouraged me to not give up on the second novel. And there are those much closer to home: my son Benjamin, who was my first listener as I read the first draft out loud; My son, Levi, with his encouragement and his technical work without which this could not have happened; Kudos to my husband, Chris, who suffered silently through untold editors and their crazy edits and my mutterings about such editors and edits. I learned much through ACFW and their courses, and Jennifer and Jane my critique partners. And foremost I praise God who prepared me through life and much more through His wisdom to write this story. May this story be a blessing to all who read it.

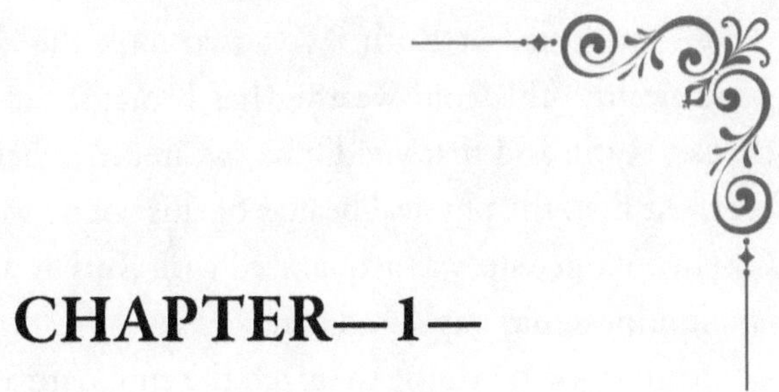

CHAPTER—1—

Gwen closed her eyes, listening to the quiet whispering of the tiny snowflakes accumulating on the large, round window at Dad and Mom MacDonald's hideaway. In her mind, she could see the plethora of wild birds flapping around the bird feeder stationed just a few feet from the window. There would be blue jays, cardinals, finches, chickadees, a nuthatch or two, and many other birds, some of vibrant colors and some of more subdued shades flitting around the feeder.

She pulled her cup of steaming tea closer, inhaling the hot, misty fragrance. She was still in wonder and awe at the peaceful swishing of the snowfall outside the kitchen nook.

After her kidnapping ordeal a few weeks before, all Gwen wanted was to hibernate away from the world, to be safe and secure. Like a child snuggling into a huge feather bed covered by a warm comforter.

A new sound came to her as Ruth O'Brien and Anna MacDonald, chattering and laughing as they stomped snow from their boots on the patio, opened the entry door. Even though she could not catch the gist of what they said, their jumbled conversation as they removed their scarves, coats, and boots were comforting sounds. She opened her eyes and turned, breathing deeply of the tingling, fresh smell, literally a breath of fresh air, wafting into the kitchen.

"We have some baking planned for the rest of the morning." Ruth set the fresh milk and eggs on the kitchen counter.

Gwen smiled at Ruth. "You two look the absolute picture of good health. This cold weather has brought out the roses in your cheeks, Ruth, and that vivid blue sweater matches the color of your eyes." At first, the physical beauty of this young woman had stunned Gwen, but once she was acquainted with Ruth it was her gentle spirit and kindness that impressed her.

Ruth stood on tiptoe to search the cupboard a few minutes, then she and Anna brought their steaming mugs of tea and a large green box with a hinged lid, a clean sheet of paper, and a pencil.

"What kinds of cookies do you like?" Ruth and Anna sat down at the table and began to dig through the box filled with file cards.

"Oh, I don't know." Gwen frowned and scrunched up her mouth. "Let's see, I like butter cookies, sugar cookies... stuff with fruit in it. Tarts, scones, shortbread, stuff like that."

"Wow, you can make those?" Anna's warm brown eyes grew large.

"Well, no, but I can eat them." Gwen laughed.

The two had stopped wide-eyed. "Do we have a treat for you." A hint of laughter smoldered just beneath the surface in Anna's eyes, and she burst forth in a musical laugh.

Gwen smiled. *Oh, God, I don't know what I did to deserve that of all the families I could have become part of, you directed my path to this one.* Her heart swelled with joy at the evidence of the true love of each other and deep love for God.

"UMMM, THE HOUSE SMELLS wonderful," Mrs. MacDonald called as she and Mac wiped their feet then hung their coats in the closet at lunchtime. "It smells like cookies, biscuits, and beef stew. We'll have to leave you girls alone more often!" Mr. and Mrs. MacDonald wandered into the kitchen. Both newcomers stopped at the kitchen door in disbelief.

"Maybe not." Mrs. MacDonald's eyes grew wide. "What have you three been doing? I declare every crook and nanny in this kitchen is stacked with cookies!"

"That's nook and cranny, Mom." Anna smirked and gently corrected her mother's spoonerism. "And look, we have lunch ready also." She cocked her head sideways and looked hopeful.

"You surely do." Mr. and Mrs. MacDonald exchanged amused glances. "I would say you three have been especially busy this morning." Mr. MacDonald raised his eyebrows.

"I would say, dears—" Mrs. MacDonald continued to peruse the kitchen and eating area. "that we have enough cookies to last until, oh, about the middle of May."

"Okay, what are you two chuckling at?" Ruth asked as the older couple continued to survey the area and its contents.

"I think it's the bandanas," Mr. MacDonald said.

"No, I believe it's the flour." Mrs. MacDonald squinted at the scenery.

"It may be a combination of that and several other ingredients." Mr. MacDonald shook his head.

"What are you two muttering about?" Anna asked.

"From the amount of flour sprinkled liberally in the kitchen and on your persons, I would guess that y'all have enjoyed yourselves immensely." Mr. MacDonald's eyes twinkled, and he grinned.

"Well, if we don't hurry and eat these biscuits and beef stew they won't be hot, and biscuits aren't near as tasty cold." Anna frowned. With a good-humored pout, she set plates and silverware around on the table in the kitchen nook.

"This smells good." Gwen brought a casserole dish of baked sweet potatoes with a marshmallow topping.

"You get the biscuits, Ruth, I'll get the stew." Anna went back to the stove.

After their Bible verse and prayer, Mr. MacDonald took the lid off the pan of biscuits. "Looks good enough to eat." He put two biscuits on his plate and passed the biscuit keeper on. After splitting his biscuits he put a goodly portion of butter on each half.

"Anything exciting happening in town, Dad?" Anna passed the sweet potatoes.

"Thank you. No, not much happening yet. In a few weeks, we'll see the Christmas lights and decorations going up." He passed the casserole on and set the bowl of stew beside his plate, then he dished out a serving of stew and passed that on.

"Oh, but Beryls' has some new fabric in and we had to stop at Juan and Laura's store to look at their new shipment of imports," Mrs. MacDonald said.

"How exciting, Mom." Anna held out a dish of broccoli, cheese, and carrots to pass on.

"Cold weather does give one an appetite." Mr. MacDonald took a healthy portion of the vegetables and began eating. After a few minutes he asked, "We're planning on spending a quiet afternoon by the fire. What are you industrious ladies doing this afternoon?"

"We are taking some of the cookies from this morning and going visiting." Anna raised her eyebrows and her nose.

"Oh, you are, are you?" Mr. MacDonald arched his eyebrows, teasing his youngest daughter.

"Yes, we are first visiting Ruth's grandfather and father, then going to Laura's and on to Donna's for the afternoon. We have been sorting through pictures, you know, and that's what we're planning this afternoon, Daddy." She smiled beguilingly.

Mr. MacDonald smiled at his daughter lovingly. "Just don't get too wild—okay, girls?" He laughed.

"We'll try not to." Ruth snickered at the idea.

MR. MACDONALD'S BIBLE and notebook lay open across the portable desk in front of him. Thinking back to his conversation with his daughter, he wondered at the child who could be so like himself and so like her mother, and then like neither of them. All of the other children had inherited his sapphire blue eyes, but Anna's eyes were brown like her mother's. She had a combination of a goodly sense of humor, a ready smile, and was easygoing, seldom getting upset, yet she could be stubborn in her own way and in matters that baffled both of her parents. He sighed.

Mrs. MacDonald looked up as he pulled off his reading glasses. "You about done with your afternoon study?"

"My eyes tend to cross when I try to study like I used to." He shook his head. "Don't know what my world is coming to. I should know everything there is to know by my age."

"That's funny, Mac. When I was younger I kind of thought I knew it all, but now, each year I think I know less..."

"Isn't that the way it goes? I've still got some studying to do, but I need some fresh air."

Mrs. MacDonald smiled. "There's plenty of fresh air outside." She stopped crocheting for a moment. "What a blessing that Gwen and Seth are back together. Have you heard of any place close for sale around here? Gwen is holding up well, but you know the old Ben Franklin saying, Company, like fish, after three days begins to..."

"Yes, I do, but God does give us grace and patience. It could be a difficult time for all of us, to be sure. I think they've passed the bad part. It took an honest and brave heart to see the truth as Gwen did, and then a lot of courage to change."

"This year has had too many close calls. I guess it's good this last one was during a slow time of the year." Mrs. MacDonald bit her lip and shook her head. "But this cold weather can be hard on aches and pains and healing."

"I think this family has had hospital time enough this year for a long, long time. Michael's accident rolling Juan's car, Joshua's two brushes with eternity, and Lewis' truck blowing up a few weeks ago was a close call. Lewis has been kind of slow recuperating but he's doing well with all things considered." Mr. MacDonald ran his fingers through his hair.

"I better see what we have on the menus and make sure supper's on track." Mrs. MacDonald rolled up her crochet project.

"We just take it one day at a time. Lewis was going to grease that wagon. I wonder if he's got it torn apart yet. I'd better go check and see if he needs some help finishing it."

"After I check menus, perhaps I'll pop in and see how the girls are coming with pictures. When Ruth first asked about our *before you moved here time*, I had some mixed feelings on the subject. Now, I believe it has done a lot of good. Donna, who was in on some of the bad times, understands things now that she just accepted before. The others are being drawn into the family in a way they never could have been, and even our grandchildren enjoy the pictures," Mrs. MacDonald said.

Mr. MacDonald stood and stretched. "My old bones seem to get set in their ways faster nowadays than they used to, Ahmanda," he drawled. Holding out a hand he offered, "You want a hand up?"

"Thanks, Mac." She grasped his outstretched hand and stood. "I guess it is time to be busy. Wrap up warm. It hasn't gotten a bit warmer out today." She hugged him.

GWEN SAT ON THE INGLENOOK beside the towering grey fireplace and held her cold hands toward the crackling fire to warm up. "It's going to take me a day or two to get used to this cold weather. It seems like just yesterday it was warm and ninety degrees outside."

"Maybe not yesterday, but it wasn't long ago, and it was much warmer." Donna handed Gwen a mug of hot coffee. "I didn't know if you wanted cream or sugar, but there is some over on the sideboard. I can have one of the kids bring it over."

"That would be great. I found a warm spot and want to warm up just a bit more..."

"Never fear, we have it covered." Ruth swooped in and grabbed the cream pitcher.

"Thank you, Ruth and Anna. You two are amazing." Gwen smiled as they brought the cream and sugar over and she spooned some into her cup.

"We were coming this way anyhow. Are you almost warmed up?" Anna asked.

"I'm working on it. This is such a nice room." Gwen gazed at the beautiful room.

"We have some before and after pictures of the house here. This used to be part of a porch." Donna pointed to part of the living room.

"Wow, that is some renovation project—and this is indeed a wonderful toasty spot." Gwen wrapped her fingers around the mug. "Are those the pictures over on that big coffee table?"

"Yes, some of them at least. Laura and Beth have the rest of them at their house. Let me have the creamer and I'll take the cream and sugar back to the sideboard." Anna set her mug down on the high surround and took the cream pitcher from Ruth.

"Such a beautiful house. I like the colors Donna has used in here. It reminds me of one of those magazines—House Wonderful or some such thing." Gwen turned as the door opened. "I guess we can get started now...hello, you two."

"Hello, hello." Laura waved and turned to hang her coat in the closet and helped Junko do the same.

Gwen, mug in hand, wandered over and sat on the large leather sofa close to the box of pictures. "I don't know how you can categorize these pictures. I guess year by year would work the best?"

"We would need to set up a timeline of some sort. Some of these pictures are getting old and need touching up. This picture is of Lyle, my first husband. We had a very small wedding." Laura handed Gwen a curled faded picture of a thin young man and a much younger image of herself.

"I didn't realize you'd been married before." Gwen studied the snapshot.

"Lyle and I had been high school sweethearts—well, even before high school. It had been his dream to do missionary work, and we began in that direction right out of high school."

"What happened?" Gwen handed the picture back to Laura.

"We ended up in Spain with a small group and worked for a few years. Lyle wasn't ever very healthy." Laura took a sip of her coffee. "At least he realized his dreams of missionary work. He continued to become less able to function and finally passed away."

"I'm sorry to hear that. As you say, at least he was able to fulfill his dream." Gwen patted Laura's hand. "Many people live a whole lifetime and can't say that. And is that where you met Juan?"

"Yes—yes, that's where I met Juan. Lyle taught him the gospel and they were very close friends. Here is a picture of them during some better memories...and me with Juan's sister and brother."

Gwen looked at the picture of a much younger Juan and an older version of the thin young man. She passed that picture on to Junko and the other ladies then perused the next pictures of Laura and several other people at a dinner of sorts. "How many children are in Juan's family?"

"Juan has an older sister, Bella, a younger brother, Manny, and here's their youngest sister Maria." Laura pointed to a picture of Juan and his sisters and brother.

"Your wedding pictures are so gorgeous! Look at those flowers..." Gwen looked longingly at the pictures of Laura's wedding. "Seth and I stood before the preacher at church with only Rachel and Lance as our witnesses. It was a very quiet ceremony. Oh, oh, Juan's estate in Spain is magnificent! We will have to invite ourselves for a visit sometime." She smiled.

Laura gave her a warm embrace. "You're always welcome—You know the welcome mat is always out." Laura wrote the date on the lid of the box, labeled it, and passed it around.

Quietly Junko withdrew a photograph from her purse and handed it to Laura. "Joshua says I should give this to you."

Laura studied the worn photograph of a young teenage girl holding a baby of about two and a toddler of three or four sitting on a bench. The snapshot had seen better as well as worse days. "I cried over that picture so much, the wonder is there is any image left to it." She touched it softly. "This picture was before when we were all together— before the stressful times. Look how cute Joshua and Seth were."

Laura sighed. "James met Lily when he began attending the high school. I was gone when most of the shenanigans she pulled happened. By the time I returned the damage had been done. Sara, Peter, and Joshua were gone. Seth and Rachel were doing their own thing, and I think Lewis was gone as well—the family had fallen apart."

"Well, Lewis was helping John Yevenski with mission work in Arizona. John came from Tennessee to work in our area at the time." Donna looked over the picture. "That's how and where Lewis and I met. A little leaven leaveneth the whole lump." Donna handed the picture around. "Lewis came back once for a short while during that time. He wouldn't talk about that visit when he came back. Something upset him, but he's never told me what it was."

"I wanted things to return to the days when life was simple—" Laura stopped and shook her head. "Just look at them. Joshua and

Seth were so cute. They were a special pair. But Lyle died, and when I returned it was like someone had taken a chunk out of the middle of the family. The six of them were gone."

"Seth and Rachel were still in the Forest City area, but after James's death, nothing was the same. Here's a picture of James and Lily just before they got married." Donna pulled out a picture from the box.

"He's quite handsome, like the rest of you guys." Gwen held the print. "Lily? Is that her name? She looks a bit plain in this picture, not at all a troublemaker."

"Lily was cute in person. She had a comical way of doing things. They look so young in these photos." Laura sorted out several more snapshots. "She could be fun. I think she did enjoy being at the farm. At least at first. Moving on to the next box..."

Anna lifted the lid on the next box of pictures. "These are much happier times."

"Oh, look." Junko held up a picture from the top of the box. "Please to tell about picture and all the names?"

"It was a sunny morning before church. You can tell that because everyone still looks tucked in and neat." Anna laughed. "Beginning in the back here is Laura, Lewis Junior, James, Sara, Peter, and in the front are Rachel, Joshua, Seth, me in my pretty little dress, and the baby is Michael." Anna pointed to each child.

"So, des is James, and des is Sara and Peter we 'ave never yet met?" Junko asked as the picture was passed around and everyone examined the group of children. "Such a nice-looking family—all dressed in their Sunday best." Junko decided at last. "How, did you ever get so many clean dond ready for church? Even the baby?" She wondered out loud.

"Joshua and Seth look full of mischief even then." Gwen pointed at the pair and laughed.

Laura put an arm around Anna and smiled, watching as the pictures circulated and the women each pointed out their special person in the different photographs.

"Look at Lewis sitting on that mule." Donna laughed as she held up a picture of a skinny tow-headed boy in baggy breeches sitting astride a long-legged mule. "I would say he needed a ladder to get up there."

"Yes, well, we were ingenious in finding a way up. We would get on a gate or a fence if Molly would cooperate. Otherwise, we would give each other a hand or a foot up depending on if we were the first child or one of the later ones up." Laura said. "That is the famous—or infamous—Molly O," by the way."

"Molly O'?" Gwen arched her eyebrows questioningly.

"Oh, look at this one." Ruth snickered and handed around another picture of the same mule, but instead of just the skinny boy, now three more skinny kids were posing proudly astride the mule.

"The first child and last were the hardest to get up," Laura said. "Lewis would reach up and grab the mane there, and I would cup my hands. When he stepped into my hands with his left foot I would give him a push up. There was a trick to getting his body up and his right leg over. Then he would reach his hand down, and James would help me get my left foot up and use Lewis' foot for a stirrup. I got talented enough I could grasp Lewis' hand and use his foot like a stirrup and swing up. James was real good at grabbing Lewis' hand and foot also, but it was tricky for Sara because she had to be careful to not pull the person off that was helping her up as well as she had to watch out that she didn't kick Molly O' in the flank."

"Okay, what was that about Molly O'?" Gwen brought the subject back to her question.

"Occasionally you hear Dad say, 'Whoa, Molly! Or, 'Whoa, Molly O." Right?"

"Yes." Donna and Ruth both shook their heads.

"That was the last Molly O'." Laura smiled. "There's quite a story behind it. You'll have to have Dad explain it."

"Oh,—" a disappointed crew chorused.

"What's this picture?" Donna held up a picture of two women standing beside a mule. They were dressed in their Sunday best, and the mule was decorated with ribbons and other finery.

Laura began to laugh. "We will put these pictures into their boxes..." She sorted them into boxes by years. "Except this one." She laid the picture of the women and the mule on the table.

"Is it supper time? I hear car doors outside." Ruth turned as the back door opened.

"Hey, is anybody home?" Seth, Joshua, and Juan brought a blast of cold air into the living room.

"Just us chickens." Anna laughed.

"Someone run up and get Daddy for me, please?" Laura asked.

"Mother. may I?" Joshua teased.

"Don't give me any backtalk, brother." Laura reached up and tweaked his nose.

"Just hold on to your boots, sis. Dad, Lewis, and Mom are coming in right now," Seth said, as another waft of fresh air announced more arrivals.

"Time for a break." Mr. MacDonald held the door and Mrs. MacDonald and Lewis came into the house. "We'll wash up and be right with you good people." The men sashayed to the washroom while Mrs. MacDonald walked into the living room.

"How about some coffee?" Lewis asked when he joined the group.

"I was about to bring some out," Donna said. "Is anyone else ready for coffee?"

"We'll come help." The three cookie makers followed Donna to the kitchen. A few minutes later they came bringing a big platter of cookies, cups, and a large pot of coffee.

"If you kids want some cookies, there are some in the kitchen and some milk as well." Donna interrupted the kids playing games. She poured coffee for the grown-ups.

During a lull in the conversation, Laura handed a picture to her father. Presently the curiosity became unbearable. "Please don't be angry, Daddy. This was just so good, I hoped you wouldn't mind." Laura tried to read his expression.

Mac studied the picture a few seconds longer then handed it to Amanda. Finally, he smiled into his daughter's hopeful blue eyes, as a glimmer of humor twinkled in his own. "Oh, chick-a-biddy, I thought you were just using it for blackmail."

Everyone scrutinized the picture, but the only ones, besides Mr. and Mrs. MacDonald that it brought back memories for were Lewis Jr. and Laura.

"I believe that was the year Peter was born. I was twenty-six, you were thirty-one. Isn't that right?" Mrs. MacDonald asked.

"I believe that's correct." Mr. MacDonald leaned back as he got into his storytelling mode. "We'd had a rough year. An old war wound had plagued me off and on, and I'd been suffering from it. I think it was the Founder's' Day Parade in 1949...I think that was right." He looked at the picture of two women and a mule as it came back to rest in front of him.

"Okay, Dad, come on." Lewis grinned at his father. "Tell the whole story."

"I'm getting there, son...Buddy Thompson and I had been doing some logging work together but with my leg giving me grief, Mom and I were in a tight situation for money."

"Boots," Seth said.

"Shh!" Gwen hissed at him.

"Buddy Thompson's ma was partial to brown, and Amanda was partial to blue, you see," Mac said leading his audience into the story.

"Them women are wearing boots." Seth pointed to the picture.

"Hush!" Gwen frowned. "I know a lot of women that wear boots."

"Not men's boots," he muttered.

"Well, it's like this..." Mr. MacDonald reached for a couple of cookies from the platter, ignoring Seth's interruption. "As I said, it was the Founder's Day Parade, and there was a prize for the best entry in the parade. Fifty dollars, I'm thinking. Anyway, Buddy came up with this great idea." He paused, enjoying the cookie and playing his listeners. "Buddy borrowed his ma's brown dress with the apron and bonnet. I borrowed Mom's blue dress, apron, and bonnet. Buddy even found a purty lookin' wig. I borrowed Molly from a farmer west of us a way off. We had everyone trying to figure out who the women and the mule were. Things were comical, but not going too badly. Look how we decorated ol' Molly there. She had ribbons and all sorts of things. But, like most mules, she could be a contrary ol' cuss. We proceeded about halfway through the route." He paused taking another swallow of coffee and lazily stretching his long legs out in front of himself.

After what seemed like an eternity, "Come on, Dad, finish the story!" Several voices pleaded.

"Don't rush things, kiddos." He finished his cookie. "Well, we got about halfway through the route, like I said, and for whatever reason, Molly decided she had gone far enough. Maybe she didn't like her trappings as well as we did, or maybe they just made her feel out of her element. Did you ever see a mule sit down? She did. Sat right down in the middle of the street and would not budge. We tried numerous things. Carrots, sugar, corn, nothing could coax her to move.

"Of course, the parade stopped for a short while, then everyone just started going around us. Buddy sat down on one side and I sat down on the other. Just sat there in the middle of the street. Even the marching band didn't encourage Molly to stir. It wasn't until Ed

Jones and his banjo pickers came along. Mules can move right along when they get the notion. Molly got the notion right then, and we made a great trio—her running down the street and us running after her.

"She ,with Buddy and I running close behind, caught up with the whole parade and almost finished first. Two gals running after a cussed mule tickled everyone's fancy. Buddy's wig got all crooked and the flower on your ma's hat got to hanging and bobbing at a precarious angle. We won three prizes that day, one for the best entry, one for the most original, and lastly one for the most entertaining." He picked up another cookie.

"Yes, and you were called before the church elders," Amanda reminded him.

Joshua and Seth both whistled in disbelief.

"What?" Joshua's eyes went wide. The idea of their father in his mother's dress and hat, as well as chasing a mule through the streets was hilarious, but that he was called before the elders of the congregation was unfathomable. Their father who was so unquestionably Christian, so upright and conscientious, almost perfect in their sight, being called before the elders?

"Naw, I don't believe it!" Seth considered the information. "What would you be called in question of, a public nuisance?"

"Some of the elders took offense at me wearing women's clothing." Mr. MacDonald smiled.

"Well, I never heard of such a thing!" Gwen's face looked unconvinced.

"Elders have a tough job." Mr. MacDonald sipped his coffee. "In the end, they decided there was no evil intent, but I was instructed to set a better example. You know the elders have a responsibility to watch for our souls." He changed the subject as he stood. "The coffee and cookies were good, and even the memory was good, chick-a-biddy." He chucked his oldest daughter under the chin.

"I'm sorry, Daddy—" Laura blinked. "I just remembered the picture of you and Buddy running after that mule. Folks talked about it for years you know. It became a standard as to how folks could improve on it. I didn't know about ..."

"That's all right, sweetheart." Mr. MacDonald squeezed Laura's hand. "Buddy and I made seventy-five dollars apiece from that parade. When the elders found out we were having financial struggles, along with prayers, suddenly there were offers of work as well. There was no evil intent in our parade incident, or your remembrance either. At thirty-one, and the father of five young 'uns, maybe I ought to have had a little more sense."

"But why did you call her Molly O?" Gwen's face crumpled up in a frown.

"Well, when I borrowed her it was from a family not in our area. Mr. Day told me her name was Molly O. At least I thought that's what he said. Buddy and I hollered it at her all the way down the street. 'Whoa, Molly O, whoa...' She never stopped. She did come to answer to it later, but I was told her name was really Suzie Q. Maybe she was mad at being called the wrong name."

He turned to his wife. "Come on, Molly, I mean Ahmanda, let's go home. Oh—shall we finish that wagon after supper or wait till tomorrow?" He pulled on his boots and coat.

"There isn't much left to do. Morning will be fine." Lewis rubbed his shoulder and grimaced.

"We need to get it done. Have you told everyone we will be opening the barn up on Friday night next week?" Mr. MacDonald asked.

"Yes, sir, we do need to get it done. No, sir, I have not had time to tell anyone except Donna," Lewis said.

"It's official then, everyone. See y'all later." Mr. MacDonald waved, and he and Mrs. MacDonald disappeared out the door.

"What's going on?" Seth raised an eyebrow.

"In the fall we try at least once to clean out the barn and open it up. We have the folks from the congregation come over, and we invite certain friends from the community as well," Lewis explained.

"And then you do a barn tour?" Seth raised both eyebrows.

"It's kind of like pot luck, except we have a singing first, then folks get out their banjos and pick a few songs." Lewis took a sip of coffee.

"That many banjo pickers in this area?" Joshua asked.

"Only Michael that I know of." Lewis selected a cookie.

"So, we all sit around and listen to Michael? Will he even be here?" Joshua asked.

"He makes it back. Thanksgiving and Christmas break—he and a friend, but there are all sorts of instruments. Fiddles, guitars, Ruth's grandpa, and a couple of other people play the harmonica. Bernie plays a mean set of bones, and someone else plays the washtub. We just have a good time." Lewis took a bite of the cookie.

"Does Charlie Anderson bring his accordion?" Joshua grinned at Lewis.

"Why, yes he does." Lewis's face scrunched up in a puzzled frown.

"Sounds like a plan." Seth stood and moved toward the coat rack. "Guess Gwen and I need to be heading out too." He began pulling on his boots, coat, and scarf. "Let me help you, sugar." He held Gwen's coat. "See ya tomorrow." He opened the door and a blast of fresh cold air came swirling in.

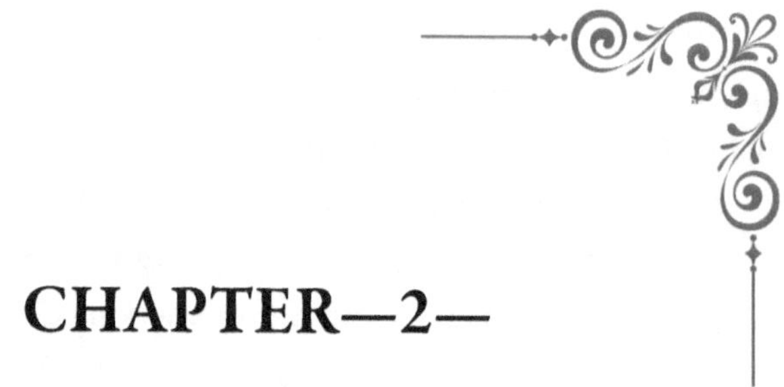

CHAPTER—2—

Ruth sighed and slid wearily into her chair beside her dad, Jack O'Brien, and grandfather Pat O'Brien. Michael winked at her and she smiled in return. She always enjoyed this once a year singing and potluck. However, they had spent a good week preparing the big barn floor by removing wagons, tools, cleaning out any leftover hay, or grain, and setting up tables and decorating.

Ruth smiled at Junko and patted Mai's tiny hand. "I remember the first time Mother and I attended one of these suppers. I was much older but probably looked like Mai—see how big her eyes are? We didn't have near this size of a group then but it was still exciting."

"Yes, Mai's eyes are big. She's thinking what all dis strangers in her uncle's barn?" Junko giggled.

"And tomorrow she'll be back playing among the horses, cows, and wagons." Ruth pointed out as Mai snuggled close on her daddy's lap, hiding in the crook of his arm.

Mai smiled and Ruth smiled back. "You are so blessed—such a darling child," Ruth whispered to Junko.

"She is our little miracle child we thought we would never have," Junko said.

"How are you, Gwen? You look marvelous this evening." Ruth leaned over and whispered as Gwen and Seth sat down. She noted the change in Seth and Gwen's relationship. There seemed to be a fire for each other and for life. Seth was still laid back and easy-going, but the lazy careless ne'er-do-well attitude was gone.

"What a bunch!" Ruth watched Charlie Anderson as he told one of his stories. "I think Charlie has found his match with Mr. M."

As the singing was about to begin, Charlie turned around and whispered something to Ruth's grandpa. Charlie and Pat both grinned and chuckled nodding their heads in agreement. Ruth stole a look at her father, who finished a conversation with Charlie's boy Chuck just as the group grew quiet. Ruth sighed sadly to herself remembering the words of the poem, "Maud Muller": "For of all sad words of tongue or pen, the saddest are these: It might have been!" She was glad the singing began.

GWEN CARRIED HER PLATE to the table and sat beside Ruth at intermission as the potluck began. "I looked up that Proverbs thirty-one, verse sixteen. Just how would Mrs. Worthy go about fulfilling that verse?"

"That man over there?" Ruth nodded toward a stooped elderly man. "His name is Prichard, Mr. Dale Prichard. He doesn't have any children."

"I see." Gwen nodded. "Is he thinking of retirement, or..."

"Moving to town. Rumor is along that line," Ruth said. She smiled as Becky from Mom and Pop's Café seated herself across the table.

"I'm so glad Reuben is coming back." Becky smiled, her dimples flashing.

"Yes, but we're not sure exactly when. Have you heard any more?" Ruth asked.

"No, but it will be good to see him. It was almost a year from when I last heard from him. Then, out of nowhere, I received a letter a few months ago and the letters have been coming regularly." Becky continued to smile, twirling a simple gold ring on her finger.

"Becky, have you met Seth's wife Gwen?" Ruth asked.

"No, I've met Joshua and his family. I have met Seth when he was in the café with Lewis and Michael. But I'm wondering where these fellas find all these good lookin' gals." Becky's dimples chased each other again as she smiled at Gwen.

"Gwen, this is Becky, a good friend of mine and my brother, Reuben. Say," Ruth exclaimed, "I guess we'd better be finishing up our food. Looks like some folks are getting things cleaned up and ready to begin."

"I just love these get-togethers at Lewis'," Becky confided to Gwen as the three women picked up their table service and carried it to a tub, throwing their paper plates in the trash.

"Nice to have met you," Gwen said. Standing on tiptoe, she spied Seth at the front of the seats and dodged around several people, just barely managing to grab his arm.

"What is it, sugar?" He took her hand.

"I didn't know you were going to..." She hesitated. "I didn't know you could play anything," she blurted.

"Well, it's been so long, sweetheart. They're taking a chance, but I reckon I'll give it a shot. Mom plays piano and Dad plays violin, and they taught us music when we were just short stacks. Wish us the best that this goes well." He grinned at her. "You know, sugar, you are the best lookin' gal here. I'm so glad you're my ..."

"Seth, your woman isn't angry at you now, and this isn't the time nor the place, dude." Joshua caught him by the arm.

"I wonder how Dad and Mom ever had children with this bunch around. Someone is always interrupting." Seth laughed. "I'll be back later, babe."

"Come and sit with us, Gwen." Anna linked her arm through her sister-in-law's and pointed out where Donna and Mrs. MacDonald were sitting.

"When I was young, I wished I had a sister. Anna, if I could have chosen a sister or even a whole passel of sisters, I couldn't have chosen better than what I have." Gwen gave an answering smile.

"Living in the same house will either bring people together or tear them apart," Anna said. "Everyone in this family has their oddities, but we try to give each other space enough to be who we are."

"You would think with this size family it would be impossible, but somehow you had to learn to work together." Gwen frowned, puzzling over the idea.

"We all grew up working together, and we learned to respect others. I'd never thought about it, but love and respect go a long way in life."

"Do the ladies play instruments also?" Gwen whispered as they took their seats.

"Yes, we do duets, solos, and often families will sing or play instruments together."

"I'm wondering..." Gwen began to voice a question that had nagged at her for the last two weeks. But with the first notes from the violin all conversation stopped. Gwen settled back in her seat with a new question.

"Wow, and I didn't even have to buy a ticket." She turned to Ruth during a break. "I've never heard such a variety of music played so well. Where did Father MacDonald study music? I haven't heard anyone able to produce the different sounds that he has from his instrument—and I mean good sounds. I've tried making music with a violin before and I did make sounds, but no one wanted to hear them." Gwen snickered.

"I know what you're saying. I've tried getting that violin to say good things, and all it said for me was, no, no, no." Ruth laughed. "But talking, laughing, and singing seem as natural for his violin as from the human throat. I don't know where he studied...I'm still learning about the family, just as you are."

"I'm sure you are ahead of me. I didn't even know Seth could play the guitar. Nine years I've spent with him..." Gwen frowned.

"Until the MacDonald family moved here, I didn't know Grandpa could play the harmonica or that Dad played the saxophone. Reuben and I took music lessons in school, but life began with us, I guess. We didn't know our own family... or ask," Ruth said. "I love the mix here. The old mountain ballads, new songs, some instrumental, some accompanied by singing. It's a good mix, especially since it's improvised."

"That guy over there—" Gwen pointed to an older, silver-haired gentleman holding an accordion while getting settled on a high three-legged stool. "He's funny. That story he told about your Grandpa O'Brien and him catching a pig...I've never heard anything so hilarious."

The group on stage began with Charlie Anderson playing his accordion, Michael on the banjo, and one of the other neighbors using a washtub for an instrument. It was about midnight when they put their instruments to bed and closed with a prayer and a hymn.

"We ran out of time. Ruth didn't sing, or your mom either, for that matter. I wonder why." Gwen mused as she and Seth crunched their way through the snow toward Mac and Amanda's.

"You're probably right. Ran out of time. That and for the same reason you didn't, babe." Seth looked up at the night sky.

"Well, I didn't know anybody, and I wasn't prepared." Gwen wrinkled her brow. "Ruth has a beautiful voice."

"You'll have to ask her then, sugar." He stopped walking and breathed deeply of the frosty air. "You were right."

"About what?" She blinked in confusion. Looking around, she realized they were at the arbor.

"This is heavenly in the moonlight."

She suddenly felt the nip of the soft breeze kissing the glistening snow as well as her nose and cheeks. She was aware of the dark velvet blue of the night sky studded with brilliant cold white lights. It was colder than she could ever remember, but there was a freshness, as if the earth had been purged of everything unclean. The tree branches whispered, softly answering the questions of the breeze.

"Oh, Seth, I'm sorry," she apologized after a short pause as they both felt the bond between them strengthen.

"Sorry for what?" His very soul throbbed with the beauty and intensity of the moment.

"I wasted all those beautiful moonlit nights this autumn when it was not only beautiful but also warm." She smiled softly, running her mittened hand over his cheek.

"Every season has its beauty, but you, sugar plum, are always beautiful to me." He softly wrapped his arms around her and gazed into her luminous eyes. "It can't be any worse than all those years I wasted."

"You didn't waste those years all by yourself. I told you about Melissa, my young seatmate on the airplane back to my estate. Her father shared an hour at the coffee shop in Chicago. He helped me see myself and our relationship in a different light." She laid her head on his chest and could feel his heart beating steadily. "Seth, I love you so very much."

"Oh, Gwen—" He bent to kiss her just as a wet snowball splattered against his hat and sent cold rivulets of snow slipping down under his shirt collar.

"Snowball fight!" a chorus of voices shouted gleefully from several different hiding places.

"Watch out, babe!" Seth hurriedly bent to scoop up snow for his snowball. "You better duck inside the arbor. I'll take care of these ya-hoos!" He emphasized as he let his weapon fly toward a dark figure.

"What? And miss all the fun?" Gwen stooped down to scoop up her own handful of snow. There was a big splat as a wet snowball splattered on the arbor where her head had been. "I'll get you, Anna

Louise MacDonald!" Gwen cried sending her snowball hurtling at her sister-in-law. A sudden good-natured howl indicated Gwen had made good on her threat.

After about twenty minutes of snowballs flying everywhere, Mr. MacDonald called a truce. "Hot chocolate and doughnuts inside, kiddos."

The group traipsed into the little house in the side of the hill laughing, rosy, and wet, but none the worse for their experience.

Gwen snuggled back into her little niche, dunking her doughnut into hot chocolate while quietly surveying the diverse group. Ever-so-polite Juan was watching over Laura like a mother hen over her chick. Donna was seated next to Laura as Lewis Jr. brought a tray with mugs of hot chocolate and doughnuts for the group. The two couples had developed a close loving relationship through the years of suffering as well as the rejoicing—the hard times and the good times together. It had given them a common bond along with their common faith in the Lord.

Michael and his college acquaintance were amusing several people with college stories. Joshua and Seth were supervising some very groggy children who toasted marshmallows at the fire. Golden-haired Anna and auburn-haired Ruth, and dark-haired Junko with heads bent together whispered seriously. Mr. and Mrs. MacDonald were wending their way through the family gathering, laughing and encouraging everyone. Within a few minutes, they found their way to Gwen's nook.

Mrs. MacDonald smiled and sat down beside Gwen, patting her hand lovingly. "I'm so glad you came back, dear."

"You'll never know how glad I am to be back." Gwen looked at her and smiled. "I wouldn't miss the next fifty years for anything."

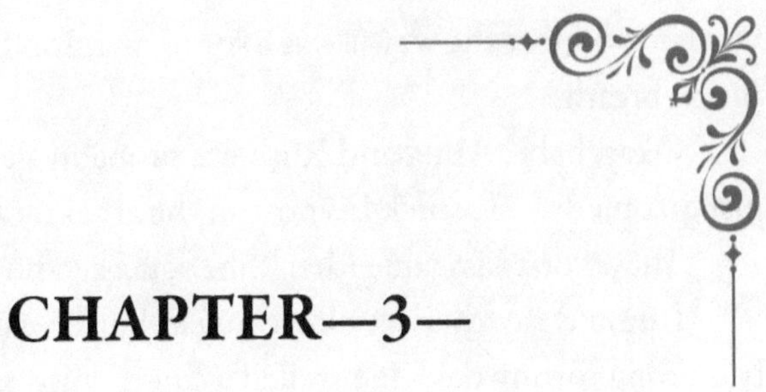

CHAPTER—3—

"Just don't wake me up, Mac." Amanda groaned, rolling over and stretching.

"Okay, Ahmanda. Go back to sleep." He good-naturedly switched off the small lamp by his dresser. As he bent to kiss her on the cheek, she peeked at him with one half-opened eye.

"You are a nut." She sat up, opened both eyes, and laughed at him.

"Guilty as charged," he said. "You are soft and warm and should go back to sleep. Some of the girls will be up preparing breakfast." He insisted as she groaned again and slid her feet into her shoes.

"Soft and warm? I feel black and blue. I'm sure I outgrew snowball fights twenty years ago!" She lamented as she turned her closet light on and found her clothes.

"We probably did, but the kids haven't noticed it yet, the rascals." His face was serious and solemn.

"But, Mac, you threw the first snowball." She stopped and stared at him.

"Imagine that." He winked, his face still solemn.

"Aye, you're the rascal." She gave him a gentle swat. "And the fruit didn't fall far from the tree." She walked out the door he held for her.

"YOU ARE ANNOYING," Gwen muttered as she pulled the covers around her head to avoid Seth. "And I don't want a kiss. The night was far too short the way it was. Not to mention I feel like I have elephant breath."

"Okay, babe, Anna and Ruth are probably getting breakfast. I'll just go quietly." He stuck his nose in the air as if offended.

"They won't kiss you either." She squeezed both eyes shut.

"I should say they wouldn't, sugar, but breakfast is a very good beginning for my day." He trailed a finger softly across her forehead and down her cheek. "Did you know—" He snickered. "—your hair is sticking up right here?" He gently tugged at a lock of her cinnamon-colored hair.

"That's great, partner. Go get your breakfast and let me sleep." She mumbled without opening her eyes.

"I can take a hint." He huffed out the door, smiling.

"Sorry, I'm so late." Seth apologized as he entered the breakfast nook. "Gwen will be out in ten minutes. Say, Mom, you have the same problem Gwen has." He chuckled.

"What's that, kiddo?" she asked.

"You look like you slept in your hair," he said.

Mrs. MacDonald looked at her husband. "He hasn't looked in the mirror has he?" She shrugged in Seth's direction.

Seth smoothed down his hair sheepishly, and turned toward the kitchen. "How's my favorite sister this morning?"

"Favorite sister?" Anna exclaimed raising an eyebrow. "Oh, I see. I'm the one with the food." She stuck out her tongue and made a face at him.

Ruth chuckled at their antics. "I have never in my life been acquainted with such a family!" She shook her head.

It was ten minutes exactly when Gwen sauntered through the living room and into the kitchen. "We missed a few things in the clean-up last night." She threw a paper plate and some disposable tableware away. Carefully she placed two cups in the dishwasher. "How can he be eating?" She pointed at Seth who was wiping up his plate with his last piece of toast. "I feel as if I just ate an hour ago." She rolled her eyes.

"I'm making up for a deprived childhood— growing up we only had breakfast, lunch, and supper," he said.

"YOU CAN'T KEEP HER secluded forever. Somebody is going to find out about her sooner or later." Nathaniel scowled at Michael. "That auburn-haired gal is a beauty, but so is your sister, and I wouldn't mind being first on her list." He didn't notice the dark look that crossed Michael's face.

Michael added his armload of chairs to the growing number on a cart they were loading in preparation for returning them to the Beetle River Community building.

"I don't keep Anna secluded, brother. She has worked as many places as I have, Australia, Spain, New Zealand, India, and places in Europe that I can't even remember. If I had known you were such a jerk, I wouldn't have invited you." Michael's brows drew together and anger showed in his face. "You don't get either one. Life and love aren't a reach and grab like a little kid after a pretty toy, or a baby after candy." He scowled.

"Don't get your dander up." Too late, Nathaniel realized his mistake. "I just can't help notice how exceptionally pretty those two are. Fine looking young Christian ladies who are not married, and if you hadn't noticed, I'm not married either." He attempted to smooth things over.

"Well." A muffled voice from the front of the wagon startled the two young men. Lewis Jr., Michael's oldest brother, spoke icily as he stood up. "I assure you, Brother Nathaniel, you will behave like a gentleman toward our sister Anna and Ruth, and every other woman in our family young or old." Lewis emphasized as he wiped his large hands on a grease rag and stood beside Michael.

"Hey! Y'all need any help?" Seth's voice called from the other side of the manger as he wandered into the barn. "Whoa, Nellie." He ran a gentle hand over the old mare's side and resting his gloved hand on her haunch, he spoke softly. She barely acknowledged him as she continued to rustle in her hay contentedly. He ducked through the manger and came out on the machinery side. Casually he walked up beside the other two brothers.

Nathaniel gazed from one to the other and came to rest on the third brother. "I honestly meant what I said," he stuttered. "If I get out of line just let me know—gently."

Seth was not quite sure what was going on, but he could add two and two. "I'm sure we will, brother. Does anyone need any help?" Seth repeated.

"Not me." Nathaniel spoke quickly and almost comically. From the look on his face, Nathaniel didn't feel necessarily reassured.

"Sure." Lewis gave Michael's acquaintance a quizzical glance. "We are just putting things in their places. Let's get these feed barrels and things over here put away."

"Say—" Seth picked up a heavy hay rope and began carrying it toward its hook. "—that meal over at Laura and Juan's that we men are supposed to be planning for the ladies? Juan has a suggestion that really has merit." Seth continued to explain the idea quietly as they moved machinery and supplies back to their normal places.

A WEEK LATER AT LAURA'S in preparation for the special supper, Ruth's attention was focused intently on the task of braiding Junko's long thick, black hair into a single plait.

"Dear Ruth." Junko smiled at their images in the mirror. "You are such a comfort."

"Why, thank you. But what makes you say such a thing?" Ruth worked the braid into a circle then secured it with pearl-tipped pins.

She fastened a wreath of pink apple blossom petals as a contrasting color that matched Junko's apple blossom pink and white satin gown. "I think that will do very nicely." She looked over her handiwork critically.

"You always seem to know what makes me feel better. Being around you makes me feel happy." Junko's words were simple.

Ruth brushed a stray hair out of her face. She had been busy all afternoon as the women prepared for the special evening meal the men were preparing down stairs at Laura and Juan's house. Yet now as focused as she was on helping Junko, there was a sudden clutching at her heart and a surge of fear that she did not understand. Was Junko just a little more pale lately? Or was she lacking in her usual energetic output? Ruth searched her memory for something. Something elusive that would have been an answer to why she had suddenly felt such a panic. She couldn't recall anything solid. However, the fear remained.

She smiled encouragingly at their images in the mirror, hers with the auburn hair, fair skin, and large blue eyes in the background and Junko, so like the perfect Japanese doll. Seated in the foreground of the mirror, she looked as if she were a painting from a porcelain plate, with her black hair and gentle, beautiful eyes.

"Oh, no!" Junko groaned as the smoke alarm downstairs sounded again for the third time in the hour.

"I knew this didn't feel right." Mrs. MacDonald, standing in the doorway, grimaced and rolled her eyes. "It was with great reluctance that I accepted this offer. It just doesn't seem right, the men preparing a meal for us, and all of us getting dressed up like this." She clucked in disapproval.

"No, it doesn't feel quite right." Donna frowned. "And tomorrow we will spend all day trying to clean the kitchen." Her words seemed prophetic with the number of times the kitchen smoke alarm had sounded. There was not much smoke, and there did not seem to be any danger of fire, so everyone continued their preparations as the men had instructed them.

"Ruth, I honestly don't know what we are going to do with you." Laura sighed and shook her head. "It's almost the appointed time for the supper gong, and Junko is right. Look at you... Beth, you and Mai run down and tell your papa we need a few extra minutes here." Laura dispatched her messengers to the kitchen. "Come on, girl," Laura said as they whisked Ruth into Laura's room. "We have to watch you almost as much as we do Mom."

"What are you talking about?" Ruth's eyes grew large and bewildered.

"Ju 'ave spent all afternoon helping all else prepare for dis evening," Junko gently scolded.

"We have all been busy this afternoon." Ruth frowned.

"You are a very lovely young woman, and anything you wear will look lovely, even that pretty Sunday dress," Mrs. MacDonald said. "However, the rules were you must wear something special."

"Shh." Beth put a finger to her lips as the two giggling girls returned from their mission and seemed about to burst. "I told Papa, he says okay," Beth repeated to her mother.

"*Muy bien, chiquita, gracias.*" Laura hugged her daughter. "This, Ruth, was for your Christmas surprise." Laura and Anna pulled a large box from Laura's closet. Lifting the lid they took from the tissue paper-lined box a gorgeous deep-blue velvet dress. As they held it up, the others in the room involuntarily caught their breath. Before Ruth had time to protest, the women had her nice Sunday dress replaced with the new special one. "Anna found this at my dressmaker's in Spain. She said it had your name all over it." Laura arranged the full three-quarter-length sleeves and pulled the tulip-shaped skirt into place.

"Oh, Momma mia!" Beth knelt to help shake out the lace-gored skirt, while Mrs. MacDonald fluffed the matching stand-up lace collar into position.

"Sit down." Laura began to pull the pins out of Ruth's auburn mane. "Mom, you start brushing here and Junko and I will go find some hair accessories. What style ought we use here?"

"Let me have the brush and comb. I don't know what style you want. I'll just brush till you get back." Mrs. MacDonald started gently combing Ruth's hair. "What do you want, Ruth, a braid, or what?"

"There are several styles pictured there." Ruth pointed to a bulletin board with current hairstyles. "Something that can be accomplished quickly..."

"Look what we found," Laura said as she and Junko returned triumphantly holding up their treasures. "We'll have this done fast enough. You start on that side, Junko. I'll work over here. Poof it up a bit more... like this—"

"I see. Dat looks nice. I like it." Junko's skilled fingers worked the hair into a simple yet elegant crown.

Laura secured Ruth's hair with jewel-tipped hairpins then placed a small golden circlet in the center.

Mrs. MacDonald inspected their work critically. She fingered the lace collar. "We need a brooch here."

Laura retrieved a silver-blue cameo from her jewelry box. "Aye," she breathed. "That is just perfect, for a perfect person." She brushed a kiss on Ruth's cheek. *"Diga a tu papai que estamos listas."* Laura sent the girls off with their message.

Beth and Mai clasped hands. Smiling and whispering, the conspirators left the room, returning almost immediately. Beth informed her mother. "Papa says everything is ready."

"Let's go then, girls." Mrs. MacDonald surveyed the group as she held the door open for them. The gong sounded to let them know it was time for supper, and they all cautiously descended the stairs just as the men appeared from the dining room.

Laura stopped suddenly. "Juan, I didn't know…" Her eyes were wide. "You look absolutely the most handsome—"

"Mr. Alvarez," Mr. MacDonald addressed his son-in-law, "I don't believe I have ever seen such lovely ladies anywhere. What do you think?"

"I believe, Mr. MacDonald, that this is true—one hundred percent." Juan took Laura's hand and smiled at her.

"Lewis Elijah MacDonald, I do believe you are the orneriest man I have ever known." Mrs. MacDonald sputtered. "Look at you—I'm almost speechless. Lovely ladies? Lewis, you look unbelievably dashing and debonaire. Was that why you men had to have that day in the city?"

"Juan's tailor was hard-pressed to get everything finished." Mr. MacDonald took her hand. "He did have to call in reinforcements."

"So, do you think they are surprised?" Seth adjusted his tie and cummerbund.

"I'd say so," Joshua said.

"Just when did you come up with this plan?" Gwen asked placing her hand in the crook of Seth's arm as he escorted her into the dining room.

"We fully intended to cook the meal ourselves. We, being bears of very little brain. However, king of the grill here, Juan, suggested the tuxedos and caterers. Much more impressive to the ladies, we decided. Much nicer than anything we might dish up," Seth said.

There was a pause as each man seated his lady, Michael attending to Ruth, and across the table Nathaniel seated Anna.

"Several things puzzle me." Gwen raised her eyebrows. "Mainly, what about the smoke and smoke alarm?"

"Ah, that was Joshua's idea. Making sure the smoke alarm is working properly." Seth winked at Gwen.

"No, no, Mother." Gwen looked down the table to where Mrs. MacDonald was seated. "Mr. MacDonald the elder cannot be the orneriest man. I'm thinking maybe his sons have caught up with him somewhere along the way."

Juan cleared his throat. "Supper is waiting. Let's have our Bible reading and prayer so we can attend to it."

"King Lemuel's mother must have had wives and ladies in mind such as I am proud to have with me here." Mr. MacDonald opened his Bible and began reading. "The words of King Lemuel: the oracle which his mother taught him..." He finished the chapter with: "'Give her of the fruit of her hands; and let her works praise her in the gates.' As the father of the most lovely ladies, in word and deed, I want to say, thank you very much."

"Lewis," Mrs. MacDonald said, "I can only speak for myself, but because of your leadership and example you have made it easier for me to be what I need to be."

"WHAT IS WRONG WITH your friend?" Ruth whispered to Michael who was seated next to her. "He seems very clumsy this evening."

"Maybe it's the suit. Or maybe he's never been around so many stunning ladies before." Michael took a sip of his iced tea and smiled at Nathaniel, seated across from him.

"I thought he was supposed to be polished and well-mannered." She closed one eye.

Michael laughed. Dropping his head, he leaned toward Ruth and whispered. "Ruth, I am so glad that Nathaniel is the only other single fellow here."

"Why is that, Lancelot?" She smiled in a conspiratorial manner.

"I wouldn't want to have to keep any more yahoos in line. You and Anna are entirely too gorgeous." Michael shrugged.

"Oh, I see," Ruth said. She watched in fascination as Nathaniel almost dropped his buttered roll.

"It's like this, my lady. Mr. Nathaniel there looks quite the part of a gentleman dressed in his tux. But there is more to being a gentleman than getting dressed up. Mom and dad have taught us how to act and given us practice in manners and how to handle ourselves, yet even then it can be a challenge." Michael sat back as the caterer removed his salad plate.

Ruth smiled at Anna who gave a slight shrug. "You may be right, but..." Ruth puckered her brow at Michael's explanation.

"And you, my lady, are beautiful," he said.

"Are you looking forward to the next semester?" Ruth ignored his comment.

"I'm certainly glad this is my last semester. How about you, Nat?" He addressed the beleaguered young man who jumped and sloshed his glass of iced tea.

"What?" Nathaniel asked as he dabbed at the small spot of moisture on the tablecloth.

"I'm glad this is my last semester. How about you?" Michael repeated his question.

"I'm glad it's your last semester too." Nathaniel poked fun at Michael.

Anna and Ruth laughed and Michael frowned good-naturedly at Nathaniel. "I guess it's unanimous at least."

"I THOUGHT THE EVENING went well," Ruth said as she and Michael strolled toward Mac and Amanda's home.

"Yes, even poor Nat warmed up eventually and seemed to enjoy himself. Did you ever notice how the stars seem so much brighter here away from the city lights?" Michael paused, looking at the sky.

"I'm glad the wind has died down. This afternoon it was almost trying to tear the roof off the house. The stars are so bright on these clear, cold winter nights I feel as if I could reach up and touch them." She stared up at the sky in wonder.

"I love the cold, crisp air. The winter here is so much different than it is back east. I guess I can't choose which I like the best. One isn't better than the other they are just different."

"Have you decided what you will do after you graduate?" Ruth asked.

"No, I've had several offers. Different places. I'm such a family person. Those decisions are tough."

"I understand. I'm not adventurous at all. Some people travel the world. For me, my home here is my world."

"I suppose because of our previous problems with James and watching things tear our family apart, I am very...maybe protective? I don't know the word. I think it makes what we have here more precious."

Michael was almost his usual self during the evening. He was courteous and funny, verbally jousting with others in his family as well as Nathaniel, but Ruth felt a difference. Now as she walked beside him, her gloved hands shoved deep into her winter coat pockets, she sensed his serious, muted disposition. In one way she wanted to shrink away from something, but she didn't know what.

"I'm sorry I made you unhappy this evening."

"Oh? When was that?" She asked.

"When I told you that you are beautiful."

"Everyone was beautiful tonight."

"That is true but... if there is one fault in your character, Ruth, it is that you are so sensitive to a compliment. You look very nice, not just tonight, but many times. Yet everyone is supposed to act as if you aren't."

"Anna was beautiful, Junko was beautiful, Laura... your mom..."

"I can't feel it would be right for me to tell my sisters-in-law they are beautiful, and on occasion, I do mention to my sisters...and mom...how fabulous they look. But I'm supposed to ignore you?"

Ruth felt the breeze stirring the fur on the hood that framed her face. She thought over his words and at last stammered, "I... don't quite...understand." her words were punctuated by little white clouds of frost. "I really don't understand," she repeated perplexed. "I am thankful for the blessings God has given me, but to dwell on physical attributes... would be vain. The Bible does admonish, grace is deceitful, and beauty is vain."

"You are right, Ruth," Michael said. "Too many people are caught up in selfish, self-worship. And like Mom sometimes says, praise to the face brings open disgrace. But all of us want to look nice..."

"Why— Michael, you are quite handsome, and you don't seem to dwell on yourself."

"Thank you, my lady." His tone was almost bitter.

"For what?" She gazed up at him wide-eyed with the wonder of his words.

"When someone pays you a compliment, all you have to do is say thank you, Ruth Kathleen O'Brien." He tickled her nose with the fringe from her scarf.

"I see you are right, Lancelot." She teased smiling at him.

"Are you sure?" he questioned lightly.

"Yes, I'm sure...wait." She held up a hand. "Sure about what?"

"That you won't marry me?"

"Thank you." Ruth's heart ached at the quiet look in his eyes.

"For what?" He looked confused.

"When someone pays you a compliment all you have to do is say thank you." Ruth used his former words.

He stopped so quickly that she had to turn back toward him. Ruth looked up into his face. Surely he hadn't grown any taller during the last three months, but he had changed. In some way, he was more mature.

"Michael?" Ruth would have preferred returning to the light-hearted relationship they previously enjoyed, but they were no longer children. She had never been afraid of Michael. He was the boy she loved— as a second brother. She was not afraid of him now, but her heart twisted within her. "Michael, what?" She was puzzled and perhaps she was a little frightened. Michael who was always so kind, funny, and thoughtful, who had always been there when she needed him—what change had taken place in him all of a sudden? Or had he changed so gradually that she just had not noticed... until now?

"Are you mocking me?"

His words sent a chill up her backbone. "Oh, no, Michael. I am quite serious. I take your offer as a sincere and wonderful compliment." She reached out to touch his coat sleeve. "I'm just sorry I can't accept," she said with sadness. Her face was framed by the dark blue fringe that only added to her beauty, for her eyes, always large and vivid blue, were even more so at that moment. Artificial color could not have made her lips and cheeks any more of a perfect color.

"I have tried to bear in mind that..." He said softly absorbing the memory of her image that evening. "...that it is important to be the kind of godly man to be worthy for a Christian woman to give her love to. Maybe in some way you don't think I've earned that right?"

"Michael Hosea—" The old familiar name slipped off her tongue easily, but with a different ring to it somehow. "I just know that you and I have things to do, and right now they don't include each other. In a short while, you will meet someone who will change your life. You must be ready for that change."

"Ruth—" He thought better of what he planned to say. "I guess I will try to become the man that is ready for the commitment to the woman I love, my lady." There was no teasing in his voice or manner.

"My dear friend," her eyes implored, "just be yourself. Just be your dear, loving self."

CHAPTER—4—

"**T**onight's the night." Laura and Junko were busy decorating the living room for the soup supper that evening. "The holidays always hold a place in my heart," Laura said. "So many pretty surprises every year."

"Are ju excited?" Junko asked. "Does all know who should, and no one who should not?"

"We have tried to be very careful, and I think we are going to be able to pull it off," Laura said. "For years we had no letters. Now since Rachel was here, it's like a floodgate has been opened. What do you think, will this red and green go here?"

"Dat look vury nice there. Try thees ribbon and maybe candy cane too?" Junko added just a touch here and there to make the decorations look professional.

"That is just right." Laura tweaked a pinecone into place. Standing back she studied the window decoration they had just finished and smiled at the overall effect. "It looks like one of those postcard pictures with frosty magic in the air. And now with our secret surprise—the world wrapped in a snowy blanket is a perfect present of sparkling diamonds and frosted silver. Just beautiful. So, has Joshua decided on a house yet?" Laura changed the subject.

"I tink so. It 'asn't been so easy, but 'e tinks 'e found a nice place. Just needs a leetle work." Junko chuckled.

"Eduardo and Juanita have most of the meal and everything planned and cooking for tonight. Juan and the fellows will meet Peter and his family at the airport in Hermon, Sarah and Bob and Rachel's families will meet them at Tweedle Dee's. Mom and Dad will be coming here shortly because I, of course, needed extra help." Laura smiled at the excuse they had used. "Oh, there they are now!" A car drove into the drive.

"Jes, Mai was supposed to catch the ride here from playing with the cosins. This cold and snow, I 'ave never seen such before, but Mai loves it and all the family, so much she loves." Junko cocked her head sideways listening as footsteps and a knock sounded at the back door.

"Anybody home?" Mr. MacDonald called as he opened the door from the breezeway.

"Come on in," Laura called at the sound of feet stomping in the laundry room, the rustle of coats being hung in the closet, and Mai's tiny voice piping away.

"Watch it, kiddo. Leave your boots over here out of the way, sweetheart." Mrs. MacDonald encouraged. "Well—" Mrs. MacDonald, at last, made it into the living room. "Say, you two have done an excellent job here. I don't see why you need Dad and me, dear." She gave Laura a one-eyed smile.

"Sometimes I just like to have you two around," Laura said. "I do need some help upstairs, and since Eduardo and Juanita are tied up with preparations for supper, it would be very helpful if Dad could get the driveway and some of the paths cleared off."

"Well, let's get at it then, girl," Mrs. MacDonald said. "We will have to hustle to have everything done by this evening."

"By this evening?" Laura stopped in suspicious surprise.

"Why, yes. That's when you want it done isn't it?" Amanda asked wide-eyed.

"Well, I guess so. It would be lovely to be all finished by this evening." Laura wondered if her parents knew about the surprise being planned for them.

"I'll carry some decorations up for you if you know what you want. I don't want you overworking in your condition." Mrs. MacDonald raised her eyebrows at Laura.

"Here, Mom, you take this box, and, Junko, here's one for you. I'll bring the dust mop." She stopped and smiled at her mother. "I have a bit of dusting to do in the big window at the top of the stairs before we hang these decorations."

"This is such a beautiful room, here at the top of the stairs." Mrs. MacDonald picked up the dust mop and started whisking the top of the upstairs window. "Talk about picturesque. You sit down over there in that stuffed chair, while Junko and I do the decorating." She leaned the long-handled duster along the wall and set up the ladder.

"I'm not an invalid— but I'm grateful for the help. This pregnancy is at the cumbersome stage. It has been quite awhile since the last baby." Laura fanned herself.

"I certainly don't want you on this ladder, girl. Junko, hand me up that string of lights, please." Mrs. MacDonald took charge.

"I tink dees lights here will look nice. You agree?" Junko held up a string of soft white Christmas lights.

"With the porcelain houses and the rest of the decorations, those will be so pretty." Mrs. MacDonald held up the lights. "Like twinkly stars— Oh, good, Mai—you came in just at the right time. You and Grandpa can help put up the houses, trees, and scenery. Then we can catch a cup of tea before heading home."

"That looks perfect." Laura smiled at her helpers. "I'm sure Juanita has some hot tea brewing. Let's call it good for now—there's the phone. Pardon me while I go...Yes—" Laura answered the phone in her bedroom. "Okay. That will be excellent, *mi amore*. Talk to you later, then. Goodbye." She replaced the receiver. "That was Juan." She joined her company downstairs. "He has picked up a few things and will be home early."

"We won't keep you long then. Thank you, Juanita." Mr. Mac-Donald took his cup of tea. "I kept the snowblower busy. I made a maze in the backyard for the children to play fox and geese tomorrow. But it is time for us to be running along home." Mr. MacDonald blew on his cup of hot tea before he took a sip.

"Just enjoy your tea, Daddy, there's no rush." Laura took a deep breath. "Mom, Junko, and I have worked diligently this afternoon, and it doesn't hurt to relax a few moments." She closed her eyes.

"Are you all right?" Mrs. MacDonald had a concerned look on her face.

"Yes, I'm fine, Mom." Laura opened her eyes and took a sip of tea. "I wish I had an instant record and replay that I could absorb the ambiance of this moment and save it forever. Spending time with you people...We do a lot of things together but too often we rush. We take our time for granted. We seldom tell those we love how dear they are." Laura smiled lovingly. "Thank you so much for helping me today, and for being here for us."

"You've been working too hard, chick-a-biddy." Mr. MacDonald smiled at her, a tinge of scolding in his voice. "We know you appreciate us, but it's good to hear anyway. Still, you need to rest and not get overworked."

"I can certainly speak from experience, dear," her mother agreed. "The first babies were not near so tiring as the last ones. Michael was definitely harder on me than you and Lewis Junior. There's a certain point when you notice things that didn't seem important before."

"Well, Mother." Mr. MacDonald drained his cup and stood. "It's time we were getting back home so we can clean up for supper."

"We'll see you in a bit. You go lie down and rest and don't get over exhausted. Junko, make sure she gets a bit of rest." Mrs. MacDonald squeezed Laura's hand and hugged Junko.

"You know they have something planned." Mr. MacDonald grinned at his wife as they walked to the car. "I'm quite sure they didn't need us to putter around Laura's all afternoon." He cheerfully backed the car around and drove out the driveway.

"Well, it's their surprise. I don't care to ruin it for them. I confess I'm concerned. Laura looks tired out. I just hope she listens to our advice."

"We need to stop by Lewis' for a moment after we are cleaned up. He said he needed me to look at something for him. We'll have to scurry, Ahmanda," he drawled.

"It won't take me long to be ready for supper. I didn't work that hard."

"I DON'T KNOW WHY LEWIS thought I needed to come in with you. I didn't think you'd be that long. We'll need to be back to Laura's in thirty minutes—no less than thirty minutes, Mac. I could've stayed in the car." Mrs. MacDonald scolded as they entered Lewis' house from the deck.

"You could have but you never know how long Junior and I will be. He wants me to look over some house plans. We're here," Mr. MacDonald called to Donna from the doorway.

"Come on in," Donna answered from the kitchen. "I'll be with y'all shortly. Have a seat by the fire. Lewis will be down in a few minutes."

"Oh, he's already here," Amanda said as they entered the living room. The figure sitting on the sofa rose to meet them. Amanda felt confused. "Lewis?" Her eyes focused and refocused and she became aware that several people entered the room at that moment. "Peter?" Her voice broke at the familiar but unfamiliar name.

"Dad? Mom?" The voice was deeper, more mature, yet still familiar.

It had been a long time ago in a somewhere else time. It had been twelve long years since Peter had left. He had never been good at writing, and after a few letters from home that went mostly un-acknowledged, communication had stopped except for Christmas cards once a year. Now here he stood in awkward silence. Mrs. Mac-Donald did not know exactly how to say, what needed to be said, or where to start.

"Dad, Mom?" He repeated with a sad appeal. Peter had always been quieter than the rest of the children. He was not gregarious even among his own family. The shortest of the boys, he was more studious and serious. He did not play the piano, violin, or any instrument well, making the excuse that some folks were better at enjoying music than making music. However, he had an excellent tenor voice.

Sara appeared from out of nowhere. She had always been vivacious and outgoing, a spokesperson for both herself and her much quieter little brother Peter. She now pulled Peter along in her tow, embracing her parents. "Dad! Mom!" she exclaimed, "It's been too long! I was so remiss about sending cards." She continued to give them hugs. "When I finally came to my senses, there was no forwarding address. You know how I'm easily sidetracked, and it was too easy to think someday I would catch up—you know, make the extra effort. Things just got in the way, and I never did. I was so excited to hear from Rachel, and then Laura. In a way, it was Rachel's way of patching things up. You know, kinda like her special gift to you and Peter and me. I doubt you would even recognize Robert anymore, and here I want you to meet our three girls," she said dragging them over to her family. "Margaret, the oldest, is twelve, Emily is eleven, and Annabel is the baby at eight."

Sara was picking up where she had left off years earlier. She still possessed blond hair and blue eyes, but of all the children, life had etched many changes into her face. She was no longer the slender, lithe young woman she had been. She looked to be older than her thirty-nine years from the lines carved on her face.

"Peter, where's your family?" Sara prompted him.

"They are right here," Peter said. Mrs. MacDonald clutched his hand tightly lest he slip away. Grasping his father by the elbow, Peter guided his parents in the direction of a short woman with expertly coiffed prematurely gray hair and a young girl. He introduced his wife to his parents as if they had never met, followed by his daughter, whom they had never seen. "This is Judith and our daughter, Mary."

"Hello, Judith." Mr. MacDonald gave her his most congenial smile. "It surely has been a long time. And Mary, is it?" He shook the young girl's hand.

"Yes, sir." Mary had a warm, friendly smile. Whereas Judith was stiff and formal giving everyone the impression she was a step up the ladder above them in some way.

"Well, Mary, Grandma and I are both pleased to meet you." He stepped aside so Amanda could greet their granddaughter.

"What a lovely name, Mary. I had a friend named Mary. She was a roguish sort of person, but she was a lot of fun." Amanda hugged her newest acquaintance. After several handshakes and hugs with Sara and Peter and their families, Rachel and her family joined them.

At some point, Lewis interrupted. "I've been informed by several concerned parties, that we need to head over to Laura and Juan's for supper, so, everyone to your cars, and let's go."

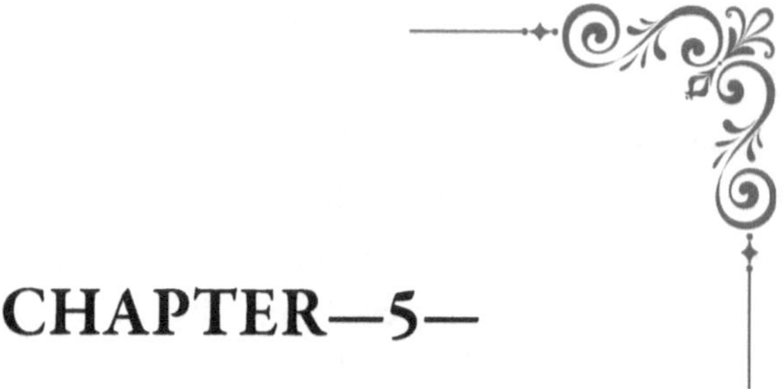

CHAPTER—5—

"Well, Brother Matthew, these are all of our arrows," Mr. MacDonald said the next evening at Bible study. "You may count as I name them. Laura, Lewis Junior, Sara, Peter, Rachel, Joshua, Seth, Anna, Michael. Our third child, James is not with us—he went to his reward about twelve years ago."

"Mr. MacDonald, I'm sorry. Back when I made the comment about arrows in the quiver, I was being flippant with something that I had no business being frivolous about. Will you forgive me?" Brother Matthew said as he looked over the small church house full to bursting with all of the MacDonalds in attendance.

"I will, my friend," Mr. MacDonald replied with a hearty hand-clasp. "Are you and your family coming over for the bobsled ride Saturday?"

"Yes, Hannah and Daniel are so excited, as well as Marie and me. This has been a wonderful visit. I'm so glad the Heides invited us for a few days. We are settling into our new work, but I doubt we'll ever find another congregation like this one." He smiled thoughtfully.

"We think it's pretty fine also." Mac and Brother Matthew watched the group that milled around, shaking hands and greeting one another. "I guess we'll see you in a couple of days then."

"THIS IS SUCH A POSTCARD snowfall." Peter helped Judith to the rental car.

"This weather just makes me so nervous." Judith observed the light snow falling as Peter opened her car door.

Getting into the driver's side Peter said, "I've driven in much worse when I was stationed in Europe, but light snow can be dangerous if a person isn't careful." He pulled onto the snowy road as they departed from the building after evening Bible study.

"I'm so glad this evening is over. I'm afraid I have a positively splitting headache." Judith frowned. "Crowds often make me feel ill." She sorted through her handbag. "I must have left my bottle of aspirin tablets back at our room." She snapped her purse shut after her search.

"What's that, Judy?" he asked.

She snapped at him, "My headache medicine." Her frown deepened in annoyance. "You haven't called me that for a good many years, and I'd be just as happy if you never did again."

"The roads aren't bad after all and we don't have far to drive." Peter either didn't hear her words or ignored them, trying instead to reassure his wife.

"I can't believe there are towns like this one. This 'bed and breakfast' as they call it is so quaint." She sniffed. "I'm glad we don't have but a few more days until we get back to civilization." She sighed.

"Judith—" Peter slowed down for the driveway at Olan and Rheba's bed and breakfast. "I know what a sacrifice it has been for you to travel out here, and I appreciate this. I'm sure it is good for Mary to meet the other side of the family, and I have missed them."

"I don't see why it would be good for her to meet your family. She has done quite well the way we are, and your family gives me a headache. They seem to be everywhere, especially after all these years, and most of them seem so—" She paused trying to find the word she wanted. "—common."

Peter sighed and swallowed the anger and resentment he had learned to suppress. *Looking down her nose at the world put her nose out of joint. It might help if she were just a little taller.* He smiled to himself.

Judith's eyes narrowed and the constant frown deepened. "I should have married Bellamy Potter... He never gave me that condescending, infuriating smile. You just don't understand." She almost growled at him. "My mother warned me, but oh no, I would not listen."

"Bellamy Potter? Didn't I read a newspaper story lately that he's been indicted for some kind of..."

"Lies, all lies," Judith harrumphed. "He's done nothing. Nothing's been proven."

"What I've heard is it's pretty serious, but you're right, everyone's entitled to their day in court." Peter nodded.

"I don't know how you could miss those people. They're just common people. Mary hasn't missed anything by not knowing them."

"But, Judith..." Peter couldn't get a word in as she continued.

"I've done my duty. Gone the extra mile. It's been twelve years since my last misadventure and twelve more won't be long enough. And in a few more days I'll be back home."

"At least it wasn't far." Peter pulled into the parking spot at the Smith's Bed and Breakfast and turned off the motor. After walking around to the passenger side, he opened Judith's door and offered her a hand out. She took his hand grudgingly. He shut the car door and she pushed past him, walking toward the steps to the front porch on the smaller grandparent house bed and breakfast. Mary jumped out of the car and grabbed her father's hand. She smiled at him her simple, sweet smile.

"I'm glad we came on this trip," she whispered. "I like everyone here, especially Grandpa and Grandma. They seem so kind and fun." Her face glowed when she smiled.

"They are kind and fun, baby. I wish we could visit more often." Peter had a sad smile.

"What are you two whispering about?" Judith demanded crossly as she mounted the steps to the porch.

"I was telling Father that this has been fun," Mary said. "Grandpa made a maze in the backyard at Auntie and Uncle's for us children to play fox and geese in. And Uncle Lewis has the biggest team of horses I have ever seen. They must be nine-feet-tall," Mary exaggerated. "And Grandma has a window that turns into a door." She continued talking, not noticing her mother's disapproval.

"I'm sure." Judith's eyes narrowed.

"THIS HAS BEEN AN UNCOMMON year for snow even for us," Lewis commented Saturday morning. He was bundling up to go out and get ready for the bobsled ride. "Can you get it?" he called to his wife as the phone rang.

They could hear Donna talking into the receiver then she replaced it. "That was Judith," she informed them. "She said they would be a little late. Seems she wanted Juan to come get them from Olan and Rheba's. She is quite positive Peter can't drive in this snow." Donna laughed imitating her sister-in-law.

"That's all right," Lewis said. "I'm not ready yet anyway. I'd better get out there and get on the ball." There was a blast of fresh air as the door opened and he disappeared.

Seth looked at Joshua and pantomimed the curled pinky finger.

Joshua laughed. "Each to his notion."

"Said the little old lady—" Seth continued.

"—that kissed the cow." Mrs. MacDonald finished the saying as she joined the pair. "What are you two talking about?" She sat down with them by the fireplace in Lewis' living room and took a sip of her coffee while waiting for the answer.

"We are just being thankful," Seth said.

"I see." She raised her eyebrows questioningly. "About what were you being thankful?"

"For our wonderful wives." Joshua lifted his coffee cup and saluted before taking a drink.

"Okay, kiddos. I'll not press the point. We should be thankful in all things. We should also pray for the weak." She sighed. "There are a lot of people that I'm glad I'm not married to. It's too bad Judith hasn't seemed to enjoy her visit. But Peter and Mary have enjoyed theirs. Are you two ready for the bobsled ride?"

"Well, we're all here at least, and I see Brother Matthew and his family are just here," Joshua said.

"And there are Peter and his family..." Seth turned as another car pulled into the driveway.

"Hello, Mary." Mrs. MacDonald grinned when the door opened and Mary bounced into the house. "How's our favorite Mary this morning?" She hugged her. "Have you eaten, and are you ready for your bobsled ride?"

"We have eaten, Grandma, but Father and I are being very quiet about the bobsled ride, you know." Ten-year-old Mary put her finger to her lips.

"Oh, I see." Mrs. MacDonald put on a very prim and proper, wise and knowing face. Looking over her granddaughter's head, she gave a warning look at her two boys. They in turn made an excuse and scattered to warn everyone else. Mary quickly exited out the back door as her mother came in the side door.

"I don't know where Peter or Mary went." Judith sat in front of the fireplace, her face screwed up into her normal cross manner. "They were coming in with me, and then they both disappeared. I just can't understand. Mary never does anything like that." Judith pouted.

Mrs. MacDonald's eyes grew wide at the sound of the bobsled bells. "Judith, come to the kitchen and help me with…" Her words trailed off as she walked toward the kitchen.

Judith rolled her eyes, but she followed her mother-in-law to the kitchen. "Where's your hired help?" she asked.

"They'll be here later." Mrs. MacDonald held the kitchen door for Judith. She didn't feel the need to explain that Eduardo and Juanita were Laura and Juan's hired help. Judith had no concept of their family situations. Mrs. MacDonald watched the bobsled slide past the house as the kitchen door swung shut behind Judith.

So it was that Peter and his daughter were on the bobsled going past the front room window as Judith drank a cup of coffee in the kitchen unaware there was a bobsled ride in progress.

"SOMEONE IS NOT A HAPPY camper." Anna giggled to Ruth the next afternoon.

Ruth tried not to smile. "I wouldn't wonder. For the last three days, we have worked very hard to keep her busy so that Peter and Mary could have an enjoyable visit. I think we deserve some kind of award."

"Well, dear little Mary deserved a chance for a few normal days in her precious life. It may be the last she will ever get." Anna's voice was regretful.

"No, Mary will come back. She has enjoyed this last week. This evening after worship services should cap things off for them. If I were a wagering person, I would be willing to bet that they have never toasted marshmallows or wieners at the fireplace before in their lives. Not Judith or Mary, that is," Ruth said.

"We might as well throw our coats on and go help Donna get things ready. I'm sure she can use the help. Everyone should be arriving soon anyway." Anna walked to the coat closet to make good on her words as Ruth and Gwen joined her.

"I DON'T KNOW, MOM. All I can say is I'm glad they will be leaving in the morning." Donna was seldom cross or out of sorts. "I don't like the feelings she stirs up in me at all. Dealing with Judith is getting on my last nerve." Her dark eyes were troubled.

"Like the 'I would like to throttle her' emotion?" Mrs. MacDonald sympathized.

"Yes, that and several others very similar." Donna grimaced ruefully.

"I think people like her are sent our way to remind us that we aren't as far along on our walk as we sometimes—smugly, I admit—feel we are," Mrs. MacDonald said.

"It's certainly a reminder to me. If I'm tempted to feel more highly of myself than I should, I will forevermore think of Judith. That will surely be a 'whoa Molly' moment for me. I never want to look to others like she looks to me." Donna sighed sadly.

Both the women looked up to see Peter standing in the doorway and were stricken with sadness. "I'm sorry, Peter." Mrs. MacDonald scowled. "I don't know how long you've been there..."

"I understand." He brought his coffee cup into the kitchen. "It isn't your fault... really. I want all of you to know how much Mary and I have enjoyed our visit. I know everyone has worked especially hard to make this work. Judith is not an easy person to, ah—" He pursed his lips as he searched for the right words. "Ah, well, she's just not an easy person to deal with, but y'all have done a wonderful job. I love you and appreciate everything you've done."

"So, is she feeling any better?" Donna asked refilling his cup.

"She will feel better only tomorrow when we finally drive in our driveway at home. When she is back in her own neighborhood with her mother and familiar friends. That is when she will feel better, and I doubt if any time before." Peter pursed his lips and stared into his fresh cup of coffee. "But that is the way things are." He looked them both in the eyes.

A whole host of sadness washed over Mrs. MacDonald. She knew it was too late. The water was already gone under that bridge. The words *I told you so*, or *we warned you*—those words wouldn't heal the wounds. It was a mother and son moment when they looked at each other and knew the depth of his hurt. She gave him a long-overdue hug. "We love you, son."

"I understand the heights of joy and the depths of agony parents feel for their children. My one bright spot is Mary. When you told me years ago—what you told me—you and dad would've spared me this suffering. All of my business success is a small consolation for our unhappiness at home. At least I provide well for my family, and I'm honest. Those are two things you guys taught me. To work well, do my best, and be honest." He sighed involuntarily and straightened up as Mary came inside smelling fresh and wholesome from her time in the snow.

"We were making snowmen, Daddy, and us girls had the very best one!" She bubbled excitedly. "I have never had so much fun." She emphasized with a big hug. "I wish we could stay here another month."

"That would be nice, but Daddy has to make a living and I'm sure your mother would 'just die' at such a proposal." He smiled, tugging at an errant braid.

Her round eyes became serious as she shook her head. "I guess you're right, Daddy, but still I have had so much fun."

Mrs. MacDonald watched, with a tear in her heart, the father and daughter moment as both accepted without words the cross they had to bear. They would do so uncomplaining. She watched as Mary and Peter smiled at each other.

—— ∽ ——

JUDITH LAY IN THE DARK upstairs room with a cold compress across her forehead. *Peter brought me some medicine as well as some frightful brewed headache tea that someone sent up. The tea was supposed to make me sleep and feel better. Ha! It was probably poison.* Judith looked at the cookies and crackers Mary had brought her. She scowled. *I can't believe they left me here... All Mary could do was rattle on about the fun she was having and they were going to toast marshmallows and awful things at the fireplace. And with a quick kiss, she disappeared... and left me here to suffer by myself while they all have a good time.*

She sat on the edge of the bed and dared to examine the room. *I've seen bigger houses than this and much more expensive furnishings*—Judith smirked—*But the decorations are rather quaint. Those curtains remind me of Shirley's designs back at Briarwood. Since everyone has forgotten me...* She tried some of the tea and crackers.

The tea tasted pleasant, and Judith took a small bite of a cookie. *Not bad at all. I don't know how they can leave me.* She thought with great annoyance— Curiosity finally won out. She crossed the large bedroom to the windows framed in opulent, dark green curtains and pulled a curtain back to peek outside, only to view luxurious panels of lace. Drawing aside the lace panel, Judith saw that the large window opened onto a balcony overlooking a frozen fairy landscape of silver and white. There stood a row of fat snowmen of various sizes and shapes grinning at her as if mocking her. She let the panel and curtain fall back into place. She walked by the fireplace hung with gay Christmas colors and the basket with a dried flower arrangement in brilliantly dyed colors, past the old-fashioned elaborate mirror hanging on the wall and returned to sit on the bed. Maybe just a splash of water would help. She walked to the spacious bathroom.

Very nice, she thought in approval, everything you could want in here. She splashed cold water on her face then dried it, carefully replacing the towel. Opening the bedroom door into the hallway, she listened to the laughter from downstairs. Someone was playing the violin. Whoever was playing was giving an excellent performance. Exquisite, she thought. She sat down in a chair in the hall by the bedroom door and closed her eyes. Someone was singing in a very beautiful soprano voice. Judith forgot herself for the moment resting in the comfortable chair. She had not realized they were going to have entertainment.

There was a beautiful Scottish ballad by the most wonderful tenor voice, and then the same tenor voice sang "Do You Know My Jesus." Judith was astonished. Just where had they found such talent in this awful, dinky little town? She lost track of the time as she sat and listened to the entertainment. After a while, it seemed to be all over, and Judith decided to quietly go downstairs. She was curious to meet the people who had performed so well. She eagerly looked down into the living room from the stairs searching for the entertainers but saw only the same faces she had seen all week.

Judith spotted her husband's familiar face. Peter stood by the fireplace conversing with Juan. She had not seen him look so happy and relaxed for a long time. She had a sudden pang of remorse. There was Mary. She, too, looked happy as if she were having a splendid time. *How could they be having a good time while she was suffering by herself upstairs?* Here among his own family, Peter looked different. He was peaceful, smiling, and dare she admit it handsome? She had not noticed for years just how attractive he was. Judith had a fleeting remembrance of the man who had captured her heart so many years ago, and it left an ache that she did not understand.

"I FEEL SO SORRY FOR Peter." Sara sighed with a wistful glance. They had all gone to the airport to say farewell to the three visitors that morning. Now everyone was breathing a collective sigh of relief.

"Peter didn't have to marry her. The one I feel sorry for is Mary." Rachel cradled her cup of coffee then laughed out loud. "Do you think Judith will ever forgive us?"

"I thought everyone did a marvelous job of keeping her occupied." Ruth came from the kitchen and joined the two who were unwinding in the living room in front of the fireplace at Lewis and Donna's. "I don't think she was aware of all the work we were doing. People like Judith are too caught up in themselves to realize other people have lives...or feelings."

"Well, I don't know about forgiveness, but I'm sure she will never forget us." Sara snickered.

"I think this is the first time we have been able to calm down this whole week." Laura sighed and nestled into the overstuffed loveseat beside Junko, as one by one, the other women joined the group.

"Robert, the girls, and I have enjoyed ourselves. I want to thank Laura and Juan for encouraging us to come, and Donna and Lewis for opening their home. How many times do people tell us to be thankful for the good things we have, and we don't seem to know what those things are until we lose them. Or almost lose them." Sara tucked a stray hair behind her ear.

"That was a hard secret to keep, but it was worth it. Thank you, Mom." Laura accepted a cup of hot chocolate and took a sip. "How did you know I needed this?"

"You and Donna need to take it easy." Mrs. MacDonald chided.

"Speaking of secrets, Gwen, how did Seth like his surprise?" Ruth asked.

"To say he was astonished would be an understatement." Gwen laughed.

"What? What's going on?" Anna sat beside Donna on the sofa.

"It has to do with Proverbs thirty-one, verse sixteen," Gwen said.

"So what piece of property did you buy?" Mrs. MacDonald brought in another cup of hot chocolate and handed it to Donna.

"How exciting. Joshua and Junko have their place, and now you two. And just where is it?" There was a barrage of questions from several voices at once.

"Does this mean you're going to leave me?" Anna wailed, throwing her arm over her forehead in melodramatic despair.

"Oh, Anna, you're such a card. It's Mr. Prichard's place over yonder." Gwen laughed at her sister-in-law. "He still has renters in the house, and it will need fixing up, so it won't be tomorrow." She smiled and patted her sister-in-law's hand. "But we can't stay with Mom and Dad forever, and I hear flower gardens are nice. Besides, my mother is finishing with our business back east, and I want her to come to stay with us as soon as she can."

"Next week is going to be a change. We've been so busy, but with Sara and Rachel's families leaving to go home...We'll have to entertain ourselves now." Mrs. MacDonald sat quietly with downcast eyes.

"I guess all will be quiet on the home front, huh, Mom?" Rachel said.

"Well, it is never quite quiet on this home front, but the kaleidoscope of our lives is different than it was fifteen years ago." Mrs. MacDonald looked up slowly. "That's all right. Things should change as we get older." She shrugged. "So, are you all packed and ready to go?" She glanced at Rachel and Sara.

"Yes," Rachel answered, "just a few things to pick up and last-minute laundry to put in the suitcases. We plan on leaving just after supper. Lance likes to drive at night. We got in that habit when the children were small. There is less traffic, and the little ones always slept most of the way anywhere we went."

"We plan on leaving first thing in the morning. Robert wants to take a few days extra to visit some of his family along the way," Sara said.

"We start school again next week. That's always difficult after the holidays. It's like 'the spirit is willing, but the flesh is weak' syndrome.

But I want to be far enough ahead that when this baby comes I won't feel guilty about taking a lighter approach." Donna sighed.

"Yes, we are working ahead as well, so that it won't be so challenging, and we'll have some leeway when the baby comes." Laura paused.

"Life never seems to run smooth," their mother added. "No matter how well we plan things out God lets us know in His way that we aren't really in control. I never planned that I would be the mother of ten children... or do one-third of the things I have. When I turned my life over to the Lord, things just went in all sorts of directions."

"Do you ever regret having ten children? I have three, and I'm so busy trying to stretch my time I don't know how you did it, Mom." Sara smiled at her mother.

"Oh, no—" Mrs. MacDonald shook her head. "No, I never regretted my ten children. I wish, of course, that some things had turned out differently, but...it was like having ten little presents." She smiled softly.

CHAPTER—6—

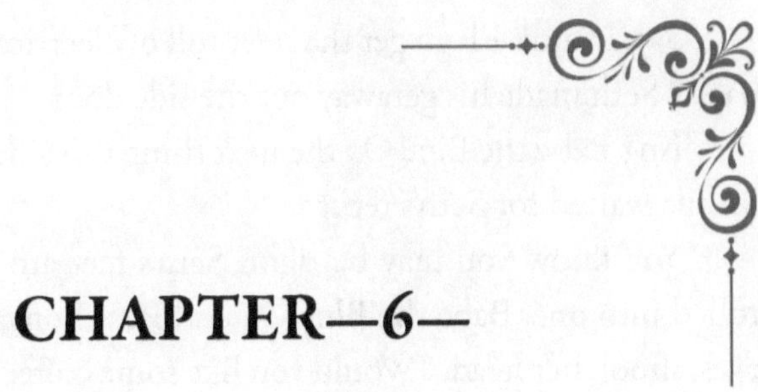

"I didn't think we were ever going to come to this point of moving in. But this house is shaping up." Seth was pleased with the progress being made on the house Gwen had purchased. "It just needed a little nudge was all." He steadied the ladder.

"What are you yacking about?" Joshua backed down the ladder and out of the attic.

"I said you are doing a fine job on the electrical work, brother."

"Yeah, I know you're probably thinking up new and pleasurable ways for me to spend my weekends." Joshua grimaced as he combed cobwebs out of his hair.

"Yeah, yeah, I'm thinking— Say, how is your place coming along? You'll be moving in pretty soon too?" Seth asked.

"Yes, sir. In a coupla weeks, you can come crawl around in my attic, brother." Joshua pursed his lips and shook his head.

"I have to help Gwen plant flowers." Seth sighed.

"Yeah, right." Joshua chuckled.

"I know it's a hard job, but someone has to do it." Seth had a pained look on his face as they came down the stairs to the living room.

"You two still at it?" Gwen raised an eyebrow as she entered the room. "You," she warned as she pointed a finger at Seth, "stay out of my flowers, you madman." She turned to Joshua. "He has the biggest feet this side of Paul Bunyan."

"Say, I think I'll go get the next roll of electrical wire. I'll be right back." Seth made his getaway out the side door.

"Isn't Babe the Blue Ox the next thing this side of Paul Bunyan?" Joshua waited for Seth's return.

"You know you may be right. Seth's feet are like both of them rolled into one, Babe the Blue Ox and Paul Bunyan." She rolled her eyes, shook her head. "Would you like some coffee? I have coffee and tea in the kitchen. Ruth, Junko, Mai, and Anna are coming to help me choose flowers, and give advice. They ought to be here any time."

"Just a half a cup would be fine." He followed Gwen into the kitchen.

"The weather has been unpredictable, but that's spring in the Midwest." She handed him his coffee.

"That's springtime in a word everywhere. Pretty soon we'll have the season of the mud—not my favorite time of year." Joshua stopped to take a drink. "I can't tell you how good it is that Junko and Mai have a place in the family. Junko had a small family, her and her brother, Saiko. Their mother died when they were young and her father died—well, it's been a little over a year now."

"Oh, how tragic. This world has its share of sorrow, but it would be hard not to love Junko. She's so gentle and sweet. Everyone from Dad and Mom down to Anna and the nieces and nephews are so kind and helpful, even for me. I was just drifting after Aunt Zoë died. I had a paid chauffeur and was traveling here and there, always alone. I met Seth when I visited at church. Everyone there, young and old, knew him and he was well-liked by everyone, so good with the children at church. Funny now that I think about it. I can't explain it, but I looked into his face and saw my future, our children, everything was there. In nine years I have had two miscarriages, and we lost one baby at two weeks old. I can't figure out how I saw our children, but I did."

"Seth told me y'all had lost a baby. I can only imagine how hard that is. We'll all pray for you. You're still young, and I know it isn't any consolation, but—maybe it wasn't the right time."

"Of course, my mind agrees with what you've said, but my heart...doesn't understand." Gwen shrugged and looked down at her hands sadly.

"We never expected to have Mai. Junko was sick at the time, then she had to fight to save the baby along with trying to heal herself... Sounds like your company is here." He finished his coffee and smiled as they heard car doors slam announcing the arrival of her visitors. "Mai was a pleasant surprise. We have thanked God for her every day." They watched out the window as Mai skipped up the walkway chattering to Sam the dog as he trotted along with her.

"You are so very blessed to have her, Joshua, she is very special." Gwen smiled and opened the door as Mai reached up to ring the doorbell.

"Howdy, partner." Mai mimicked her uncle Seth. She bounced in the door with a dolly tucked under her arm.

"Mai!" Junko exclaimed softly in a horrified voice, "That is no way to speak to your Aunt Gwen."

"Sorry, Auntie 'wen." Mai was only partly repentant.

"She is so like her father." Junko sighed blushing. "I just don't know what to do with either of them." Junko's eyes implored the other ladies for understanding, and Mai ran straight for her daddy, holding up her little arms so he would pick her up.

"Hmm, sometimes our past does come back to visit us..." Joshua cleared his throat as he held his little girl. "I think Seth must have gotten lost. Where is he? Didn't he find that roll of wire yet?" He looked for his delinquent brother as the ladies laughed.

"Yep, I'm coming." Seth appeared in the doorway. "Let's go check the outlets on the other side of the house."

"Have a good visit, and I'll keep Paul Bunyan out of your flowers today." Joshua laughed and set Mai down.

"COFFEE? OR TEA? WHICH would you like?" Gwen asked and began filling the cups. "I've gotten several catalogs lately besides the ones I had early right after Christmas. How did they know to send these?" She spread the catalogs out, and everyone chose the one that caught their attention.

"The companies send them out to occupants in hopes they'll find an old customer or a new... buyer." Anna searched for an acceptable word. "This is my favorite way to spend an afternoon in springtime. Do you have any idea what kind of flowers, trees, and plants you're looking for?" She sighed as she leafed through the brightly colored books. "When is your mother supposed to arrive?"

"She is making sure all the dots are dotted and ts are crossed. The foundation is set up for my estate, and now all she has to do is pack her little suitcase and fly out. Should be... oh, next week." Gwen squinted at the calendar.

"That soon? I'm sure you're looking forward with anticipation to her arrival," Anna said.

"You can bet your boots I am. Although I have been back and forth the last few months, it will be terrific to have her here. We can just settle in and enjoy some time to relax." Gwen smiled.

"The weather will warm up soon and it won't be long before you can plant these flowers. Aren't you going to have your caretaker—Ralph, isn't it? Is he coming out for a visit and to give you some advice?" Ruth asked.

"Ralph refuses to fly. He says if God had meant for him to fly he'd have been born a bird. But he and Gerald, my butler, are driving out in a car." Gwen snickered. "You know how stubborn people can get." She smiled patiently as she might have smiled at an errant child.

Laura and Donna's babies are sure growing fat and doing well." She changed the subject. "Who would have thought?" Her eyes grew wide. "Laura's little Noah is such a doll with those big brown eyes, black hair, and chubby cheeks. Donna sure has her work cut out for her! I don't know how she handles twins. They are as cute as a pair of buttons with their big brown eyes and that naturally curly hair."

"The boys spoil those babies." Anna chuckled. "Those two girls aren't going to know what legs are for."

"Either that or they will just believe they have four legs." Gwen chortled. "I guess I would take twins if the good Lord saw fit to give them to us." Her voice was wistful, and her face softened.

"We all have to bloom where we are, take what we get." Ruth squeezed Gwen's hand. "As for your garden, you may want to wait a bit and see what flowers are already here. Mrs. Pritchard had some very nice flowers at one time. She was sick for a few years and cut back on them but I think there are still some roses and early spring crocuses... I'll be excited to see what Ralph has for advice. Do you have the room ready for your mother? This isn't the same as your estate out east, just a nice-sized old farmhouse."

"Yes, Mr. Pritchard told us he was born in this house, and he had five siblings, so it's not a small house. At one time this was a busy farm, but everybody has gone their own ways. He and his wife had three children, but their boy died, and the girls aren't interested in anything to do with the farm."

"I can see you'll be doing some remodeling. Maybe have to build an addition for Ralph and Gerald for when they come?" Ruth asked.

"I'd never thought of that. We may need to. Alice, Ralph, and Gerald are all on the advisory board of my estate foundation, but they are also semi-retired now." Gwen's brow wrinkled in thought. "Alice, of course, being my mother—and we've always been close—will be with me. But I can't think of anyone I'd rather have with me as well as Ralph and Gerald.

Junko and Mai have been such helpers in preparing for Alice." Gwen touched Junko's hand. "I'm sure mother will just love her room. Juan and Laura have helped also, advising me on different things. Helping me order furnishings. Everything should fit into place before she gets here. You will have to come back next week after the new furnishings come in and see what we've done." Her face lit up with expectation. "When will you start moving into your new house?" Gwen looked at Junko.

"We should have everyt'ing moved in and set up in a week. Maybe less." Junko said. "Everyt'ing 'appen at once."

"As we say here in the States when it rains, it pours." Anna sighed.

"It is often so. There is much work to do yet." Junko exhaled. "These pictures make me want to start planting. Look at all these pretty flowers and trees."

"I'm making my list." Gwen held up a notepad with pages and names of items on it. "Seth has something of an idea for a small orchard laid out. Of course, we'll have to run it past Father MacDonald and Ralph..."

"We 'ave an old remnant of an orchard, but much trees are too old. So much fun," Junko said.

"I guess it is about time to be heading back. It will soon be time to prepare supper." Ruth squinted at Junko. "I'll be over to help clean cupboards for you tomorrow—you look a bit peaked today. Have you been getting enough rest?"

"Ruth, you always ask me that." Junko chuckled. "But I would appreciate your help. Sometimes it is lots of work and a help lifts the load."

"I'll come help too." Anna finished her cookie and tea. "If one person helps, two will be better. I can help with upstairs closets while you work downstairs."

Anna and Ruth exchanged glances. "Here, let me put your dishes in the washer, Gwen. Then we need to be off." Ruth began to pick up the cups and carry them to the sink.

"Thank you so much for your help, advice, and company." Gwen carried the plates, following Ruth to the counter.

"Goodbye. Thank you for coming." Gwen waved as everyone walked back down the sidewalk in much the same manner as they had arrived with Sam the pooch escorting Mai and her dolly to the end of the walk. Anna, Ruth, Junko, and Mai all loaded into the minivan, and Anna drove out the driveway.

"IT'S UP TO US." RUTH leaned back in the passenger seat after leaving Junko at Laura's house and heading back to Mac and Amanda's hideaway. "Laura and Donna are occupied with the babies. Mrs. M will be a help, but she's not a spring chicken any more. Gwen will be tied up with her affairs and getting things settled on her front."

"I can see you're right, of course, but are you sure? I don't want to make something out of nothing." Anna busied herself watching the gravel road in front of her.

"I've been suspicious ever since the supper last year. I've watched, and as you say, I don't want to make something out of nothing. I can't tell that Junko is more pale, but she does seem to tire more easily."

"She did seem a bit peaked today, as you pointed out. And since you mentioned it, I think I've noticed a change." Anna pulled into the drive.

"I wish I were wrong. I don't know where it's going, but it doesn't hurt to help and be proactive. If I'm wrong, I've just been very helpful and no harm is done." Ruth shrugged her shoulders, hoping against the odds she was wrong. "We can pray that I'm wrong."

"We'll keep it to ourselves for right now. What time are we supposed to be at their house tomorrow?" Anna parked and picked up her purse.

"Bright and early after breakfast and morning chores." Ruth slammed her door and followed Anna into the house. "Mm, smells good in here." As the girls walked into the house, the smells of an evening meal met them.

"It sure does." Anna opened the coat closet door, and they both hung away their coats and scarves and changed into slippers. "Mom, we're home," she called out.

"I'm in here, girls. Glad you're home. Can you two take over here?" Mrs. MacDonald met them at the kitchen door. "I need a shower and to clean..."

"Mrs. M. What have you been doing? You look like you've been playing in a can of paint." Ruth stopped and stared.

"I *have* been playing in a can of paint...green paint. Doesn't it look good with my outfit?" Mrs. MacDonald showed off her paint-smeared clothes.

"'Fess up. What have you been doing?" Anna squinted, her lips set in a straight line.

"Now, now, don't get too excited. I was helping your dad."

"I thought he was on our side." Ruth grimaced.

"Oh, hello, girls. You've made it home. Did you get all the flowers and trees picked out?" Mr. MacDonald wandered into the kitchen smelling like he was fresh out of the shower.

"Dad, I thought you were on our side, but here mom looks like she's been dipped into a can of green paint." Anna's eyes were wide.

"You know how Mom paints. That's exactly how she looks after painting almost anything. At least it's a nice color, don't you think?" Mr. MacDonald winked at his daughter. "You go ahead, Ahmanda, and get cleaned up. You might want to get that green paint out of your hair."

"So, what have you two been up to?" Ruth watched as Mrs. Mac-Donald scurried off toward the bedrooms.

"Joshua and Junko are planning on moving things into their new home, and I told them we'd do some of the painting before they move. Mom and I were working in the kitchen, dining room, and living room today. That way it will be ready whenever they are. Joshua had the paint chosen and so that's what we were doing."

"We need to finish up the supper here. You go sit by the fire and read a bit. There isn't any getting ahead of you two, is there?" Anna clucked at her dad. "Ruth and I are planning on helping Junko tomorrow—washing out kitchen cupboards, dusting and mopping, and maybe putting dishes in the cupboards."

"You're good girls." Mr. MacDonald hugged Anna. "Junko works very hard, but she's not as sturdy as she looks."

"Thanks, Dad. We've had good examples." She smiled up at him.

"IT USUALLY TAKES LONGER than I think it will to get everything loaded and drive where we need to be, but here we are." Anna and Ruth pulled into Joshua's and Junko's driveway and parked.

"I'm glad there's just two of us...no children, and we can set our own pace. I'll grab this box of supplies, you grab that bucket with its supplies, and we'll get after this project." Ruth and Anna walked up the sidewalk to the wide front porch.

"Hello, hello—" Anna called as they entered the downstairs. "Ruth and I made it, Joshua." They continued through the living room, dining room, and into the kitchen.

"I love this color of green. It looks much better on the cupboards than it did on Mrs. M last night." Ruth looked at Anna and snickered as they unloaded their cleaning supplies.

"Here are some things to put in the cupboards." Joshua brought in a box and set it in the corner of the kitchen. "Junko appreciates your help. She'll be over in a bit. Mom and Dad helped speed things up painting yesterday. I didn't expect them to slip over here and do that but you know those two."

"Yes, we do know those two. You should have seen this nice green paint on mom last night. It's definitely a good color for her, just not all over her." Anna finished wiping out one cupboard and moved on to the next. "I got a letter from Michael yesterday."

"How's he doing?" Joshua asked.

"He's had several job offers. He's considering some options, but didn't sound like he'd be home much this summer."

"It will be different not having Michael around. Where's he thinking of working?" Joshua asked.

"We will miss him during the summer. We've taken him for granted because he's such an old reliable. I guess there's a mission group working in India that has asked him to be a part of their work after he graduates." She turned from the cabinets. "I'm finished washing, you want me to put dishes in here?"

CHAPTER—7—

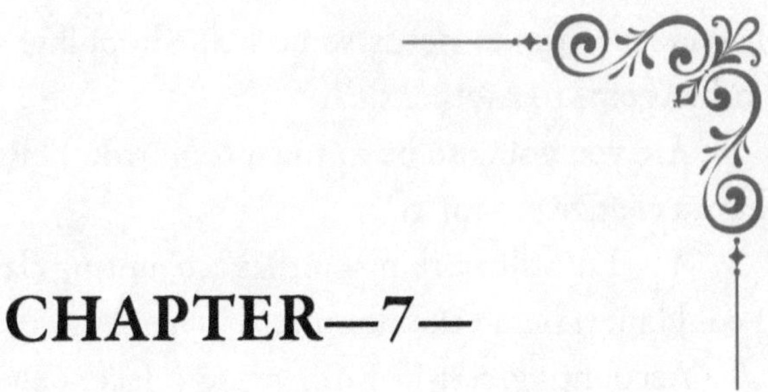

Ruth's hands kept busy moving with activity but her mind went in its own direction as she listened to Joshua and Anna's conversation. Her thoughts went back to late July last year and her conversation with Michael. *"Michael, what are you going to do when you're finished?" "I think I'll start my own business," he'd said.* Well, what had she expected? Her heart ached thinking about the pain in his eyes the last time they had talked about marriage. Why couldn't he understand it wasn't him she was rejecting? They needed to be doing what God wanted them to do, and marriage wasn't in her future at this time.

"I'm somewhat surprised." Anna began putting plates and cups in the cupboard. "Michael hasn't ever really expressed a desire to work overseas."

"The experience won't be wasted, but when I've asked him before, he has always talked about coming back here. It's good to see the world. I've seen more than I ever wanted to but... Don't put any dishes in this lower section here." Joshua pointed. "I've got a partition here where I'm going to put the dishwasher. We will pick the dish washer and the fridge up from the store tomorrow. I've got the stove hooked up, and now I'd better go check out the upstairs bathroom." He retrieved some of his tools from the closet.

"This will be a very nice kitchen. Just the right size. They'll be able to have a small table out here for breakfast and small meals.

I wonder if Junko needs some help shopping." Anna moved past Joshua's tape to another shelf.

"Are you going to be in town tomorrow?" Ruth was relieved to have a change in subject.

"Yes, I'm still working on that accounting class I've been taking. I could meet her in the afternoon."

"Accounting class?" Ruth made a face. "Eww, math has never been my strong point."

"Not mine either, but if I ever need to run my own business, I'll need accounting... Oh, here's Junko and Mai." Anna heard the front door open and a little girl's chattering.

"Oh, here, let me help you—" Ruth put down her cleaning cloth and hurried to the front room. "This is too heavy for you." She scolded as she took a box with kitchen spices and supplies from Junko. "We didn't hear you drive in. Is there anything else you need me to carry in?"

"Tank you vury much. Mom and Dad, Lewis and Donna are bringing some furniture right behind us."

"You look bushed, love. Sit down on those stair steps until we get someplace for you to relax. It won't be but a short minute. I wish we'd brought some tea or coffee..." Ruth fussed over Junko.

"Right here." Gwen stepped inside off the porch and Seth followed her carrying a hamper. "I brought a picnic basket with a bit of food, just in case Mr. Bunyan here needs to make up for his deprived childhood." They stood at the doorway with a large basket.

"Furniture is coming, and I'll be right back with a cup of tea..." Seth said over his shoulder on his way to the kitchen.

"You sit still and tell us where you want the furniture." Joshua came down the stairs and stepped around Junko. He hurried to hold the door open as the dining room table and chairs made their way onto the porch, and then for the sofa and chairs as they followed.

"And look what else we brought." Mrs. MacDonald held up a doll cradle as Mr. MacDonald carried in a box full of toys.

"Here you are." Gwen brought a cup of tea for Junko. "This living room will be so nice. I do like these nice wood floors—here, put the sofa over by the window, the end table there and the coffee table right here—come sit down in the chair and I'll put your tea right here. You can rearrange after you've rested, Junko."

"Thank you so much. Joshua has worked to get dees floors sanded, stained, and back into shape. They were vury rough...and the porch, but it 'as come together so nice—and Mom and Dad, the paint is just right." Junko took a sip of her tea as Mai squealed with joy and pulled a musical toy out of the toy box.

"We should have everything set up and in the house by the end of the week. Thanks." Joshua took the cup of tea Seth handed him. "The work won't be finished, but we'll be able to settle in. It'll be easier to finish then."

"We'll pass out a few sandwiches and get some of this furniture in place before heading on to bigger and better things, bro. Gwen has the food on the table. All we need is someone to pray over it." Seth winked.

"THERE IS SO MUCH TO do. Things were a bit quiet after the first of the year, but with planning the gardens, and ordering garden supplies it picks up steam like a locomotive moving down the tracks. How is Alice settling in, and what about the new addition you're putting on?" Mr. MacDonald asked.

"Alice and Gwen have been close even before Gwen knew the details of her birth, so this hasn't been difficult. Except Alice has to get used to a smaller charge coming from Gwen's large estate...and our landscape is windswept and barren compared to what she's used to." Seth helped himself to another cookie. "When Ralph and Gerald join our repertoire, it should be interesting."

"They should be here any day now, shouldn't they?"

"Yes, they are getting close. They are following a load of Gwen's horses. It's been fascinating. They don't want to travel too fast." Seth munched on his cookie thoughtfully. "We don't always understand our blessings."

"That's true, son, but which blessing are you talking about?" Mr. MacDonald smiled.

"When Joshua and I went to work last year—in disguise—I had a chance to meet Alice, Ralph, and Gerald. I got to experience their world firsthand as they would see it. I even have a better understanding of Gwen and her perspective after last fall."

"Not a lot of folks would call that situation a blessing." Mr. MacDonald's face scrunched up. "In some ways you got more than you bargained for."

"It was an insight from a different perspective. Gwen and I spent nine years in my world. It wasn't a bad thing to spend some time in her world."

"So, I can come over tomorrow morning and help with your project. What tools ought I to bring?"

"I'm finishing up on the outside, so your help with the siding would be appreciated. The inside is ready for painting. Gwen thinks she'll try her skills at that."

"Does she want Mom to come help?" Mr. MacDonald guffawed.

"Mom can come, but Gwen and several other people would probably have me drawn and quartered if Mom ended up dipped in paint." Seth grimaced.

"Maybe Alice and Mom could gang up on Gwen?" Mr. MacDonald wiped his eyes after his hearty laugh.

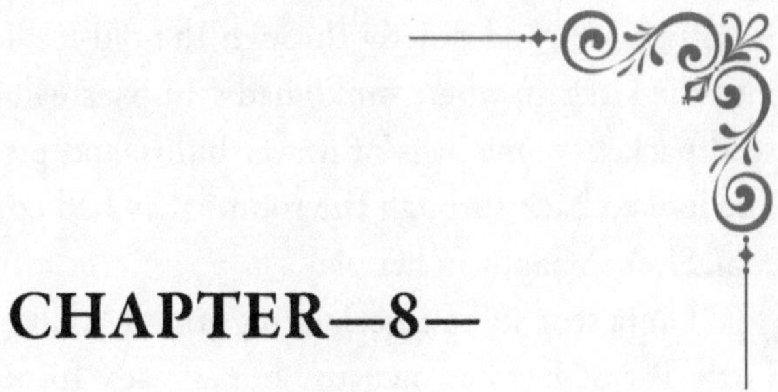

CHAPTER—8—

"Ruth is planning to come over and we will start planting new flowers." Junko glanced at the kitchen clock. "It should not be long before she comes. Gwen say her caretaker, Ralph, will be over and give us some landscape pointers. Maybe after supper?"

"That should be fine. Seth and I are finishing up a roofing and siding project over on the other side of Beetle River today. Hopefully, we'll be done early this afternoon." He turned to his little girl. "Mai, you be a good girl for your mommy, okay?" Joshua picked her up and hugged her. After setting her down, he brushed a quick kiss across Junko's cheek. "I need to get my tools and load the truck so we can get that job done today and—you know what?" he stopped in mid-thought. "All that is good, but I want you to know, you and Little Parrot are what make this and every day special." Joshua wrapped his arms around Junko in a loving hug. "I am so glad we've come home. I'll be back about two-thirty this afternoon."

RUTH SET HER BUCKET of tools on the porch by the front door listening to Junko's footsteps pattering across the living room floor in her new house. "Good morning," Ruth smiled when the door opened.

"Come in, come in." Junko stood aside and welcomed her into the spacious front room.

Ruth followed quietly through the old-fashioned dining room into the kitchen, where Junko had set up a small card table and laid seed packets, some bags of flower bulbs, and pictures on the table. She looked back through the rooms they had come from. "Look at Mai. She's so happy in her play."

"Laura sent some especial t'ings that Mai like to play with. Now Little Parrot has her own toy box already furnished with favorite toys." Junko poured the tea. "It is so nice to be in our own home. The springtime is so beautiful and green after the much snow of winter."

"Let's see what you've got here. I'm ready to help plant flowers, and did you say you have some small landscape projects?" Ruth picked up a flower picture and examined it, determined to be cheerful as well as helpful. "This has been a long winter, and I am ready for spring and for the bright jonquils, crocuses, tulips, and all that other stuff." She smiled. "Some of the bulbs and things should have been in the ground last fall." She shrugged. "However, we do what we have to do."

"Dis is some of what I have. It still isn't warm out but can these grow?" Junko asked.

"Some things will have to wait for planting," Ruth said. "Sometimes the weather throws a snowball right at the last moment. But it is a good time to plan our projects since we can see the bare landscape and have an idea of where we want to go. We can take some of these things out and plant them and put stakes for where we want other things." Ruth put some seed packets in a bucket. Then she picked up the bucket with items off the table and they traipsed back through the house to the front door. She pulled on her jacket and waited while Junko found her coat and scarf.

"To come out on the porch, Mai, you will need your coat. You may bring some toys onto the porch but no farther," Junko cautioned. "The air out here is so fresh and clean...I love Laura's flowers and just everyt'ing." They stepped out onto the porch, and Junco breathed deeply. "Mom and Dad's, Lewis and Donna's too, dey 'ave such pretty places. I feel when I come here from da very first dat I 'ave come home. Such peace and rest." Junko sighed.

Ruth picked up her bucket of tools and they walked down the steps. "This will be a very lovely home. Look, there are already some volunteer spring flowers. Some grape hyacinths and snow crocus poking their tiny little heads out of the sod. We'll need to be careful where we plant flowers." She put down her bucket and paused a moment. "What we need over here is a garden rake to pull some of these weeds back. I'm sure this is where the old garden spot was. Ah, yes, there's a garden rake." She walked over to where the rake leaned against a post. "After my mother... died... that's exactly what I felt when Mr. and Mrs. MacDonald took me into their home. I felt like I'd come home."

AS JACK O'BRIEN DROVE into the lane leading up to the house, he looked over the landscape. This property had been abandoned for almost ten years now since Mr. and Mrs. McGuines had passed. The farm ground was being farmed, but the house and grove had continued to deteriorate slowly. It reminded Jack of the fairy tale of the sleeping princess that had a hedge of thorns growing all around the castle.

Joshua had leveled the driveway leading to the house, and put in several loads of gravel—a good thing since it had been full of ruts and was rundown. Now as he bounced up the lane, it was evident there was much work being done, not just on the lane, but on the entire homestead. It had been a lovely house, barn, and building site shortly after the turn of the century, and there was still some good life here.

He stopped his pickup and parked outside of the yard fence. The two young women working in the yard were intent upon their conversation. The dark head of the little Japanese woman and the auburn head of his daughter were bent together over their work, and they had not heard his pickup. He watched them for a few minutes and sighed. His daughter was such a lovely young lady, in spite of himself, he thought with a pang of regret. He had tried to make things right before his wife Diana's death, but had worked even harder for the last few years.

"Good morning, ladies," he called as they both looked up startled when they heard his pickup door slam. He sauntered toward them with his hands stuck in his jacket pockets, taking a deep breath of air. "You two look as if you're enjoying this fresh spring morning." He wondered at the healthy glow on both their faces. *Surely the whispered rumors couldn't be true that Joshua's wife is not well.*

As he continued walking up the sidewalk towards the house, Mai came flying off the porch and down the porch steps, her pink high-heeled slippers tapping out a clap-clapping sound. The pink lacy dress she was wearing over her outfit of lavender lilacs was two sizes too large—which added to her impending danger as she tripped.

"Mai, watch out!" Junko cried out in alarm. Too late, Junko scrambled toward Mai as the little girl fell into Mr. O'Brien's providential arms.

"Whoa, Nellie Belle. That was close." He held her up with a laugh.

"I no Nellie Belle." Mai screwed up her little face in wonder that Ruth's daddy would get her name wrong.

"Oh, is that so?" He frowned as if thinking hard. "Well, is it Billy then?" He teased.

"No, it not Billy either, Mr. 'Brien."

"Okay, I have it now. It must be Rumpelstiltskin." He nodded.

"Dad, are you teasing Little Parrot?" Ruth asked as the two women walked over to the sidewalk.

"Now, would I do that?" His blue eyes showed crinkles at the corners when he laughed.

Mai, out of habit, patted his face and smiled at him. "Gran'pa Ma'Donald has little lines here too." She tickled the sides of his face.

"Snuccck." He snorted and bit at the end of her finger playfully.

"Hee- hee- hee." She squealed in delight.

"Okay, down you go, Ethel." He placed her back on the sidewalk.

"I no Et'el e'der." She pouted.

"Go play now." Her mother gave Mai a gentle swat. "Don't bother Mr. O'Brien, Mai."

"She's no bother, ma'am." He smiled at her. "I brought some flower bulbs and things Dad thought you all might be interested in."

"Thank you vry much. I'm sure that will be nice." Junko smiled her thank you.

"You are very timely. We were just planning where to put a water fountain and a small pool. You know like the one Mr. and Mrs. MacDonald have?" Ruth waved at the landscape.

Her father grinned at her. "You know, Ruth, I don't believe I have ever seen the one that Mac and Amanda have. Is it like the one at Laura's?"

"Pretty close." Ruth's brow furrowed as she thought. Turning, she walked toward where they had in mind. "We were thinking over here." She indicated a spot under a nearby tree.

Jack squinted in thought. "You know that would look nice, but why not on the other side by the weeping willow?" He pointed.

"MERCY, THAT HOUR WENT fast." Ruth blotted her brow after they had laid out a landscape plan for herbs and a pool to go with the fountain. "But we've made progress even if it's almost lunchtime. Dad, you sit there on the porch. We'll be right back."

Jack O'Brien obediently waited on the porch as the two young women disappeared inside with much talking and laughter.

Could it be that six weeks from now will mark the first anniversary of the coming of Julius C. Armstrong to the small town of Beetle River? The community would never know what they owed to that young man. Only two people from the community—himself and the police chief of Hermon, Dave Mallory— really knew. Jack O'Brien did not remember how he knew that undercover agent Julius was also Joshua, the son of Mac and Amanda MacDonald. At least by the time of the airport shooting, but only he and Mallory knew. The MacDonald family were all good folks. Jack's mind wandered as he thought through their family.

Jack's face wrinkled up in further thought as he puzzled over the Ruth and Michael question. Michael had come to him and asked his permission to ask Ruth THE question, whereas most young men would have gone to the girl first.

Michael and Ruth were so close, he guessed everyone kind of expected them to marry. He knew Michael would take good care of Ruth, but nothing seemed to have come of the question. There wasn't someone else in Ruth's life, and...Ruth and Michael made a good pair, but— he sighed and frowned in thought. Who could figure about women? They all appeared to have a timetable all their own, and no one was going to interfere with it. He shook his head as he pondered.

"Oh, ho, you girls have outdone yourself." He smiled as Ruth and Junko brought out some tuna sandwiches, tomato soup, tea, and cake. Mai brought a tiny glass of water with two small violets she had gathered that had bravely popped up among the jonquils and the snow crocuses. "Now I won't be able to go harass Mom, Pop, and Becky at the diner," he teased them. "I'll just have to go harass poor old Dad."

"How ees your Father?" Junko asked.

"Better. He had a bout with a cold or some such thing, but you know them old Irishmen are purty tough old codgers. Thanks for asking."

"Does Grandpa need me to run some errands for him?" Ruth asked with a concerned look. "I cleaned the house for him yesterday, and he looked awful peaked. He said he felt better."

"You always brighten up his day. Just a visit would be nice, I'm sure." He dipped his cake into his cup of tea.

Mai watched him, fascinated. "Mr. 'Brien, whadyadoin?" Her eyes were wide, and her face wore a droll expression.

"Come here, Peaches." He motioned, a smile on his face and a twinkle in his eyes.

She looked a question at her mother.

"Jes, go on, sweetie." Junko shook her head.

Mai slowly dawdled up to Mr. O'Brien and stood beside him not sure what to expect. He looked down into her questioning little face. As carefully as he could with his rough, work-worn hand, he stroked a stray hair out of her eyes. He picked her up gently and sat her on his lap, he smiled at her.

"Did anyone ever tell you what a little doll you are?" he asked.

"I no dolly, I's a little girl." Her eyes were wide and serious.

Jack just roared in laughter as Mai watched him enthralled.

Wriggling down to the floor, Mai ran to Ruth. Clinging to her she whispered loudly, "Woofie, is oo daddy okay?"

Ruth smiled affectionately at Mai, hugging her. "Yes, precious child, my daddy is okay. He just means you're a little sweetheart," she explained.

"Oh, okay." Mai nodded. Running back to him, patting him on the knee, and looking into his face. "Oo okay, Mr. 'Brien," she consoled him.

As he wiped his eyes, there flashed through his mind the picture of Ruth and little Mai. How much he had missed when his daughter was that age. Then there was another picture of Ruth and little Mai that sobered him up. Suddenly the cloud disappeared. The picture became clearer. These people—all of them would need Ruth before the end... still the hand of God.

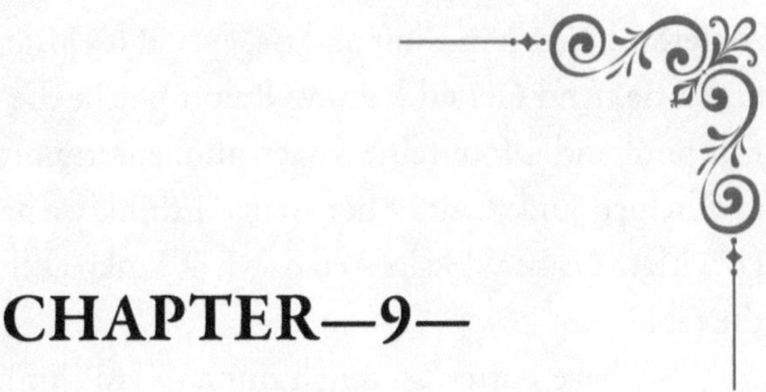

CHAPTER—9—

"Look at how this is turning into so lovely a home." Junko sat in a chair watching as Joshua worked to put up a swing on the porch. "Before it was a house—just a property. Gwen's caretaker, Ralph, has been such a help. I jes love her people. Dey are so funny."

"Yes, they are good folks." Joshua turned with a smile as Gwen's former caretaker, Ralph, and the butler from her estate, Gerald, worked to set some of the landscaping projects in place in the front yard.

"Alice, do we need to go help those two?" Gwen and her mother walked out of Joshua and Junko's house.

"No, I think they can argue...I mean *discuss* the projects without us, but we could call them in for a rest." Alice put an arm around Gwen and smiled.

"Who would've thought life would change so dramatically?" Joshua said as he finished putting up the support for the porch swing and put his tools away. "It's been less than a year since our meeting with y'all, and here we are still keeping each other company."

"Who would have thought the few weeks you spent working as an undercover cook at my estate would turn into a lifelong kind of commitment?" Gwen chuckled as Alice walked over to the two working on the project.

"I certainly wouldn't have, but you know those two—" Joshua shrugged toward the caretaker and the butler. "They're good people. Gerald was always so formal it seems a juxtaposition to see him in something less than a suit and tie, even if it's just a pair of dress slacks and a tie. And Gerald helping Ralph put in the foundation for the fish pool and a fountain? That's pure entertainment." Joshua stood and helped Junko out of her chair. "I think we have some iced tea to go with the cake?" He looked down at Junko as they walked inside to the table.

"We have gotten so much done today." Junko sat at the dining room table.

Gwen put plates of cake on the table and brought some glasses for tea. "Everyone sit up to the table and try this carrot cake Alice and I've made. It's the first real cake I've ever been involved with." She smiled as Ralph and Gerald came to the table after washing their hands.

"It looks real good, Missy." Ralph's face crinkled up in a smile.

"Carrot cake? You can't beat Alice's carrot cake with a stick. I think we've got your fish pool and fountain centered, and we'll come back and work more tomorrow." Gerald took his cake.

"Why would ju beat Alice's cake with a stick?" Junko's face had a horrified look.

"No, my love—" Joshua's eyes twinkled. "—no one's beating the cake with a stick. Gerald just means Alice makes a very good carrot cake."

"Oh. I see." Junko's brow puckered in thought.

SITTING IN THE KITCHEN at Mac and Amanda's hideaway the next week, Junko closed her eyes for a moment. She opened them and took a sip of her tea. "I very much find this spot peaceful and so pleasant here. Ju 'ave large family, but also so much love for each other. My father and brother and I were very close. I was concerned when my father die for Joshua to make tings better with his family. I felt not just my family was important, but he needed to patch tings together. So important for Mai to meet her other family. We 'ave not known you long, yet I feel as if I 'ave known all of you forever."

"We missed our family and prayed for their return." Mr. Mac-Donald pulled at his bottom lip. "This last year has been amazing. We are thrilled that you and Joshua are getting settled into your new house. The next few months will be exciting."

"We've been working v'ry much to get settled in. It is looking so much better with all the help we've had. Tomorrow Ruth is coming over to look at some furniture I've got new. Ruth and Anna, such good to me..." Junko sighed.

Joshua stirred his tea then put the spoon down. "I've wasted too many years and possibly would have wasted more, but we came to realize—even before God threw me through the door and back into my family—that I needed to make amends with you. Thankfully, God is in control, and I'm grateful for his hand in this." Joshua stopped and took a deep breath. "Six years ago, Junko and I used to jog together, but it became harder for her to keep up. She seemed so tired all the time. She had tests and was told it was cancer. She did all of the things she was supposed to do, and it has been in remission. However, remission is not cured. At her last check-up, the doctor found something. He isn't sure what, but there is a possibility it has returned. She needs more tests..." He struggled, not able to look them in the eyes.

"Oh, no!" Amanda gasped. "These things aren't supposed to happen to us." Her eyes were large and sympathetic. After placing her teacup back into the saucer on the table, she took Junko's hand and put her arm around her shoulders. "We will pray, my dear. And you know we'll be here for you."

"I know dis." Junko laid her head on Mrs. MacDonald's shoulder.

Mac opened his Bible and began reading Psalms one hundred thirty-nine. "O Jehovah thou hast searched me and known me." He finished reading with, "—And lead me in the way everlasting." Taking Joshua's large hand in his and Junko's small hand, he led them in prayer. "Lord, help us to know thy will, do thy will, and accept thy will. In Jesus's name, amen."

RUTH WAITED AT THE front door, again listening to the soft patter of Junko's slippers across the wooden floor. The news hadn't been as much of a shock as of a sadness. She had prayed these long months that what she saw with her eyes was not happening.

"Oh, Junko." When the door opened, Ruth wrapped her arms around her friend in a hug. "I don't know what to say." Then like a flood, she began to weep. "I'm so sorry—"

Junko shared the box of tissues with Ruth. "I was alone the first time I was sick." She wiped her tears. "My father was sick and my brother was away, only Joshua was with me. There was no Mai. We did not believe we would have children. When Mai was born, it was two miracle. She has been a tiny joy, a very much funny bone." Junko smiled softly as she watched her only child playing in the living room as the early morning sunlight streamed through the window. "Leave your shoes here, and come look at my flower seeds and tings I 'ave gotten. I have a pot of tea just brewed."

Leaving her shoes at the door Ruth replaced them with slippers and followed Junko to the kitchen. "You are not alone anymore." She sat at the kitchen table and cradled her cup of tea. "When I lost my mom it was Mrs. M who took me in. I don't know what I would have done without her. We cried together, then she said to me, now that we've had a good cry, we need to stand up and pick up our lives. It isn't that we won't ever cry again, she said, but we needed that good hearty bawl."

"Mrs. M?" Junko rolled the sound around. "Dat would work— Mrs. Mom—Mrs. MacDonald? So much wisdom and no better friend." Junko sighed.

"From the first time Mom and I met Mr. and Mrs. MacDonald, I—Mom and I both felt it—like we had hit the jackpot." Ruth sipped at her tea. "Let's look at your flowers. We'll just do the best we can from here on out."

"YOU REST, DEAR PERSON." Ruth finished setting plates and silverware on the table for supper. "We have everything done here. Come now, I'll help you get comfy...If you want to sit on the porch and enjoy your spring flowers and the cooler breeze...Mrs. M and I will finish putting the food on the table."

"It was so good of Joshua to make a porch swing into a bed. I do enjoy the fresh air. I tink it helps me feel better." Junko waited as Ruth rearranged some pillows and helped her get situated in her swing.

"Let me move these pillows. How does that feel?" Ruth asked.

"That is just right. Thank you." Junko closed her eyes and drifted off to sleep.

Ruth tucked the cover around Junko as Joshua came up the steps. "We're getting the last of the meal on the table. When you're ready, let me know. We'll wait."

"Thank you. I'll let her rest a few minutes, then we'll be in." Joshua brushed a kiss across Junko's forehead and sat beside her in a wicker chair, gently caressing her hand. He looked out across the front yard with its new plantings of flowers, trees, and shrubs. *Who would have seen this coming? A year ago I was wondering if Junko and Mai would like it here. I wondered if they would accept this family and if they would be accepted. I almost died last year, and there've been so many changes. Yet, here we are today in a way I could never have foreseen.*

"Look at how beautiful things are becoming." Junko's eyes were still closed. "We are working at Donna's tomorrow on strawberries." She opened her eyes.

"You have some pretty high goals there. Are you sure you're up to picking strawberries?"

"I don' ave to pick strawberries. I jes oversee." Junko snickered.

Joshua smiled and patted her hand. "I know. Those rascals, they won't let you do anything. Are you ready to go inside now?"

"It is so good of Mom and Ruth to come help with supper dis evening. They have even helped with the garden. They 'ave shown Mai how to plant flowers today."

"Flowers are important. What kind of flowers?"

"Sunflowers. Giant sunflowers. Mom and Ruth were picking some peas and der Little Parrot was patting something into a row she had made and watering it in with her toy water pitcher." Junko sat up slowly.

"That should be real nice. You like sunflowers. Were they some of the seeds you had bought?"

"Jes, they were some I had bought...big flowers and red. She put them all in three foot of row. Dis will be interesting to see."

"Three-foot row? I would think that will be... interesting." Joshua blinked, rubbed a hand over his face, and looked at Junko.

"Such a child..." Junko smiled and then they both laughed heartily.

"Well, let's go see what's for supper." Joshua threw the cover over the back of the swing and took Junko's hand.

"WHAT CAN I SAY, DAD? Each set of these treatments leaves her drained. I'm so thankful this time around we have family and friends to help." Joshua ran his hand through his hair and sighed. "Last time she was sick there wasn't much help. The ladies from the church here have set up a rotation for meals, and of course, you guys visit and help with shopping, cleaning, and other things." He sat in the shade of the rose arbor over the patio at his parents' hideaway. It was peaceful with the birdsong and the few bees buzzing in the distance.

"A burden shared is a load lightened. A joy shared is happiness increased," Mrs. MacDonald reminded him. "That's a good token of what family is supposed to be. Here to help and support each other. Her treatments are done for now?"

"Yes, she's a trooper. I hope it will be the last, but right now we're waiting to see. Everyone has been so good. You can only guess how comforting it has been to be able to remain in our own home and not disrupt our lives any more than necessary. Anna and Ruth are so good at helping. They've been taking nursing classes, haven't they?"

"Yes, this year has seen many changes. They've been taking classes, Michael's working overseas. This is the first summer he's not been home." Mrs. MacDonald looked down at her hands with sorrowful eyes. "We can't hold onto everyone forever, but the parting is..." She stopped, not knowing what to say.

"'Such sweet sorrow'—Shakespeare, I believe." Joshua smiled. "We all had to go for a while. Even Lewis and Laura had to do work away from you, but the saying is 'Let them go, if they love you, they will come back. If they don't it was never meant to be'... or some such thing." Joshua sat back and took a drink of his tea.

"That is true. It helps to ground a young person in how and what they want. It gives people new eyes," Mr. MacDonald said.

"I've never thought of it as new eyes. But we do see things differently. Junko has so enjoyed the gardens and the seasons. There have been so many changes this past year. A year ago, Seth and I were leading double lives as we followed Gwen to her estate and worked on solving her mystery."

"What did they ever do with that Franklin Greene person?" Mrs. MacDonald asked.

"With the diaries and such documents, it was shown that what took place was planned and executed by Franklin's brother, Frederick. Even the kidnapping was Frederick. Franklin did have some psychiatric counseling, and he's been doing well."

"Lewis had a close call when his pickup blew up. We were afraid we'd lose him. Those were some frightening times. People like Frederick...they're evil beyond comprehension." Mrs. MacDonald took a drink of her tea and changed the subject. "We'll be gathering in pumpkins tomorrow and picking apples to put in the cellar this week. Will you feel up to joining us? We begin at Lewis' on the big wagon for the pumpkins and squash tomorrow, and by the end of the season, we'll end at our orchard with apples."

"We do plan on joining in. Junko says she only has to supervise, and she wants Mai to be part of the things going on. When she feels the lowest, someone seems to show up... I've noticed Ruth has a second sense." Joshua soberly rubbed his forehead.

"Ruth has a loving heart and a gentle touch—like Junko. They are much alike. I think we focus a lot on how much the doer does and we don't always see how much a graciously accepted gift gives in return." Mrs. MacDonald touched his hand gently.

"I'd never thought about it, but it is a humbling experience on both ends." Joshua smiled.

"We all would help Junko, but we can't. Watching as these treatments take everything from her is heart-wrenching and a difficult time. Yes, and Ruth is so tender-hearted watching others suffer, she grieves. With everything Junko has lost, there is a translucent beauty that takes its place." Mrs. MacDonald's face softened.

"She is determined to carry on so that Mai won't miss out. She's been there to make strawberry jam, and preserves, canned green beans, and at the time of canned tomatoes. In helping Mai it connects to what you said about a gift graciously received being a blessing to the giver. Junko has a deeper bond through being at events.

Even if she just supervises, as she calls it. Well, I'd better get back to the house." He finished his glass of tea.

"I guess we'll see you tomorrow for the pumpkin harvest then—here, I'll take your glass, don't worry about it."

"Thank you, and we'll see you then if not before." He hugged her.

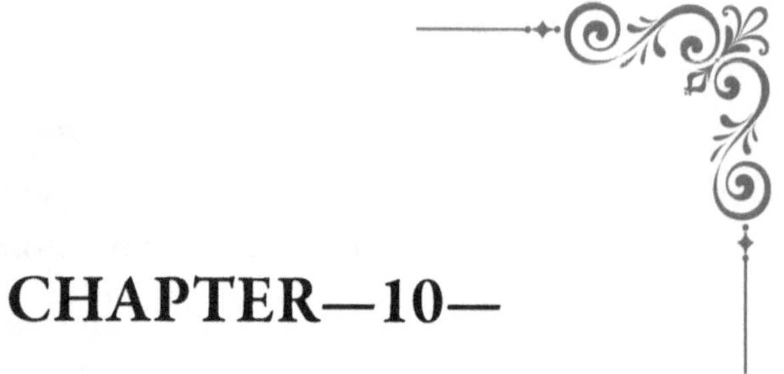

CHAPTER—10—

"Happy anniversary!" The assembled group gathered around as Gwen and Seth cut their cake.

"How many years is this?" Jack O'Brien asked Seth as they sat at the large table.

"Technically it's number eleven. This last year was our first real year, and it has been a good year. Thank you." Seth moved back as the waiter placed food on the table in front of him.

Gwen took a drink of her water. "Last year we were at my estate back east. I didn't know where Seth was and I was wrestling with all sorts of things. I can't comprehend how different my life is now. God took all the pain and sorrow from that old life and gave me this new one."

"This is a very nice venue." Ruth waved a hand. "It must be satisfying to have your mother, Alice, here with you, and Ralph and Gerald as well."

"Yes, for our wedding it was a quiet affair. Just Seth and myself and Rachel and Lance—and the preacher, of course. This is quite a mark of how far we've come. We wanted something a bit special for this year." Gwen pushed her salad bowl away. "This food has been very good."

"I'm looking forward to the apple picking party. This year was a good apple year, and we should have a terrific crop to put in the cellars. I think that's a great omen." Seth finished up his baked potato and cut a piece of steak.

"I think you're right. I like baked apples, applesauce, apple...can't think of anything apple I don't like." Gwen laughed. "I've been obsessing over apples lately."

"You need to be careful with those cravings. I used to crave beets when I was..." Mrs. MacDonald's eyes went wide, and she stopped speaking and became thoughtful.

With a twinkle in her eyes, Laura looked across the table at her mother. "Mine was green peppers."

"Chocolate and mint." Donna smiled.

"In a few weeks, we'll be back to having our singing and barn potluck," Lewis Junior said to Seth.

"Umm, it will be an occasion to celebrate. Won't it, girls?" Mrs. MacDonald smiled at Laura and Donna.

JOSHUA AND JUNKO RESTED on the bench at Lewis's orchard. "We seem to have one thing after another. Last week it was Gwen and Seth's anniversary party, this afternoon we're here in the orchard. We won't want to stay out too late. The weather gets more than nippy at night."

"I am so glad that we return. I feel much better here with your family." Junko leaned her head against him and relaxed into his arms.

"This has been kind of our anniversary too. You've been here a bit over a year now. And I've been retired coming on a year...if you count my intervention with Seth and Gwen's situation." Joshua held her tenderly.

"We were so afraid for all of you. Especial after Lewis' accident. Father MacDonald was trying to contact you and then he had to come 'ome right away..." Junko shivered at the memory.

"It worked out, but yes, it was touch and go. Good to have my memory back—most of it at least." Joshua grimaced.

"It is pleasant sitting here. It's warm enough and cool too. Just right for a jacket and the sunshine makes me happy..." Junko's words trailed off.

"The days grow short, the leaves are falling, but the peace and beauty of this moment is priceless." He watched as time hung, suspended like a leaf that has left the safety of the branch and is drifting softly, very softly on an unknown current to settle and eventually rest on the ground. "Thou art fair, my love, behold thou art fair," Joshua murmured as they watched everyone laughing and picking apples.

"Jes, and you are my turtle dove— Do you hear the music?" she asked.

Joshua listened as they were both quiet for a time absorbing the life around them. "I hear the breeze. I hear people picking apples, and laughing, and teasing, and singing—I guess I do hear the music."

"I tink if we sit here we appreciate more how sweet this is around us."

"To be part of the family, and yet a part from the group. How special to be allowed to look out from one perspective, yet look into it as well." Joshua pondered in thought.

"Please be thankful for what we have today—and yesterday, and for all of our years together. But someday you should tink of remarrying to some fine Christian girl. Mai will have many good examples here, but to remarry would not be bad." She sighed softly and closed her eyes.

"Don't speak like that. You have to give yourself time to heal." Joshua frowned.

"Sometimes we 'ave to look painful tings in da face." She wagged a finger at him.

"Today I have the Scarlet complex." He avoided the subject. "I'll think about it tomorrow."

"I will feel better if we talk about it instead of pretending that there will be many tomorrows." Junko chided him softly.

"O'ka-san!" Mai ran to her mother. "Mi'te! Kidei ringo desu, O'ka-san!" she exclaimed. The little red and white jumper accentuated her peach complexion and the pink cheeks that were shining with excitement. "Look! A pretty apple, O'ka-san!" her thick black hair hung down her back in two crisp French braids. "'Bout ready for the big fire, Otoo-san?" she turned to her father with excitement in her every fiber. "We're back from the hayrack ride."

Joshua lifted Mai onto his lap and held both his girls firmly yet gently. Mai reached her delicate little fingers to his face. "Why you cry, otoo-san?" Tracing the tears on his cheeks she wondered aloud. "Otoo-san? Nande shikku shikku naku no?"

"Aa, musume! Watashi ga anata-tachi totemo aish'teru. I love you and your mother very much," he repeated. He hugged Mai and set her down. "We will wait till after the prayer then I'll take your Mamma home. Can you ride home with your Uncle Seth and Aunt Gwen?"

"Yes, I can, Papa. Auntie Gwen has good news." Mai was excited to be telling what she'd heard. "We are going to pray over Mamma and Auntie. I brought this apple for mama." She rattled on from one subject to another, holding out the perfect red apple to Junko.

"There you are, now." He took the apple. "You run back. Ruth will help you toast your hot dog and there will be some s'mores too. I'll wait up for you at home."

THERE WAS A LIGHT GLOWING in the living room as Mr. MacDonald knocked on the door and held it open for Mai. "Made it home safe and sound. I expect you need to run up and get ready for bed, honey," Mr. MacDonald said, and then walked toward the kitchen. "Hello? Joshua?"

"Yeah, I'm out here, Dad," Joshua called from the kitchen.

"I brought your little person home. I think she enjoyed herself." Mr. MacDonald's face lit with a smile.

"Mai has the distinct ability to enjoy life. She is so much like her mother. You want a cup of coffee?"

"Sure, I've got time. I left Mom at home. I think she's worn out with all the activities. The anniversary, now the apple picking, before that the pumpkin and squash gathering." Mac sat at the kitchen table.

"How are Seth and Gwen doing? I bet they're excited." Joshua brought the coffee.

"Yes, but it's just been confirmed, so it's early. The baby isn't due until April but with their history, there is no time to waste before we start prayer. How are you doing?" Mr. MacDonald asked.

"We're doing. One day at a time." Joshua set the cups on the table.

"It's been a while since the last treatment. How long before you know where you are on this?"

"They will continue to monitor and do some follow-up work. Junko is a fighter, but she's not coming back like she did the first time." Joshua was anguished. "I don't know, she... has a different outlook on things. I can't seem to talk her out of this foreboding attitude."

"That makes it tough. It's hard on you and hard on her. Is there anything—any basis for her feelings?"

"That's what makes it aggravating, we don't know, and it's too early to know one way or the other."

"You don't need advice. You already know all the words I could say. I noticed you both enjoyed this afternoon...at least you looked like you did?"

"Yes, today was a beautiful day. Since I'm working my own business I have the luxury of taking time when I need it. I blocked off a whole day and spent it at home. I made waffles for breakfast, read to Junko for an hour before lunch, played some of her favorite music while Mai and I played some board games in the afternoon...and of course, the late afternoon in the orchard."

"These are the things that will linger in your memory—Time taken, and life well spent. We could have lost Lewis last year. We almost did, but we didn't. Every day when each one of us wakes up, we should remember to thank God for another day."

"Coming from my previous line of work..." Joshua stopped and took a sip of his coffee. Clearing his throat he continued. "I should be well aware of that philosophy, and I am, but I see how difficult it is in our current society. Most people find a job then build their world around that job."

"Last year when Gwen was struggling, before she left us to go back home, she asked me why we live this way. Because yes, it is simple in some ways, but not as simple in other ways. I think she asked why do you work so hard to keep your life simple? I told her we choose to live this way, partly so we can control more of our lives. I guess I better be getting on home." Mr. MacDonald drained his cup.

"Thanks for the conversation, Dad. It's supposed to be quiet until next week, right?"

"Yes, the soup supper, and then we're having the barn jamboree so it will be quiet until then. Michael's supposed to fly in Friday morning as well. Mom is happy about that. His absence has been a terrible sorrow for her."

"YOU LOOK SO NICE TONIGHT. I think at last you're gaining back some ground." Ruth carefully brushed Junko's hair and braided it.

"I 'ave been feeling better. Dis soup supper will be just right for me. Laura always has the best suppers...Juanita is such a good cook."

"Edwardo is no slouch either. He's been working for Juan all of his life. Edwardo's mother was orphaned, and Juan's mother took her in and gave her a home when she was abandoned. Edwardo's mother eventually married one of the men employed at Juan's estate. Edwardo is very loyal to Juan, closer than a brother," Ruth said.

"Juan is so quiet. He and Laura are good together." Junko looked in the mirror and smiled. "Dear Ruth, you are such a comfort." Junko caught Ruth's hand and gave it a gentle squeeze.

"Why, thank you." Ruth smiled.

"You know exactly what makes me feel better." Junko stroked Ruth's hand.

"I have thought of taking more nursing classes—but I don't know if I can bear the suffering." She gently pushed a pearl-tipped comb into Junko's hair.

"Poor Ruth. The suffering is hard." Junko's eyes held a sad, faraway look. "It is good Michael is home for the holidays, jes?" She changed the subject. "Dees summer was v'ry long with heem gone overseas with the mission work."

"Yes, it is good that Michael is home for the holidays." Ruth's eyes were troubled and sad. "He and his team have had quite a bit of success with their teaching efforts."

"Ruth, you do not find Michael good to look at?"

Ruth smiled at Junko in spite of the question. "I don't know any of the MacDonald men or women who are not good to look at."

"But he does look v'ry 'andsome. I tink 'e 'as, how would you say, become the man?" She searched for the right words.

"Yes, he is quite handsome. And we say that a young man has grown up or matured." Ruth frowned. "There, your hair is just right and you look very nice. Let's go now."

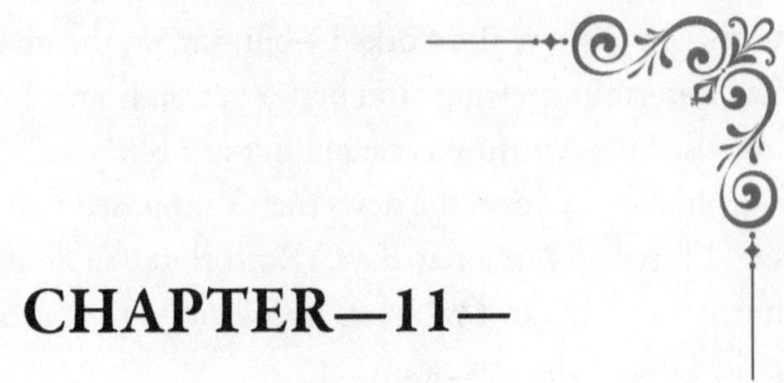

CHAPTER—11—

"Thank you, Ruth, for helping Junko." Joshua hung his coat in the closet and shut the door. "She loves decorating but now that the big holidays are past...and the year will be starting anew it's good to put some of those decorations away."

"No problem— you know I enjoy spending time with Junko and Mai. Anna will be here tomorrow, and I'll be back the day after—Supper's in the warming oven, and I can't think of anything else right off." Ruth looked over the living room and picked up her purse.

"You have a special bond, a special touch. It must be that you are so much alike."

"I don't know...alike how?" Ruth asked.

"Junko is a fighter. She lost her mother when she was small, and her father passed away just two years ago. Now this," he said. "Junko has a black belt in Karate, and has won several competitions."

"Incredible!" Ruth's eyes widened in astonishment. "No? I didn't know—I can't put the idea of Junko and a black belt in Karate in the same sentence. They don't go together."

"Yes, the first time I saw her, I was at a competition for a friend of mine. She was there competing against someone else—a larger opponent. But it's based on skill."

"So it was love at first fight?" Ruth snickered and pulled her keys out of her coat pocket.

"For me maybe, but..." He smiled at Ruth. "I didn't think I'd ever see her again, let alone meet her. A few weeks later I blundered into the shop where she worked—but, say, on the news they're talking like a storm is brewing. You better get on home. I came home early because I don't want you caught out in a blizzard."

"It's been all over the news there's supposed to be a blizzard coming. I'll see you in a few days." Ruth shut the door behind her and hurried to her car. *Oh, great, it's starting to snow*. She frowned and pulled out of the driveway.

A mile down the road, the snowflakes came down thick and fast and the road became a blur. *A good thing it isn't far to Mr. and Mrs. M's*. She bit her lip, fighting panic. After a fourth of a mile more, she rolled down her window, watching to keep her bearings. *Oh, good grief—Lord, help me, how can I be driving on the wrong side of the road?* She began to drive at a crawl. Had she traveled another mile? *It can't be much farther.* Her eyes were glued to the whiteness in front of her as she looked for the driveway. Just as she reached the drive, her car began sliding sideways into the lane. It came to a stop in time, then crept slowly toward the garage. Shaking from the strain, she heaved a sigh of relief when she pulled into the garage and put the car away. Sitting for a few minutes to stop shaking she breathed a prayer. *Oh, dear Lord, thank you for safety.* She slammed the car door behind her and gratefully opened the door into the house.

"What a blessing!" Ruth stopped and inhaled the good smell of cooking food and the comfort and warmth of light and heat. "Hello, I'm home!" She called out. "And none too soon to suit me. It sure smells good in here."

"I'm so relieved to see you." Mrs. MacDonald was setting the plates on the table for supper. "Michael called. He and Juan are on their way home. That was an hour ago." She placed silverware beside the plates. "Joshua had left early so he could send you home. Michael was concerned if you had made it. That was an hour ago." She repeated with worry. "And I have been— not worried exactly— but praying for you ever since. Now I guess I had better increase my prayers for Michael and Juan." She frowned as she finished her task.

"Things are deteriorating out there. When I pulled out of Joshua's driveway, it wasn't long before the storm began in earnest. I'll give Laura a call, see if they have made it that far." Ruth picked up the phone. "Don't worry, but... Okay," she spoke into the phone. "I'll let them know." Hanging the phone back on the hook, she turned to Mrs. MacDonald. "They just made it to Laura's. Laura tried to persuade Michael to stay there, but he has to send in some information and all his stuff is here." Concern was evident on her face.

Mrs. MacDonald watched as Ruth's face blanched. "Well, it isn't worth risking his life." Mrs. MacDonald scowled and draped a kitchen towel across a chair.

"It's only a little way. He should be all right." Ruth grimaced and furrowed her brow.

Mrs. MacDonald picked up the phone and punched in a number. "Mac, number ten is on his way home from Laura's, and Ruth says... Okay." She hung up. "Mac has everything under control."

"Oh?" Ruth said.

"He and Lewis are going to hitch up the team and go after him. Those horses are so good they can find their way back to the barn even in a storm."

"We had better have some hot coffee and soup ready when they get here." Ruth busied herself in the kitchen.

Working energetically for the next thirty minutes, they finally heard the door blow open. Mr. MacDonald and Michael whooshed in, bringing cold frosty air and a partially frozen body, well-wrapped in a blue blanket.

Michael deposited the bundle in the blanket in a chair by the fire. Mac left several items by the chair and went back to help Lewis put the team away for the night.

"Put another log on the fire, Mom. Ruth, is there any hot chocolate or coffee or something?" Michael was shivering and trying to warm himself. "One of the Christianson girls was sideways on the shoulder of the road. I almost rear-ended her vehicle when I came along. She wasn't dressed for this weather." His teeth chattered with trying to stop his shivering. "I don't know what's the matter with folks. I had some extra clothes and things along. Praise the Lord, or she would have frozen."

"Here, Michael." Ruth handed him a cup of coffee.

"Let me take this scarf and the gloves." Ruth unwrapped Michael's scarf from the young woman's head as Mrs. MacDonald brought another cup of bouillon for their unexpected visitor. "Here's a cup of bouillon. Be careful. I've wrapped it in a napkin." Ruth put the soup on the coffee table and helped remove the heavy gloves so the visitor could grasp the cup. "Can you hold that now...Ada, is it?"

"Yes, it's Ada. And I'm warming up a bit." Her teeth chattered.

As Ada continued to thaw slowly, bit-by-bit they removed Michael's oversized coat but wrapped a warm afghan around her. Her short, stylish skirt, open-toed high heel shoes, nylon stockings, and a very flimsy feminine sweater were—as Michael had summed up—quite inappropriate, especially for this type of weather.

"Anna is going to stay at Seth and Gwen's this evening." Mrs. MacDonald bustled into the living room after answering the phone.

"Good, good, that's wise," Ruth said. "Mrs. M, this is Ada Christianson. They live around a mile and on over east."

"Ada Christianson? Why, yes, I know the place. Over by the Heide's, I believe? Not to be bossy or anything, but Ada, you had best stay here for the evening. Mac and Lewis flagged your car. Just give your people a call and let them know you're safe. If you need help getting out, tomorrow will be soon enough," she said. "You can take a warm shower or bath. That will help warm you up, and Ruth will get you some warmer clothes."

"I don't want to put you out—but I guess until this storm's over, we'll all need to stay put. Thank you." Ada replaced her empty cup on the table. "That sounds great."

"Follow me, then. We have a spare room here." Ruth pointed as they walked down the hall. "Here's the bathroom, and I'll get you those warmer clothes."

AFTER THE STEAMY SHOWER, Ada Christianson dried herself quickly and pulled on a warm plaid flannel skirt and a fleecy pullover sweater. She looked in the mirror as she brushed her shoulder-length, silky blond hair out of her face and pulled it into a ponytail. So thankful she had grabbed her purse to bring with her. Ada applied a light touch of powder, then appraised her reflection one last time. Her eyes narrowed as she decided that the girl—she couldn't quite remember her name—had chosen colors that complimented Ada's complexion as well as being comfortable and warm. She replaced the items in her purse and set the purse in the spare bedroom after exiting the bathroom.

Ada walked back past the bathroom and a couple of other doors before she found her way to the kitchen. "I am so grateful to all of you for your help. I don't know what I would have done if..." here she hesitated trying to remember a name.

"Michael." Mrs. MacDonald supplied.

"Yes, if Mike hadn't come along."

Mrs. MacDonald's brow puckered. "The phone's right there on the wall. Why don't you call home and let them know you're all right?"

Mr. MacDonald came stamping in the door at that moment. "B-r-r-r, it's cold out there." He shook the snow off his coat and gloves. "Sure smells good in here, Ahmanda," he drawled as he hung his things away. Giving his wife a peck on the cheek and a hug, he teased, "So what's for supper, sugar pie?"

"I was just suggesting that Ada here call home, then we can have supper, Mac. I'm sure she should stay here for the night."

"She sure should." He shook his head in agreement with his wife's judgment. "It's bad out there. I must say, Ada, you look much better now. Let me go get washed up, Ahmanda, and I'll be ready to eat a horse."

"Lewis MacDonald—" Mrs. MacDonald gasped. "—We aren't having a horse for supper." Mr. and Mrs. MacDonald continued to tease each other even as they headed off on separate missions.

"Those two like to tease." Ruth smiled at Ada. "I do hope that skirt and sweater will be all right. I usually wear it with a scarf and brooch."

"It's fine. I am just glad to be safe and warm," Ada said. "I don't know what I would have done if your brother hadn't happened along."

"AH... MICHAEL'S—" RUTH started an explanation. Ada was close enough to Ruth's age, surely she should know Michael was not Ruth's brother, Reuben.

"Time to sit up," Mr. MacDonald called before Ruth could finish speaking.

"—The providence of God—" *How do I explain this situation tactfully? Well, truthfully I am his sister-in-Christ.*

After the Bible reading and prayer, Mr. MacDonald looked down the table at Ada. "I don't believe we've had very good introductions here. I did hear a name—Ada?"

"Yes. Ada is right," she said.

"Well, then, Ada—may I call you Ada?" Mr. MacDonald chuckled.

"Mac, this is Ada Christianson, from down around by the Heide's." Mrs. MacDonald realized there had been very little introduction. "I'm afraid we have overlooked the names part. I'm Amanda MacDonald, and this is my husband, Lewis Senior. And our son, Michael, and you know Ruth O'Brien." She pointed and continued as the food was passed from person to person.

"This is the best chicken pie you've ever made, Ahmanda." Mr. MacDonald took a bite.

"You always say that, Mac." She laughed, her eyes twinkling at him. "But thank you anyway."

"It's always true. You just keep getting better." He winked at her. "So, Ruth, how was Junko today?" He became sober.

"The holidays weighed her down. They were almost too much. She was very tired today. I helped her with laundry and housework. She always insists on doing more than she should. I feel as if I should be able to see right through her, she's so thin." Ruth bit her lip and blinked back the tears.

A mutual look of understanding passed between Mrs. MacDonald and Ruth. "She is so precious." Amanda sighed and changed the subject. "You say there is no use to call home, Ada? No one is there any way? Surely there is someone you need to inform of your safety?"

"No. Dad is staying in town. My sister, Cyndi, will be in Hermon this evening as well. My other two sisters live out of state." Ada listed.

"Well, I guess at least you're safe. Would you like some more chicken pie, Ada?"

"That's the first time I've ever had homemade chicken pot pie. It is so good, but I think I'm full and more..."

"Hopefully you've saved a spot for dessert?" Mrs. MacDonald turned as Ruth brought the peach kuchen.

"So, how was your day, Michael?" Mac turned his attention to Michael.

"Just so-so, Dad. Since I'll be leaving this week I'm kind of in limbo. I spent the day at Juan's store. That was a trot down memory lane." He smiled thoughtfully. "It's been a vacation to be home, but I'm needed back at the mission work. You know it's like night and day difference from here to there." He took a large helping of the dessert as it came to him. "The home-cooked meals, spending time with everyone...all of it has been super. But I can only handle so much downtime. Makes it hard to... Say, this peach stuff smells really good." After pouring cream over his dessert, he took a spoonful. "This is delicious. My compliments to the cook." He smiled looking at his mother.

"Thank you, son, but Ruth made that while we were waiting for you." Mrs. MacDonald grinned at his compliment.

"Well, my compliments to the cook anyway." He waved his spoon in Ruth's direction. "Sorry you had to wait," he apologized. "Those roads were nasty. Did you have any trouble getting home from Junko and Joshua's?" He looked directly at Ruth.

"Yes, it was terrible. It took me an hour to get home, or close to it. I almost slid past the driveway when I got here." Ruth winced.

"What were you out in this kind of weather for?" Mr. MacDonald asked Ada.

"I was coming home from work. I started a new job in Hermon," she said.

"Oh, where do you work?" Mrs. MacDonald asked with a smile.

"I work at Mimmi's Fashions. I was promoted within the store. I had been a salesperson, but now I'm the manager over what we call 'soft lines.' Those are items such as clothing and soft accessories." Ada watched Michael out of the corner of her eye.

"That is a lot of responsibility for someone your age isn't it?" Mr. MacDonald asked.

"This kind of weather brings out the best and worst in human beings." Michael barely glanced at their guest. He had not been following the conversation. With the second helping of dessert, his eyes kept straying back to Ruth.

"You must enjoy working there." Ruth attempted to cover Michael's faux pas.

"I took two years of business school after high school, and I worked there part-time at the same time. It is interesting, but mostly it fills the time and pays the bills." Ada shrugged non-committally.

Ruth looked down at her plate, trying to think. *After Ada's mistake of thinking that Michael's my brother—she doesn't remember me at all. Well, that is to be expected maybe. I'm not Reuben. The Christianson girls might have remembered him...but none of them, neither Ada nor Ada's sisters had anything in common with quiet old me.*

Yes, they might have remembered my brother, Reuben. He was like dad. A good-looking hunk that had followed in Dad's footsteps with his football prowess. It would have been amusing if Ruth hadn't seen this reaction before. *And Michael is,* Ruth sighed, *good to look at... and he had literally rescued Ada from freezing to death.*

"Time to move into the living room by the fire—who's ready for a rousing game of Aggravation?" Mr. MacDonald pulled the game out of the closet. "Michael, can you still pop corn?"

"I'm not sure. It's been over a year since I popped any popcorn, but I'll give it a try." Michael walked out to the kitchen.

"What color would you like, Ada?" Mrs. MacDonald asked.

"I—I don't know. I've never played—Aggravation?"

"Well, pull up a chair here, and we'll get started. What color marbles would you like? Put your marbles here." Mr. MacDonald waited for everyone to put their marbles out before explaining more to Ada. "Then you have to get all of your marbles around here and back home. Simple as that." He smiled.

"Yeah, simple as that," Michael said. "Except Dad there, and Mom, and Ruth have a way of getting in the way..."

"And Michael always wins." Ruth laughed. "You would think Michael is all kind and helpful, but he's Mr. Heartless when he's playing a game. Don't get in his way, let me warn you."

"Grab your popcorn and let's get started." Mr. MacDonald scooped up the first bowl of popcorn and began passing them around.

MICHAEL GROANED, HOLDING his head in his hands. Had the blizzard messed with his mind or what was it? He had done well during his vacation until this evening. He could not help but watch the way the light danced off Ruth's auburn hair like a halo, the way her face was so alive when she smiled, and the vivid blue of her eyes. These things left an ache in his heart.

Michael flew in late for his vacation to limit his time at home. Burying himself in his work far away from home had helped him avoid the bittersweet emotions her presence brought. However, that did not lessen his yearning. He missed sharing problems, sharing ideas, the camaraderie and friendship that they had enjoyed in the past, and wondered if she ever missed him. He tried to put the longing away and focus on his work.

At this rate, he might as well have stayed at Laura's till the end of the blizzard. *Focus. I need to focus.* He sat back, looking at the computer then looked into his manual. He began following the step-by-step instructions, but after thirty minutes he came to a dead end.

Dear Lord, what do I do now? Sitting again with his head in his hands, he fantasized about ways to throttle that computer. He looked up at the screen and chuckled silently. Who in their right mind would want to choke an inanimate object? *Okay, well—*he started again.

RUTH WOKE WITH A START. She was usually a moderate sleeper, but the storm seemed to lull her into a deeper sleep. *What was that?* She sat up suddenly, listening intently. There, she heard it again. *What a relief, it's just Michael at the keyboard.* Should she let him work it out or go help him? In times past she would not have hesitated, but tonight it would serve him right if she just let him fight through it on his own. There he went again. She slipped her robe on and pushed her feet into her slippers. It did not take long before she was headed for the office with two steaming mugs of cappuccino.

"Here you go, my friend." She handed him his mug. She was saddened that he had been avoiding her ever since their conversation a year ago. Ruth had missed Michael, yet his absence made it easier for her to do the job she had to do, but at the same time made it harder for her. The family was accustomed to his absence during the school year, but this year he had been gone during the summer also. Ruth knew it pained Mrs. MacDonald that he was absent, and they all three knew why he was gone. He had only returned for the annual potluck and holidays, allowing just enough time before scheduling to leave again at the end of the week.

"Thanks." He accepted the mug. "I've been agonizing over this for hours." He groaned, running a hand characteristically through his hair.

"Why," Ruth laughed, "do all of you MacDonald men do that? I've seen your dad do it, Lewis, Jr., even Joshua, and Seth—"

"Do what?" He puzzled raising his eyebrows at her.

"Run your hand through your hair so that it stands up on end like this—" She reached unthinking and ran her fingers lightly through his tousled hair. Too late she realized her mistake, and quickly she returned her hand to grasp her mug. "Well—" She blundered on. "I thought about letting you stew all by yourself. What must our visitor think? You ignored her all evening."

"I didn't think she was my responsibility," he said sharply. The agony that her touch had caused was evident in his face. "I rescued her from freezing. Wasn't that enough? Besides, I have nothing in common with her." He frowned.

ADA WASN'T AT ALL A light sleeper, but tonight she couldn't even get to sleep. She felt like the princess in the story of the princess and the pea. The turmoil from the storm, the unfamiliar surroundings, the strange bed, the strange family, the strange emotions, it all kept her tossing and turning.

Why did she let me think he was her brother anyway? The angry thought ran through her mind. *And what's wrong with me? I've set my feet on the path to being my own woman—an up-and-coming young businesswoman. I'm not going to be anyone's fool, especially some good looking...* She fumed at herself for her feelings, especially that this young man didn't pay *her* any attention. That was something she wasn't used to. He just sat and made sheep eyes at that O'Brien woman. Angry, muddled thoughts swirled in her head, but she would never have admitted any of this.

Ada could hear voices droning in the room next to where she was tossing and turning. This was a well-constructed house. Not a board creaked as she moved silently. The office was between the two bedrooms, and it was the simplest thing in the world for her to hesitate at her door. She had never read from her Bible that eavesdroppers never hear anything good about themselves.

"I have nothing in common with her..."

"Did I hear that right? The nerve of that man—" she fumed. *"What is a man and woman supposed to have in common anyway? Didn't have anything in common, humph!"*

"Ruth, you know my feelings. You know that I would care for you. I am committed to the work that I am doing, but it isn't forever.

Others are training, and will be ready to help in this work soon. We could marry in the fall. Mom and Dad would be happy. You know they love you like a daughter already. Your dad and Grandfather have given their consent..."

"My dad— my Grandfather? Michael, what are you saying?" she gasped, the color draining from her face only to return in a crimson blush.

"You don't think that I would approach you without asking your father first, do you?" He drew back as if she had struck him. "I told you..."

"Yes, I know—" She spoke quickly to stop his words. "—I just never thought..." Ruth stammered. "I love you and your family very much. You all have given me a gift I can never repay. But this would only make our families happy if it were right."

Ada moved slightly, just enough to observe the scene at the far end of the room. The O'Brien girl was almost the same age as Ada, but that was where the similarity ended. How could anyone be that lovely this time of the night— at least not without a lot of work? She sat like a queen wrapped in an exquisite blue velvet robe trimmed in gold embroidery and lace. At suppertime, her hair had been pinned up and neatly contained, but now it hung in a loose braid down her side almost to the floor. The young man seated at the desk looked as if he had been agonizing over something, and there was a glow of light in the background that contributed to the surreal atmosphere.

The young man slid to his knees and picked up the young woman's hand. "Ruth?" His heart was in his eyes. "Do you find me so repulsive, so unacceptable?"

"Michael, do not tempt me further. I do love you, and I would do almost anything rather than to see you unhappy." She stroked his hand lightly then looked into his eyes. "I find you misguided, but not repulsive."

"Ruth, if you'd give me some idea. Some direction where to go?"

"Last year when Gwen left, I knew she needed Seth and Joshua. She was in danger. I don't see anything now, only a mist that I'm walking through one day at a time. I can't tell you any more than that. One day at a time, Michael."

What's wrong with those two? Ada frowned. *What did he mean by intentions?* Surely they were old enough to make their own decisions without either a father or grandfather. She'd heard that these people were different. She remembered her dad speaking about them and tried to remember what he had said. Ada was so confused. This whole affair had been one strange experience after another. When her car had first slid sideways and she was unable to get it under control, had she inadvertently uttered words something to the effect of *Oh, God, please help*? Stories of people found frozen in their vehicles flitted through her mind.

In this part of the country what people called Mother Nature was unforgiving. One mistake was all you needed to make and there was no second chance. She might have uttered another cry for mercy as in *'Oh, God, please help me!'* No one from her family would check to make sure she was alive. It could be days before she would be found. By then it would be too late. Ada remembered the feeling of relief that flooded over her when a rescuer appeared out of the swirling whiteness. He supplied warm clothing and a way of escape. She also realized even in her distress that he was strikingly, good-looking, and wondered just where this hunk had been hiding.

What were these two people talking about? Ada's head reeled attempting to understand. In her world, you just took what you wanted, and gave whatever you felt like giving. Character didn't count for anything. Whatever you do just don't get caught, was the motto for her and her crowd.

If I had a guy like that, I wouldn't even think twice but... Something sifted into her consciousness. What was it he had said? Something about —*Besides I have nothing in common with her.* The contrast between her lifestyle and this world was stark. There was no restraint in her world, but these two were controlled by something greater than the moment in which they lived.

"Do not tempt me, Michael." Ruth looked intently into his eyes. "I want the things that you want...children, a house, a home, a family. I want all of those things, but I don't see them in my future at the moment. I could—by saying yes to you—easily have those things. But I can't. It isn't the time, Michael. You and I both have things to do before we can commit to marriage, and we must trust God in this matter. I have missed you. Please don't stay away so long again."

"Ruth, if you would just give me some encouragement. You may be walking in a mist, but I feel like I'm groping in the dark. I have tried to be worthy of you. To live honestly and with integrity before God, but I don't know how to win your favor. Tell me, is there someone else?"

"I don't see anyone else. I'm not looking for anyone else. I can't give encouragement where I don't see it. One day at a time is all I can see right now."

Kiss him, you fool, Ada thought, *or you're going to lose him*. She couldn't stand any more. She fled for refuge to her bedroom. For some reason that Ada could not comprehend, she cried herself to sleep that night.

CHAPTER—12—

Ruth sighed, and her mind wandered as she tried to study for her class. Her days were packed full as she studied medical classes and took care of Junko. She closed her book and turned to look out the big kitchen window at Mac and Amanda's hideaway.

Mrs. MacDonald stuck her head in the doorway. "Oh, there you are. Would you like a cup of tea?" She strolled into the kitchen.

"That sounds great." She sighed again and continued to look out the window at the mounds of snow piled high on the other side of the glass. "This winter we've had enough snow. January and February feel like the world is closing in. I've made it to my classes during the week, but prefer staying in the rest of the time."

"I know. I'm ready for spring already." Mrs. MacDonald brought two cups of tea to the kitchen nook.

"I've been pondering over our two invalids." Ruth stirred her tea.

"Invalids?"

"I know there is only one true invalid, but Gwen has been somewhat housebound. She was feeling sorry for herself Sunday because—well, in that condition you don't need any real reason. So they tell me." Ruth studied the birds at the bird feeder while she thought.

"Maybe we should have a party." Mrs. MacDonald brainstormed.

"I think that would be just what the doctor ordered. We could call it a leap year party. Have cupcakes, hot chocolate, and a sleigh ride—the girls need some fresh air." Ruth smiled.

"I'll talk to Mac and see what he thinks. What's your schedule? Any afternoons available?"

"Anna and I have a test tomorrow, and we have the rest of the week free. So, we're good to go." Ruth looked in her book.

"COME IN, COME IN." Donna opened the door as Alice and Gwen came across the deck. "Lewis hasn't gotten Pete and Dolly hitched yet. We thought we might have a few games in front of the fireplace. Find a comfy place to sit."

"Is everyone here already?" Gwen left her boots at the door while Alice took her coat and scarf.

"Ruth and Anna came down early to help set up a few tables for the games, and Mom came a bit later to help get coffee and punch set up. Joshua, Junko, and Mai just walked in before you did. Watch those babies..." Donna hurried off to catch one of the twins.

"We call those two babies 'the artful dodgers.' I've heard it said there is nothing on two feet that is faster than a toddler who is evading capture." Ruth laughed at the scene taking place. "I do believe Donna's nicknames for those two are pretty accurate."

"Yes, this little punkin' is Running Dear One, and that little punkin' is Running Dear Two." Donna came carrying a baby who had a cupcake in both hands, cupcake all over her face, and a big grin.

"I am grateful," Laura said, "that Noah is more placid. He's quite content to let someone bring him his bounty, as opposed to the grab and run trick."

"None look like dey are lacking." Junko smiled. "Thank you. Dis punch is v'ry good. Dis party is so nice."

"It is nice. This winter feels longer than last winter. I'm looking over my seeds and flowers, and this year I have more help. Who's playing in this game? I'm kind of rusty here, so maybe I should just watch." Gwen took a sip of her punch.

"Mr. Ralph and Mr. Gerald have so much help been. Dey come for a visit ev'r'y Tuesday when Joshua gets home from work. Dey play chess and tell stories." Junko sat back in her comfortable chair.

"NOW THAT WE'VE EATEN too much, it's time to try to stuff us into coats. Maybe we should've done the ride first." Gwen laughed.

"This was such a good idea, no matter how we do it." Anna held Junko's coat and helped button it securely. "Here's your scarf." She wrapped it around so no cold air could bother her.

"This is a challenge at this stage of the game." Alice hovered over Gwen, trying to get her wrapped up. "I don't think I've done as well as Anna." She glowered.

"I hear the sleigh bells coming." Ruth stopped to listen as Anna and Alice continued to bundle their charges for the outing.

"I will 'ave so much clothing on I'll never bend. I'll be like a mummy." Junko chuckled.

"I don't bend well anyway." Gwen picked up a pair of mittens. "But I'm ready, and this should be fun."

"The bells have stopped." Ruth opened the door out onto Lewis and Donna's deck. "Lewis is waiting. We'll get you tucked in."

"It has been a long time since I've been in a sleigh." Alice laughed as she helped Gwen get settled in the big sleigh. "This should put some roses in your cheeks, lamb." She rubbed Gwen's mittened hand.

Anna smiled at Junko. "Here, let me tuck that blanket in better..." Her brows drew together as she made sure she had the blanket anchored well.

"If everyone's in and settled, hold on. We'll go around the mile and return." Lewis shouted back to his passengers. "Get up there, Dolly. —C'mon, Pete." He clucked to the team, and they tossed their heads, manes flying, and the bells began jingling again. The horses seemed to enjoy the outing as much as the passengers.

"Oh, look, there's Ada, that got stuck and had to stay at our house." Ruth noticed Ada's car traveling homeward, and they all laughed and waved.

Just being outside in the fresh air made their faces glow. Their spirits brightened considerably as the big team pranced down the snow-packed road around the section then toward home.

"You do look rosy." Laura waited as they pulled to a stop. She held out a hand to help first Gwen, and then Junko out of the sleigh.

"Such beautiful animals. Dis one's named Dolly?" Junko stopped to touch the large animal, running her mittens over the shaggy coat. "The horses are so big but gentle." Junko leaned her head against the withers.

Dolly bent her head down and gently nuzzled Junko's hood. "Look, she knows how I love her..." Junko sighed. "This has been such a good day. To have good family and good friends is treasure. What a wonderful ending for this delightful day."

"Thank you, everyone." Joshua helped Junko into the car then slid into the driver's side.

"I'll be over in the morning." Ruth waved as he closed the car door. "What a wonderful day, Mrs. M. It was so pleasing to see how happy everyone was. Junko has been kind of peaked lately, and this was so amazing."

"She isn't getting better, is she?" Mrs. MacDonald took Ruth's hand as they walked back into Donna's house.

"The doctors have told her if the last treatment didn't work, they wouldn't guarantee how long she had left. This is very hard. Jesus' words in Matthew about 'Take therefore no thought for the morrow: for the morrow shall take thought for the things of itself. Sufficient unto the day *is* the evil thereof'—certainly applies." Ruth wiped the tears from her cheeks.

"None of us is guaranteed tomorrow. We will take every day we get and rejoice in that day, Ruth." Mrs. MacDonald stopped and wiped the tears from Ruth's face and hugged her.

"SING TO ME OF HEAVEN..." Ruth sang softly a cheerful hymn as she put dishes away in the cupboard.

"It ees so happy." Junko brought in a load of towels from the dryer. She rested a few minutes then began to fold the towels and put them in the drawer. "To 'ave you to sing—Even Mai like to sing. Sunday she sat her dollies around the coffee table and taught them to sing her Bible song, 'Jesus Loves Me.' She listens to you, and I laugh to see her tuck her dollies to bed then sings dem to sleep. She is so solemn. She will be a good momma someday."

"She is so sweet and serious. That's what makes her so cute. Howdy, partner." Ruth imitated Mai. "Then she acts like that's normal, that everyone says howdy partner. It just slays me." Ruth laughed and put the last dish in the cupboard. When she'd hung the towel up to dry, she picked up the broom to sweep the kitchen floor.

"Slay?" Junko blinked. "We rode in Lewis' sleigh?"

"English. It's two different words. One is the sleigh you rode in and the other means to fight the wild beast and kill or slay it." Ruth, with her broom, pantomimed a sword fight.

"I tink I understand." After a pause, Junko asked, "You and Michael 'ave come to the understanding?"

"Yes, we have," Ruth said without explanation as they moved into the living room.

"I see great sorrow in heart of my friends." Junko walked to the living room and sat on the sofa. "I wish I could 'elp."

"For some things, we have to leave the solution in the hands of God... There is no earthly help. I am going day by day. I wish you, my friend, would recover and live a long, happy life. Are you ready for a rest?" Ruth hugged Junko and helped her lie down then covered her carefully.

"The doctors do not know how many months. Already through prayers of my Christian friends and family, I live almost six month longer. I pray to see the time of the singing of birds, as the Bible says.

I would like to hold Gwen's baby to be born in May. I go day by day too." She closed her eyes and smiled. "Michael ees not 'appy either." She returned to her original thought and the frown returned.

"Life isn't cut and dried." Ruth picked up her knitting. "Everyone had our lives laid out—Michael and me, that is. Sometimes—" She paused thoughtfully before continuing. "God has other plans that we don't understand. Right now, I can't see beyond today. I'm here helping you, Mai, and Joshua. Learning medicine, and healing, taking classes. That's where I am supposed to be. Michael is in India helping in the work there, and that's where he's supposed to be."

Junko rested for a time. "There is someone else then for Michael?"

"I don't understand." Ruth stopped knitting and raised her eyebrows.

Junko opened her eyes and looked gently at Ruth. "You couldn't marry Michael because of someone else?"

"I couldn't marry Michael because... I don't know why anymore. At first, it was like we were friends and..." Ruth's brow wrinkled. Her emotions were a confused jumble.

"Ruth—" Junko spoke slowly. "—my friend, don't be hasty. Don't lose the love of a good man for something you don't understand."

"You are right, of course... and you must rest now." Ruth tucked the covers around Junko. Watching Mai playing, Ruth picked up her knitting and sang softly. She tried not to think of Michael, but unbidden thoughts would come now and then as she wondered how he was doing. Of course, he wrote to his mother and others in his family on occasion, but how could she claim to love him like a friend when their relationship was such a jumble? He had stopped writing to her. They never exchanged letters anymore. He never returned home unless he was required to return. And the last time he had been here even Ruth knew something had changed. As Junko had said, Michael had matured. He had grown into a godly young man. Ruth sighed as Junko's words echoed in her mind. *Don't lose the love of a good man for something you don't understand. Oh, God, don't let it be a voice of prophecy.*

"ADA, THAT TIME IN THE snow must've frozen your brain. You haven't been the same since."

"You're making a mountain out of a molehill, Cyndi. All I said was I'm thinking about visiting that little church out there." Ada frowned crossly.

"What's wrong with where we always go?" Cyndi's eyes narrowed, and her face puckered up in a pout.

Ada laughed sarcastically. "Always go?" It wasn't a question.

"Well, whenever we go to church somewhere, that's where we go." Cyndi frowned defensively, still pouting.

"Easter and Christmas." Ada sneered.

"Well, what's wrong with it, anyway?" Cyndi's jaw tightened in rebellion.

"You really want to know?" Ada put aside her mask.

"Sure." Cyndi looked anything but sure that she wanted to know.

"That evening was a different experience. I felt something, saw something, and it made me see myself differently than before. I saw my way of life as cheap and shallow. I saw something I'd never seen before..."

"Ada, what you saw was a man, and you've been brooding over him ever since." Cyndi puckered her lips and raised an eyebrow. "One of them MacDonald men, I'd betcha. Is he single?" she asked with half-closed eyes.

"Cyndi, I'll be straight with you. There were two men, but—Yes, there was a man there, and yes, he is kind of single."

"What do you mean 'kind of single?' Does he have a paper saying 'until death do us part?' If he's just seeing someone, he's still available, baby." She smirked.

Ada sighed. She knew her sister's way of thinking. Not long ago it was her way of thinking also. Her heart sank. She just couldn't explain to Cyndi.

"Here, let me pick out an outfit for you." Cyndi rifled through her sister's closet. Pulling out a short, bright red skirt and a lacy sweater she laid them on the bed then went back to the shoe closet and dug through the shoes bringing out some high-topped leather boots. "Here you go." Cyndi winked slyly at her younger sister. "Let me do your hair and make-up. We'll make sure he takes notice of you."

Yeah, he'd take notice, and I'd stick out like a sore thumb. Everyone would notice. A lot of good it did Cyndi, Ada thought cynically. *She's on her second divorce and eyeing another man already.* "Why don't you go down and get some coffee ready? Let me take care of this," Ada said.

"Well, sure, baby. I just want to see you happy is all. You get dressed and come on down. I'll even go with you into the lion's den." Cyndi made a generous offer.

Ada eyed Cyndi's choice ruefully. How was she going to wear what she had planned and not hurt her sister's feelings? Well, there was no help for it. *Why did Cyndi have to be here today? She always stayed in Hermon on the weekends.* Ada's face clouded with a scowl. Putting the skirt and sweater back, she kept the boots. She took the dress she had just purchased the day before out of the closet. It was dark red with a lace collar and long sleeves. It accentuated her slender figure. It was still fashionable without flaunting anything, unlike her sister's choice.

She looked in the mirror. *What do I do with this?* she thought, brushing her hair. It was at the in-between stage. *It looks kind of funky like this. Hmm.* She frowned and pulled some of it up. It was cut with the idea of just hanging in place... It would be easy to give it up, she sighed. *No, I'm not turning back.* She set her lips in a straight line. Brushing her hair back, she pulled it into a loose ponytail. She found a poufy knitted beret hat. *Not too bad*, she muttered.

Cyndi's eyes widened with surprise when she saw Ada in the doorway. "Oh, baby, that don't look too bad—but that isn't any way to catch a man. I don't see..." She stood back, paused, and surveyed her sister. "It is pretty, but...I don't see anything." Her face was full of wonder.

Ada knew Cyndi meant well. She had tried to be both mother and father to Ada, her little sister, since their mother had passed away. Their father had always left the rearing of the four girls to his late wife, and he either didn't know how to raise girls or didn't care. Either way, he just let them do what they chose and paid them no mind. The first two girls were old enough that they'd married and gone their ways, leaving Cyndi to take care of Ada.

Cyndi shook her head. "I just don't know what has gotten into you, girl. You'll never attract him like that."

"Maybe he's a different kind of man than you are used to," Ada said gently.

Cyndi blinked in surprise. "I don't know what you mean, Ada. What other kind of man is there?" She tried to consider the idea of any other kind of a man. "I just want you to be happy is all." She fell back on her standard response.

"Are you happy, Cyndi?" Ada spoke almost too bluntly before she thought.

Cyndi stopped, the cigarette halfway to her lips. The pain in her eyes spoke the truth. She squashed out her cigarette in the ashtray. "I'll go get my jacket. Is yours in here also?" she asked, rummaging in the downstairs closet.

"No, I have mine." Ada picked up her new matching sweater.

RUTH WALKED TO THE living room window and watched as the last of the visitors drove out of the driveway. She picked up a cup and a stray glass and walked back through the living room smiling at Anna and Alice as they entertained Donna's twins. She set the cup and glass on the counter. "There were quite a host of visitors for our shower—Junko's living room was full of a goodly crowd of ladies."

"When Ruth said we should have a chower I don't know what to tink. I wonder do we wash the baby or ourselves." Junko made a joke.

Ruth laughed. "The English language is wonderful to experience. What do you think?" She smiled as Junko tenderly touched the soft baby face.

"I tink this is the most beautiful baby ever— except little Mai, of course." Junko held the baby and cooed happily. "She is so soft. Newborned babies 'ave a smell all their own, and they are so soft." She continued stroking the baby's little impish face. "She look just like you, Gwen."

"Why do babies sleep when you want them awake and are awake when you want to sleep?" Gwen lamented good-naturedly.

"Little Zoë Junko MacDonald has to sleep now so you will get used to being up all night for the next eighteen years." Mrs. MacDonald laughed heartily at her joke.

"It's funny, all those people came to do homage to Gwen and little Zoë, and Zoë was oblivious to all the excitement and bustle that was being had in her honor." Donna chuckled.

"That little cherub just slept most of the afternoon. Didn't matter that she was passed from one set of arms to another. But no, tonight she'll be awake and want to be entertained." Gwen sighed.

"This 'as been such a delightful afternoon." Junko breathed softly. She snuggled the tiny baby lying on her chest. "I feel so contented and peaceful." She touched the soft flannel baby blankets, smoothing them ever so gently.

Gwen smiled at her sister-in-law. "I have waited so long for this day—In more ways than one—and I'm so glad we made it together." They sat together, enjoying the peace after the party.

"Everyone has left but us cleaner-uppers." Ruth came back from another foray into the living room.

"Ada Christianson has become a regular at services, hasn't she?" Donna continued to dry and put dishes away.

"Yes, and the change in her demeanor is welcome." Mrs. Mac-Donald and Ruth portioned out the remaining cake. She and Ruth shook their heads.

"How is that?" Donna asked.

"When we unwrapped her from Michael's extra clothing, she was...well, she was underdressed. It's a wonder she didn't freeze to death." Mrs. MacDonald cleared her throat.

"Oh, my!" Donna's eyes grew wide. "Surely you exaggerate?"

"Not much. The Lord works in mysterious ways." Ruth washed up the cake plate and wiped up the counter.

"What do you mean?" Donna finished putting glasses in the dishwasher.

"They have been neighbors for many years, and we have hardly met them. But quite frankly, if anyone ever needed the Lord, that family does." Ruth picked up the broom and swept up the crumbs.

"Her mother died shortly after we moved here, didn't she?" Donna furrowed her brow trying to remember.

"Yes, I think she was in a car accident. I remember taking them a basket of food when it happened. They seemed very thankful," Mrs. MacDonald said. "There were just the four girls, I think?"

"Yes, there were four girls. The two oldest were in the same grade for some reason..." Ruth's brow wrinkled in thought. "They weren't twins, but they graduated at the same time and pretty much married at the same time."

"Cyndi is pathetic, isn't she?" Donna sighed with a sorrowful look.

"She always makes me sad. I don't know why." Ruth sat down.

"That's what I feel too." Mrs. MacDonald grimaced. "Some people are their own worst enemy, and there isn't a thing you can do for them."

"I feel that Cyndi is just floundering. At least Ada is looking for something," Gwen said, watching the baby.

"I jes hope it da right ting, she look for." Junko looked curiously at Ruth.

Ruth's eyes grew large, and she looked away. Glancing around at the tidy kitchen, she changed the subject. "Well, I guess we're done here. I wonder if Anna and Alice have the living room and dining room straightened."

"I think they've just been playing with the babies." Mrs. Mac-Donald chortled.

"Well, let me tell you," Donna said, "that in itself is enough work to keep five people busy. What those twins can't get into hasn't been discovered yet."

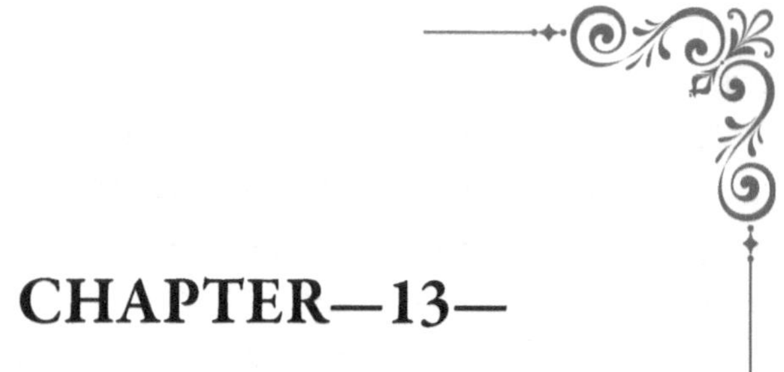

CHAPTER—13—

"It is only right that you and I can be of more help to Junko. I'm still concerned for Laura. She had a difficult recovery from the pregnancy and delivery." Ruth set the pan of enchiladas on the counter.

"She always overworks herself for the holidays, and this year was no different. The doctors told her after Noah was born to rest and take it easy." Anna's brow puckered as she chopped onions and carrots for the evening meal. "We should have a surprise party for her."

"We should have something special for Laura and Junko. Take lots of pictures, have cake and ice cream and...one more time—" The tears that Ruth wouldn't allow when she was with Junko rolled down her cheeks.

"Don't cry, Ruth..." Anna put down her knife, wiped her hands, and wrapped her arms around Ruth. "Don't cry," she repeated as the tears started down her own cheeks, and they held on to each other.

"There is no shame in having a tender heart." Mrs. MacDonald came into the kitchen area. "The real shame is in not having feelings for others. This is a difficult time for all of us." Her heart ached for the family. Sorrow wasn't anything new for her or Mac. There were many loved ones in her life that had gone on from this existence, but the young ones such as their son James, or Ruth's mother, Diana, and now Junko's sickness. These things always wrenched at the heart more fiercely.

"I THINK THE GIRLS HAVE a good idea." Alice sat thinking. "It doesn't have to be a big party, just a small get-together. We can host it over at Gwen's, and I'll be in charge."

Gwen smiled. "Ralph and Gerald are back from their mini-escapade and have done some more landscaping. We can use it as an excuse to show off some of our new trees and fire pit. It's a bit of a challenge trying to get a caterer out here, but if it can be done, Alice... Mother can do it— if it can be done."

"That settles it." Mr. MacDonald took a sip of his iced tea. "Next week at Gwen's pagoda."

"We better get going if we're going to be ready." Alice picked up her handwork and folded it into her bag. "This should be enjoyable—a new project. Grab that baby and let's go."

"DIS HAS BEEN A GOOD day." Junko sat under the large umbrella sipping lemonade.

"The kids have had so much fun today." Laura smiled. "It's nice to just sit—although I feel like I've been sitting too much lately."

"Not to worry, deary, you've earned a rest now and again. It's good you have Beth to help with Noah. She's so patient and good with children." Mrs. MacDonald squeezed Laura's hand.

"Jes, she's so good with Mai. Dey like sisters...and even Lydia like a sister to Mai." Junko smiled.

"I didn't have any sisters, and now I have them all over. We've needed little people in our lives, haven't we, Alice?" Gwen chuckled.

"That was one thing we missed at your mansion. The sound of little feet." Alice looked tenderly at Gwen. "Your little feet grew up far too quickly, but now we're making up for lost time."

"It is so uplifting to have family return. We didn't have near the faith we should have had. We prayed and prayed but never saw coming what happened. The Lord works in his own ways." Laura sipped her tea.

Mrs. MacDonald laughed. "The improvised polo game Ralph and Gerald thought up for the kids is so fun. Who would have thought? Six children, six ponies, and the two older—gentlemen on horses—and brooms for mallets to scoot a large beach ball to the goals. What a game."

"Alice, where did you find those ponies?" Junko pointed as the ponies were brought up to the fence. "I tink Mai has become a pony whisperer. Look how she takes to that little spotted one."

"Ralph and Gerald are quite the pair." Alice shook her head. "All these years they've been so quiet and done their jobs respectfully like Ms. Zoe would expect, and now they are off like two kids. Finding ponies—Like you said, who would have thought? They found a pony farm out west a way. If you don't mind, maybe they can bring one back for Mai?"

"I tink that would be good—Joshua, what do you tink?" Junko asked as Joshua ambled up in conversation with his father.

"What's that?" Joshua sat beside Junko and put his arm around her.

"Junko wonders if Ralph and Gerald could find Mai a pony?" Alice asked.

"I imagine that would be fine. We have a double-sided shed with a few paltry chickens in it... A pony in the other side would balance things out. Go nicely with the pooch that showed up on our porch a week ago."

"A stray dog, huh?" Mr. MacDonald asked.

"Yeah, now all Mai needs is a flying pig." Joshua smiled at Junko.

"We find some old blankets and a bed for Taro. He's 'appy and Mai is 'appy." Junko rested her head on Joshua's chest. "The house, it becomes a home." She closed her eyes.

"Are you ready to head for the hills?" He caressed a stray lock of hair back into its braid.

"Head for the hills?" She opened her eyes and looked at him quizzically.

"You look tired out. Are you ready to go home?" He raised his eyebrows at her.

"We'll get a few more pictures first before you leave." Alice beckoned to Ralph and Gerald. "Bring the ponies and the kids up for pictures, you two."

"You get the pictures and I'll get some goodies for y'all to take home." Gwen hurried into the house to fetch a box. "It has been nearly a perfect day for this party. We'll be over tomorrow, Junko, in the afternoon."

"Dat is nice. Mrs. Rudd comes in da morning to 'elp. She 'as so many stories. We are making a recording for her grandson."

"She has lived most of her life here local, hasn't she?" Gwen closed the box and put it in a sack.

"Jes, she say she has been born and raised in dis area since 1898. Much history she has."

"Well, we'll bring Zoe' and be over." Gwen gave Junko a hug and a kiss on the cheek. "Get some rest."

"Tomorrow, then. Mai, carry the sack, okay?" Joshua handed Mai the goodies and gently scooped up Junko.

"WE'RE ALMOST FINISHED cleaning this pagoda and area out here." Alice held a full garbage sack and began tying it shut. "Things have changed for the better, I'd say."

"Why is that?" Gwen picked up a cake plate, a sandwich holder, and a spatula and put them in a cart of items going back to the house.

"When I was young, many people shunned others who had certain illnesses. Today was a testament to at least some progress," Alice said.

"Yes, it is difficult enough bearing the burden of sickness let alone being shunned for it. There was some sort of epidemic when I was young—" Mrs. MacDonald furrowed her brow trying to remember. "I was pretty young and don't remember what it was without asking. My mother seemed to have immunity, or she was just fearless. Anyway, she went around to help neighbors and others. But you're right, Alice, there were some diseases, like cancer, where people were shunned because no one knew any better. The known facts weren't true."

"And cancer was so mysterious. Many people thought you caught cancer. I'm thankful we can come together and support each other at this time." Alice's face was sad and sober.

"We hurt enough through this time, but thank God we aren't afraid we'll catch it. We can pull together. We will have these memories to keep in our hearts. Will it ever hurt less?" Gwen continued cleaning up the few stray leftovers.

"It will change, and the time should come when we can think of it without as much pain. But not today—and it only changes." Alice patted Gwen's hand.

"Ruth is suffering deeply. I don't know any way to help her." Gwen sat down to rest.

"She's lost so much. First, her mother and—" Mrs. MacDonald motioned helplessly. "When Diana, her mother, was killed, Ruth and her brother lost the hope that their mom and dad would get back together—the hope that they would be a family again."

"I'm glad she and Anna are so close. Is her brother coming home?" Alice waved to attract Gerald's attention. "I could use some help here, now that you two have those ponies back in the stable."

"Yes, he's supposed to be back in a week, I think." Mrs. MacDonald stopped and counted on her fingers. "It depends on how long it took his letter to get here."

"Today was worth a million, trillion, bazillion dollars. Just watching Junko's face while she laughed at the kids on the ponies playing polo with brooms and the big plastic ball." Gwen laughed.

"And Ralph and Gerald on bigger ponies acting like mother hens keeping everything moving in the right direction. I never saw this transformation in those two coming." Alice snickered.

"Scriptures say a merry heart doeth good like a medicine. I believe that's why we've been blessed to keep Junko with us longer than those doctors predicted." Mrs. MacDonald loaded the last of the table service into the cart and surveyed the area. "And I think we've got everything in the cart for Gerald to wheel back to the house."

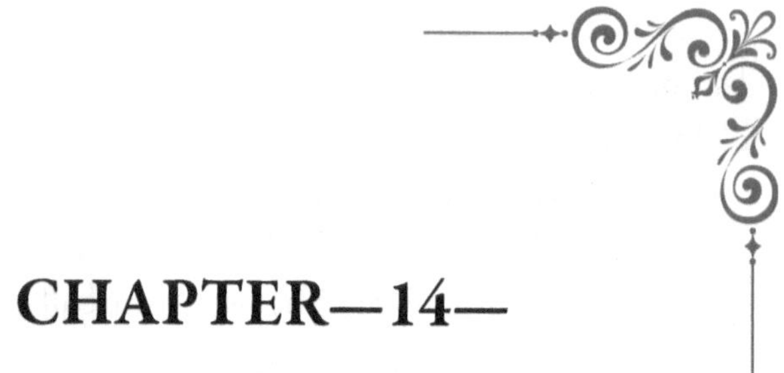

CHAPTER—14—

"I think this pony looks like it should do well." Joshua ran his hand along the little pinto's neck under her mane. "You did a fine job picking a pony, Ralph. Mai will be happier with this pony than she would be with a flying pig. There's enough chill in the air yet. Junko's still inside and Mai isn't awake yet—We'll tie this pony here in her stall for a bit and you come on in and have a cup of coffee."

"I've had a bit of experience in picking horses an' such like. The owner says dis pony is real good with children. He says his grandchildren played with her and rode her a lot. Only ting he says, she's a bit of a prankster." Ralph looped the lead rope around the tie-up at the manger and gave it a good tug.

"Prankster? How can a pony be a prankster?" Joshua shut the stall door and latched it before they walked to the house.

"I don't know, but he says she's not mean, and the kids will miss her." Ralph slipped out of his shoes at the door and left his hat on the coat rack.

"You sit here, Ralph, while I grab a couple of mugs and I'll bring us a tray of coffee." Joshua slid his feet into his slippers before heading to the kitchen.

"Ms. MacDonald, and how are you dis fine day?" He settled into the leather recliner.

"I am doing well. It is windy out, I tink?" Junko sat up slowly.

"Here, I have some coffee and doughnuts for you. Ralph, I thought you use cream and sugar..." Joshua set the tray on the coffee table. "Junko takes cream and sugar, so here you are."

"I do like a little cream and sugar..." Ralph waited until Joshua fixed Junko her coffee then he scooped a goodly portion of sugar and poured an ample amount of cream into his mug. "I'm tinking da wind has picked up considerable from all the noise outside." Ralph's brow furrowed and he took a pastry.

"Dis is v'ry good pastry." Junko took a bite. She put hers back on her plate, resting as she chewed.

"Reminds me of pastries we used to have back east at Gwen's mansion..." Ralph stopped and looked closely at his pastry. "Not really a doughnut?"

"Well, these are some pastries and things that Alice sent home from the other afternoon, so your guess is as good as mine where she got them or if she made them herself." Joshua laughed. "You're right, Ralph, that wind sounds pretty strong. I hope the dog is well anchored. The wind is loud enough, it must have awakened Mai." They heard the patter of feet coming down the stairs.

"Good morning, Mai. You're up bright and early..."

"Oto-san?" Mai ran to the front door. She stood on tip toe to see out the window in the door. "Okaa-san, visitor?" Mai threw open the door and the screen door.

"Mai!" And an audible gasp from three adults as a pinto pony placed her two front hooves onto the welcome mat on the gleaming polished wood floor, and the head of a very confused golden retriever dog appeared between the front legs of the pony as the dog looked on with a question.

"O-O-O-Oh." Joshua and Ralph looked wide-eyed at each other.

"O-O-O-O-O," Mai squealed, eyes wide in delight.

"Ah-h-h." Junko was wordless, not sure if she should laugh or cry. At last, the laugh won out, and she spoke quickly in Japanese. "Out, out, get that silly pony—and dog— out."

"MI AMOR, YOU WORRY about too many things." Juan gently scolded Laura.

"That is easy for you to say—and I'm not worried about it." Her face puckered.

"It sounds like worry to me." He raised an eyebrow at her.

"No, worry is a sin. I'm just concerned about it. I need to..." She hesitated, searching for the right words. "It's important to do what I can. Since Doctor Howser wanted me to take up a relaxing hobby, tomorrow I'm taking my easel over to Junko's and spend some time over there painting. Everyone else takes their handwork or needlework, so..."

"Do not fret." Juan put his arms around his wife and held her quietly. "Has no one ever told you how important you are to all of us?"

"Well, I'm sure maybe someone has." Laura remembered several incidents where that happened.

"Has no one ever told you how you are not just important, but you are loved, and you work too hard, and many of us are what you call, concerned about you?" He continued the embrace. "I will help you get your easel set up tomorrow, but you must remember now, Junko has a *perro* on her porch and at times a *caballo*, and a *loco pollo*."

"Why does she have a dog, a horse, and a crazy chicken on her porch?" Laura looked up in wonder at Juan. "I've heard about the stray dog, but—?"

"Remember the ponies Ralph had for the other afternoon? Well, Junko thought Mai would like a pony and it would be good therapy, you know."

"I think that's a good idea. Mai did take to that pony the other day. But on the porch? They have a shed." Laura sighed and continued the hug.

"The story is rather funny. Ralph went back to the man with the ponies and got a good price on another pony..." Juan continued to tell the story.

"So, you mean that by the word *prankster* the man meant the pony is an escape artist who can untie ropes, unlatch gates, and almost open doors? And the pony likes cookies, dogs, and roosters that she finds along the way?"

"And little girls, especially ones by the name of Mai." Juan smiled.

"This should work well." Laura smiled back. "I'll join the menagerie on the porch. And thank you, *mi amor*, I think I needed your words of comfort."

"They are true words. Words that should be said more often. I know them as true, and I believe you would know them too. But unless they are said, how would you know?"

"WHATCHA DOIN', TIO Juan?" Mai watched as her uncle brought up an artist's easel the next afternoon.

"I'm setting up an easel to make you ask questions." He smiled. "It worked too."

Mai's eyes grew wide. "Auntie, whatcha doin'?"

"I'm setting up my paints and going to do some painting, deary." She smiled at Mai. "I brought Beth, Lydia, and Noah to play."

"I can show them Maybell, my new pony. Come on, let's go see my new pony." Mai grabbed Lydia's hand and ran toward the shed.

Beth carried Noah, following behind. "My pony does tricks. I call her Maybell, but daddy and Ralph call her Trixie."

Laura laughed, watching the kids run across the lawn. "I heard about your first encounter with the new pony." She sat down next to Junko and looked up at Juan. "Anna will run us home after bit, Juan. You and Richard and Aaron can run on now."

"Okay." Juan bent for a quick kiss. "Come on, boys, let's go. Jump in and buckle up. You'll have to see the pony next time."

Amid a chorus of disappointment, Juan backed the van around and drove down the lane.

"Juan had quite a few errands to run. I don't know why the boys wanted to see this pony so badly. It's not like they don't have their own horses." Laura chuckled.

"Not like dis pony I tink." Junko nodded. "Da pony with t'ree names. Trixie, May, and Bell."

"Why three names?" Laura's eyes narrowed, and she squinted at Junko.

"I not sure. Joshua and Ralph, of course, named her Trixie, because—"

"—I kind of figured the Tricky Trixie connection, but May and Bell?"

"Mai, she call her Mable, but she tinks it May Bell." Junko shrugged. "Who knows, little people get some funny ideas."

"That's certainly true. When I was young, we had quite a few gravy songs."

"Gravy songs?"

"'The song that says up from the grave he arose'...we never heard it quite right. It wasn't until we could read that we saw it wasn't gravy." Laura smiled.

"English 'ave some tricky words." Junko sighed.

"Let me help you lie down. Is that pillow comfortable? And the cover?" Laura sat in the wicker chair closest to the swing. She gently rocked the swing as she talked and Junko slept. "Communication is such a difficult thing. I want you to know, you are important and loved—So much help to me before Noah was born. My dear friend..." Laura continued the gentle motion, rocking the porch swing as Junko slept, knowing she didn't hear most of what was said. "Still, I'm thankful you've been part of our life. I do wish it were for much longer." Tears quietly slipped down Laura's cheeks. "I'm sorry. I should have been here sooner." She wiped them away as Anna joined her.

"Glad you made it, sis. We've been concerned." Anna sat in the chair beside her sister.

"It has been difficult—I've struggled since Noah's birth. That was tough. And I watched as Lyle struggled and grew weaker, and yes, it's been more than ten years now, but..."

"Laura, you don't need to explain. You were so young, in a strange country..."

"And so alone. All I wanted was to come home." Laura's tears flowed silently, and she blew her nose. "But some days we have to face our fears. We can't live in the past. The present life isn't the same as the past. I'm not alone now. I have enjoyed good memories with Junko. We laughed together at the ponies the other day. I realized then it was important to change my path or someday I would find myself regretting what I had done— or not done. Regret is a poor companion."

"My dear, Laura. Do not worry. I unnerstan'—it's okay," Junko spoke without opening her eyes.

Laura's eyes grew wide as she glanced at Anna. "We've had lots of good days the last two years, and I'll be here for the next however many that are left." Laura caressed Junko's hand gently. "I make my pledge to you."

"YOU'VE BEEN WORKING on that painting now for over a week. It's coming along." Mrs. MacDonald gave the painting a one-eyed frown.

"I know, Mom, it's not exactly like I want, but no matter what I do it just looks weird." Laura stood back as far as the porch rail would allow, frowning at her canvass.

"From over here it looks v'ry nice." Junko sat on her swing sipping tea.

"At least you are looking chipper today." Mrs. MacDonald sat in the chair beside the swing.

"Today 'as been a good day. Joshua was 'appy you and Dad to come over. He's working to put a window in da shed for Trixie-May-Bell."

"It's time for a break. Mom, would you like some tea?" Laura put her brush into the odorless thinner. "I'll go get some. Do you need more, Junko?"

"I'm okay," Junko said.

"How's that pony working out?" Mrs. MacDonald asked.

"Someday I could, how you say—clobber da pony— but Mai is 'appy and pony is 'appy. So, what do we know?" Junko chuckled and raised her eyebrows.

"She's still showing up when she wants?"

"Jes, she like to surprise ev'ryone. Da other morning we find her sleeping on da porch with Taro da pooch. Her and Henry the rooster."

The screen door slapped shut as Laura brought a tray of tea and cookies out and set it on the small table. "Here you go, Mom. Let me warm your tea up, Junko. I brought some hot tea this time—isn't cold out here, but still just right for some brewed Irish tea. Would you like a little lemon and sugar?"

"Mai like to paint. She like the water paint, like I do when I was young." Junko pointed to a painted picture taped on the porch railing.

"She's done a good job. At least her flowers look like flowers and not globs of color like mine." Laura scanned the colorful picture with narrowed eyes. "Juan says Ralph is training Trixie-Maybell."

"Jes, he say ponies like her are—he doesn't call it hard, but dey too smart. Some can be a partner and will work with you, but others are too smart and will never be good for anyting."

"Some people are like that too. They are so smart. or think they are, and they can't see the truth if it was sitting on their nose and spit in their eye." Mrs. MacDonald took a sip of tea.

Junko chortled. "Dat's funny. I can almost see that—please to 'elp me lay down now?"

"Here, do you have enough cover?" Mrs. MacDonald took Junko's cup and picked up the afghan while Laura plumped up the pillows. "I thought I'd play some piano while you rest?" Mrs. Mac-Donald poured herself another cup of tea, and Laura held the door for her to go into the house.

"And I thought I'd just sit here if you don't care?" Laura took the chair beside the swing. "I haven't heard Mom play for quite some time now. All I need now is Dad and his violin—that's been even longer." She closed her eyes, just listening, as the first few notes sounded.

"Tank you—" Junko held Laura's hand and closed her eyes as well. "—v'ry much."

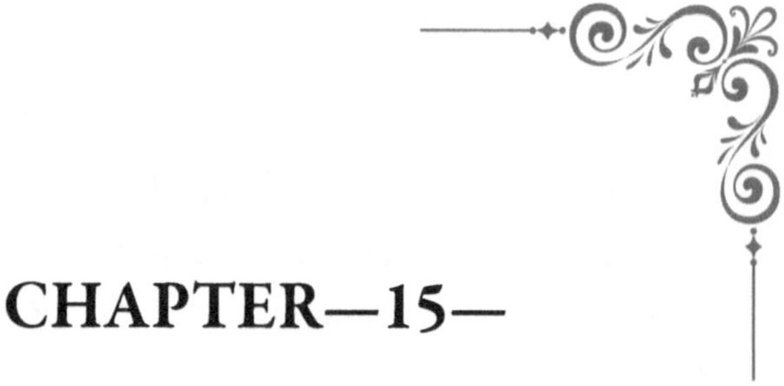

CHAPTER —15—

Ruth smiled at Junko as the sunshine dappled through the living room window. "The weather this spring has been so unpredictable, but we're past the freezing part. We are well past May eighth which is our last frost date. The flowers are positively radiant and the breeze is so gentle and warm. Summer will be here before we know it."

"I am so tired, Ruth." Junko sighed. "Maybe we go outside on my swing?"

"Such a beautiful day—fresh air and the sunshine would be pleasant and do a world of good for you." Ruth wrapped up her knitting. "Mai, honey, we are taking Momma out to her swing. Get your toys, sweetie." Mai gathered things to take with them. As Ruth lifted Junko into her chair, she noticed how frail she was and held back the tears.

"We need a new goal." Ruth dared to bring up the subject. Now that Junko had reached her goal of seeing and holding Gwen's baby, and the time of the singing birds, she was surely slipping from this world into the next.

"A new goal?" Junko's eyes widened in surprise.

"Oh, look, Gwen and Alice are here with little Zoe' Junko." Ruth helped Junko sit in the swing. "You'll want to hold the baby before you lie down and get comfortable— Hello, hello," Ruth called as they got out of their car.

"Just showing up for our visit." Gwen came up the steps. "Bringing Zoe'. She's become quite a social butterfly..." Gwen laughed. She carefully laid the sleeping baby in Junko's arms.

"Smile." Alice snapped a picture of Junko and Zoe'. "Treasures." She didn't need to explain. She blinked back the tears as she quietly slipped into the house.

"I was telling Junko we need to set new goals. Like they do with babies?" Ruth said.

"Yes, babies they measure month to month—I'll put little Zoe' inside in the bassinet." Gwen brushed a kiss across Junko's cheek as she scooped the baby up.

Ruth could see in the visitor's eyes the truth they all knew but wouldn't say. They each came daily for a visit, aware that Junko's time was drawing to a close, and that each day might be her last.

Ruth helped Junko get situated and spread the coverlet over her. In the golden warmth of the afternoon sunshine, she lay in the large porch swing that Joshua had constructed. He knew how much his ailing wife loved being in the fresh air with the sunshine, flowers, and birds, and the rocking of the swing comforted Junko far better than any medicine.

Mrs. MacDonald and Mai came out of the house. "Hello." Mrs. MacDonald sat in the padded wicker chair beside Ruth, who was gently rocking the swing. "I've brought some embroidery to work on while we sit and chat." She held up a bag with her hoop and some floss. "I still feel such joy at being able to see again. I just feel like stopping folks and warning them to enjoy what they have. Savor moments when there is peace and beauty all around you. And right now I see Mac coming up to the house with his violin under his arm. Laura suggested the other day he should bring his violin and we should play some duets. It's been too long since we've done that. I'll wait till he gets here."

They listened during the wait as Mai sang to her dolls. She put her finger to her lips to make a shushing sound. "Oo need to sleep now, babies." Mai placed them carefully in their little cradle. "Woofie, can I bring out my water paints now?" she asked.

"Sure, sweetie. Do you need me to help you get them?"

"No, I can do it myself," she insisted and ran inside.

"Isn't she just perfect?" Mrs. MacDonald asked. "So many folks are in such a hurry." She shook her head sadly. "They miss the really important things in life like watching their children grow up, being there for friends...and family. I have seen it too many times over the years." She stood and laid her embroidery work aside. "You made it, Mac, shall we go play for Junko? She always enjoys it."

The piano and violin began to play Clair de Lune softly from the living room. Mai brought her paints out and began a picture of flowers and butterflies for her momma. After a short time, she brought the finished picture to Ruth. "Woofie, can I put this here for Mommy?" She held the picture up and indicated a place on the pillar. Ruth smiled her permission while listening to Mac and Amanda as they played softly in the background.

"So Mommy can see it when she wakes up." Mai brought a dolly and tucked it in beside her mommy.

"Hello, Grandpa." Ruth greeted Pat O'Brien as he walked up the steps and sat in a wicker chair by the table. "So glad you came for a visit."

"Hello. Just making the rounds. Finished at Mom and Pop's, so here I am."

"Would oo like some tea?" Mai brought her little tea set to the table.

"Sure would. What kind of tea do you have today?" Grandpa Pat asked with a serious pose.

"I 'ave berry good tea." Mai pretended to pour into his cup.

"You do have very good tea." He took a pretend sip of tea. "And you have just the music for a tea party. What are you doing today, Mai?"

"I 'ave been taking care of the babies and painting pictures. Woofie and I baked cup cakes this morning. I love my mommy and my Woofie." Her eyes were large and serious. "There's my daddy and Auntie." She slid off her chair, running for the porch steps as a car pulled up and stopped in the driveway.

Pat O'Brien's heart ached to watch the blithe little spirit running down the sidewalk. He'd been through this scenario too many times. First when his Priscilla had passed, and then when Jack's Diana had died so suddenly.

"Ruth?" Junko stirred and called for Ruth.

"She just stepped inside, honey. I'm here, and Joshua and Laura are coming up the sidewalk with Mai. Ruth'll be here in a minute." Pat reached out and touched her hand softly with his gnarled fingers.

"It looks like Joshua and Laura are here." Ruth came out onto the porch and smiled at him.

"They are and it's a good thing. She's been asking for you, Ruth." He stood as the group ascended the steps. "Howdy, neighbor."

"Glad to see you. How's it going?" Joshua extended his free hand as he carried Mai on his other arm.

"Not too bad on my end. I've been havin' tea with a certain little charmer, there. She informed me that she had berry good tea." Pat O'Brien smiled.

"Ruth?" Junko asked softly again.

"I'm right here." Ruth touched her shoulder and caressed a stray hair out of her face.

"She's been askin' for Ruth." Pat O'Brien stepped aside.

Joshua, with Mai in his arms, knelt, and then sat in the chair. "It's Joshua and Mai." He took her hand and held it gently.

"My love…" it was more like a sigh. "Is Ruth here?"

"Yes, she's right here. Do you need anything?" He smoothed her cheek.

"Do you remember my poem?" she asked.

"When the snow sparkles on the mountain? Is that the one?"

"Jes, dat ees it."

"And the morning is everywhere." He rocked the swing gently.

"When evening's glory is in the valley,

And night birds are singing a prayer.

No matter where you go, my love,

My heart will follow you.

No matter where you go, my love,

My heart will meet you there." Joshua quoted. "Junko?" He kissed her hand but could say no more. Words wouldn't pass the lump in his throat.

She raised her finger to his lips. "My time is short. Please do not sorrow long. Please... for you and Mai... open your 'eart to another. Take care of Ruth and Mai. Mai—let me hold my baby."

Mai laid her little head on the pillow close to her mother. "I wuv oo, okasan." She patted Junko softly.

"Mai, be good girl for your daddy, Momma loves you too. It be a long time...before we see each other again."

"Okasan, do you hear the bells of heaven?"

"Jes, my dear one. I hear the bells of heaven. I will wait for you." She kissed Mai softly. "My favorite people." She paused for a rest as Mr. and Mrs. MacDonald, Laura, Ruth, Gwen, Alice, and Pat joined Joshua and Mai on the porch. "Take care of Joshua and Mai, please." Her face was peaceful. "Joshua, when... we used to jog... together... then I so tired. I 'ave to sit and rest. I would say 'You go on... I catch up later.' Now is my turn. I go on... you catch up... later."

Somewhere a bee buzzed and a bird sang, and a gentle breeze caressed each grieving person as Junko bid them farewell.

BROTHER MATTHEW CONSENTED to lead their farewell as they all gathered at the little cemetery surrounded by the new spring life. There was a drizzle in the air muting the day. The apple blossoms perfumed the mist as family and friends gathered to lay Junko to rest. The beautiful flowers bloomed everywhere, some in soft shades, and some in a bright profusion of color in tribute to the one who loved them so dearly.

"'For love is as strong as death,'" Brother Matthew quoted. "As Solomon reveals in Song of Solomon chapter eight verse six. In verse seven, Solomon continues, 'Yea, many waters cannot quench love, neither can floods drown it.' —We loved our gentle sister Junko. To say that she will be sorely missed is only to state the obvious. She was a gentle flower here in this garden of life. We might also ask, as Solomon did in the first verse of the same chapter, 'Whither is thy beloved gone?' We know she will not come unto us again in this life, but we may go to her in the future.

In Romans chapter eight verses thirty-seven through thirty-nine, we are encouraged by these words, 'Nay, in all these things we are more than conquerors through him that loved us. For I am per-suaded, that neither death, nor life, nor angels, nor principalities, nor things present, nor things to come, nor powers, nor height, nor depth, nor any other creature, shall be able to separate us from the love of God, which is in Christ Jesus our Lord.' We also know that in First Corinthians chapter fifteen verses fifty-five and fifty-seven we are told, 'O, death where is thy victory? O, death where is thy sting? The sting of death is sin. But thanks be to God who giveth us the victory through our Lord Jesus Christ.'" As he began quoting I Corinthians, the clouds parted, and a ray of sunshine pierced the sky, sending rainbows sparkling throughout the cemetery. A thrush be-gan to sing joyfully and was joined by a meadowlark. "Let us pray." Brother Matthew raised his hands, and they bowed their heads.

CHAPTER—16—

"Why do you cry, Woofie? Okasan said we need to be courageous." Mai's eyes were large and sad as Ruth brushed and braided her hair.

"Oh, sweet baby, Okasan never said we wouldn't miss her, and courage doesn't mean we won't cry. We loved your mommy. It is good that she is past the pain and suffering of this life, but we cry for ourselves because we miss her." She stopped, blew her nose, and wiped her eyes. "There you go, precious child." Ruth tied a ribbon on the end of Mai's braid. With a sigh, Ruth thought of the song, "'Day by day.'" It was hard sometimes to find the strength she knew God had promised her.

JUNKO'S WORDS ECHOED in his mind—*"I am so glad you are 'ere with your family"*—as Joshua stood on the steps absorbing the warm sunshine that early morning. The bright sunshine sparkled everywhere, much as it had the first Sunday he had attended here, and many other Sundays in the past two years. The providence of God had brought him this far, and he trusted that it would continue to lead him. He heaved a sigh as he thought about all of the oddities in those first days of his arrival at Beetle River. How he had, as an undercover agent, walked back into his own family. He remembered Seth's arrival as well a few weeks later. He flexed his arm muscle. His leg and arm were completely healed on the outside. However, they still ached at times just before the weather was about to change.

Everywhere he looked this beautiful morning, the vivid colors from the green grass to the blooming flowers, to the bright colorful birds singing reminded him of how much Junko had loved this country and the people she called family. She and Mai had felt at home from the very beginning. He took a deep breath remembering what she had told him—*for you and Mai... open your 'eart to another*—but his heart was aching and raw, and it would take quite some time for it to heal. Joshua and Mai had spent the last few days at his mom and dad's hideaway. The people were friendly and compassionate. The familiarity was comforting to be with friends and family at church that Sunday morning. The church house door opened, and he felt a presence rather than saw a form.

"It's time to come in, Jo." Seth put a comforting hand on his shoulder.

"Just thinking, Seth. Remember the first time you came here?"

"Yeah, things sure have changed, haven't they, brother?" Seth shook his head.

"Things haven't changed as much as we have, Seth. I'm glad to be here with our family. That was one thing Junko was thankful for. That we had come home."

Seth opened the door. "I'm glad to be home too. Let's go in, Jo."

MICHAEL SURVEYED THE group. There was a full house that morning as he attempted to get a headcount. Now as everyone sat down, he could get a better count. He had decided to take a few extra weeks off after the funeral to help where he could. He had been away so long, there were people here he did not recognize. Thirty-nine, and forty including himself. Quite a difference from where they began.

In the beginning, they started with his mom and dad, Lewis, Donna and little Mark, Laura, Juan, and baby Beth, and of course Anna and himself. Ten whole souls. It had been slow, but that was one thing he appreciated about his parents. They had an unwavering commitment first to God, and then to others. What was it his dad had said so many times?

"We could pick and choose what we want to teach, and yes, it would be more popular. It would be more palatable to the world. Our audience might be larger. But Jesus didn't go to the cross to be popular or to have a fine audience. He went there so we could have salvation. We will not compromise with sin. We will not cheapen Jesus' sacrifice."

He wrote the number down so he wouldn't forget it then went to his same old seat. Ruth smiled at him as he sat beside her. It was time to focus on the service—for both of them.

"THERE WAS QUITE A GATHERING this morning. Who was that young woman in the green dress?" Michael sat at the potluck later with his dad watching the horseshoe pitching competition. Everyone had finished their meal except some of the children who kept going back for the cookies.

"Well, now, I don't rightly recall anyone in a green dress, son." Mr. MacDonald scratched his head in puzzlement.

"There she is over there." Michael motioned toward the picnic table.

"Oh, yeah, now I see her." Mr. MacDonald nodded and chuckled. "Say, do you remember that snowstorm last winter?" He seemed to change the subject.

"Sure do. That was a lifetime away." Michael thought of something entirely different than what his dad mentioned.

"Well, that is Ada—Ada Christianson." The laugh lines crinkled at the corners of his eyes as he observed the look on his son's face.

"Are you pulling my leg, Dad?" Shock and disbelief were written all over Michael's face.

"No, I certainly am not. And remember your mother's excellent advice, son. Close your mouth, you're not a cod."

ADA HAD BEEN STUDYING and growing in the Lord just waiting for when he returned. She was not sure why she was waiting for him. He had been quite clear that they had nothing in common. *Maybe someday*, she thought wistfully.

He looked pale and thinner than usual. Ada had heard he had picked up a bug somewhere, but there he was. Then her sister Cyndi's words made her wince. *"What do you mean 'kind of single.' Does he have a paper saying death do us part? If he's just seeing someone, he's still available, baby."*

Ada set her lips in a straight line. Gathering her Bible, purse, and notebook after Bible study Wednesday night, Ada made her way toward the door. Michael was standing by the tract rack. She touched his sleeve. "I am so sorry about your brother losing his wife."

He looked up. "Yes, it has been a sorrow for all of us."

"How long are you planning to be at home?" she asked.

"I'm not quite sure. Another week, possibly two. I can't be gone from my work indefinitely, but I'm sure things will work out soon." He tried to look nonchalant, but the change was almost overwhelming.

"I never did get to thank you for what you did during the snowstorm." She had practiced this pitch for quite some time.

"Think nothing of it," he cut in. "I would have done it for anyone. I'm just thankful that it ended well." Michael brushed the compliment aside. "How long have you been attending church here?"

"Oh, about three months now." She stopped to count. "Well, I just wanted to pass on my condolences and welcome you back, even if it is only for a short time. Maybe I'll see you around since you will be here for a while." Ada had changed outwardly, but she was no fool. Besides, she had the distinct impression that he was amused at something.

Mrs. MacDonald sighed heavily and Mac's eyes followed her gaze. They exchanged a look, and they shared the same thought.

"We would like to think not," he whispered to her. "But we need to pray—fervently. Not quite like a rerun, or—could it turn into a similar nightmare?"

"The change in Ada was very sudden and drastic. I was stupefied when she first showed up at services, and then she agreed to study... However, I rejoiced when Ada came forward to confess her belief that Jesus is the Son of God and to be baptized." Mrs. MacDonald sighed.

"We can't prejudge someone else and their belief. I believe she honestly is seeking something better." Mr. MacDonald searched for the right thoughts. "We have always trusted Michael to do the right thing, and his love for Ruth. And I still do trust those two things."

"WELL, WHAT COULD SHE expect?" Ruth chided herself as she watched Ada and Michael. Other girls had attempted to interest Michael in the past. Did she think he would be like a puppy dog always following her around, waiting for her to answer yes? Did she think he would never find someone else? She hurt. Everything about her hurt. Ruth's heart ached for Joshua and Mai. She missed Junko with an unending sadness, and she hurt for Mr. and Mrs. MacDonald, as she watched their uneasiness grow over the next two weeks. During his remaining time at home, Michael did not seem to notice their apprehension and appeared to enjoy Ada's attention, for occasionally he sought her out. She knew the answer, at least in part, was to be more fervent in prayer, yet the more she needed prayer the harder it seemed to pray. *Lord, your grace is what we need here...*Ruth sighed in frustration.

"SO, HAVE YOU GOT YOUR man yet?" Cyndi asked.

"I have found something better than a man, Cyndi," Ada said.

"I suppose you have found God." Cyndi snorted.

Ada was quiet for a time then smiled at her sister. "Why, yes, I guess you could say that."

Cyndi's eyes narrowed as she quietly appraised her younger sister. "That Michael fellow, he's sure a catch." She tried a different tack. "He's about my age, isn't he? I don't know why I've never seen him around before." Her face puckered in concentration. "Isn't he the one that came along when you had car trouble last winter in the snowstorm?" Her eyes were still narrowed, and she fished for answers.

Ada winced internally but knew it would be unwise to let on that her sister had hit a nerve. "Yes, he is good-looking, and he is also the one who gave me a ride to his parents' house." She tried to sound non-committal. "Have you noticed how genuine and nice those people are?" Ada worked away from the original conversation.

"All of those MacDonald men are good-looking." Like a bulldog that won't let go, Cyndi continued. "That brother of his, the one that lost his wife. I've kinda had my eye on him. He's been around the world and home again." She winked at Ada. "If ya know what I mean."

Ada had grown fond of Junko MacDonald. She was a sweet, endearing woman, quite shy until you came to know her. It made Ada flinch to hear Cyndi talk about these people in that way. There was no question about it, no wonder at all. Yes, Ada had been as callous and senseless as Cyndi. She had been just as wicked. *What was it that brother MacDonald had preached on just the other morning? Something about an evil woman and her beauty, and on account of a harlot is a man brought to a piece of bread?* It reinforced her conclusion of how cheap her former lifestyle was, and the more she studied the Bible the more she marveled at its wisdom.

She sighed. "Do you want to study the Bible with me, Cyndi?" She already knew the answer but she asked anyway.

Cyndi made a face. "Not hardly, baby. That stuff just gets in my way. Are you sure that church isn't a cult or something?" She studied her sister through narrowed eyes. "I know you're not smoking anything—and yeah, those folks are nice. Anyway, I guess you're happy and that's what I've always wanted. You've changed, and I miss you, baby, I—" She stopped to take one last drag on her cigarette. "—I hope you get your man." She squinted through the smoke as she squashed the cigarette out in the ashtray. Cyndi wasn't sure she liked the new Ada.

"MICHAEL," MR. MACDONALD said. "I had hoped never to have to speak to you in this manner." His face was serious and stern. "I don't know what has passed between you and Ruth. But remember anything that concerns our family is a concern to your mother and me, and..." He hesitated to choose his words slowly. "I am concerned with your behavior lately. We always assumed you would speak to Ruth's father and were under the impression that you had done so. Lately, it appears as if you are leading another certain young woman to believe you are interested in her. Michael, this is not acceptable behavior, but perhaps we have misjudged, or is there a mistake?"

Mr. MacDonald waited. He had been loath to broach the subject with his youngest son, but he could not ignore the problem. Michael was due to fly back to his work, and according to some people he had agreed to write to Ada Christianson. Michael had been his usual helpful self, taking up his old place in the family affairs. However, it appeared as if Michael had been spending most of his spare time in Ada's company for the last two weeks.

"I don't know what to say, Dad." Michael's face darkened. "I went to Mr. O'Brien just before I finished my training and I asked his consent, but when I spoke to Ruth, she refused with the reasoning we each had something to do. That or something wasn't right...or not the right time, maybe. So I waited and asked again just after Gwen and Seth returned. Then I asked again when I was home during the snowstorm. Still the same answer. I still love Ruth." He paused in thought. "How many times do I ask? I have not intentionally led Ada to believe I was interested in her romantically. She has Bible questions, and I answer them." His face was clouded, still in a scowl, with doubt and frustration. "I just don't know what to do anymore."

"Can you honestly move on to someone else when your heart belongs to another woman?" Mr. MacDonald asked. "When I spoke to your Grandfather Stewart and asked for his daughter's hand in marriage, he refused. He flatly told me he didn't want... a country bumpkin for his daughter's husband. He predicted I would just drag her off onto one of 'those mountains' and she would grow old in a few years and die barefoot and—" His father's next words struck Michael like a slap, but he could only half appreciate how they had hurt his father as a young man. "—pregnant." Mac finished with a swallow. "But I honestly knew I could never give my heart to anyone else, for it was already Amanda's, and Amanda's it would remain until I died."

"I wasn't moving on to someone else, but I guess I have some thinking and praying to do, don't I?" Michael's scowl deepened. As he characteristically ran his hand through his hair, the troubled look grew deeper. "I didn't know Grandfather Stewart, did I?" Michael asked.

"No, he had health issues. He had his heart set on a well situated young man as a match for your mother, but when your mother told him in no uncertain terms that in order to honor his wishes not to marry me, she would never marry anyone, he began to reconsider. Between that, and your Great-grandmother Jenny, telling him he was an interfering old goat... She was a force to be reckoned with." Mr. MacDonald chuckled. "The final notch was when the doctor warned him that he was sick and perhaps dying. He relented and gave us his blessing."

"Thank you, sir. I know this conversation must have been hard. It took a lot of love," Michael said. "I haven't moved on, but I will need to pray and maybe trust more. I don't know how you in your situation could go on with your life knowing—or at least believing—there was never going to be a point of closure for you and Mom."

"It wasn't an easy place to be, son, but life isn't about being easy. It's about being right."

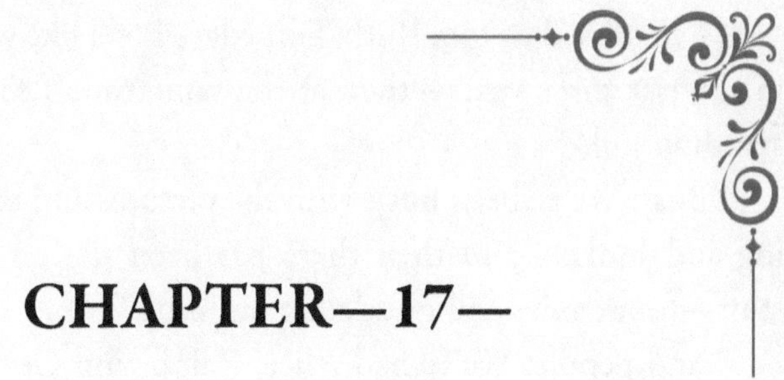

CHAPTER—17—

Ten minutes after Ruth disappeared out a side door of the Mac-Donald hideaway, Mrs. MacDonald followed the same path around to the entryway of the barn.

"I thought I might find you here." Mrs. MacDonald arrived just as Ruth finished brushing her chestnut gelding and reached for the saddle blanket. "Mind if I come along on the ride?"

"No, of course not—I should have asked you before. I've been thoughtless and selfish—" Ruth blushed.

"No, no, don't blame yourself. We're still trying to rearrange our lives." Mrs. MacDonald led out her mare and gave her a quick brushing. "It's been different in the last few weeks. Especially since Michael left, and now Joshua and Mai have moved back to their own home..." She threw the saddle blanket on.

"I've felt at odds—I've lost my bearings. I'm finished with my studies for a few months, but...so much has changed, and I feel listless, limp like a wrung-out rag." Ruth frowned.

"Mac has been busy, and I've been keeping too close to the kitchen lately. And I'm hankering for a good ride. Thank you, Ruth. That five-hundred-pound saddle keeps getting heavier for me—" Mrs. MacDonald stood back as Ruth threw her saddle on top of the blanket, helping her arrange the saddle and tighten the cinch.

"That saddle isn't five hundred pounds, but there is a fair amount of finagling to get it up on the blanket with no wrinkles." Ruth stopped her activity and smiled. "Mrs. M, I've missed our *us* time."

"I've missed us too, Ruth. Somedays I feel like we've come so far in the last three years—then at the same time I feel like I've been standing still."

"Busy. We've been busy, with the pictures and the family returning and Junko—and then there has been the un-normal, normal stuff—four babies being added to our mix..."

"And people. We've had Alice, Ralph, and Gerald become part of the pudding around here."

"I can handle most of the addition, but the loss is almost unbearable. I'm hurting beyond words at the loss of Junko. I know Joshua is hurting as well, but I'm having difficulty understanding where Mai is at right now." Ruth's brow furrowed as she finished tightening her own horse's girth and checking the saddle.

"Mai was born for such a time as this."

"What do you mean?" Ruth's eyes grew wide. She stopped in stride as she led Harley, her horse, to the doorway.

"Mai was a God-given blessing for Joshua and Junko. She gave a new meaning to their life when she was born. She gave Junko a legacy now, and Joshua a tie to the past and the future. Yes, we need to pray for Mai. We need to love and cuddle her, but also teach her how to stand and walk—like you have learned, precious girl." Mrs. MacDonald gave Ruth a quick hug.

"I will have to think on that, Mrs. M. That is profound." Ruth stood for a minute at the doorway in concentration. "But...I just don't know what is wrong with me." Exasperation showed on her young face. "It isn't just that there is so much inside work—it's that some days being inside makes me feel like the world is closing in on me."

"There will always be work to do, Ruth." Mrs. MacDonald had a good idea of what was wrong, but some things were best left for the individual to discover. "Let's go, kiddo," she said as they both stepped into their stirrups and swung into their saddles.

"What a beautiful afternoon." Mrs. MacDonald inhaled deeply, filling her lungs with the sweet perfume of the growing crops, the mown hay, and the summer flowers. "I wonder why I don't get out more often."

"It has been so wonderful for the last two years after Joshua came. Since he solved the crime wave problem, I've been free to ride and not have to worry about being followed or stalked. Before, I was a free captive, always looking over my shoulder. Someone always had to be with me." Ruth sighed. "Yet now I don't feel right. I'm free but ...I miss Junko very much, and ... it's something more than that." Ruth glanced around at the familiar landscape. Their horses stepped quietly down the peaceful country road and their saddles creaked occasionally. "These last two weeks I've taken to riding or wandering through the pastures and woods on foot after my work is finished. The peace and quiet soothes my heart, but only for a short time."

"People often think of youth as a time of freedom because young folks don't have the worries of adulthood such as paying bills and rearing children. But young folks have the burden of choices." Mrs. MacDonald stopped. Bending down, she pulled a tall pasture weed. Stripping all but the end leaves off the weed she used it to shoo flies away from her horse's ears. "Stupid deer flies. I don't know why God made deer flies..." She and Ruth laughed.

"I see, Mrs. M, that was one of those instances where God needed your opinion, right?" Ruth snickered as she followed her friend's example and made a swatter out of another pasture weed.

"Well, all they are is a nuisance, and a nasty one at that..." Their horses continued walking quietly along with their riders occasionally swooshing the ugly flies away. "Well, back to the choices aspect. Those choices will often follow them through life. That's hard, because too often, they carelessly make monumental choices in youth that will carry through into adulthood. It is those choices that make life in adult years either easier or more difficult. Ruth, you have been weighed down by choices— by burdens that much older people would find hard to bear. Maybe you need a change." Mrs. MacDonald swooshed a fly. "Anna is going with a group of medical missionaries this fall. You have taken courses in medicine and could be a help. Why not go with them?"

"You know—" Ruth pursed her lips thoughtfully. "—I think you're right." They reined in at a small bridge spanning a shallow creek, stopping for a moment to watch the leaves floating in the water around a branch. The leaves became entangled before they broke loose and continued downstream. "I could do that, and it would be something of a break. I'm not a traveler, and I'm kind of reluctant to leave Joshua and Mai. Especially little Mai." She frowned. "But it would be only for a short time."

"Ruth O'Brien, don't frown. It will give you bad wrinkles." Mrs. MacDonald laughed. They rode over the little bridge and continued their ride. "Have you heard from Michael?" She dared to raise the specter of the past.

"No, I haven't." Ruth's face was sorrowful.

"We get so little news from him—mostly through his newsletters. It sounds as if they are quite busy." Mrs. MacDonald almost wished she had not mentioned her son. Ruth's miserable countenance stabbed at her heart. "Ruth, I don't want to pry. You know we love both you and Michael. I wish... you know Mac spoke to Michael before he left, but we only got a sketchy explanation. Maybe you could help us so we know what the problem is?"

They rode along the dirt road in the dappled shade of the leafy overhang from the cottonwood, chokecherry, soft maple, and mulberry trees. After a long pause, Ruth spoke slowly. "I'm so confused. I'm struggling with what love is, I guess. Michael asked me three years ago in August to marry him when he got out of school that next spring. He did a rather poor job of it the first time, and I didn't take him seriously. When he was back for the holidays—it was after the supper that the men had catered—he asked me again. It wasn't the same boyish request as it had been the first time. It was...well, it was very sweet and gracious. But I couldn't give him the answer he wanted then either. Then during the snowstorm, he asked for encouragement and wanted to know if there was someone else. I couldn't give him an answer to either question. There was someone else, but it wasn't the way it would appear." She swallowed unshed tears. "Now he seems to have changed his mind. I can't find fault with his behavior— but I'm confused. Can you love someone and not know it? Can you love someone then stop loving that person and love someone else?" Her large brilliant, blue eyes set in a vivid face became more beautiful in her troubled state of mind.

"Martha, Martha, you are cumbered by much serving," Mrs. MacDonald chided.

"What do you mean?" Ruth's brow furrowed.

"You have too many concerns for one so young. Your questions are valid, but—" Mrs. MacDonald hesitated. "—answer me truly, is there another man in your life?"

Ruth's face colored, and she answered slowly. "No, not really."

"It's the 'not really' part that we need to work on." Mrs. MacDonald continued to swish the few flies gently away from her horse's face. "You know Joshua has been thankful for all of us helping with Junko, and Mai loves you like a mother. But, my dear, please listen to me." The older woman stopped her horse for emphasis. "Don't confuse need for love. Joshua will have a struggle to move past the pain of losing Junko. You miss her—we all miss and continue to love her. However, we, including Joshua, will have to move on with our lives. He may remarry someday, or he may be like your father and grandfather. He may stay single for the rest of his life. He will need all of us, the whole host of us, but...you will have to let them go. Joshua and Junko. Mai will always belong to all of us."

"But Joshua was there when I needed him." Tears slid down Ruth's cheeks. "If it hadn't been for him, we all would still be fighting the Meechams and their control. And he almost died for us."

"Well, yes. We all owe him a great debt in that matter, but he would not want— nor require— you to give your life away in return. Do you understand that?"

"Yes, I do. I can see that now." She was quiet, pondering over these new ideas.

They rode along lazily for several minutes then Mrs. MacDonald addressed Ruth's other questions. "As for the question of can you love someone and not know it—and the other questions you raised— the answers to those questions are probably simply yes. I have never loved anyone like I love Mac. From the moment I first saw him, he was my hero. Our love changed through the years, but I could never have loved or married anyone else."

"You and Mr. M do have a unique relationship. I think Mom and Dad had a one-of-a-kind relationship as well..."

"Mac and I are not everyone. And your mom and dad, for all of their problems, were different as well. However, if you truly love someone, you won't stop loving that person and love another. That would be more of a passing fancy than love. Can a person love again after the death of a spouse? Surely they can. I know several widows and widowers who have remarried after their first spouse passed away. But it isn't that they have ceased loving the other person. They just love the second one. Differently."

"So, that brings me back to my first dilemma." Ruth sighed. "What is love? What is the right kind of love to have between a husband and wife?"

"One of the basics is respect. Never marry someone you don't respect." Mrs. MacDonald laughed as Ruth blinked. "You expected me to say never marry a man you do not love didn't you?"

"I guess I did, but my question was what love is, so I don't suppose that would have been a right answer." Ruth raised her eyebrows.

"No, it wouldn't have been. You don't want to marry someone who does not respect you either. Respect is basic."

"Respect?" Ruth's face looked doubtful. "How do you know if they respect you?"

"How do they treat the people around them? Do they listen? Do they weigh the needs of others?"

"Of others? Why others?" Ruth raised her eyebrows.

"People can put on a good show when they're trying to impress and win someone's favor. Usually, the show is limited in scope to close friends and family, but especially to the person they're trying to impress. Some people say watch how they treat people they won't get anything from."

Ruth's face was pensive as she thought. "Lewis and Laura teach their children godly principles but more along the lines of how to treat other people. It's not just the person you're interested in romantically. It goes back to considering other people as—people. Laura and Lewis have such good marriages, contrasted to say...Peter and Judith."

"Yes, well—you can tell some people, but that doesn't mean they listen." Mrs. MacDonald cleared her throat. "Let's stop and give these animals a drink."

Mrs. MacDonald dismounted at another stream surrounded by a grassy bank and let her horse drink. "Back to what is love. Love is more than a warm tingly feeling. Christ had the ultimate love that gave itself even while we were undeserving, and that is a part of a husband-and-wife love. And each partner must give one hundred percent each, not the puny fifty-fifty percent some people talk about. I always felt with Mac that no matter what, I could trust him with anything and everything. One thing I've always stressed to my girls was to never marry any man that you cannot feel comfortable saying 'yes, sir' to."

"That goes against—I mean—that sounds extreme, like archaic?" Ruth's brow furrowed.

They sat down on the grass while their horses grazed peacefully. "Well, hear me out. It does go against everything we hear today. With equality this and empowering women and all that, but in First Peter, it tells us that Sarah called Abraham 'lord.' I've heard people joke about that, but it's not a joke. Anyone looking for a little boy they can push around the rest of their lives won't like themselves and they won't like the person they choose." Mrs. MacDonald looked down at the grass a moment in thought. Then looking back at Ruth, she smiled. "Strong women need to look for strong men who will be worth the title, and men need to strive to be the kind of man to deserve it."

"It takes a lot of trust to put someone in that position. You wouldn't want to trust your life with just anyone—I've seen some women in bad situations."

Mrs. MacDonald swatted the air with her pasture-weed swatter. "Most of those women wouldn't be in those situations if they had paid closer attention before they married. No one should live in fear for their lives or their children's lives. God wants you to put your husband as the head. If you can't put him there, he's not the one you should marry."

"It could mean either you aren't ready for marriage...or he isn't either." Ruth mused as she pulled several stems of grass and examined them minutely. "I've seen couples that fight continuously because at least one of them can't remove themselves from their tower of self."

"That's a funny way to put it, Ruth, but, yes, that's true. Respect and honor work both ways. Since God wants the man to be the head of the family, the man needs to be able to lead physically and spiritually. If he isn't mature enough to do that or has to drag his woman kicking and fighting him all the way—hopefully figuratively speaking, no one will ever be happy. And in this day and age, I can't believe any of us will be called on to say *yes, sir*. It's an attitude of trust." Mrs. MacDonald smiled.

"But my question is..." Ruth's face was troubled. "You see, I miss Michael very much, but is it because he's been a part of my life for so long, or...? I thought it was like a brother and sister love, but—it isn't the same as I love Reuben. I missed Reuben, and it was great to have him back. We had lots of fun, but when he asked Becky to be his fiancée I was glad for them. Really happy..."

"When you think of Michael, what are your thoughts?—feelings?" Mrs. MacDonald pursed her lips.

"Michael? Michael was a pleasure to be around. We used to talk kind of like brother and sister, but we shared lots of things. We laughed a lot together. He used to call me his lady, and he was Sir Lancelot..." Ruth sat quietly for a few minutes. "I've never been concerned with safety or purity around him. He's so..." Ruth searched for the right word. "good. That's the best way to describe him, I guess. And the interesting thing is, he's that way by choice."

"By choice? What does that mean?" Mrs. MacDonald's face showed puzzlement.

"Some people are too weak, so they 'go along to get along.' Michael, on the other hand—I think you described Joshua once as being biblically meek—strength under control. Michael is like that. But apparently, I've discovered all of this a might too late." Ruth's bearing was still sad.

"Or maybe his first attempt was more like he wasn't ready, and you weren't either?" Mrs. MacDonald asked.

"In looking back, that's right. It was a bit premature, and I did need to be with Junko. Although I don't know how I knew that. God called me to minister to her, but now, I just don't know."

"We can see that it was the case. At the time we didn't see where it would end," Mrs. MacDonald said.

"And now I feel empty, and... restless. It doesn't seem to make any difference anyway, I suppose." Ruth's eyes narrowed as she was still occupied with a blade of grass. "For apparently, as you have said it was a passing fancy, and Michael has changed his mind." She heaved a sigh and dropped the grass.

"Ruth, I would never have thought it possible of you." Mrs. MacDonald's eyes grew wide, and she gasped softly.

"What is that?" Ruth looked up in surprise.

"To be so unfair. We know that things aren't always what they seem. There may be a purely logical explanation and what we think is going on is not. Do not impute to Michael something that in my lifetime I have never seen in him. His mind and his heart don't change easily." She looked into the deep pools of despair mirrored in Ruth's eyes.

"Oh, my friend." Tears slid down Ruth's cheeks. "I'm just so... It's my fault, and I'm so sorry, but there seems to be no answer."

"Of course, there is an answer. We must pray and trust—"

"And be brave enough to accept God's answer may not be the one I want." Ruth wiped the tears away. "That's what I'm struggling with now."

"At least now we will struggle with it together." Getting to her feet, Mrs. MacDonald continued. "I wish this conversation had taken place much earlier. At least we will wrestle with the angel together." She hugged Ruth. "And look here, that silly horse of mine has eaten the tassel off my fly swisher. I guess it's time to mount up and head for home."

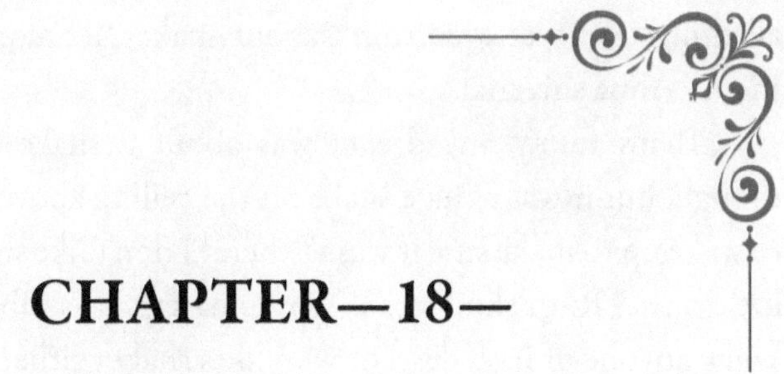

CHAPTER —18—

"**A**re you all packed?" Anna asked Ruth

"I've packed and repacked, but at least I think I'm ready. I keep trying to stick in odds and ends that might come in handy. I probably won't need any of those things and will find too many of the things I do need I've left at home." Ruth fretted looking at her list.

Anna smiled benignly. "Don't worry, Ruth. Although you're probably partly correct. Generally speaking, however, the idea of need and true need are usually not the same. The things that would be handy get left behind, but we can survive on much less than what is truly handy."

"What time will we be leaving in the morning?" Ruth nervously still tried to pack and repack her carry-on bag.

"We will be leaving here early at six o'clock. Our flight will leave, or should I say is scheduled to leave, Hermon at eight o'clock," Anna informed Ruth. "We will pick up the rest of the crew in Dallas, then fly on south." Anna checked her bag as well.

"I don't think I'll sleep a wink tonight." Ruth grimaced. "I'm not sure if I'm in a state of excitement or dread. I had the awfullest dream last night."

"I was the same way the first time I went by myself without Dad, Mom, or any of the family—and I've never gotten over it completely. You know, last night I had a dream about snakes. Snakes, of all things! I never even think about snakes, let alone dream about them." Anna shivered.

"That's funny, my dream was about a snake also. Only one though, but it was a huge snake on the ceiling above my head. I had to wake up to make sure it wasn't there! I don't like snakes—not even little ones." Ruth shuddered. "Grandpa says it is inborn. He doesn't know anyone of Irish descent who likes snakes either."

"We need to head down to the barbecue and prayer meeting. I must confess even though I have been on several of these trips I still get nervous. I appreciate the prayer meeting. It makes me feel as if God Himself has wrapped me up and hid me in the cleft of the rock." Anna finished zipping her bag and put the lock on it. "I guess that's that."

THE AUTUMN PROMISED to be full of brilliant color. Joshua's life had settled into a routine that only slightly covered the raw ache of losing Junko. He watched as the other members of his family ate their barbeque sandwiches, laughed at jokes, and carried on their lives. He felt alone with his grief. Ruth had quoted to him from the Psalms once, something about the heart knows its own sorrow, and a stranger doth not interfere therein. He sighed. Strangers or not, each one has to bear their own sorrows in their own way, just as he did.

Ruth brought over a plate for him and little Mai. "Do you mind if I sit here?" she asked.

"Mind? Why in the world would I mind?" His face showed surprise at her question.

"I was being polite." She smiled. "Any last-minute instructions from the travel expert?"

"Do you have one suitcase full of food, and another one full of toilet paper?" He looked at her with raised eyebrows.

"Well, I do have some food, and some of the ah—some of the other article." She blinked in an attempt to be discreet. "But I don't have a whole suitcase dedicated to each of them. Why? Should I?"

"It all depends…" He laughed. "Seriously, Ruth, Mai and I will miss you, and we certainly will be praying for your safe return." He reached over and squeezed her hand. "I have been thankful for how well you cared for Junko and Mai. I'm glad you are taking this trip. You have put your life on hold for us far too long."

"Odd, your mom and I talked about …" Ruth hesitated and appeared to search for the right words. "I'm struggling—you know I don't like traveling. And the wonder is that I signed up for this trip. I'm nervous, Joshua. I feel that I need to go on this trip, but I have a terrible premonition, and I'm quite frightened." Her eyes were large.

"It might be just first trip nerves." He tried to quiet her fears. He took a bite of his barbecue, grasping at ideas to help her get grounded and used to the idea of their journey not being frightening. He could feel her fear as if it were something tangible. "Ruth, you're not a wimp, and your courage to face the unknown and do the right thing, no matter how difficult, has been inspiring to us ordinary blokes. I wish I could go with you girls on this trip, but that's impossible. You know we'll be praying without ceasing." *How absurd*, he thought desperately, *she's going on this trip with only my little sister for protection?*

"You must stay with Mai, for one thing, and two we know you aren't an ordinary bloke, Joshua." Ruth raised an eyebrow at him.

"Has anyone heard from Michael?" Joshua was hesitant to ask. "I think Dad and Mom got one of his newsletters from their mission work, but that was at least six weeks ago… or more." He was trying to muster an idea.

"Joshua, I appreciate your concern, but I'm sure Michael is busy in his work. I find it interesting that even with the added people—your family and Seth's family—we still find ourselves short-staffed. Look, Seth and Gwen just had their first child and now after all this time of no children, she's expecting a second child." Ruth had a look of wonder on her face and in her voice.

"True, and even though Michael is a good help. And he and Seth are smart, but they don't have the connections I have and they wouldn't be the help since I've always been the instigator...oops I mean, brains behind our endeavors." Joshua smiled.

Ruth snickered. "I'm hoping you understand this in the right way...and I'm sure you will. I love you and Seth. You two make me laugh. Even in bad situations, I draw strength from you and all of your family. I have truly been blessed to know all of you." She sat looking at her hands quietly for a few minutes, and then looked up and smiled at Joshua and over at little Mai.

Mr. MacDonald stood, and everyone became quiet. "We have come together tonight to pray for the safe departure of Anna and Ruth, for their safe journey, and their safe return. Let us pray."

As prayers were offered up, Joshua thought back to the time when he asked himself, *How can a blind woman, a young man, and a young woman possibly be of any help in a case like mine against a corrupt crime syndicate?* At that time it was a blind woman who reminded him God has often used unusual people to accomplish his goals. *I guess I'm still working on believing and trusting in God and His providence. Lord,* he prayed, *help thou my unbelief.*

Seth came over and took a seat on the bench beside Joshua during a break. "Sitting on this side of my life I wonder at how much I threw away." They watched Mai playing with the rest of the kids.

"How's that?" Joshua leaned back.

"Life is somewhat different at this stage of my life than it was when we were teenagers, but we still had prayer meetings and whatnot back then." Seth motioned with his hand.

"Yes, we did, but there was a difference." Joshua frowned in thought. "I don't know what the change is. I would say the disparity is between us then and us now."

"Probably. Since we now know that we don't know what we thought we knew back when we knew everything..."

"That's what I'm saying." Joshua laughed. "As young people back in the day, we didn't know that what we had was something uncommon and very precious."

"We used to hear the phrase, 'Life is tough; handle it with prayer.' We knew it was, but we just weren't prepared for life or even for a life of prayer for some reason. This has been a good time. We all need these prayers." Seth waved his hands in a wide gesture.

"It's like a gift. A gift isn't just for the person who receives it. The person that gives the gift receives a blessing in giving the gift. Prayer isn't just for the object of the prayer. The one...or ones who pray receive a blessing as well." Joshua rubbed his chin. "And you're right. I've never felt so helpless. Anna and Ruth are poised to fly off into the unknown, and I'm grounded...as well as yourself."

"Do you think there is something...Should we be concerned?" Seth smiled as Gwen, holding baby Zoe, came over and sat beside him.

"Normally? I would generally say no. Just first flight nerves."

"So, what's up?" Seth's eyes narrowed.

"Ruth and I had a conversation a little while ago—" Joshua sat in thought before continuing. "—She's afraid of something. It could be pre-trip nerves, but knowing Ruth—it's a premonition of something."

"Oh, no." Gwen sucked in her breath. "Ruth doesn't like traveling, but she's not...well, she's not a scaredy-cat—and they just got word from Michael's team leader. He's been deathly ill for three weeks now. Michael wouldn't let them notify anyone until he was on the mend."

"That numbskull. What was he thinking?" Seth exclaimed.

"Probably didn't want to upset anyone—reminds me of several others I've known." Gwen frowned as she stared intently at Seth and Joshua.

"The team leaders should have known better, no matter what Michael wanted." Joshua's brows drew together. "There's probably more to the story than we have...Oh, sounds like we're going to have a few more songs then finish up so we can get everyone an early-to-bedtime." Joshua smiled and hugged Mai as she ran up and snuggled onto his lap.

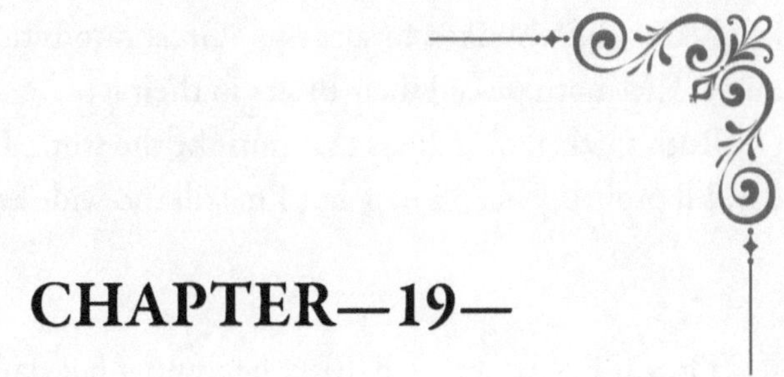

CHAPTER—19—

Ruth gripped the handle of her carry-on bag and closed her eyes. Even just sitting in the aisle seat as the plane taxied down the runway seamlessly lifting off the ground and soaring into the blue sky felt full of danger.

Opening her eyes, she sighed. "I've never understood the idea, and it doesn't make sense how something so big can hang suspended in mid-air. And not just suspended in midair, but swimming through it. No, thank you, I don't want to sit by the window. I'll stick with the aisle seat."

"It's good that we aren't arguing over the window seat." Anna looked out the window. "After the initial lift-off, I enjoy watching the airport and everything on the ground grow smaller and smaller until it looks like a miniature town and a piecemeal of country fields. Kind of like toys. And the slight ground fog in low-lying areas? Could be of snow or possibly cotton batting rolls from one of Mom's patchwork quilts."

Anna sighed and leaned back. "You know, watching through the small window, I feel as if I'm sitting still and the world below me is a moving picture rotating below." *Funny, Anna thought, we are moving at an incredible speed, but it's the ground that appears to be moving.* "I don't know, Ruth, I think trust is like boarding a plane—not like a blind leap into the unknown at all. Unlike a plane, faith relies on there is never operator error on God's part." She turned, rummaged in her carry-on bag, and pulled her Bible out. She looked up and laughed as Ruth blinked in surprise. "Great minds think alike," Anna said as they both placed their Bibles in their laps.

Ruth snickered. "I guess that must be the truth. By the end of today, I'll probably need a nap, but I'm still too wide awake."

RUTH OPENED HER BIBLE, beginning her daily Bible reading in Proverbs. She moved into Psalms, taking comfort from Psalms 134. Every once in a while, she glanced past Anna out the window. The view looked innocent enough, and it didn't raise any alarm in her mind. At last, she nodded off for a short nap.

She woke with a start—*Mercy, she thought, I didn't expect to get that comfortable. Well, it is the taking off that bothers me more than the flight or the landing.* Returning to her Bible, she continued her reading by musing on the scriptures that Brother Matthews had used at Junko's funeral. She reread, "'For love is strong as death; jealousy is cruel as Sheol; the flashes thereof are the flashes of fire, a very flame of Jehovah.'" *Oh, God, how did my life become so confused? Why did it become so mixed up? Was this supposed to help me understand Dad and Mom's situation?* She sighed as she read and took comfort in the next verse, "Many waters cannot quench love, neither can floods drown it." *Mrs. M is such a wise council. I'll need to trust she is right. Things aren't exactly as they appear. At least, who can separate us from the love of God? No one but ourselves.* Ruth sighed again as she read and pondered.

"Sometimes patience is not so easily won, is it?" Anna asked with a sad smile.

"No, I guess not." Ruth continued without raising her eyes. "I'm reading in 'Ecclesiastes 7:13: "Consider the work of God: for who can make *that* straight, which he hath made crooked?"' I'm wondering how things become so confusing. Everyone thought when

Meecham was dealt with, all of our troubles were vanquished. Ha. That didn't happen." Her lips twisted into a sarcastic grimace.

"That's often the way it is. Satan doesn't give up. He may take a holiday, but he always comes back." Anna shrugged.

"Not that I have been jealous concerning Michael and Ada, but it does go along with the situation to be cruel just like the first part of the scriptures put it. It's been said, and it seems to be true, this world is a land of tragedy and woe. Some things are the working of Satan from others, but I am convinced that the biggest tragedies are the ones we perpetrate on ourselves."

"There is no sense to keep beating ourselves up over mistakes, but we do anyway. Ruth, may I speak a word in Michael's defense?" Anna spoke slowly with hesitation. "I don't want to butt in where I shouldn't be, but I'm positive that there's a mistake in our understanding, and that it will all turn out right in the end. He has loved you far too long to not love you now. Before, even when we were plagued with interference from Phil Meecham—things in the past... Well, I know my brother. So many times he has instructed me to find something— a present here or there for you. Even then he was always thinking of you, and I'm convinced he still does. This misunderstanding breaks my heart."

"Thank you, Anna. I am so blessed to have friends and family that are so thoughtful. Your mother told me the same thing a few weeks ago. I find it odd that no one except Ada has received much correspondence from him. At least I don't seem to be the only one." She sighed heavily. "Anna, why have you never married? I don't want to be sticking my nose in either, but I know you aren't averse to marriage, and I know that opportunity has knocked, so why are you still waiting?"

"I suppose it is my parents' fault." Anna smiled and raised her eyebrows. "After watching them all these years, I don't want a halfway marriage. When I compare the young men of today to my dad—" She spoke as if the subject was standing in front of her, "—they come up short. Of course, it isn't the physical attributes. It's their childish way of approaching their faith and ...in approaching me as well. I don't know if I'm supposed to be honored that I'm on their list of those whom they are seeking their wife from."

"I know. Your mom and I had a long talk a few weeks ago. I felt bombarded by so many different descriptions of love, and I was confused. She answered many questions that I have. Many young men don't care who I am. They only look on the outside, and I'm a whole lot more than just my outside."

"I suppose Mom told you about respect." Anna smiled. "Dad doesn't do anything without weighing how it will affect mom spiritually as well as physically. It makes me realize how difficult it is to be the head of the family. It's an awesome responsibility, and I for one am glad it isn't my role. This brings me back to why I'm not married yet. I want a man who approaches marriage with those ideals. Marriage is serious business, not something decided on physical appearance alone."

"You mean you haven't found that man you can answer *'yes, sir'* to?" Ruth asked with a one-eyed smile.

"Exactly right," Anna said with a shake of her head. "We have a generation, males and females who don't see beyond themselves, even though they need to see far enough for at least two people, and prospectively for several more somewhere down the road."

"That is scary—oh, look." Ruth pointed out the window as their plane made a dip. "Just look at how huge that city is. Quite a bit larger than Hermon." She caught her breath in wonder.

"I should say so." Anna gazed out the window. "I've been in some cities that stretched so far—and at night all you could see were lights—lights extending as far as the horizon."

"I'm just a country girl from out in the sticks." Ruth pursed her lips. "But on the other hand, I don't mind. I don't want to live in the city. I suppose you could say I'm content to live in the middle of nowhere."

"I'm glad there are folks that like to live in these cities. That way there aren't so many living out where I want to live." Anna laughed.

"I'm with you." They listened as the stewardess came on the intercom and made her announcements. They buckled up their seat belts and waited as the plane landed. Ruth stood and let Anna into the aisle, and they picked up their belongings.

"Hopefully our luggage comes with us. Sometimes it takes a trip by itself into outer space." Anna grimaced, rolling her eyes as they marched into the terminal.

"I took advice from Mrs. M and traveled light. Although at the last minute Joshua said I ought to make sure I had a second suitcase with...well, stuff in it." Ruth snickered at the thought. "Wow, was that only last night?" she asked. "What a hoard of people..." Ruth's eyes widened as she looked at the crowds milling around the terminal, the sights and sounds as well as the smells. "So many people and they must be from all over the world. How long do we have until our next flight?"

"We have a good three hours before our flight." Anna dug in her purse.

"Let's go find someplace for a cup of tea," Ruth said. "Where are we supposed to meet the rest of the group and when?"

"This layover may look long, but believe me—" Anna stopped to look at her instructions. "—by the time we find the gate and where we're supposed to be, it won't seem long enough." Anna held up the map and pointed. "Here is where we are. Here is where we need to be. Restroom first, then let's find our gate and our destination, after which we will find that cup of tea."

"At least we don't have much to carry. I'm also glad to be in good physical condition." Ruth maneuvered through the oncoming traffic. "That must be why I've been walking all over the farm this summer."

She turned abruptly to avoid a man pushing a cart. "Are we almost there?"

Anna laughed. "You're nearly as bad as traveling with Laura's kids. We are making headway, but as far as being just about there..." Anna pointed down the corridor. "We have to go this way, and there's another mile of walking first before our gate. It's down this way." She waved as they continued toward their goal.

"You are a Godsend, Anna. I don't know what I would have done without you! This traveling business is more work than putting in fence posts. Personally, I'd rather put in fence posts, and I've never been fond of doing that." Ruth sighed.

"And here," Anna said steering Ruth through the door of a small shop, "is a good place for a cup of tea after our long walk."

"Let me look at that list again, Anna. Which of these people do you know?" Ruth asked as she perused the list of their fellow missionaries.

"At the top here is the main man, so to speak. That's Doctor Dan, or Dan Spears. Everyone likes Doctor Dan. He's serious when he needs to be, which is when he's working, but he can be funny when he isn't. And he is pretty much always nice. Eileen Williams is next on the list. I have only worked with her one time. However, she was pleasant. Mostly. She's about ten years older than I am, she's quiet, and knows her business. Raymond and Mary Sewart are a lot of fun. They're an older couple. Not old, but not young. I guess you'd call them middle-aged. Davis Brown and Don Simons I don't know. They may have been on other trips, but I haven't been on the same ones if they have. Doctors Kenneth and Margo Grunn are older than middle-aged but similar to Dad and Mom. They are a real encouragement. They work tirelessly and never complain. I have worked with this woman, Robin Beech, and like the bird, she's kinda flighty. She wasn't hard to work with, but she didn't always finish her tasks according to protocol, and Doctor Dan had to speak to her sternly.

Frankly, I'm surprised she's on this trip. I'm not familiar with Kathleen Atkins, and there are local people I don't know who have volunteered, and a local doctor who's helping arrange medicine supplies, and someone is arranging transportation. And the last person here—you remember Nathaniel Crowl? He was the young fellow Michael brought home that time on break."

Ruth looked at Anna and they both snickered. "I don't know what happened to him, but he sure was nervous most of the time he was visiting." Anna checked her watch. "We are where we should be waiting. They should start to arrive soon." She looked around the terminal. "There, I see Kenneth and Margo. What did I tell you?" She nudged Ruth as the older couple spotted her and waved.

"Ken and Margo," Anna greeted the tall gray-haired couple as they approached. "How has your trip been so far?" She hugged them. "I see you have found some of the others. Ruth, this is Doctor Ken Grunn and his wife Doctor Margo." Anna stretched a hand out and introduced the other people. "Eileen Williams, Raymond and Mary Sewart, and Doctor Dan Spears—this is Ruth O'Brien from our Beetle River congregation." She indicated Eileen Williams, a tall, thin woman of forty-something, another couple, Raymond and Mary Sewart in their fifties, and lastly Doctor Dan Spears, an agile-looking man in his mid-thirties, not tall but not short—just average.

"And this is Davis Brown and Don Simon." Doctor Dan announced as two new guys joined the group. "Davis and Don, I think you know everyone except Anna MacDonald and Ruth—Ruth O'Brien? Is that right, Anna?"

"Yes, that's right." Anna shook her head.

"That means everyone's here except Nathaniel Crowl, Robin Beech, and Kathleen Atkins." Doctor Grunn looked at the list. "We've had enough time to hit the restroom, but now Margo and I are going to grab something to eat then we'll join everyone in our designated spot over there." He gestured in the direction of their gate.

"Okay, two groups, eating and waiting." Doctor Dan laughed. "We'll wait for you over there." He led the waiting group over to their seats. "Nathan is flying in and should be here soon. Robin and Kathy are from this area, so any time they should be here."

He sat in a corner chair and soon became absorbed in a medical magazine. He glanced up and nodded as Ken and Margo rejoined them after their lunch. "Hello, hello." Doctor Dan stood, and greeted Nathaniel, followed shortly by the last two stragglers, Robin and Kathleen. After introductions, he said, "We have all made it to this stage of our journey. We have people waiting for us at the other end. Let's have a quiet prayer before our flight."

NATHANIEL SAT DOWN beside Anna. As he rubbed his whiskered chin, he smiled at her. "I guess your brother was right."

"Oh, how's that?" Anna asked.

"He said you had been all over on these mission trips, and he wasn't hiding you anywhere." He continued to smirk self-consciously as he recalled his conversation with Michael three years earlier.

"Well, yes, he would know." Anna raised her eyebrows at him, puzzled.

"Your brothers can be quite intimidating. I'd never encountered a situation like that before. But you do indeed look quite capable of taking care of yourself."

"Well, thank you—I think," she said giving him a sideways look. "I guess—I'm not sure what I owe the compliment to. When we travel, we all depend on the providence of God to bring us where we are going."

"I've re-examined my life choices since I visited that year, and changed several things in my life after that. I've been traveling around the states. But it wasn't until I met Doctor Dan last year that I found out about this trip. I've been anticipating this journey ever since— Oh, that's our flight." Nathaniel stood and picked up his bags to board the plane.

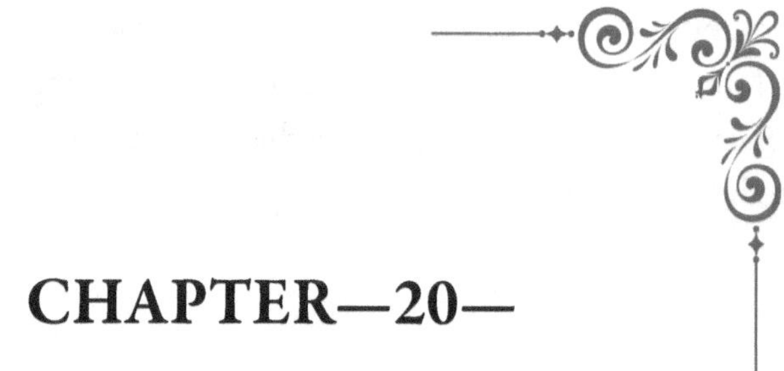

CHAPTER —20—

Ruth looked at her plane ticket and realized that the airline had shuffled their group slightly. "I guess we won't be sitting next to each other on this part of the trip." She showed her ticket to Anna.

"We'll just have to make the best of it. I suppose that's one way to get to know some of the other members of the team." Anna smiled.

"And I'm too set in my ways. I think that's part of what I need to learn. I'm a real introvert but I can and I *need* to branch out at least a bit." Ruth's lips were set in a straight line.

"It'll be alright. Our seats were all bought at one time. We'll be with members of the group so you've met whoever you'll be sitting with. I'm up here and you'll be back a couple of seats over there." She pointed Ruth in the right direction. Anna slid into her seat beside one of the new members. "Hello—Davis, is it?"

Ruth looked at her seat number, which was just down and across from Anna's seat. "Hello, I'm your seatmate, I guess." She sat down beside a petite youngish woman with light brown hair and pretty blue eyes. "My name is Ruth O'Brien." She smiled at the other woman.

"My name is Kathleen Atkins. Everyone calls me Kathy. I'm really nervous. This is the first mission trip I've been on and I'm wondering why I was so sure I wanted to come on this trip."

"I know exactly what you mean. I'm committed but, yeah, I'm not sure why I'm here." Ruth's eyes were wide. "We should have enough time on this flight to settle down. I even had a little nap on the first flight."

"I came off a shift from work, so I'm a bit tired. I hope you didn't want to sit by the window. I enjoy watching the scenery float by, but if you want I could change with you."

"No, no, that's fine. I'm not much of a traveler and certainly not a flier." Ruth held up her hand. "You may enjoy the scenery with my blessings. So, you're from the Dallas area?"

"Yes. I work at a retirement center. I'm a dietician." Kathy smiled at Ruth. "Imagine that."

"Oh, that is fun. Have you done any research on Guyana diets?" Ruth raised her eyebrows.

"A little, but there isn't much call for a dietician at this point that I can see. Here we go…" Kathy sat back in her seat as the plane began to taxi down the runway.

"There is a call for willing helpers, no matter from where." Ruth continued the thought. "Anna MacDonald and I have been studying and taking classes in healthcare this last—almost a year now. I'm thinking of working toward a nurse practitioner license. You look like you could use a nap. If you relax you can get a decent rest. I may try to get a bit more sleep as well." Ruth smiled at Kathy as she noticed how droopy her seatmate's eyes were.

"Thank you. I don't want to be rude. I'm not falling asleep because I don't want to listen."

"Not to worry. I didn't sleep well last night, you know nerves and all. If you've just come off a shift, it's time for you to get some rest. We had to get up pretty early to catch our first flight. Now that we're in the air, I can relax."

Kathy snickered. "Yes, I don't know what it is, but the pilot has to have me help him get the plane off the ground—at least in my mind." She leaned back in her seat and drifted off to sleep by watching the countryside float quietly under her window.

"YES, MY NAME IS DAVIS Brown. I don't believe I've had the pleasure of working with you before?" Davis assessed the beautiful young woman sitting beside him.

"Anna—Anna MacDonald. I was telling my friend, Ruth, I hadn't worked with you or Don, or Kathleen."

"This is my first adventure in this arena. I work as an EMT in the Dallas area. So, this isn't your first rodeo?" Davis looked at her quizzically.

"No, I've been on a number of these rodeos." She smiled at him. "I started going on mission trips back with my father and brothers. It was just a normal part of life." Unlike Ruth, Anna was more outgoing. She enjoyed the exchange of ideas and camaraderie from these trips.

"What luck, an old-timer that looks like a million bucks—oh, I didn't mean to sound like that—" His eyes grew round and he apologized. "I don't know why I said that—I mean like I said it. You know it's my first trip and you'll be able to give me some pointers, and you're not a sour old woman—or man for that matter and..."

"That's okay, your apology is accepted." Anna tried to hide a laugh, but finally gave up and the laugh won.

"Oh, good night, I am so embarrassed. How about you just call me Davis, and tell me to shut up whenever." He ran a hand over his face then smiled at the pretty young woman.

"We could start with how did you come to be here and what pointers are you looking for?" She stopped laughing, gasping to catch her breath.

"Don was coming on this trip, and it sounded interesting to me. I've been to several places in the military. Picked up some knowledge that could be helpful, and me in medicine, you know and whatnot." He shrugged. "Pointers? Any pointers will be appreciated."

"At least you've traveled before, so by the time we get to Guyana and through customs and find out if our luggage has come with us, it will be at least ten o'clock this evening. And by the time we make it to our hotel rooms, it will be midnight at least. Our local contacts will have a minibus waiting and the rooms rented, so that part isn't a biggie."

"So, our main thrust will be medical care?" He asked.

"Sometime before Monday morning, we'll have to sort out who's doing what. Of course, the doctors will do the doctoring stuff, but we'll need someone to screen the people—take down their information, make them a file, so to speak. Keep records. And then others will do some prep work. Everyone will need to keep an eye out to find enough time to talk to the patients about scriptures, sing Bible songs, and tell Bible stories during the day. In the evening an evangelist will hold a teaching session at one of the congregations we are working with. Sometimes we also hold a Vacation Bible School for the little ones. Our time has been set up so we'll have tomorrow—Saturday—for rest. Sunday we'll have worship with singing, prayer, Lord's Supper, and normal Sunday stuff. Monday is when the work begins."

"I WAS A BOY SCOUT. That's why I've got my flashlight." Davis brandished his small flashlight as the group walked back to the hotel after church Sunday evening.

"Is that so?" Kathy laughed. "You're funny, but I'm glad you brought your flashlight. We have just enough light with Doc Grunn and his flashlight leading, you and Doctor Dan on each side, and Ray scouting along behind."

"Four flashlights are welcome, but this light is unpredictable. I'm glad it's not any farther." Anna watched as they carefully walked toward the hotel.

"The sun just dropped over the horizon and it got dark." Ruth surveyed the ground intently. The light danced around as they moved along the street.

"We are in a different world almost." Margo Grunn grimaced.

Anna took Margo's arm in hers and whispered. "Let's walk together, Margo. Between the poor light and this ground, walking is a bit unstable. Thanks for helping me with the children's class tonight."

"This ground and our lighting situation makes me nervous too." Margo smiled at Anna. "I haven't ever been asked to lend a hand with children's classes before. I didn't think I'd enjoy helping as much as I have. I don't know where you girls came up with those visuals but the kids really like them."

"Ruth and I worked for weeks on these visuals, and our family helped prepare them as well. It helps when you've been on these campaigns before. We have one suitcase for visuals and we have one for food and—supplies." Anna smiled at Ruth.

"And then we pool the last suitcase for clothes." Ruth chuckled.

"That doesn't leave you much room for clothes." Robin's eyes grew wide.

"We bring enough for what we need. We can hand wash some things." Ruth shrugged.

"How sensible. I never thought of that." Kathy raised her eyebrows. "That just makes sense." She stubbed her toe. "Oh, oh..."

Davis reached out and caught her. "That makes a lot of sense. Travel light and fast. That's the Boy Scout motto."

"That's not the Boy Scout motto. The Scout motto is 'Be prepared.'" Davis's friend Don laughed good-naturedly. "Brown, you have a habit of mixing your mottos and your metaphors."

"Regardless, here we are." Ken Grunn switched off his flashlight. "Now we can work up who gets what chores for the next week." He held the hotel door open as everyone filed into the lobby.

⁂

"THIS HAS BEEN QUITE the week." Doctor Dan sat on the edge of a desk as he watched the last of the patients, a young mother with two children, gathering her possessions to leave the clinic.

Doctor Ken looked over the top of his glasses at the other doctor after sorting through some paperwork. "Yes, it has been a week. For all the people we've seen, our group has done well keeping information and getting people in and out of the clinic. We have a big day planned for tomorrow with an evangelist for morning and evening worship, and the girls will continue their excellent work with the children for Bible school."

"I noticed your wife was even helping with one of the small children's classes the other evening. She looked like she was enjoying herself." Dan chuckled.

"Margo isn't a children person, but something about this trip and the girls have touched a spot, and she has enjoyed the kids' class. It's been good for her." Ken put his papers into a file box with the rest of the information folders.

"How's your son doing? His wife was sick for a time, wasn't she?" Dan handed his partner the rest of his papers.

"Rolly's doing well. His wife was sick, but she's pulled through and is doing great. How about you? You and your fiancée ever set a wedding date?"

"No, we parted on friendly terms—or maybe just ambivalent terms. Some days a miss is as good as a mile."

"Well, that can be so." Dr. Ken raised his eyebrows. "Not as compatible as you thought then?"

"That was about right. Macy resented the time I had to spend at the office, but she did like the money."

"Life sometimes gets in the way, I guess." Dr. Ken stood and picked up the box with the files. "I'll leave these here for this congregation's records. Monday we'll move our next clinic to a different congregation—Monday and Tuesday, then Wednesday, Thursday, and Friday we'll move out to that place— canal something or other— about an hour out of town."

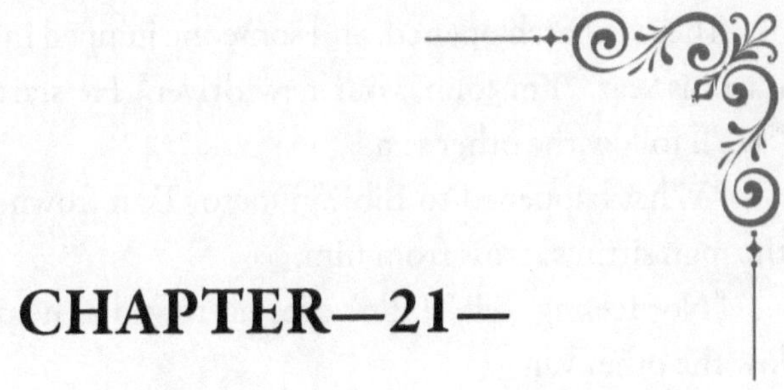

CHAPTER—21—

"It's a good thing there aren't any more of us than this." Doctor Dan breathed deeply as they finished loading the medical supply crates into the back of the minivan and closed the hatch. "We'll divide up. Grunn—" He motioned to Doc Grunn. "You take that van, and I'll take this one. Everyone jump in, and let's go." He placed his backpack in front and slid into the passenger seat waiting for the driver. Davis, Nathaniel, Kathy, Ruth, and Anna stowed their packs as well and scrabbled into the back seats. The remaining members clambered into the other van with Doc Grunn, watching for their drivers to come out of the building.

"This'll be the last leg of this journey. I'm glad I came on this trip, but I can't say I'll be sorry to be heading home Friday. I have enough food for the rest of this job." Davis looked through his backpack then zipped it shut.

"I'm really tired. If I don't see another case of...well another case of anything for a long time, I won't miss it." Kathy frowned.

Anna looked at Ruth and raised her eyebrows. "I told you—" She mouthed wordlessly. "I think she's not feeling well."

"Are you feeling okay, Kathy?" Ruth asked.

"I've been a little under the weather is all. Once I get back home, I'll rest up." Kathy sighed.

"As a professional EMT, I'd say you need a vacation from your vacation." Davis shook his finger at her.

"You're funny, but I appreciate your concern." Kathy smiled.

The rear hatch opened, and someone jumped in as the driver slid into his seat. "I'm John, your new driver." He started the minivan. "We'll follow the other van."

"What happened to Bibi?" Doctor Dan frowned and appraised the man sitting across from him.

"Not feeling well." John's eyes narrowed as he pulled out to follow the other van.

Davis looked back at Nathaniel and frowned. He had tried to get a look at the person who had jumped into the back of the van but wasn't able to see them, either from poor light, or the person just didn't want to be seen. There was an uneasy quiet as everyone settled in for the remaining part of the journey. No one talked, and there felt like a drawing together, a kinship that grew up among the six missionaries.

"Spears..." a garbled message came from Doc Dan's walkie-talkie he carried to communicate with the other group.

"Didn't copy. Try again." Dan waited but there was no more message. "That happens, but it's usually when we are farther apart." Doctor Dan frowned at his walkie-talkie. "Grunn, are you there?" When he looked back up, he realized the other van was no longer visible. "Where'd the others go?" Again he frowned at the driver.

"They're up there, not far. I've got them in sight." John continued to drive.

DAN SPEARS DIDN'T LIKE this situation. He knew at that point they were in trouble, but wasn't sure how to get out of these circumstances. They had about forty-five minutes until they should be at their destination, but what would that destination be? The other van was not in sight. That much he knew. While he had appeared to be reading a medical article, he had been praying. He hadn't been able to get a glimpse of the person who had jumped into the back of

the van. Did these people want the medicines? What was the reason behind this activity? And where were they going?

"SOMETHING'S NOT RIGHT." Ruth's eyes were wide. She leaned her head toward Anna and continued to whisper. "We aren't following the other van any longer."

"We should know what's going on pretty soon," Anna whispered back. "The traffic has thinned, and I'd think we should be..." She stopped whispering as the minivan pulled off to the side of the road.

"We are here. Everyone out." The driver pointed a handgun at Doctor Dan.

"No need to be violent. What do you want? Take the medicines and leave us alone." Dan tried to reason with the man.

"We've had sickness in our compound. We need medicines and care—workers who know what to do. We have a boat to go upriver where we need to be. Everyone must come." John frowned and waved the gun for all to get out. The person in the back rose out of his concealment. He had a larger gun that put to rest all arguments.

"Okay. Just take us men. Leave the women. The three of us can take care of sick people. Do the right thing and leave—" Dan tried again.

"—I said all must come." John growled. "Now, everyone out! And don't try to be a hero."

Without any more conversation, Dan opened his door and slid out, hanging the walkie-talkie on his belt and pulling his jacket down over it. Quietly Davis slid the van door open, grabbed his backpack, and helped Kathy out. Ruth slid Kathy's pack out to her, and everyone got out and made sure they had their possessions.

"The boat there— Down that path. Take the medicines." John motioned. He was a man of few words. Everyone grabbed a tote, and

John led Dan down first with everyone following carrying their treasures.

They made a chain of people and passed the totes of medicine to the man on the boat. There was a plank that ran between the land and the boat, which made it tricky not to lose anything, especially since they were under duress.

"I'm not able to walk that board. I know I'll fall." Kathy turned pale. Her eyes grew wide in panic.

"Get on the boat." John scowled, his face darkening.

"I'm afraid of water. —I can't, I just—"

"Come on, Kathy." Davis took her hand. "I'll help you. Spears, you get in the boat and I'll help the girls to you."

"Okay." Doctor Dan scrambled down the plank to the boat. "Ready, Freddy—or Mister Brown," he called back.

"Just call me Scout. I was a Boy Scout..." He firmly held Kathy's hand. "Trust me." He smiled at her reassuringly.

"Thank you." Tears streamed down her cheeks as he guided her steps.

"Here you are." He handed her over to Doctor Dan. "You're the man, Doctor Dan." His words were jesting, but he didn't smile.

"We're all in this together—Scout."

"There you go." Davis stepped back as Nathaniel gave Anna a hand to get started down the plank.

"This isn't a good way to start." Nathaniel and Ruth waited till Anna stepped into the boat.

"Walking the plank didn't ever end well in the pirate stories." Ruth glared. "I don't like this with someone standing behind us with a gun. It isn't walking the plank that bothers me. My brother and I used to walk the rafters in our grandpa's barn. The problem is the man with the gun."

———— ⟡ ————

"WHAT A DAY THIS HAS turned into. After two hours of riding in the boat—now, we get to hike through the jungle. It seems like we've walked for hours—" Ruth wiped the sweat from her brow, exhausted. Her nightmare was all around her. She saw a snake in every tree.

After their two-hour boat ride, they had stopped along the bank and unloaded the medical supplies and themselves. They had been met by three other men who were to carry supplies. John, their abductor, walked ahead of the group chopping foliage with his machete, enlarging the faint path into a wider path through the dense foliage. The other man with a rifle, who had been more of a silent shadow, covered their back. Those carrying the supplies were behind them.

"Hey, hey, John. The ladies need a short rest." Doctor Dan called to their guide. "You must remember, we are not used to this heat, humidity, and the jungle."

The guide held up a hand and shouted. "A short rest." He stopped and came back. Taking a long drink of water, he looked the group over. Everyone was drenched with sweat.

"What kind of sickness do your people at the compound have?" Dan took a drink.

"You will see," John said.

"Just curious. It helps plan for whatever is needed." He sighed, still not believing this was happening.

"I DON'T LIKE THIS," Anna spoke quietly to Ruth as the girls refreshed themselves.

"Nobody likes this. I don't think anyone knows quite what to do." Ruth grimaced.

"He gets less friendly and cooperative the further we go, and he wasn't ever friendly." Anna scowled.

"This isn't right, Crowl." Davis looked at something he held in the palm of his hand

"What isn't right?" Ruth overheard their conversation.

"We don't know the direction the village is from where we were, but this direction is way out there." Davis slid his compass back into his pocket. "I've done rescue work, and I carry some rude instruments just in case, you know, so I don't get lost, or so I can get found if I do get lost."

"That's because you've been a Boy Scout?" Ruth teased.

"Well, yes it is." His blue eyes twinkled at her. "We are very far from where we began, I surmise."

"Of all the things that could happen, I never saw this coming. You often hear of strange things occurring, but they usually strike someone else. Or they should at least." Nathaniel rubbed his chin.

"Humph, in this case, I guess it will happen to someone else in the view of people back home." Davis wiped his hands on his dungarees and took a drink of his water.

"Scout, you sure have a different way of looking at things." Nathaniel wiped an arm over his brow.

RUTH JOINED ANNA AND Kathy. "How are you feeling, Kathy?"

Anna wiped the log carefully, then sat beside Kathy. "You look like a strong wind could blow you away."

"I was a bit tired this morning, you know. All this stress has been nerve-wracking." Her voice faltered. "I had those two hours on the boat to rest. I felt fine when we started, but now I'm light-headed. It's just the heat and not enough water. Nothing to be concerned about." She did not sound convinced herself. "What are Davis and Nathaniel whispering about?" She put her elbows on her knees. Her eyes were closed as she cradled her head in her hands.

"No one is happy about this situation. But there isn't anything we can do about it." Anna pursed her lips and shrugged.

"I don't have a good feeling about this." Kathy frowned to herself.

"We'll find out what's going on in a little bit. It must be somewhat of an honest need. And if it's this hard on us younger ones of the team, it wouldn't have been good for the older ones of the group," Anna said.

"We were so close to going home." Kathy sighed. "I'm thinking of all the packing I've gotten done. Pretty much everything was ready so tomorrow I could throw the last of my necessities in my bag and leave."

"Most of us were counting the hours, but at least there won't be a delay in knowing something is going on." Ruth grimaced.

"They should be looking right away. I hope the other driver is all right." Anna looked concerned.

"Why wouldn't he be all right?" Kathy opened her eyes, looking at them closely before taking a long drink of water.

"When Doctor Dan asked this guy what happened to Bibi, he said he wasn't feeling well." Ruth reminded her.

"I have a feeling these are not nice people. Do you suppose they are related to those people we heard about on the news in that gang?" Kathy's eyes widened.

"Ho." Nathaniel joined the three women. "Dan told the guide that Kathy here is sick and that we need to get her back to the compound."

"So, what did he think?" Anna asked hopefully.

"It is a no-go. Are you girls about ready to travel again?" Nathaniel asked.

"We've come too far anyway. These people wouldn't care about Kathy." Ruth touched Kathy's arm. "Are you feeling better, Kathy?"

"Yes, a little anyway." She stood up slowly.

"It's time to go." The guide, John, became irritated and grabbed Davis, who was the closest person to him. "It is time to go!" He held up a wicked-looking machete. "We go on—together—to my village. Now!" He gave Davis a shove.

"Everyone where you were." He motioned for everyone to take up their previous positions. The man with the rifle was between the missionaries and the people carrying the supplies, while the guide was still in front leading. "March now, no talk." He turned and began cutting his way through the jungle.

"As if we could talk." Nathaniel picked up his and Kathy's packs both heavy with supplies, and he threw them one over each shoulder. "The girls are just about finished in this heat. How long before someone passes out?"

In fifteen minutes Kathy crumpled on the ground. "You." John pointed to Doctor Dan. "Carry the woman."

"You know," Dan said. "We will need to redistribute two packs. In this heat and humidity, everyone is going to need to be carried at this rate." He challenged their abductor.

"Not far, there's a good path...very close, only short way to the village." His brown eyes were angry and harsh. He turned back to chopping, but true to his word, it was not far until they came to a well-used trail then shortly to the village, as he had termed it.

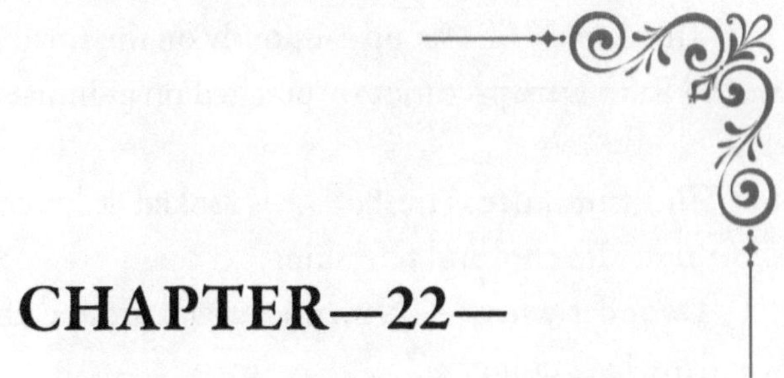

CHAPTER—22—

"Halt!" they were challenged. "Password?"

"John!" Their guide answered crossly, adding in a few other words under his breath.

"Ah, come in and wait here." The guard waved them in and blew sharply on a whistle. Shortly another man dressed in military-style clothing came up and showed the way to a block cabin. He pushed open the door and waited for everyone to enter. The door was slammed shut and they heard a lock click.

"Whew!" Davis exploded, thankful to set down the packs he'd carried. "That was sure a long trip...and close too!" He helped Dan place Kathy carefully on the cot. Nathaniel eased the two packs he was carrying to the floor and helped Anna and Ruth lower their packs as well.

Someone fumbled with the lock and the door opened to reveal a man in military-type garb. "After your long trek, maybe you'd like something cool? Some refreshments?" His voice was soothing and pleasant. After placing the food on a low rough table, he scrutinized the group of three men and three women. He took note that the young women were quite attractive, even under these circumstances, before he backed out and relocked the door.

"The pineapple and juice should help." Davis passed out the fruit and poured a cup of juice. "After that march...Here, drink this." He handed Kathy the juice.

"Thank you." She sat up cautiously on the small military cot. Anna and Ruth were precariously perched on a similar cot under a window.

"This fruit juice is fresh." Davis looked at his cup of juice after a short rest. "It's cool and refreshing."

"I wonder when—" Nathaniel gazed around the building. "—I wonder what's going on."

"John said they needed medicines and people who knew how to use them. I guess that's us." Dan took another long drink of water then checked Kathy's pulse.

Everyone's eyes were drawn to the door as the sound of heavy boots crunched toward their cement block cabin. There was the sound of several people sucking in their breath at the same time as the lock rattled. The door was unlocked and swung open.

The man in the doorway was young. A guess would put him in his mid to late twenties. He was immaculately dressed in dark colored slacks and a button down shirt. He exuded a presence that indicated he was used to giving commands. In short, he was familiar with authority and comfortable with it.

His eyes examined the group quickly. "Which is the doctor?" He spoke but singled out Dan with his eyes. "You?" he questioned.

"Yes, that is I." Dan stood erect from where he had been kneeling beside Kathy's cot.

"Come with me." He stepped back and let the doctor pass through the door.

"Well—" Davis blinked in surprise. "—that was...quick."

"Quick? I guess so." Nathaniel's eyebrows shot up in amazement. "Quick might not be the exact word I would have used. Unexpected maybe?"

"We have entered into a new realm here. I know what my daddy would do in a situation like this." Anna's face was pale and serious.

"I can guess." Nathaniel wiped the perspiration off his forehead. "But go ahead and tell us." He folded his arms.

"He would pray." She looked up and her brown eyes challenged him.

Nathaniel's eyes narrowed as he took stock of the situation. "I'll lead the prayer." He removed his hat and took a deep breath.

"Thank you," Anna said after the prayer.

Anna and Ruth both removed their pocket Bibles from the small pockets inside their vests. They passed the time reading quietly to themselves. At intervals they closed their eyes, their lips moving silently in fervent prayer.

"NOTHING TO BE SEEN out of the windows." Nathaniel looked through the bars covering the windows. He continued in thought as he studied the scenery. Within his view, he could observe a semi-circle of five cement block cabins—six including their structure. Their cabin was situated between the much larger structure, which was slightly set off by itself, and the other five cabins.

"You two must have nerves of steel." He turned his attention back to Anna and Ruth. "Sitting there reading your Bibles like nothing's going on. I don't know if I'm amused or amazed." He shook his head. "How're you doing, Brown? When that guy was waving that machete around, I was concerned it might get ugly, but you seem to have come out in stride. Kathy still looks peaked though."

"You're right. Kathy is still looking puny." Davis began to rummage in his backpack. Finding what he was searching for, he pulled it out. "Here." He handed Kathy a power granola bar. "Eat this—and don't talk back." He insisted roughly, but with a smile.

"Thanks." She opened her mouth to protest then she smiled at him.

"What a way to celebrate your first half a year as a new Christian." Nathaniel sighed.

"It's memorable at least." Davis sat on an empty cot. "Don was telling me about his missionary experience, then he said, 'It'll be fun you should come with me. It'll get your mind off your troubles.'"

"That's the one phrase you need to stay away from. The one that goes like, 'It'll be fun. You should try it.'" Nathaniel snorted. "Just stay away from it."

They were startled as a loud groan came from the large house to the right of their cabin. All five occupants of the rude cabin stood and stared with concern toward where the sound had originated.

"What do you think?" Davis walked to the window and stood beside Nathaniel.

"I don't know. I've been searching in my mind. Do you remember the news story to do with the bandits and that shootout we heard about a couple of days ago?" Nathaniel asked.

"Doc Spears mentioned that. But why bring all of us up here?" Davis's face puckered up, disturbed.

"John didn't ask for volunteers. He couldn't just waltz in and say, 'Our fearless desperados were shot up pretty bad and we need some doctors and medics to fix 'em up. Who wants to volunteer?'" Nathaniel grimaced.

"I guess not." Davis nodded slowly. "Shh. There they come." He held up a cautionary hand as they heard boots crunch outside their door. All eyes were glued, watching as the door was unlocked and swung wide. Doctor Dan was framed in the doorway, and behind him stood the young commander.

Dan walked across the room and grabbed his pack. "You—Nat, and Anna." He twitched his head toward the door. "—bring your packs, and come with me." He heaved his pack over his shoulder. "The rest of you go with Ricardo here." He turned and they were all three gone with the same speed that the commander and the doctor had left the first time.

"Bring your *cosas* and come wid me." Ricardo had a heavy accent. "De boss say dis is no place *para las mujeres*—" He seemed to search for the right words. "—for de weemin." His words were not unkind, and he motioned toward the house. "*Vamonos, andale.*"

The three remaining captives quickly collected their belongings and followed Ricardo. Davis followed Kathy and Ruth across the space between the two structures. He could feel strange eyes watching as they mounted the steps and crossed the porch.

Davis stood in the doorway a minute to adjust his eyes to the difference between the brightness of the outside contrasted with the dimness of the dark, shaded room. They were literally blinded for a few moments.

"What needs to be done here?" Kathy gazed around at the large dining room. The table had been pushed up against the wall and there were many cots containing the wounded on them.

"*No comprendo.*" Ricardo waved his hands.

"*Nosotros necesitamos saber como ayudar*?" Ruth frowned and attempted to remember her Spanish. "I sure wish Anna was here. She could just rattle it off, but my muddled brain." She shook her head. "I don't know if I've got the right words."

"*Yo comprendo.*" In spite of her stumbling, he shook his head in the affirmative. "*Si, si, ellos necisitan mucha... ayuda.*"

With Ricardo's help, Kathy, Davis, and Ruth began treating the wounded. Davis and Kathy did the examinations while Ruth made notes on each person and what they needed. Then they began in earnest with the worse cases taking precedence.

"I'm praying we have enough of the right medicines. This isn't like what we were dealing with at the clinics. We don't have medicines and supplies for a battlefield of gunshots, knife wounds, and these types of wounds." Davis showed Dan, Nathaniel, and Anna around the dining room three hours later as they joined the three in the dining room team.

"We'll just have to do the best we can with what we have." Dr. Dan sighed. "The one upstairs was worse than these. We did a good job on him, all things considered. We'll have to leave him in the hand of God." Dr. Dan examined a head wound then started to clean and suture the wound.

"*Madre mia! Mori y me fui al cielo? Mira, angeles.*" A wounded man hallucinated as Ruth and Anna finished up his bandage.

Anna smiled at Ruth. "He thinks he's died and gone to heaven. He thinks we're angels. No, no—" Anna spoke gently to soothe the distraught man. "—You are still in the land of the living. We're only servants of the Lord, not angels."

"I believe we are done for the time being." Kathy dropped wearily into a chair. "This has been more than a day." She handed Davis a roll of gauze.

"Armando?" Dan called.

"*Señor?*" The cook stepped out of the kitchen.

"I am looking for Armando," Dan said.

"*Ah, un momento, por favor— Señor, le gustari'a que le traigo uno taza de café', mientras que voy al buscar al Armando?*"

"*Gracias.*" Dan swiped a forearm across his face. Turning to the others on the team he said. "Well, now that I've used all the Spanish words that I care to—I haven't seen this many wounded since..."

"I was a Boy Scout." Davis filled in quickly.

"Shhh." Anna put a finger on her lips. Don't mention the word military here."

"I wasn't going to use the M-word, but you're right. Mum's the word." He smiled at her. "And don't show off any unnecessary española, either." He winked.

"Okee-dokee. Gotcha." She raised an eyebrow.

"Could you all try speaking English?" Nathaniel took a sip of his coffee.

"I think what they are saying—" Kathy kept her voice low. "—is there are certain things it is best if they do not know. Things that might be held against us or other things that might be an advantage for us. If they thought we didn't know their language, they might not be so careful..."

"Ah-ha. I see." Ruth voiced what the others were thinking. Everyone was quiet, weighing new ideas. "As long as we don't have to be dishonest." Ruth remembered Mrs. MacDonald's dilemma and how they had laughed at her predicament a few years back. "They don't have any grand ideas about my Spanish-speaking ability." She grinned sheepishly. "The Lord does work in mysterious ways."

"Shh." Davis held up a hand as they heard soft footsteps approach. Six pairs of eyes turned and watched and waited for the person to appear.

"My name is Armando. I have met some of you already. I regret—" He hesitated momentarily. "—that our hospitality is somewhat lacking at the present. I also regret the circumstances under which you were brought here, but it was urgent." He spoke in excellent English. "The cook will bring you something shortly. You can rest and eat. After you finish eating, I will show you to your rooms. There is one room for the women and one room for the men. I will return soon. Eat and rest."

"*Gracias.*" Dan smiled as the cook's helper brought in plates and food. "*Como se' llama?*" he asked.

"Robert. My name is Robert." He looked at Dan in a puzzled way and set the plates on the small table.

"Thank you, Robert—Davis? Lead us in prayer, please." Dan bowed his head and after the prayer, he began to fill plates. "I don't know. We seem to have two groups here, one Spanish speakers and others of English speakers. Who wants to take the first watch?" Dan questioned with a frown.

"I'll take the first watch," Nathaniel volunteered.

"Anna, why don't you take the first watch with Crowl there. Ruth and I will do the second watch, and Davis and Kathy you take the last watch. This will be a crucial time. Let's check these patients again now. Some of us can get a few hours of much-needed rest. This has been a difficult day, and I'm thinking the night won't be much better. We are all exhausted." He finished by running his hand over his tired face.

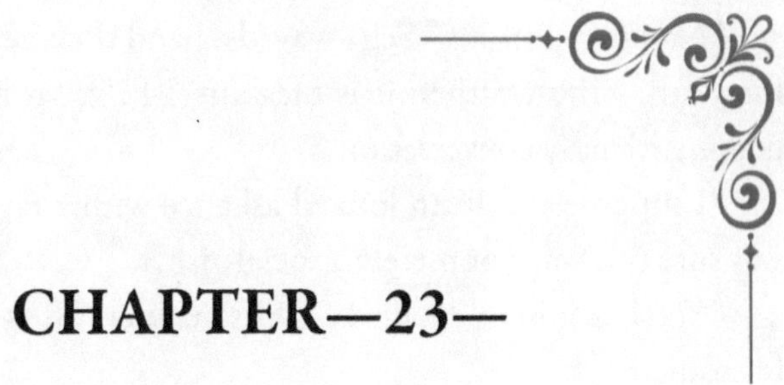

CHAPTER —23—

"What we did here was to help people. Some of these men would have died without our help. But we must fight evil, Anna. We must not submit to it, no, not for one hour." Ruth waved her forefinger.

Anna glanced around the room. "We've been here long enough—a week and a half by my calculations— I'm sure we should have been found."

"Anna, you lead the prayer then." Ruth and Kathy bent their heads while Anna petitioned the Lord in a simple prayer.

There was a quiet tap at the door before it opened noiselessly. "You." Armando motioned to Ruth. "Felix would speak with you." He held the door open for her to pass. She walked down the hall a short way to Felix's room, not far from the other rooms. Armando tapped again and, opened that door.

"Do you ever get tired of holding doors for other people?" She looked up into his blank, dark eyes. She wished she could read his mind. She knew he had watched them as they went quietly about their duties, but his face was always a blank, as if he wore a mask.

"For some people, yes, but not for you, senorita." He smiled now.

Ruth's eyes searched his face, wondering if she saw a spark of life in it somewhere. She sighed and looked away as she entered the room. Armando was difficult to read, but Felix was not. Ruth resented the calculating way he sized her up. Whatever his intentions were, they weren't good.

"No interruptions." Felix waved a hand then he indicated a chair for Ruth. "The weather, it is pleasant?" Felix sat back in his chair, making friendly conversation.

"I suppose so." Ruth looked askance with a raised eyebrow. She was sure this was not merely a social visit.

"You like it in our country?" His manner was as if he were fishing for something.

"Quite honestly, no." She gazed out the large window at the trees swaying in the distance.

"Why do you not like it here?" His English was not as polished as Armando's.

"It isn't home. —I guess it isn't what I'm accustomed to." She still evaded his eyes.

"I see. You are missing your servants?" He was getting to the real question.

Ruth's eyes opened wide in surprise, and she laughed. "No, no. We're farmers. There are no servants in our home—only ourselves." She added, finally bringing her gaze back inside yet still avoiding his crafty observation. "At home, we would be bringing in the apples for the winter, and harvesting grain and gardens. Have you ever been to America?"

"I ask the questions." His brows drew together and his face became angry. "You are a very beautiful young woman. What is wrong with you? Why you are not married?"

"I have chosen not to marry yet. Do you have family...children perhaps?"

"I tell you, I ask the questions." He slapped the desk with his hand, his countenance still angry at her persistence. "You have chosen not to marry? Do you have a—" His brow furrowed. "a lover?"

"A lover?" Ruth gasped. "I should hope not!" She sat up straight in horrified disbelief.

"Maybe..." He pursed his lips thoughtfully. "...perhaps... a sweetheart?"

"No." She looked down at her hands folded in her lap.

"Why does your father not insist you marry?" His mouth puckered into a frown, and he looked intimidating.

"Could you force your daughter to marry?" She looked unaffected by his antics. What was the look that flitted across his hardened features, Ruth wondered.

He muttered something under his breath that sounded very much like, "*'Americans, aiee!'*" There was a pause as Ruth continued to watch him from lowered eyes.

He finally asked the question he had been dancing around. "Your papa—he will pay much money for your safe return, yes?"

"Do you think only rich people love their children? We are not rich—only farmers. My papa doesn't have *much money* for my safe return. Surely you have some concept that not all people in America are rich? Only the ignorant people from other countries believe all Americans are rich." Her eyes narrowed and challenged him.

"I am not ignorant." His eyes blazed at her. "You may go." Again he slapped the desk and raised his voice.

She stood and walked to the door. Opening it she stopped suddenly just short of bumping into Armando. "Excuse me—" Had he heard the conversation, she wondered? Was that a look of amusement or admiration? It was replaced by his usual blank stare. "What do you folks want?" She asked annoyed. "Surely you don't believe all people in America are rich too, do you?"

"No, *se', senorita*. But many Americans are more affluent than most in this country." He opened the door to their room, and Ruth entered. "You—" He quietly motioned to Anna and led her down the hall and opened the door into Felix's room for her.

ARMANDO HAD NOT BEEN back to his home country very long before his brother Felix began integrating him into Felix's businesses. At first, the work had looked like bona fide business, but the more Armando observed the dealings Felix had, there was a subtle gap. Now that Armando found himself sucked into the midst of the murky mess of Felix's life, he felt trapped. It was lucrative—plenty of money—but not what Armando had imagined for his life. He could afford an extravagant home, beautiful things for a beautiful wife, and a beautiful family, but at what cost? Did he want to become hardened and cruel like his brother?

He waited in the hall for the young lady, Anna. Many of the wounded men had taken to calling the three young women "the beautiful angels of mercy." The young women had at all times tried to be quiet and respectful. Armando had noticed the difference between them and many young girls he had met. These three tried not to draw attention to themselves, yet they were so young and lovely, it would have taken someone made of stone not to have noticed. For all of his outward appearance, Armando was not made of stone.

"WHAT DID HE WANT?" Kathy waited until the door closed as Anna left.

"Money, mostly. Maybe answers. I'm not sure what all he was searching for." Ruth shrugged. Then she removed her Bible and turned to the Psalms.

"I am afraid, Ruth." Tears slid down Kathy's cheeks. "I don't like Felix. He looks cruel and just gives me the creeps the way he looks at us. And honestly—" Kathy's lips trembled. "—I don't have anything someone like Felix would want. No money, no family. You and Anna are pretty and—"

"—Sometimes things aren't exactly what they seem." Mrs. MacDonald's words popped suddenly into Ruth's mind.

"How's that? Do you think my fears are ungrounded?"

"No. The threat is very real and very great. A dear friend told me this not long ago, and it just came into my mind." Ruth fingered her small Bible. Kathy was technically right. There was nothing really impressive about her. She was a quiet, petite young woman with straw brown, blond hair. But she had a genuine quality. Ruth tried to put a name to it to no avail. "So, what are you planning to do when we get out of here?"

Her question seemed to soothe Kathy's fears. "I'm not exactly sure. Go home, look around, and I guess make some decisions. Funny how these crisis situations can put things into a different perspective." She wiped the tears away and blew her nose.

"You're right on the button there." Ruth prayed, *Lord help me help her in this time of darkness.* "What decisions are you making?"

"My husband and baby were killed in a car accident a year ago. Right after the accident, I was so lost and so in shock. I just wanted to get away, to leave everything. Especially anything that reminded me of...before. I guess I was kind of like the walking dead. I just went on numbly acting and reacting. One day I was looking at the bulletin board at church as Robin was putting up an announcement. We struck up a conversation, and that is how I ended up here. Do you think we'll get out of here?" Her blue eyes sought reassurance.

"I'm so sorry about your loss." Ruth's eyes grew wide and her face paled. "I do believe we'll get out of here. I know there are a lot of people praying for us. I also believe that no matter what, I will trust in God." Ruth decided it was sweetness, maybe a form of guilelessness. Kathy was a good one to have pulling for you.

"Thank you, Ruth. You and Anna have been such encouragement to me. You two are so good and gentle."

"We have our rough spots like everyone else. I don't know how Anna and I have encouraged you. It is enough just to know that we have."

"Well, I never!" Anna exclaimed as the door opened and she was ushered back into the room. "The nerve of that man!" She scowled, and her brown eyes snapped in a fury. "He wanted to know how much I was worth to my papa! I told him even the poor can value their children. I asked him just how much his children were worth to him. He kept repeating that he was the one asking the questions and pounding the desk."

"I'm surprised that he didn't..." Ruth stopped speaking remembering Kathy's words, "I have nothing Felix would want." "I wonder ..." She stopped, deciding she had best keep that idea to herself.

"DOCTOR DANIEL SPEARS." Felix's voice droned as the doctor finished checking his bandages. "We are asking a million dollars for your ransom. What do you think of that? We value you very high, huh?"

"I'm impressed. I'm impressed that you value me so highly and your life so little." Doctor Dan's eyes narrowed as he continued to pick up the supplies and throw away the old bandages.

"Armando!" Fernando shouted so suddenly that Dan dropped his scissors.

The door flew open and the person in question stepped in quickly. "Si?"

"What is there to do with these Americans? They do not understand their position here. What to do? I think I will have this one beaten and his right hand crushed. Yes, that is good, but wait, he is too valuable to us. Maybe we should beat the women. He would not like that. Then he would take things serious, I think. But then I think we don't want to damage such valuable merchandise. That leaves the other two. They may be valuable, but probably not. So what to do with them? Huh?" His eyes narrowed as he contemplated. "Perhaps we cut off their little fingers—just as a warning."

Dan's face flamed with anger. "Yes, drag innocent people through the jungle, and after they have saved your life and the lives of your comrades, repay them for their selfless efforts. Cut off their fingers, beat them, or crush their hands. What kind of barbarians are you? We're non-political doctors and medical persons caring for the poor in the name of Christ. We're doing something good for these poor people. Then bullies like you..."

Like lightening, Armando's hand shot out and slapped him across the face. "You must remember your manners." He spoke quietly, his face not changing expression. Crossing the room to the water bucket, he poured water into a container, and wetting a cloth in cool water, handed it to the doctor to stop the bleeding on his lip.

"Armando, I wonder how much this doctor is worth to his friends and family. I thought one million, but maybe it should be two? Maybe we can bargain, say take the price we get from the women off of his price?" Felix puckered his lips and frowned, leaning back in his chair.

"What Armando said is true. I need to remember my manners." Doctor Dan struggled to regain his composure.

"Now he is listening to reason. Is he not?" Felix smiled a self-satisfied smile.

"I wish there was some way to remind you to remember yours as well—if you ever had any." Dan's hand moved quickly to block a reminder from Armando. "I'm just asking you to hear me out. Don't go getting slap-happy, as my granny used to say. Maybe I'm important to you. Maybe I'm valuable to my friends and family, but so are the other five members of my team. God loves and values them. Since I'm their leader, I'm responsible for them. You can't have any of them. I will stand in their stead. Let them go." He finished speaking with a steady eye and a firm voice.

"You talk easy." Felix's eyes narrowed into sly slits. "If the knife were at your fingers, would you still be so brave? Eh?"

"That's a good question. I would pray so. You see, a Savior stood in my stead many years ago, and I was much less deserving than these that you have in your possession. Jesus did much more for me than I could ever repay. What do they call it? Noblesse oblige? I am obligated by a noble calling. Yet I wonder—" Dan mused softly, more to himself than his captors. "Even if you left me crippled for the remainder of my life I would be much richer than you could ever dream of being. Your body is mending very fast, sir." His voice was quiet and steady. "—But there is something terribly wrong with your soul."

"I DON'T KNOW IF IT is the mountain air, or if you have the constitution of an ox." Later in the day Dan again checked Felix's wounds. "Whatever the case, you are healing very quickly. Most people would require more than two weeks to heal. You don't need me to dress this wound, really, and the rest of the wounded are the same. Everyone needs to be careful, but no one still requires care. Crowl, just a light bandage there, and we'll call it done." Doctor Dan snipped off the last of the stitches.

"You still do your duty even after our conversation of this morning." Felix mulled this over as if it were a new idea. "Maybe we could sell just one woman. Beautiful women are worth much, especially in such fine condition."

"What kind of men are you?" Nathaniel spoke in disbelief. "The Bible speaks against people who buy and sell others. Men stealers, it's called. I know the family of two of the young ladies. If any of their men were here, even if you were in prime condition, you would not touch a hair of these girls' heads."

"So, they are fighters, eh?" Felix's eyes gleamed.

"Come to think of it." Nathaniel pursed his lips, considering the question carefully. "I have never seen a one of them physically fight.

However, I can honestly say I wouldn't want to be on the other side of a fight with them."

"And why do you say I would not touch these women?" Felix frowned.

"That is a good question." Nathaniel finished the bandage. "The women seem to have a guardian, and maybe it isn't just their men. You know—and this is just a word to you, sir. Those young ladies are just that. They aren't trash to be bought or sold like so much merchandise. The guardian of which I speak is their God. If I were in your shoes, sandals, boots, or whatever you wear, I would be very careful in the decisions that I make concerning them."

"You would threaten me? Ha! You need to take a care. I am the one in control here." Felix scoffed. "What does God care about our little affairs here? So far, I leave Him alone, and he leaves me alone. I like it that way." He nodded with a self-satisfied smile.

"No, I wouldn't threaten you. Just be aware that God is not bound by any agreement you think you have with him." Nathaniel shrugged. "Often the people you don't suspect are the ones you should be wary of. Just telling you the truth."

"THIS IS THE LAST ONE to be seen." Davis checked the list as Ruth unwrapped the bandage from a head wound.

"He is so much better." Anna observed as she stepped over to help.

"This man won't need our attention anymore." Ruth took off the last of the bandage. "You are all better." She attempted to relay the news to the patient.

"*Que, senorita? No comprendo, lo siento mucho.*" He shrugged his shoulders.

"*No esta' infermo? Todo bien?* I don't know—" Ruth rolled her eyes. "—am I saying anything that makes sense?"

"*Hermosos angeles, gracias. Muchos gracias,*" he said gratefully.

"*Da nada.*" She smiled. "*Buenos tardes, señor.*"

"Thank you, sir." Davis took the cup of coffee that the cook brought. "You girls want one too?" he asked.

"I have been fasting and praying today." Anna reminded him.

"Me too." Ruth nodded.

"Maybe I should have been too." Kathy raised her eyebrows self-consciously.

"No, you should not." Three voices spoke in unison.

"We don't want you to pass out again. Whatever you do, you need to eat to keep up your strength. You may need all your strength and more before we get out of here." Davis frowned at her sternly.

"I don't understand." Emotions struggled across the surface of Kathy's face. "I have always believed that when you do a good deed for someone they are grateful. I—I just always believed that. Not everyone has always said thank you, but in some childish way, I just thought it was an oversight. Now I'm so confused."

Davis chose his words slowly. "Even apathy would be better than the cruel insensitivity of Felix. Doctor Dan warned us, Crowl and myself, that these people would probably look for various ways to extract money from the situation. They are seemingly ruthless, calculating, and unprincipled."

"You sum it up very well." Armando entered escorting the other two men into the room. "An operation like this always needs money." He shrugged. "We know that doctors always have money. We also know the price of beauty." He paused, purposely not looking at the young women. "And those who are willing to pay for it." His features never registered emotion. "I am sorry, but that is the way it goes."

"Señor?" Kathy asked boldly. "We would like to ask a favor."

"You may ask." He noticed her eyes were vivid blue, and how innocent and pretty she was. Much too delicate to be in this situation, not bold like some of the women of his country. Her eyes were gentle and her smile was winsome.

"We would like to go home."

"I didn't say I would grant to you what you asked." Armando didn't know whether to smile or sigh. If he had his choice... but it wasn't his choice. "Only that you may ask what you wish."

EVENING DEVOTIONS WERE part of every missionary trip that Dan Spears organized. The time spent together in singing and prayer and the Bible lesson kept the spirit of the group focused and helped the local people understand that these were not just doctors and medical people ministering to the physical needs. These people were here to show Christ and His love for the spiritual as well as the physical needs. It was quite a blessing that Dan and Davis had brought their Bibles in their packs, and Nathaniel had a songbook and a small Bible among his things.

Dan gave the Bible lesson that evening. Anna had worked with this dedicated doctor on other missionary trips and had never failed to be impressed. He was only medium height, and his features were pleasant, but he would not be considered compellingly handsome. Just an average guy. However, when he opened his Bible and taught, his love for the Word of God was evident. She had never had the opportunity to ask, however, she wondered why he had not become a preacher.

The group sang well together that evening. Nathaniel led the songs, and unbeknown to them, there was an audience. Some were listening outside as well as inside as the mission group sang, and after the final prayer, all was peaceful.

"There is a Spanish section in this songbook." Nathaniel sat quietly thumbing through the book. "I wish I knew how to sing in Spanish."

"Let me see it—" Anna took the book. "Maybe we can sing some." She looked through the section and chose two songs. "Look, these tunes are familiar. Nathaniel, you've taken some Spanish in high school—it goes like this." She sang the first verse.

"I can do this." With a little practice, he had them worked out, and the group followed their example.

"I think we did a fair job of following the leader and singing those songs," Davis said.

"I didn't know Anna was so good at Spanish." Kathy sat quietly thinking. "That must have been what Dan meant about not using much Spanish."

"I have heard her rattle off Spanish at the compound, so I guess I knew she was pretty proficient. I wonder why Dan didn't stop her, or any of us for that matter, this evening." Davis cocked his head sideways.

"It doesn't make any difference now." Ruth looked at the ones gathered. "They will do what they will do, no matter what."

Nathaniel, Davis, and Kathy understood the truth of Ruth's statement. They looked at each other soberly, wondering what was to come for them.

Anna sat by herself reading her Bible then she picked up the songbook again and began searching through it. Her countenance was calm and accepting.

Nathaniel and Davis went to speak to Dan. Their heads were bent together in serious conversation for a few moments. Dan went to speak to Anna as Nathaniel and Davis came back to the others.

"Spears agrees with you, Ruth. He thinks tonight is a turning point," Nathaniel whispered to Kathy and Ruth. "They have threatened some of us, hinted at unpleasant things, but we don't know. Whatever they are going to do, this is our plan—"

There was a moment of silence as the four pondered the information and the plan. They looked up as Dan and Anna began to sing the hymn "Love, Love, Love..." in Spanish. It was a moment of revelation to the entire group.

"Well, I'll be." Davis summed it up for all of them. "I guess I have heard Spears speak some Spanish, but I never would have guessed he was fluent."

"That song is awe-inspiring the way they are singing it." Nathaniel scrunched up his face listening thoughtfully. "I think we can do this—" He began singing an echo in English of what they were singing in Spanish. The group joined in—softly at first, but each time they sang the song through it got a little louder. The illusive haunting melody of the song rose and carried throughout the house and out into the night. When they finished the last stanza, there was a long, prayerful silence. Each person sat wrapped in prayerful contemplation.

"Thank you, Anna. You have the most beautiful voice." Dan heaved a sigh.

"The feeling is mutual, sir. I couldn't have done it without you." Her countenance wore a troubled look.

"Are you frightened?" he asked.

"I feel more like I'm in limbo. I've passed the point of fear. For a while I was, but I know there are a lot of people praying for us, and..." She hesitated. "My parents raised us on the Bible and trust, and I know that God can do anything. I remember the story of Shadrach, Meshach, and Abednego. How they told the king 'Our God is able to deliver us, but *even if He doesn't*, we will not serve thy gods.' Well, I know that God is able, and we are clay in His hand. Who knows what good we have accomplished here? Perhaps more than we will ever understand."

"I will cherish those words for a very long time—or as long as God gives me time." Dan wiped a hand over his weary face. "I want to thank you guys for being who you are. I couldn't have chosen a better group to work with—and under these circumstances. No matter what, remember: go with God." He picked up the small candle, and everyone followed, knowing that their movements were monitored.

Anna, Ruth, and Kathy filed into their room. "Well, what next, I wonder?" Kathy shivered when she heard a click of the door being locked on their room. "I feel on needles and pins."

"I guess we try to get some sleep." Ruth pulled empty water bottles and wrappers out to rearrange her backpack. "Let's have a short prayer first."

"I can't sleep. I'll just lie here wishing I could sleep." Kathy scowled. "And for the last two weeks, every waking hour has been spent in prayer."

Anna glanced at Ruth's efforts with her pack. "Ruth, that's a wise idea. We came in here with full packs. I can lighten this pack up quite a bit. Kathy, tell me something about yourself while I work." Anna began repacking as well.

"I'm twenty-seven years old and my birthday is next month." Kathy followed Ruth and Anna's example, removing unnecessary clutter from her pack.

"Okay, your turn, Ruth."

"I'm twenty-two years old. I have a brother named Reuben who is planning on marrying his sweetheart in the spring." She smiled at Anna.

"Hey, I didn't know that!" Anna smiled back. "Well, let's see. I'm twenty-nine, I have the greatest family there ever was. Your turn again, Kathy."

"Until the last two weeks, I didn't realize how much I wanted to live. After my husband, Albert, and Bertie junior were killed in the car accident, I thought my life was over. But now, it isn't that I have forgotten them, or that I love them less. I just think maybe there is something God has left for me to do."

"Kathy, there is something God has left for you to do. I feel it very deeply." Ruth's eyes teared up. "I have a confession to make. Last night I had a dream. It was so real. My dad was here in this room. He spoke to me saying, 'This is for all those years and for all those times I should have been there for you, your brother, and especially your mother, dear daughter of mine.' He filled the whole room, and he smiled that wonderful smile when he makes you think the world is full of sunshine and roses. Anna, when I thought I had lost Michael to Ada, it seemed like I could see nothing ahead of me but a black void. During last night's dream, Dad's sunshiny smile blurred into Michael smiling at me like he did when we were still—" She paused looking around at their room with the three cots and the few furnishings. "I realized just how much I have missed him these last few years, and how much I do love him...even if it is too late."

"Ruth, I have a confession too." Anna fumbled removing a necklace. "Here, my dear friend." She thrust an object into Ruth's hand. "Remember the year Joshua and Seth showed up? Laura and I were in Spain? Well, Michael had us, Laura and I, pick out a nice gift for you, and this is what he wanted. It's hard to see in this light— or lack of light, but he said if there was a time when you were ready for this, that I was to give it to you with all his love, with all his heart, and his devotion."

Ruth looked at the object and gasped. Even in the faint moonlight it shimmered and glowed. It was a small gold ring with an emerald, a ruby, and two pearls encircled by a swirl of small diamonds.

"Oh, Anna." Ruth breathed, softly caressing the ring. "but what about..."

"Ada?" Anna smiled a one-eyed smile. "I told you there was a mistake in our understanding. I know Michael meant this ring for you. He asked when he came home last time if I still had it. When I said yes, he just said to take care of you for him."

"Oh, Ruth, that is so sweet and special." Kathy's eyes shone even in the muted light. "Before we came on this trip, I felt alone. My family and I are close, but they don't live close. They tried to help after the accident, but our lives are so busy." She shook her head. "I've grown close to you two. I don't feel alone any more. I know that everything will turn out right for all of us. Davis has been a real encouragement to me, and he lives close. Even if our relationship doesn't blossom, it has come with a sense that maybe there is hope for another life."

"I thought Davis was married." Ruth admired the shimmering of the ring.

"No, he came home one evening, after five years of marriage. She had left a note explaining that she had loaded up her stuff and left. He admitted he felt so utterly stupid. She had been carrying on for about two and a half years with this other fellow. He never even suspected. In true Davis style, he said even being a Boy Scout didn't prepare me for that." Kathy shook her head and smiled.

"He hasn't been a Christian long, has he?" Anna asked.

"No, less than a year."

"What about Dan?" Ruth asked.

"He was engaged the first time I worked with him. But I haven't heard him speak of his wife or family. He doesn't wear a ring. So I don't know." Anna shrugged.

"Oh? He was engaged? That's news to me," Kathy said. "I'm sure Davis said Dan isn't married. Neither he nor Nathaniel is married according to Davis. I'm sure that's what he told me."

"I knew Nathaniel wasn't." Ruth smiled. "He told me on one of our watches why he was so nervous the year he visited us. You remember his visit three years ago, Anna?"

"I remember the visit." Anna finished putting everything back in her pack and zipped it shut.

"He made an unwise statement at some point in his stay, and you know how your family is about that sort of stuff. The boys put him in his place and on his best behavior." Ruth stretched.

"That's funny. I wondered at the time," Anna said.

"You see, Kathy, Anna has a large family. And several brothers are keen on treating women with respect, especially the ones in their family." Ruth finished her pack and closed it up.

"That seems to be a lost art." Kathy moved a pile of wrappers and empty bottles to the floor in front of her cot. "Do we just leave this excess stuff here?"

"That's where I'm gonna leave mine." Anna swept her pile into Kathy's.

"Nathaniel had never considered that there was anything wrong with his behavior before. He changed his habits and was looking for someone who knew the value of a Christian home and family. Someone who would appreciate a godly mate." Ruth added her trash to the pile.

Kathy yawned. "This should make these packs much easier to carry. I don't know how we'll be able to get these out of here but...I believe I could go to sleep now. I wish this cot were someplace else though." Perched on the edge of the cot, she scowled.

"Yeah, like back home in America." Anna laughed softly, following Kathy's example.

"I guess I couldn't have been marooned with a better bunch. Who is going to lead our prayer?" Kathy sighed.

"I'll start it." Anna bent her head.

"We're game." Kathy and Ruth closed their eyes and bowed their heads.

After the prayer, Anna tried to fluff up her pillow. "There isn't any possibility to toss and turn on these accommodations."

"That is one thing about these beds—" Ruth stretched out on her cot. "—but the day started early, and it's now late."

Anna heard peaceful breathing from the other two as they fell asleep. Ruth's suggestion of her dream inspired Anna to dream of her father, except her dream had overtones of strife and turmoil and was not reassuring.

THE NIGHT DREW ON, and the faint moonlight became no moonlight. The night sounds grew silent waiting for something. There was a slight movement here and there as if a gentle breeze stirred the leaves of the trees, except there was no breeze. Suddenly the rat-a-tat-tat of gunfire erupted throughout the camp. The doors on the cabins were kicked in, only to find them empty. The whole camp was empty.

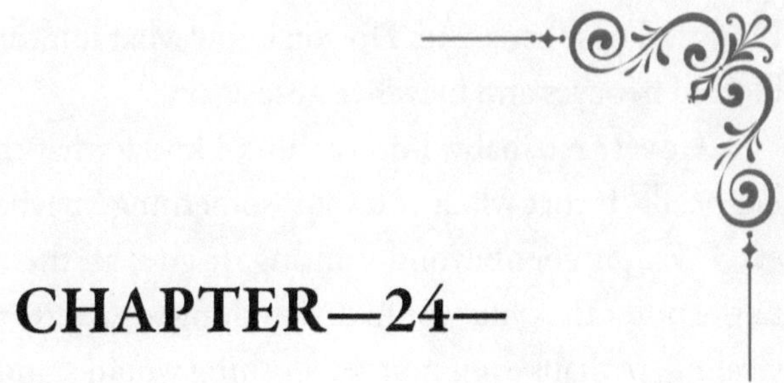

CHAPTER —24—

"What's the matter, baby?" Cyndi sat down on their couch and gently massaged Ada's back. "What's the matter? Somebody make you unhappy? You can tell me, you know. Stop crying, baby...I can't stand it when you cry." She bit her lip, feeling her sister's pain.

"Oh, Cyndi, I appreciate your concern." Ada sobbed, trying to control her tears. "But...well..." She sniffled. Blowing her nose she began again. "Yes, someone has made me unhappy."

"I knew it!" Cyndi almost crowed. "I knew them folks at that church would do something. What was it, baby?" She held her breath.

"It was someone at the church." Ada trembled and reluctantly admitted. "Someone really stupid, and mean and two-faced." She pummeled the couch pillow.

"Who was it, Ada? Some nasty woman?" Cyndi frowned. This was better than a soap opera, and she was ready.

"Yes, it was a nasty woman, Cyndi. It was me." Ada burst out sobbing again.

"What?" Cyndi screeched. "What are you talking about? What in the world do you mean?" She searched her sister's tear-stained face.

"Some time ago you asked me who I had seen that made me change. You hinted that I had seen a man, and that was the answer.

I'm so.... I'm so ashamed. Do you know what it means to covet?" Ada blotted her eyes and blew her nose again.

"Covet? No, baby, I don't think I know what that is." She shook her head. "Is that when you want something, maybe?"

"Well, it goes beyond wanting. It goes all the way to desiring it to the point that you would do anything to acquire the object. Lying, stealing, perhaps even murder, nothing would stand in the way."

"Well—" Her sister wilted slightly. "—you haven't murdered anyone have you?"

"No, but it is almost that bad. You see, I never told you exactly what happened during that blizzard. When Michael came along—if he hadn't come when he did, you and I wouldn't be sitting here talking. I would have frozen to death, and that's the whole truth. In a sense, he was my savior. He wrapped me up in his extra clothing, and then his brother and father appeared out of nowhere with Lewis' team and sled and took me to their home, gave me food, shelter, and... something else. From the moment Mrs. MacDonald and Ruth began to unwrap me from Michael's clothing, I received nothing but care and concern from every one of them." She burst into tears again, sobbing broken-heartedly.

"There, there, baby. Don't cry. They're good people, the Mac-Donald folks are." Cyndi patted her on the back.

"I know ... know ... know they are." Ada stammered wiping her nose again. "That's the problem. Mr. MacDonald is so kind and funny. Mrs. MacDonald is so warm and sweet. Ruth is so kind and ... and... and... good." She spluttered out.

"What about... What's his name?" Cyndi's face twisted cynically. "Is he kind and funny, or warm and sweet, or kind and good?"

Ada began sobbing again. It took some doing before she finally got a grip on herself. "He's all of the above."

"Oh, no, those are the worst kind," Cyndi muttered under her breath. "Okay, baby, out with it. Just what is this all about?"

"They thawed me out, as I said, gave me all of those things. I don't recall ever sitting around a table eating with our own family. Mrs. MacDonald and Ruth had a wonderful meal prepared. Mr. MacDonald asked how everyone's day had gone, and he really listened. They didn't any of them understand that I had no one to inform that I was okay. And Michael sat and watched Ruth all evening. He was home for just a little vacation, and he wanted her to set a date for their wedding, but she wouldn't for some reason. And... he loves her... like I wish... someone loved me." Ada would have cried all over again, but she buried her face in the pillow. Her tears were all cried out.

IN THE QUIET PAUSE, Cyndi held Ada and stroked her hair. "Oh, baby." She crooned as her own tears silently slid down her cheeks. She thought about the truth of Ada's words, how right her sister was. She clung to her sister as they rocked back and forth. She couldn't ever remember sitting as a family and eating a meal, and she was older than Ada. She couldn't remember anyone, especially her father, ever asking how her day had gone or listening even when she had tried to tell someone. She felt weighed down by the sadness of being so alone— so very alone. She squeezed her eyes shut.

"So," she asked, "where are you going with this, Ada? What does this have to do with your crying and carrying on?"

"I wanted what they have. I could see why they were different, and I figured if I could become more like them, I would have it." Ada sniffled and took a deep breath.

"It seems logical, girl, but it isn't something to cry over. Why, just look at you. You really have done well, but I thought you were happy." Her brow furrowed in thought. "You aren't though, are you?"

"I would be but ..." Ada shrugged.

"But what?" Cyndi's eyes narrowed as she waited.

"But I haven't left that old man of sin." She looked down at the wad of tissues in her hands. "Not only did I want what they had ..." She hesitated.

"But you wanted him as well?"

"Yes," Ada whispered. "Yes, and I set about to do anything I could to have something in common with him."

"Sometimes you don't make a lick of sense, girl. To have something in common with him?" She drew back, and her eyes became wide as she raised her eyebrows.

"Well, that night in the spare bedroom, I could hear something happening in the office room next to the bathroom." Ada took a deep breath. "Curious, I kind of eavesdropped— on Michael and Ruth. He had been working on some papers and she had brought him some coffee or something. I was so angry with her for not accepting him, for not even... Well, I understand some things now, but she could have given him a better answer. When she scolded him for not being a better host to me at supper, he told her, —'I have nothing in common with her,'—and he was right. I looked at myself and saw how cheap I was. A good man who would make a good husband and father would have nothing in common with me as I was that night."

"Well, that is kind of enlightening. I guess." Cyndi cleared her throat uncomfortably. "So, what is the moral of this story?"

"Before he left this last time to return to his work, I connived." She choked on the word. "I connived to get him to study with me." She repeated. "Then he promised to send me more information on certain subjects that I asked him about." Her face blushed with shame at the memory. "For some reason, others believed that he was writing to me, or at least corresponding with me, and I let them believe it." Her eyes were downcast as she confessed her final shame. "He was not and never has been interested in me romantically, and he never led me to believe he was. He and Ruth belong together, and I have repaid her goodness to me by returning sorrow to her. Now she has gone with that medical missionary team, and we don't know if she will ever return. So I have repaid all of them evil for their goodness." The tears began again, softly this time.

Cyndi floundered helplessly. "I don't know what to tell you to do. I don't know what advice to give you, baby."

"I know what I'm going to do, but it won't be easy." Ada balled up her right fist and punched it into her left-hand palm with resolve. After washing her face and composing her self-control, she addressed her sister. "It's too late tonight, but in the morning, I'm going to call Mr. and Mrs. MacDonald. I'm going over first thing in the morning to make things right."

The color drained out of Cyndi's face. "I'm coming with you. If you can do such a thing knowing full well they'll probably cuss you out and hate you forever—I'm gonna stand beside you, baby."

"If they did all of that it would still be better than what I deserve. I would miss my guess if they do, however. That just makes it harder. It's like beating the dog, and instead of being mean and ugly and trying to bite you, he just hangs his head. It makes you so ashamed that you feel like handing him the stick and saying, 'Okay it's your turn. Just whack away.'" Ada sniffled.

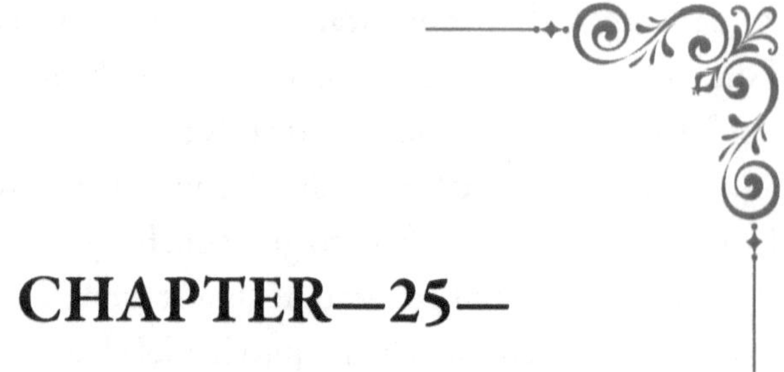

CHAPTER—25—

In the darkest night, the saying goes, there is a light—but not this night. Ruth wasn't sure how all three of the women managed to get into the supply closet just off of the kitchen. The second question was how they had gotten out of the closet and evaded the bandits brandishing weapons.

But they had slipped out of the closet and made it to their agreed on rendezvous spot with the other members.

"Scout, where's the rope?" Dan and Davis busily tied one end of the rope around Davis's waist and the other around Dan.

"Everyone hold on to the rope and form a chain," Davis hissed just loud enough to be heard by the group. "Kathy, Crowl—Anna, Ruth." He motioned for them to grab onto the rope in a line to make a chain.

"Halt—" Davis called after a short run. "Catch your breath." He listened but didn't hear anyone following. "Let's move again." He helped them pick up their packs before they moved out.

"I'm so glad we lightened those packs. These are difficult enough." Kathy sat down after several more short runs and rests. "How do you know which direction we're moving, Davis?"

"We've followed this main path that brought us into the compound. We're going in the opposite direction that we came in on. We'll move far enough off this beaten path to be hid, but we'll stay there for the next few hours. I'll know our direction better at dawn."

Davis leaned up against his pack. "Follow me, and we'll construct a makeshift camp then we'll rest."

"Let's get it done, Scout." Dan stood and everyone took their place along the rope as they moved off the path far enough to be safe.

"We all need to get a bit more sleep. We'll have to move fast when daylight comes." Davis stopped and untied the rope. "We have three hours before sunrise. Anyone want to take a watch?"

"I'll watch. I'm used to being up at odd hours." Dan wiped a weary hand through his dark brown hair.

RUTH WOKE SLOWLY AS she felt movement around her. Kathy stirred slightly as well when Ruth cautiously stretched. Davis moved about pounding on something. Nathaniel had built a very small fire in a pit. Dan was resting after his morning watch while the other two busied themselves.

"Good morning— guess we've overslept." She tentatively sat upright from leaning against her pack.

"Nothing you were needed to do. Rest is a duty as well." Nathaniel's chin stubble had grown into an almost respectable beard. "There's some hot water here if you'd like something hot to go with your power bar."

"Thank you. I have some tea bags if you'd like tea to go with your hot water?" She pulled out a plastic sack and they added some tea to the hot water. Ruth looked around in alarm when Anna moaned as she moved. "Anna? What's wrong?" Ruth turned to her friend.

Anna sat upright, pain etched on her face. "Last night…" She rolled up her sleeve on her long-sleeved blouse. "In the excitement of the moment—"

Ruth sucked in her breath and her eyes grew wide. "You've been shot? You never said…"

"Everything happened so fast, and there wasn't time. I think it was a ricochet while we were in the closet." Anna cringed.

Dan sat up bleary-eyed. "Who's been shot?"

"Anna's been shot." Nathaniel pulled the tea bags out of the hot water.

"What? When?" Dan came awake quickly.

"Last night when we were in the supply closet. I thought that shot hit pretty close to us." Ruth gingerly held the sleeve away from the wound.

Dan brought the now warm tea bags, cleaned the blood, and soothed the wound. "You should have said something last night, girl. You of all people know how easily these things can get infected and become life-threatening." He scowled at her.

"It happened so quickly then we had to get out fast and everything. I didn't know I'd been hit— it's just a flesh wound, you see?" Her worried eyes asked him to understand.

"Oh, Anna, Anna—" Dan was at a loss for words. He should be angry, but how could he look in her pleading eyes and not understand? He sighed. "Anyone got meds for this?"

She suffered silently, only flinching as he finished cleaning the injury and applying medicine and a bandage.

"That should take care of it for now." Dan stood and took a cup of tea and a power bar. "Thanks, Crowl. Got your navigation yet, Scout?" He turned to where Davis sat with his tea and breakfast bar.

"Should be good to go. I've got north, and we're looking for a creek that'll lead us to a river." Davis finished his breakfast.

"Well, let's get moving. Stay together and don't get lost." Dan bent to clean up his trash and they stowed gear in their packs. Nathaniel had already put out the fire and covered the remains.

Shouldering their packs, they moved out in the same single-file formation they had the night before. Davis in the lead, Kathy,

Nathaniel, Anna, Ruth, and Dan at the end, they silently hiked through the jungle which pulsed with life.

WHO WOULD HAVE THOUGHT? Nathaniel marched along between Kathy and Anna, wondering how in the scheme of life he had come to this situation. How ironic that after the experience of three years ago and his examination of his life, his religion, and his decision to change, God had put him in this position. Was it a test, or was it because at this time he was a more worthy person?

He knew in some way there was an unspoken tie between Michael and Ruth, so she was not a prospect for him, but Anna was a jewel. His unwise words at that time of *I wouldn't mind being first on her list* still haunted him. They would always be a reminder of where he had been and where he should be—a goal to aim for.

"LET'S HAVE A REST." Davis stopped after a two-hour trek. "One thing we need to remember is to take a break on occasion. We've been making good time...not great time, but good."

"For our mix of physical training, it's not been too bad. We're keeping up. I need a walking stick. Anyone else like a walking stick?" Nathaniel began cutting on a dead branch.

"Good idea. Spears, you check Anna's wound, and we'll work on some sticks." Davis joined Nathaniel.

Ruth helped roll up Anna's shirt sleeve while Dan checked on the wound. She watched his face for any sign— good or bad— but he was a professional at what he did. He cleaned and redressed the wound without comment.

"Here." He pulled out some aspirin and handed it to Anna. He wiped his face with his sleeve and took a big gulp of water. Turning slightly back to the group he waited for his walking stick. "You know one thing that puzzled me on this foray."

"What's that?" Davis asked.

"They never searched our belongings." Dan's eyes narrowed and he pursed his lips.

"I noticed that as well. I don't know if they trusted us, or didn't view us as a threat," Nathaniel said.

"Now that we have our walking sticks, and we've had a short rest let's keep moving. We should be getting close to water." Davis picked up his pack and hefted the machete they had garnered from the compound as they left. "It didn't take us long to get from Georgetown out here, but we had more than just our feet for travel. It'll take us much longer to get back by our feet."

"And we weren't being pursued coming out—" Dan dared to remind them of what they didn't want to think of.

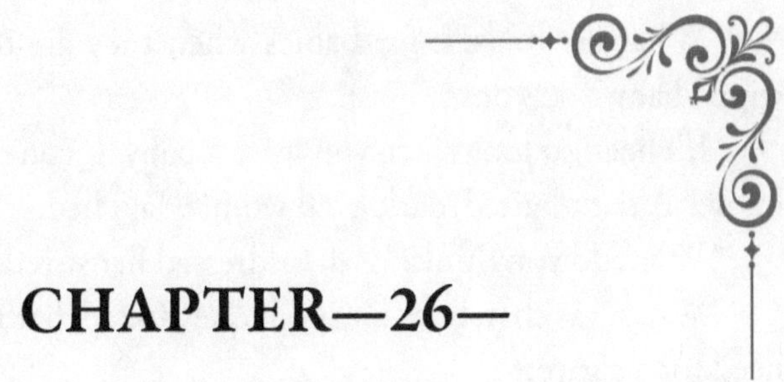

CHAPTER—26—

"What a surprise." Mrs. MacDonald answered the doorbell Saturday morning. "Ada and Cyndi, come on in. We were about to have coffee. Come on in and join us!"

"Whoa!" Cyndi elbowed Ada as they stood in the entryway. "I've been to the potlucks and stuff down yonder where it was set up for barbeque, volleyball, and other activities, but I've never been here... This cottage is so well camouflaged I never guessed it was here. What a peaceful, homey place."

"Oh—" Ada's eyes opened wide. "I didn't know you were having company. There was just a matter I wanted to discuss with you and your husband."

"This isn't company." Amanda smiled. "It's just the girls, and they're all family. Come on in. There is always room for more." She opened the door wider. "Mac and the boys are finishing up now, and he'll be coming in shortly."

Cyndi blinked in bewilderment. Just the girls? Just family? The whole house was busy. Babies were walking or crawling all over the place. There must be twenty people here—Perhaps that was exaggerating, but there seemed like a lot of hustle and bustle for just family. Always room for more? What a strange thing to say.

Seated at the breakfast nook with a cup of coffee and a choice of cookies or donuts in front of her, Cyndi nervously felt the need for a cigarette—but this was neither the time nor the place.

"What do you use for babies when they are teething?" Gwen wiped baby Zoë's nose.

"It's been so long since you were a baby, I won't even pretend to know." A dark-haired, dark-eyed woman laughed.

"What do you think?" Ada addressed her sister.

"What was that, baby?" Cyndi questioned, her mind still on the need for a cigarette.

"What do you use for babies when they are teething?" Ada repeated the question. Ada knew the names, not just of the grown-ups, but the children as well, and was conversing in a language Cyndi did not understand.

"Oh—" she caught herself just in time, "—I mean, I don't know. Cinnamon, I think, or something. No, I think Mom used cloves, but they have that wonderful stuff at the drug store that works really well. It has something that helps with the runny nose and fever that comes along with teeth." Cyndi felt like a fish out of water.

Mrs. MacDonald tapped her fingers on the table. "I believe cloves is what my mother-in-law used also, but Cyndi's right. The stuff at the pharmacy has ingredients for the runny nose too."

"The next question is, how do you keep them from getting into everything?" Gwen asked.

"Oh, that's easy." Mrs. MacDonald waved a hand in the air. "Just crawl around on the floor for a while."

"What?" Gwen, the woman with the cinnamon-colored hair, blinked in surprise. "Crawl on the—?"

"After you crawl around with Zoë awhile, notice all the things there are for her little hands to get into, and then you get up and put all those things you don't want her little hands into somewhere that her little hands can't get into... like on the ceiling." Mrs. MacDonald laughed.

There was gentle laughter at the advice. Even Cyndi laughed. She could almost feel comfortable here at that, she mused to herself. Some of Ada's desire faintly seeped into Cyndi's consciousness.

Just what made them so different? Was it the aura of welcome and calm? Whatever it was, there were too many families bankrupt of whatever that ingredient was.

"I think I'll go down and start getting food ready." Donna, the dark-haired woman with dark brown eyes, picked up her cup and took it to the sink. "Anyone coming with?"

"You go with Donna, Gwen. We'll watch the babies up here while you get the playpens up down there. Are you game, Beth?" Alice smiled as Laura's young daughter, Beth, played with the little children.

Cyndi gazed, fascinated at the sweet fresh beauty of the young girl. There was a touch of red to her natural dark brown hair, and her beautiful blue eyes twinkled merrily. Cyndi knew other girls that age, and none of them impressed her so profoundly.

"Yes, Miss Alice. I can help watch the babies." Her laugh was like a tinkling brook.

"Okay, we'll put up the playpens so when y'all come down, they'll be ready." Donna walked to the door. "I'll locate one of the boys and send them to help."

"That should work, Donna." Miss Alice smoothed back her hair.

The front door closed behind Donna and Gwen as some of the activity picked up in the living room.

"I declare, Gwen will surely have her hands full when the next baby comes. I'm so glad you have come to live with Seth and Gwen, Alice. You and your daughter get along so well, and she needs you at times like these." Mrs. MacDonald smiled, a warm light in her eyes.

"I am just happy to be here. For so many years I had very little contact with her, but now I hardly remember those days at all. Being with my darling girl and helping her and helping with little Zoë—it does make some of the hard days fade away." Alice looked down at her hands. "I wish I could help you at this time. I know how you must feel, Amanda. When Gwen was in danger, at least I was with her. The not knowing where your daughters are, your daughter and Ruth, I just couldn't bear it."

"They are both my daughters, Alice. I couldn't love Ruth any more if she had been born to me. It was heartbreaking for us when Gwen left us as well." Mrs. MacDonald leaned her forehead onto Alice's.

"Oh, Mrs. MacDonald—" Ada spoke soberly, "—we are so sorry also. I have been praying for your family as well as Anna and Ruth. I can't express how sorry I am. Are you ready to go, Cyndi? I'm sure we are intruding, and it is time for us to go. I just want you to know how very sorry I feel." Ada began to pick up her purse and keys to flee.

"Grandma?" A young boy spoke from the front door. "I came to help carry little people." Twelve-year-old David came into the kitchen. His tousled blonde hair and blue eyes were exactly like his father's, although his facial features were reminiscent of his mother. He was tall and slender like his oldest brother Mark, and he had an irrepressible smile like his cousin Beth.

"Ah, to be sure, it is time to be taking the little ones. Laura, are you ready also?" Miss Alice hurriedly took her cup and plate to the sink. "Beth, dear," she called, "do you have the diaper bags ready?"

"Yes, Miss Alice. Mai helped me, and we are just ready to go." Beth popped the last item into a bag. "I've got Noah's bag too, Mom."

"What dears you children are." Mrs. MacDonald gave them all a round of heartfelt hugs. "And, off with you then." She good-naturedly shooed them towards the door.

"I'm going too, Mom." Laura grabbed her little Noah. "I'll see you in a little." She kissed her mother on the cheek and slid out the door with the rest of the crew.

"Now, Ada—" Mrs. MacDonald turned to the pair who were left. "You came to speak to Mac and me, and, my dear, you don't need to be running off. Just sit tight and he will be here any minute. Cyndi, how are you doing anyway?"

"I...I'm fine." She blinked caught off guard. "Yep, I'm doing all right. I guess." She nodded her head lamely.

"Your job at the ..."

"Garage. I work for T-N-T GARAGE in Hermon. It's going fine."

"You don't have any children, is that right?" Mrs. MacDonald asked.

"No, not any kids. Except for Ada here, and she's gettin' kinda uppity like she doesn't want to be babied anymore." She gave her sister a gentle nudge with her elbow and smiled.

"They all go through that." Mrs. MacDonald smiled and winked. "Sometimes they outgrow it though. Do y'all want some more coffee?" Mrs. MacDonald took her cup over to the pot and began filling hers and another cup.

"Sure, we'll take another cup." Ada brought the two cups over and waited while Mrs. MacDonald filled them. "Thank you," She carried them back to the table.

They heard the front door open and close. "I'll just wash my hands and be with you in a jiffy, darlin'." Mr. MacDonald wiped his feet and headed for the bathroom.

"Fine, Mac. Your coffee's ready when you are."

Ada smiled at Mrs. MacDonald. "How do you two do it?"

"Do what?" Mrs. MacDonald's eyebrows rose in a question.

"You two are always so pleasant— to one another and most everyone else." Her heart quaked as she shrank from what she had to say. It would be harder than she had ever imagined. She sat quietly gazing into her nearly full coffee cup and picking at her half-eaten sweet roll.

A silent minute elapsed before Mr. MacDonald slipped into the room. He smiled at his wife and sat down in front of his cup. "What's up, Ahmanda?"

"Ada had something she wanted to discuss with us, dear." She patted his hand gently.

"Well, Ada." He smiled encouragingly at her. "We're all ears." He wiggled his ears faintly at her, a trick that never failed to make people laugh. "I learned that from my pappy." He leaned over and confided to the visiting women, who both snickered.

"Lewis MacDonald!" Mrs. MacDonald scolded gently, trying to conceal her laughter. "You are incorrigible." She admonished with a roll of her eyes.

As they sat waiting for Ada to speak, she suddenly burst into tears. "I don't know where to start." She sobbed. Mrs. MacDonald handed her several tissues.

"Just start at the beginning." Mr. MacDonald pulled his coffee cup toward himself.

"I'm not sure where the beginning is—" Ada closed her eyes. "I...I guess the snowstorm was where it all began. I remember being so afraid when my car was stuck, and then Michael showed up. I was in shock, I think. The whole ordeal was so unnerving."

"I'm sure it was, dear." Mrs. MacDonald squeezed her hand.

"The biggest shock was...well, your family." She began to weep again.

"There, there, what do you mean?" Mr. MacDonald tried to comfort and encourage her.

"What Ada is trying to say is, you see, there isn't much to our family. Even before our Mom died, there wasn't a whole lot of good to it. Always bickering and fighting and all that." Cyndi frowned. "Then she saw your family. They all seem so loving and helpful."

"That's right." Ada looked up. "They were just so good. Talking to one another and listening to one another. And I saw you two. I don't know how to put it into words, but there just seemed to be so much love and caring. There seemed to be a moral compass that pointed them to do the right thing, even if it was hard to do."

"Yes, go on." Mr. MacDonald took a sip of coffee.

Ada's face colored with shame. "I eavesdropped that night and...it wasn't my business, but Michael and Ruth were speaking and some of it was about me. Ruth chided him for his manners, and he said he didn't have anything in common with... me."

"Oh, Ada, I'm so sorry." Mrs. MacDonald gasped, and her face creased in sorrow. "I'm sure he didn't mean it unkindly."

"That was rather blunt." Ada kept tearing at the tissues in her hands. "It did hurt, but it was actually what started me on my journey. That and—" She paused, her face coloring with embarrassment again. "—and I couldn't figure out... If I had been in Ruth's place, things would've been different. At that time, I didn't know anything about morality, such as purity and keeping oneself pure for your mate. I didn't know anything about love— true love, that is. Michael was so right. He didn't have anything in common with me. That is why he wanted someone like Ruth to be his wife. The mother of his children, the keeper of his hearth and home, not someone like me." Her eyes were teary and miserable when she finally looked up, hoping for understanding.

Mrs. MacDonald sat back with a sympathetic sad face. "We understand."

Cyndi winced for her sister. She had never heard anyone so blunt and so honest, especially about oneself. Knowing what was coming, she wondered if these people would be so kind in a few minutes, when Ada admitted her deception and made her confession. Cyndi prayed silently, *'Dear God, if you are there,'* she added just in case, *'please don't let these folks crush her. She is just a child.'*

"Now that we have the whys out of the way—" Mr. MacDonald had a sad smile. "—you need to unburden your heart, don't you, Ada?"

"Yes." Ada began sobbing and wailing, pathetically covering her face with her hands.

Mrs. MacDonald was at Ada's side holding her and rocking her like a small child. "Go ahead, Ada. Cry it all out, darlin'. We understand, don't we, Lewis? You wanted what Michael and Ruth had, or could have, but you felt confused."

Ada's wailing subsided to sniveling as she wiped her eyes. "Yes, I was confused. I confused what I wanted with Michael and Ruth. I know now it is wrong to covet, but that is what I did. Ruth didn't seem to want to marry Michael, but..." She needed to say no more.

"You wanted to marry someone like Michael, and couldn't understand why, if you changed... just maybe?" Mr. MacDonald filled in for her.

"I wanted the husband, the home, the family, those things I saw here, but I had never had. And Ruth didn't. At least that is what it looked like."

"God is merciful." Mr. MacDonald ran a hand through his hair. "We have to start somewhere. So, where does that lead us?"

"Now I know what I wanted wasn't right—Well, what I wanted may have been all right, but what I thought I wanted was Michael, and that wasn't right. When he was back the last time, I used some before-Christian tactics to finagle him into studying with me, and he promised to send me some information. It was innocent on his part. He never led me to believe he was interested in me other than as a sister in Christ. For a time I did hope. But as I changed, I realized that I had just caused them both pain and sorrow. Ruth has never been anything but kind and gracious to me. I don't just like Ruth, I love her." The storm had passed, and Ada quietly looked into their faces. "I know others thought he was writing to me, and so did Ruth, and I just let them think that. He wasn't. Ruth has been his guiding star all along. He told me that as we studied the Bible the day before he left."

"Thank you for sharing that, Ada. I spoke to Michael before he left the last time. This helps me understand some things." Mr. Mac-Donald tapped his fingers on his cup.

"They belong together and that is all there is to it. Now we don't know where Ruth is or Anna either. I feel like at least part of it is because of me." She looked down and studied her hands quietly, not daring to look at the older couple lest she see their disapproval or something worse.

Mrs. MacDonald's arm remained around her shoulders. "God works in many different ways. —It took a lot of courage to come to us."

"And we know where they are." Mr. MacDonald ran a hand over his tired face.

"You do?" Ada's eyes opened wide full of hope, as she stared at him.

"They are on that continent right there." Mr. MacDonald pointed to the large map hanging on the wall.

Cyndi gasped. "South America is a very large continent, Mr. MacDonald. I'm afraid you still don't know where they are. How can you take this so—so lightly at a time like this?"

"But we do know. They are in the hands of God. 'Whom shall I fear? Jehovah is the strength of my life; Of whom shall I be afraid?'" he quoted.

"Oh, children's fables!" Cyndi exploded. "They could be dead, or...worse." She jumped up hysterically. "Why are you clinging to false hope?" Her eyes flashed.

"Cyndi!" Ada's eyes grew wide, and her face showed shock and dismay. "How dare you say such things?" Ada frowned. "God can do anything, and it isn't just fables. Look what he's done for me."

"That may be true, baby, but you were a consenting adult. On your part, you undertook to change. I've read the papers. Those folks are robbers, thieves, murderers, and ... worse." She leaned on the table.

"That's true, if you can believe everything that is printed in the papers." Mrs. MacDonald's face blanched. "—But God can protect His own. 'But I trusted in thee, O Jehovah: I said, Thou art my God. My times are in thy hand: Deliver me from the hand of mine enemies, and from them that persecute me.'"

"It isn't just children's fables, Cyndi. I have seen God work in our lives in ways that I could never imagine. What you said could be true, but it isn't. If you just stand back and watch, you will see." His words were kind, and he spoke with conviction.

"Come to the cookout this evening at Lewis Jr's." Amanda reached a hand toward Cyndi. "I know you doubt, but if you will just wait upon the Lord, he will show you what you seek."

"I had plans for this evening." Cyndi hesitated, rubbing a hand over her brow. "But this is far too important. Yes, I will come, and I will wait," she challenged. "We need to run home and do some errands. What time is the cookout?"

"We will begin about six to six-thirty." Mr. MacDonald looked at the clock.

"We'll be there. Come on, Ada, I have things to do if we are to be back here in time." Cyndi snatched up her purse and grabbed her sister by the arm.

"COME ON, SIS. IT'S a beautiful afternoon and we need to be heading to that potluck." Cyndi placed a casserole into the back of the car. A short drive later they pulled into Lewis' driveway and parked. "There's quite a gathering today." The two women sat watching the activity of family and friends collected together.

"Cyndi, what you said this morning was out of line." Ada frowned at her sister. "I'm not saying I agree with you, but even if their belief was— even if it was horse feathers or pie in the sky—it would be better than believing what you suggested they believe."

"All I can say is, it's better to prepare for the worst. I don't believe those women are safe, taking into account the type of men that kidnapped them. The men they will probably hold for ransom...but I can't believe the women will be safe from what..."

"That's enough." Ada rebuked her sharply, shuddering at the alternative. "That's not what is eating you at all is it?"

"If there is a God—" Cyndi's words were bitter her mouth twisting downward. "—Where was he when Mom died? Where was he when I needed him? Just why didn't he answer my prayers?"

"People die. That's part of life. Why Mom died when she did, I don't have all the answers. You're talking about Allen, aren't you?" Ada's eyes narrowed, and she sighed.

"I guess I am." Cyndi jangled her keys. "I try to forget about it, but sometimes in my dreams it still haunts me." She shivered.

"Mom never liked him. I remember her telling you to stay away from him. Why did you go out with him at all?" Ada asked. "He always gave me the creeps." Her lips curled distastefully.

"I don't know." Cyndi shrugged. "I think it was because I wanted Dad to say something. To take a stand for something. Maybe show he cared about me...or us. But he never did." She sighed. "Sometimes he would slap me around, and it made me feel like he cared, but..."

"Dad slapped you around?" Ada's eyes opened wide.

"No, not Dad, Allen. Anyway, Allen would slap me around, and at first I thought it was because he cared. You know, he was very jealous. What a joke." Cyndi raised her eyebrows. "That wasn't love. I was a possession to him, along with half a dozen others."

"Even after you were..."

"Yes, even after we were married. He never stopped playing the field. Or adding to his flock...I felt like such an idiot." Cyndi shook her head.

"So you divorced him. What about Steve? He didn't seem quite so bad."

"He wasn't in love with me. He was in love with himself."

"What?"

"We don't even want to go into that." Cyndi held up a hand and shook her head.

"Bill? What was wrong with him?" Ada asked.

"I wasn't ever really married to him. We just, well, you know..." Cyndi grimaced.

"Is it men you hate, or just what?"

"The question was, where was God?" Cyndi reminded Ada.

"Right where he's always been. When we ignore him, why do we think we have a right to ask him for favors when we need something? Do we think God is a big Daddy O who we just snap our fingers, and he supplies?"

"He has my attention now. I'm watching with bated breath, so to speak. If he brings these people back as good as new, I'll..."

"You'll what, Cyndi? Will you believe? Will you change? Just what will you do?" she prodded. "Whatever it is, you better be careful because I'll hold you to it, woman, and so will God. Let's go. The grill is hot and we don't want to miss the cookout."

Ada noted the late afternoon was lazy, with a hint that autumn had settled in. The food smelled good, the company was good, yet sadness hung over the affair. Ada recognized almost everyone here. Some of them were from church, and some were from the community, like Pat O'Brien and his son Jack.

After the meal was over, Lewis Junior began by leading several songs. Then someone by the name of Lance led a prayer and more songs. The afternoon dipped into early evening as the first stars appeared in the still blue sky. Someone passed out a few songbooks, though most of the songs were familiar. They did not need prayer books. Those came from the heart.

"I didn't know it was going to be a religious service," Cyndi whispered to Ada.

"There is a pressing need—" Ada massaged her temples. "We should be ready always to pray. There is a definite need and we are answering that need."

"Friends and family." Mr. MacDonald raised his voice to the group. "I appreciate each one here this evening. I appreciate your prayers on behalf of our dear daughters and their companions who are in danger. As most of you know, Michael has been ill, but is better now. We ask your continued prayers for our sakes. —Jack and I are scheduled to fly out in the morning to join Michael in this next endeavor to seek those who are lost. I speak for Amanda and myself when I express my love for each one of you and our gratitude as we have gathered together to petition our God for our loved ones. And if we never meet again this side of heaven may God bless us in his service. Now let us pray."

Cyndi's mouth fell open as Mr. MacDonald knelt, and like a ripple in the water, everyone there followed his example. *Well, if there is a God, he simply would be compelled to listen. If he didn't listen, then there is no God.'*

CHAPTER—27—

"We must pick up the pace." Davis wearily leaned up against a small tree.

"That isn't possible. You know it, and so do I." Dan tried to keep his voice low so it wouldn't carry.

"In the long run, our pursuers are going to make better time. That means unless we get to civilization soon—which is highly unlikely—we will have to stand and fight," Davis murmured back to him.

"That's not a cheering thought." Dan frowned at him.

"What are you two figuring?" Ruth called from where the others sat resting, eating a small lunch and drinking their water.

"It's like this…" Davis started but stopped when Dan shook his head. "No, we need to be prepared, and so do the girls," he whispered to Dan.

"You're right, of course." Dan took a deep breath. "Go ahead, and we'll talk about it."

"It's like this. We can't move fast enough to keep ahead of our pursuers. One way or another, unless we get to safety in the next few hours, we will need to fight whoever is following us." Davis laid the facts out, and everyone looked downhearted.

"Maybe we could climb up in the trees and they'd keep going?" Kathy suggested hopefully.

"That's possible, but not likely. Try to remember to stay together. That's important—and if you girls get separated from us, keep to the water. Follow the water. We aren't far from a stream or river now, and...even a stream should lead you to a river and a river should lead you to civilization." Davis took a deep breath. "Our supplies are running low, so we'll need to ration our meals somewhat and keep moving."

"I don't know how effective one machete will be against men with guns. I've heard you should never bring a knife to a gunfight." Dan shouldered his pack, watching as Kathy shakily picked up her burden. "Here, let me have that." He reached out for it.

"No, I should be able to carry my own load." She lifted it, but was unable to throw it over her shoulder.

"You didn't sign up to be a packhorse on this mission." Dan smiled at her. "That doesn't mean there's something wrong with you. I'll carry it for a time." He took it from her.

"Thank you. No sense wasting time or energy arguing." Kathy sighed as she picked up her walking stick.

"HERE WE ARE." DAVIS pointed ahead through the trees.

"That mission is accomplished then." Ruth stood at the edge of the bank looking where the water flowed a few feet away.

"Creek. Now just follow this north..." Davis pointed.

"Hey-y-y-y!" Dan shouted suddenly. Davis, Nathaniel, and the girls whirled around as out of nowhere a massive ball of fury rolled at them from behind. Their pursuers came at them from what seemed like every direction.

Standing close to the creek bank, Ruth grabbed Kathy and Anna and slid all of them down the bank out of the fight. "Shh-h." She cautioned, finger placed on her lips.

"Shouldn't we be up there helping?" Kathy hissed, her face a jumble of emotions.

"We'd just be in the way. None of us is going to make a difference up there at this juncture. Anna's wounded, you're just hanging on...they'll be better off not trying to watch out for us, and someone should watch out for you two."

Kathy blinked in confusion. "Watch out for—us?"

"Shh." Ruth held up a hand. She leaned back, listening as the sounds of jungle life pulsed around them.

"Are you all right, Ruth?" Anna lay back, silently cradling her arm.

"It's my dream come to life. The noises, the feeling of strife—this is just like being in the belly of a huge beast." She shuddered. "I'm afraid to look up. I'm afraid that big snake will..."

Someone on the bank above growled to a companion. "I know there were more in this group. Just where did they go?"

"Dunno—look something's slid down here."

The girls held their breath and tried to shrink their bodies back into the dirt.

"I see it too. Betcha if we follow..."

The words were cut off and sounds of a struggle followed then died away. Ruth peered up through the foliage to where they had come from. She heard movement and hunkered back even more.

"Anna, Ruth, Kathy," Nathaniel's voice hissed at them. "You can come up now. It's safe."

The three young women let out a collective sigh of relief. Ruth stood and helped the other two up the bank. "Take it easy. Anna's arm..."

"Oh, no! What's happened?" Anna covered her mouth with her hand.

"Dan got knocked out at some point but—he's coming around." Nathaniel soothed her fear.

"It was quite a struggle. Say, Crowl, you're pretty good there." Davis continued to help Dan sit up.

"I'd say that for both of you. If I had to choose who to have with me on this terrific journey, I couldn't have done better." Dan gasped, still dazed.

"Will these..." Ruth motioned with her hand at several bodies on the ground. "...will these men..." she didn't know how to ask the question.

"I don't know." Davis stood and started to pick up his pack. "But we need to get up and get going. The ones that ran—they'll be back, or someone from their group will be."

"We're just going to leave them here?" Kathy's eyes were wide and unbelieving.

"We don't have any option. They came looking for us, remember?"

"I guess that's right—" Kathy's face was pale and stunned.

"Scout, you take the girls and get a head start. Dan here is still dazed and a bit slow. We'll be along and catch up once he gets his wind back." Nathaniel handed Davis a walking stick.

"Let's go, girls. We'll just follow the creek here." Davis waited while everyone oriented themselves, turning to follow the water—picking up their own walking sticks, putting their packs in order. "See you in a little bit."

FELIX LOOKED DOWN HIS hawk-like nose and waved his hand lethargically. "I'm sorry, sir, these six missionary people—They have disappeared without a trace." His face was a mask as he mentally kicked himself for showing up so soon after his surgery. He remembered the older, tall blonde man with brilliant blue eyes. He should have paid attention when that medical man had spoken of the daughters and their families. When he had been much younger, Felix had encountered Mr. MacDonald years before. He would never forget that face, those eyes, or the man.

Felix's eyes moved to the auburn-haired man. Even though he had never seen him before, he would have recognized him as the father of the second young girl. Lastly, the younger man of the group resembled Mr. MacDonald.

"You are searching for your daughters?" His eyes narrowed and he spoke smoothly.

"You misunderstand." Mr. MacDonald squinted. "We are searching for six people. But two of them are our daughters."

"This report says—" Felix pursed his lips and flipped through the papers in front of him. "Three men and three women, all medical missionaries from the United States have disappeared. I have been absent from my office for a slight… recuperation." He continued perusing the report.

"You have been ill?" Mr. MacDonald asked.

"A simple operation, but I am not young." Felix sighed. "And I returned only today. Perhaps you could come back tomorrow?"

"I don't believe that will be possible." The auburn-haired man's words were pleasant and congenial.

Felix stopped scanning the papers. These weren't American tourists with a complaint. Their quiet manner belied something. He sensed something unnamable, something exciting— perhaps even dangerous. He wondered if the old man had lost any of his vigor over the years. He had seen him in action years ago and respected his courage at the time.

"Why not?"

"Our flight out leaves in a few days. We expect to be on it with our friends and family, sir." Jack O'Brien's quiet attitude gave his words more emphasis. Rising to his full height, he nodded toward the official. "Good day. We will not waste more of your time or ours. Here is the hotel we are staying at and our room number. If by any chance you learn anything, you can leave a message at the desk."

On cue, the other two stood, nodded toward the official, and followed Mr. O'Brien out the door. Felix sat studying the patch of blue sky outside his window pondering as he heard their boots making a dull echo across the waiting room, and then dying away.

Years change people. Did the old man recognized me? Didn't look like it. Would it change the outcome of the situation? Who could say? Only God knew. Felix moved slowly toward the phone. "Aye!" He clutched his chest. "Armando!" he barked into the mouthpiece. Still in a pensive mood, he growled, "Armando—" He slapped the phone down and sat back wearily in his chair.

"HE WASN'T TRUTHFUL, was he, dad?" Michael closed his eyes.

"No, son." Mr. MacDonald shook his head. "And he's not improved with age, either."

"You know him?" Jack turned with a startled stare.

"I have not been back to this particular spot for many years. When I last saw him, he would have made an excellent convert... even a preacher. I don't believe he's made good choices since then." Mr. MacDonald frowned.

"We all make choices." Jack looked up and down the street. "Life is full of them day by day, hour by hour. For instance...where do we go now?"

"Grab that taxi for us, Michael. We need to go back to our room." Mr. MacDonald ran his hand through his hair. "If I'm not mistaken, there will be something or someone waiting for us."

They were quiet while riding precariously through the traffic. Michael never did trust these taxi drivers, but they must be fairly proficient. They almost always got where they were going, and...almost always, everyone came out fine.

"Thank you." He paid the fare before they entered their hotel. *What a blessing it wasn't a long trip.* Michael sighed.

"Mr. MacDonald?" The desk clerk called as they passed the desk.

"Yes?" Mr. MacDonald hesitated.

"Someone is waiting for you." The clerk nodded toward a private sitting area.

"Thank you." Mr. MacDonald nodded at the clerk.

A well-groomed, dark-haired man in his mid-twenties stood at their approach. He acknowledged the older tall, blonde man by extending his hand in greeting. "Hello, Mr. MacDonald. Armando Gohmer—How are you?"

"I'm doing well, and yourself? How are you doing?" Mr. MacDonald shook the offered hand. "You speak English very well."

"Yes. I went to college in your country. I learned many things very well." His voice carried a cynical tone to it.

"Do you want to talk in our room, or over a meal?" Mr. MacDonald offered.

"I know of a restaurant with very good food, and a very private atmosphere."

"Very good. Let me introduce my cohorts first. Mr. Jack O'Brien, this is Armando Gohmer. His mother, Maria, and Amanda and I are close friends. Armando, my friend, Mr. Jack O'Brien, and this is my son, Michael." Mr. MacDonald finished the formalities.

A short time later they were all seated at a cozy family restaurant. Armando sat back after he had ordered.

"The last time I saw 'Mando here, I dandled him on my knee." Mr. MacDonald's face lit with a smile. "I don't s'pose you recall that, do you?" He laughed in a friendly manner. "How's your mama? Is she still living? I think we exchanged Christmas cards last year."

"Yes, yes, she is still alive. She is getting on in years now." Armando shook his head. "No, sir, I do not remember sitting on your knee. But Mama has a picture she has treasured these many years. A picture of the handsome American with the bluest eyes she ever saw, and his precious wife. She has it framed on the mantle." The pleasure showed in his eyes.

"I would sure like to visit your mama—Ahmanda would be so pleased. Would it be at all possible?"

"Perhaps." Armando hedged as his brow furrowed. This had not been in his brother's plans, and Felix had a mean streak that Armando did not want to cross.

"Is she in good health? Is all well? I wouldn't want to bother her..." Mr. MacDonald leaned forward.

"Yes, all is well. She would enjoy a visit, I am sure." Armando's countenance cleared. "Mama would be ecstatic. You know how she loves a visit, and by someone... Of course, she would want to see you."

"I don't want to interrupt your plans, and I have only this day. Is she still at the same address? It's too short a notice, I'm afraid, to just pop in for a visit." Mr. MacDonald shrugged.

"No, it would be no trouble. I'll call now and make arrangements. After we dine, we'll go." Armando excused himself to make the call.

"LEWIS MACDONALD, MY friend. My dear, dear friend!" Her face glowed with excitement. Maria Gohmer rose from her large, comfortable chair and greeted them warmly. "Come in, come in and sit down." She gestured at several chairs. "How ees the saintly wife of yours? Why you did not bring her along? Shame on you." Her voice was surprisingly deep and melodious for such a tiny person. "I should never forgeeve you— but I will." Her once abundant black hair had turned white, and it emphasized the burnished, warm glow of her skin. As she stretched forward and firmly gripped his hands, he could see the fire still burned in her coal-black eyes.

"Ah, Maria, our little bird." He smiled at the wiry woman. "You have not changed." He held her childlike hand in his large one. "She was the one who came to our aid when we were lost in the city. Just Americans—so green you could have planted us in the ground and we would have grown." He laughed and gestured to Jack and Michael. "See how small she is? But inside here—" He tapped his chest over his heart. "—this is where it counts. She has a way to make even important people listen to her." He smiled at Maria.

"Ah, Lewis—" She shook her head sadly. "—no more, no more. I am just an old woman dat no one leesens to. Not even my children. Dey don't even leesen to me anymore. Dey tink, ah, she's just an old woman, what do we care? Is that not right, Armando? You do not leesen to your mama, eh?"

"Now, Mama, don't be so harsh." Armando smiled fondly at her. "Of course, we listen to you."

"Yes, yes, dey leesen." She walked back to her chair. "Eet come in dees ear and out here." She pointed to one ear then the other.

"Children are a challenge." Lewis sat on a sofa and Jack and Michael sat beside him. "They are a blessing and a challenge. They have their moments don't they? Maria, I would like you to meet my friend and neighbor from back home. This is Mr. Jack O'Brien."

"I am so glad to make your acquaintance, Mr. O'Brien." Maria held out her jeweled hand. "I thought you were de most 'andsome man dere could ever be—but your neighborhood is blessed to 'ave the two most 'andsome men there could ever be," she spoke to Mr. MacDonald, and then smiled warmly at Jack as he rose and took her hand in greeting.

"You are so kind, but I'm not sure my neighbors have come to the same conclusion you have, ma'am. Maybe I'll have to explain it to them." Jack smiled his wonderful smile and returned to his seat.

"And this young man here?" Lewis motioned toward Michael. "He's our baby, our youngest son, Michael."

"Aye, 'e looks just like ees papa." She squinted at him. "So young and 'andsome. 'As he a family? A wife and children?" She wheedled.

"No, we are looking for his wife." Mr. MacDonald sighed.

"Eh? So young and good looking, are you 'aving trouble finding him a wife?"

"No, nothing like that." Mr. MacDonald rubbed a hand over his forehead.

"Ah, thank you, Pachabel. Would you like some tea?" She offered her guests some refreshments. "Well, what then? You never did tell me why you are come to dees country, an' why you do not bring your wife." Her black eyes were troubled.

"When we were here last, we had nine children, if you remember. I had trouble tearing Amanda away even for a short time. —Remember our baby girl, Anna?" he asked. "Well, here is her picture taken a few months ago." He held out a locket containing Anna's picture.

"Oh, so beautiful!" Maria breathed softly as she examined the likeness. "She 'as her mother's beautiful smile and her lovely eyes. You must be so proud of her?"

"We certainly are proud of her. She is a jewel of our heart."

"Does dees 'ave to do weeth your viseet den?"

"Yes. You see, a few weeks ago, Anna and another dear girl, not a daughter, in fact, but a daughter in heart, Mr. O'Brien's girl, Ruth, were on a medical missionary trip here in Guyana. Perhaps you've heard of the six of them who were abducted?"

"I 'ave 'eard of dees. Dey are being held for ransom?" Mrs. Gohmer raised an eyebrow, her black eyes shrewd.

"That's what we are here to find out, as well as to bring them home." He took a sip of tea.

"Aye, Lewis, you are always so—make it 'appen. Like magic." She waved her hands in the air and snapped her fingers. "Dees things are not always so easy, you know." She scowled. "Dere are so many wicked and cruel people! I no understand! How dey can be so." She spoke angrily, her face dark and outraged. "Your young man—dees

Ruth is hees sweetheart? Yes?" Her eyes became knowing, and she spoke intuitively.

"The course of true love never runs smooth." He sighed, and his eyes answered hers.

"Aye, yes." Shaking her head sagely. "My Fernando and I— we had our—" She paused contemplating the correct words. "little disagreements." She smiled. "God rest his soul, he has been gone from me now many years, but we loved each other very much. It was always the hot tempers. You understand, yes?"

"That is often the way. To make a long story short, yes, when we find our friends, Michael and Ruth will have an understanding." Mr. MacDonald smiled.

"Do you 'ave a picture of dees young woman Ruth? I would like to see her that causes one to travel around de world to find. Her papa I can understand, but..." Maria took the picture Michael handed her of Ruth. "Ah. Yes, she is a most beautiful young woman." She smiled at Michael. "A worthy woman who can find? Eh, Lemuel? Is she as good as she is good to look upon?"

"Ruth has been my guiding star. I have tried to live in a way worthy of her love and trust." Michael leaned forward and received his picture back.

"That ees as it should be." She shook her head energetically. "What do you now, my friend?" she asked.

"Where we left off. —It's too late this afternoon, but at daybreak, we will try to reconstruct their steps. We know where the van stopped that day, we know the boat that was hired to transport them, and we'll go on from there... on prayer and God's providence." He set his teacup and saucer back on the end table.

"Very good tings to go on and with. I will add my prayers to yours then. I need a word with Armando. If you would lead a prayer before you leave?"

"I will." Mr. MacDonald bowed his head. "God, our heavenly Father, we ask your blessings on our dear friend, Maria, her home and family. Father, protect them and help them to always do the right things according to thy will. In Jesus name."

"Thank you, Lewis. We will say prayers for you, your family, and your journey." Maria rose and bid them farewell.

"As you will be in ours, dear friend. We'll wait in the courtyard." Mr. MacDonald led the way outside.

"It was a nice visit. Look at these beautiful flowers. They know how to build things." Jack took note of the vivid flowers as they sat outside in the elaborate courtyard.

"Yes, it is good to see friends, especially after so long. The first time we were here, Amanda and I were caught amid some sort of unrest. It was Maria who grabbed us and whisked us out of danger." Mr. MacDonald opened his locket and looked at his daughter's portrait absent-mindedly. "I wonder what Maria needed to speak to Armando about." He closed the locket and replaced it in his pocket.

"Dad, do you get a feeling that something is out of kilter?"

"Only in our view. I don't believe it is a mere chance that things have fallen out the way they have. God is answering prayers, but I feel as if I am groping in the dark." Mr. MacDonald frowned.

A door opened somewhere in the large house, and they heard a voice speaking, *"Los padres de los hermosos angeles de la misericordia."*

"Hmm, that is curious," Mr. MacDonald muttered.

"What's that?" Jack asked.

"Someone just said, 'the fathers of the beautiful angels of mercy.'" Mac translated.

"That is curious." Jack tapped his fingers on the patio table.

"And still we grope in the dark." Michael took a deep breath.

"Sirs—" Armando approached. "Mama suggests I send someone to help in your search." His words were smooth as butter, but his face was dark and foreboding.

"That's all right." Mr. MacDonald waved a hand. "We don't want to trouble anyone. We'll just—"

"—No, you do not understand, sir. Mama complains we do not listen to her." He smiled with a rueful twist to his lips. "—When we do not, she still has her ways." He lifted his eyebrows. "Being the youngest child in a family of ten…" He looked at Michael, "is not always a comfortable place to be. I sometimes find although I am the youngest, I am in the middle."

"It has its challenges." Michael snorted with a wry smile.

"I will send someone to your room early." Armando opened the car door for them to slide in.

"I remember how forceful your mama can be, and we don't want any trouble." Mr. MacDonald shook his head. "We will want to leave early in the morning. Tell your mama Hebrews chapter six, verse ten, please."

"TELL US YOUR STORY." Mr. MacDonald offered his guests a cold pop.

"We were about to head out to canal number two for a clinic. We were winding down our campaign and had our medicines loaded. There were two vans, one with the medicines and the six workers. There was Dan Spears, the doctor of the group; Davis Brown, an EMT from the Dallas area; Kathy Atkins, from the Dallas area as well; Nathaniel Crowl, and your two girls in that van with the medicine crates. The rest of us were in the other van." Ken Grunn recounted the day. "We were waiting for our drivers. Our driver showed up, and we moved out into traffic. It had been about thirty minutes, maybe, when of a sudden the other van disappeared. We tried to get a message to them, but they never returned an answer."

"The rest of your group… Have they all made it home?" asked Jack.

"Yes, all but my wife Margo and I. We remained to give the local authorities any information we could, and to give their conscience a stab. The official in charge has been indisposed for over two weeks, and no one else could do anything until he returned." Ken snorted in a disgusted voice. "We're sorry, sir." He imitated with a nasal twang.

"A very good impersonation." Mr. MacDonald wiped a hand through his hair.

"I can repeat it in my sleep." Ken scowled.

"We talked to the man earlier today, and he didn't know any more than anyone else." Jack took a drink of his pop. "'Come back tomorrow.' I'm sure tomorrow is a favorite word. But a body could use up all of their todays waiting and never see all of their tomorrows."

"We traced our van to a site beside the river, and we even found the boat that had been hired to transport them down the river." Steve Spade, the local preacher, finished his part of the story.

"We have transportation. Would it be possible to hire the boat to take us downriver to the same spot tomorrow?" Mr. MacDonald asked.

"We already thought of that and made arrangements. The owners of the boat have agreed to take you to where they took the others, and they'll be ready at daybreak," Steve said.

"I'm glad to turn this over to you three. I need to get back to the States. Steve will meet you in front of your hotel in the morning, then, if you don't have any more questions." Ken rose from his seat.

"If that's good with Steve, it'll work for us." Jack finished his bottle of pop. "No use you traipsing through the bush with us, Steve. Will you have a place to wait down at the river?"

"Yes, there is a small village just a few kilometers from the spot." Steve stood as well.

"Tomorrow, then." Mr. MacDonald shook hands as Ken and Steve filed out the door.

CHAPTER—28—

In half an hour, the morning sun would be peeking over the horizon. The three Americans greeted Steve Spade on the sidewalk in front of the hotel.

"Do you have plenty of water and supplies in your packs?" Steve asked.

"Yes, we are prepared for this journey...as prepared as we can be for an unknown journey." Michael scowled. "The transportation should be here soon."

They were rewarded as an older but competent Land Rover zipped up to the curb. The man in the passenger seat jumped out and extended his hand. "Hello, I'm Oscar, this is Alphonso." He waved at the driver who, had grabbed their few packs to tie them on the top of the Land Rover, allowing more room inside as the four men squeezed into the back.

"*Por que trajiste a esos viejitos?*" The driver looked over the four passengers in the back.

"Get in and shut up," Oscar growled at the driver, hoping none of the four understood what the man had just said. The two older men looked preoccupied in conversation, and they appeared as if they were not listening. The younger two men were getting situated in their seats. "When you are in and ready, we will go?" Oscar said.

"Let's do it then." Jack looked up from his discussion, and Alphonso pulled into traffic. Mr. MacDonald turned and spoke to

Steve. "We don't know what we're doing on this journey. We may not make it back tonight. All things hinge on what we find."

"I understand that. Our communications in the jungle are unreliable." Steve crossed his arms and leaned back in his seat.

"I'll leave you some money to cover our hotel and the river travel here. If we aren't back in time, don't hesitate to return. And I'll leave a phone number and address in case you have to get in touch…"

"Surely it won't ever come to that!" Steve's eyes narrowed, and he shrank back from the idea being voiced.

"Of course, we pray not, but life isn't in our hands," Mr. MacDonald said. "And we don't know what will serve God's purpose."

"When we get to the river, Oscar, can we park the Rover until we come back later?" Mr. MacDonald asked.

"It will be fine until we come back." Oscar nodded. He clutched the side of the seat as they bumped along toward the river.

"Michael, you look a bit peaked already." Mr. MacDonald's brows furrowed as he gazed at his son.

"The boat ride ought to give him some time to rest if not sleep. It's supposed to be a two hour trip," Steve said.

"Here we are, and a two hour boat ride could be relaxing." Jack hopped out his side of the vehicle.

Mr. MacDonald slid out and stretched. "Relaxing or not, we need to keep moving. Grab your stuff and let's get going—Hello." He turned and extended a hand to greet the boat owners.

"I'm Jim and this is Joe. Grab your packs." The taller of the two men shook hands all around. "We're ready to move out."

"MICHAEL." MR. MACDONALD nudged his son awake. "Time to wake up, we're here." He held on as the boat jolted into the shore.

"So, this is where they got out?" Jack looked at the jungle landscape from the shoreline.

"Yes," their guide Jim said. "There's a village further up along the coast not far but they were headed into the jungle. I overheard the leader say he had arranged for someone to help transport the medicine crates and the time would be about an hour's walk into the jungle."

"And did someone meet them?" Mr. MacDonald's eyes narrowed as he thought over the information.

"Yes. Three or four men. I didn't see exactly how many," he said. "We take tours up and down the river regularly. We didn't think it odd to be hired in this case—until afterward."

"Y'all just stand here by the shore." Mr. MacDonald warned Oscar and Alphonso. "Mr. O'Brien and I want to look around. Just us. If y'all get to milling around, some of us... *esos viejitos— old men* won't be too very happy."

Oscar glared at Alphonso as they watched Lewis and Jack carefully scout around the site. The two men ended at a spot in the trees. They thoroughly examined the ground, the trees, and the foliage.

"This leader, how far did he say their destination was, and in what direction?" Jack wrinkled his brow.

"He said it was within a morning's walk. That they should be able to reach it by noon. We didn't pay much attention to where they went after we got back in the boat, but I think it was in that direction." The boat owner indicated with his hand.

"You know—" Mr. MacDonald turned away from the group and spoke in a low voice to Steve. "I don't know the two men, Oscar and Alphonso. They were supplied by my personal friend, Mrs. Gohmer. I would trust her with my life, but not her sons or these two men. Let me give you the address of Maria Gohmer, my friend. If we do not return, go to her. Don't trust Felix or his brother Armando." He wrote out the address on a slip of paper and handed it to the preacher. "And here's the money I promised you. We'll see you later, one way or the other."

"If we're not back by six o'clock head on back, Steve." Jack looked at his watch. "Let's get goin'. Daylight's-a-wastin'."

"WELL—" MR. MACDONALD began to arrange his pack with his supplies. "—perhaps being an old man has its advantages."

"How's that?" Jack and Michael followed his example pulling out a bottle of water and putting it in a pocket then organizing items.

"When we were starting, Alphonso wondered why us 'old' men were coming on this journey. But at least we brought supplies…Too bad those two didn't think to bring some food or water." Turning to the others, he spoke louder. "Jack will go first in line. I'll follow Alfonso here, and Michael will bring up the tail end after Oscar. Now—" He focused on Oscar and Alphonso. "—you need to be ready to stop suddenly. If Mr. O'Brien or myself call a halt, you must stop immediately."

They all looked up as the boat motor roared to life. "We'll see y'all later." They waved in farewell then directed their attention to the jungle. Hoisting their packs, they threw them over their shoulders and pointed their steps toward their destination.

IT WAS HOT AND HUMID, and the trail was difficult to follow. Thankfully, Jack and Mr. MacDonald had brought machetes. The trail wasn't old, but it wasn't fresh either. It was a constant clearing and cutting for an hour. Michael was grateful for the two-hour nap he had enjoyed while the boat sped up the river. Now he slogged along one step at a time, watching his father and keeping an eye on their *helpers*.

The quiet manner of Jack and Mr. MacDonald covered a well of strength that came with age and maturity. It was ironic neither man spoke about their military training. Their judgments were solid and sound because of that training. Ruth's father had been in the Special Forces in the military. Both men had qualities that were covered by the farmers' plain blue jeans, work boots, and crisp cotton shirts. Michael knew they both had distinguished military records.

"They had a rest here." Jack pointed and looked about for signs.

"Here." Mr. MacDonald pulled out two bottles of water and handed one to Oscar and the other to Alfonso. "You two stay here while we look around. Michael—" He took him aside and pointed. "—You see this log has been disturbed, and—" He carefully moved some leaves. "—There were some deep boot prints here." Moving cautiously to the other side of the clearing he pointed, and in a low voice whispered, "Notice Oscar is quite acclimated to this journey. Alphonso isn't. He's tiring." Speaking louder he said, "Someone lost part of a wrapper here."

"Time to go." Jack picked up his backpack and slung it onto his back. "Are you ready, Alfonso?" He asked as Alfonso lagged.

After a short trek, Jack stopped suddenly and Alfonso bumped into him. "Sorry, buddy, but you must stop when I stop." He pointed to some matted grass beside the trail. "One of the girls is having trouble here, probably Kathy what's-her-name. She's shorter and lighter than either Anna or Ruth. They had a short rest."

"Look, notice our direction keeps changing slightly but not radically? They continue to bear slightly to the north?" Mr. MacDonald motioned. "It is my estimation we will end up going north exclusively soon. We are making better time than they did, probably because Kathy is holding them back."

Michael blinked struggling to cipher his father's and Jack's hand and facial signals that accompanied their words. Oscar's face was a different kind of study. Just what did Oscar know, and where did he fit in this story? Michael's eyes narrowed as he observed him subtly.

"Halt!" Jack held up a hand half an hour later. "There's a scuffle here. They've had to rearrange packs." Jack pointed to the deep tracks on the ground.

"We're almost there...and we're heading north along a ridge." Mr. MacDonald wiped his brow. "In this heat, only a fool would force people to try to carry that much extra. Look at the tracks where the second man picked them up. Those packs had to be heavy. The rain and time would have filled the tracks up some since they were made." He shook his head. "Y'all stay here a minute. Jack—" He twitched his head toward the edge of the clearing. "If we have to split up, don't hesitate." He spoke in a low voice to Jack, pointing to the ground as a distraction. "Better they only get one of us, or we all get away in different directions. I don't trust these two..."

"We can use the hoot owl call as a signal." Jack rubbed his nose.

"That'll work." Mr. MacDonald shook his head. "I'll pass the word to Michael."

"All right, let's go." Jack took the lead again for a short while, stopping when they came to a well-traveled path. "Now which way?"

"Right. Go to the right." Mr. MacDonald decided after looking the trail over.

"Then right it is." Jack turned and followed the track. A few minutes later they were standing at the edge of the deserted camp. "Well, I'll be." Jack stood still surveying the layout. "This wasn't put up in a day. Where are we, Oscar? Is there a local name for this place?"

"Yeah, like camp Mittchigumi?" Michael muttered.

"NO, SIR, NO NAME FOR this place." Oscar shrugged, and his eyes narrowed. He hoped his face didn't show his surprise. Like Alfonso, he had wondered, *What are these old men going to do out here in this heat? In this terrain? The older one had to be in his late sixties, probably even older. The red-haired fellow? He was as hard to read*

as the older man, but surely he was in his fifties. But these two were good, really good. Great tracking. Maybe all Americans weren't lazy and spoiled.

"What do you say? If we start on that end, Alfonso, Michael, and I will take that one, Jack you and Oscar take the second, etcetera, and we'll go through the six cabins in that manner. We'll meet at the main house over there by lunchtime." Mr. MacDonald took his hat off and wiped his face with a sleeve.

"NEBUCHADNEZZAR THE king made an image of gold, whose height was threescore cubits, and the breadth thereof six cubits: he set it up in the plain of Dura in the province of Babylon..." Michael read Daniel chapter three for the Bible reading before they sat to eat lunch in the large main building.

After Michael finished reading, Mac worded the prayer for them. "Our most holy God, we petition thee this day for continued safety, for continued blessings, and continued providence in our matters here. Our heavenly Father, we ask that you remember that we are but flesh and blood here on this earth. We need thy guidance as well as forgiveness. May we only do all to your name's honor and glory. In Jesus's name, Amen."

"That story is very good." Oscar ate the food that was shared with him. "My mamma is very pious. She goes to mass often, and to the church every day to pray. The priest told us many stories. We liked them very much."

"THEY WERE BROUGHT HERE to minister to sick people all right...sick people that were shot up very badly. They did a good job of ministering, for everyone must have pulled through." Mr. Mac-Donald finished showing Michael the upstairs. "When they left, they disappeared. They just vanished. There are tracks around the camp, but they weren't friendly tracks. Some of the doors have been kicked in, and there are bullet holes here and there."

"Where does that leave us then?" Michael spoke wearily. "We don't know who has them or where they are."

"Somewhere in the middle." Mr. MacDonald ran his fingers through his hair. "If we weren't saddled with those two yahoos there, we would be further ahead." He frowned. "Alfonso would like to throw a stick in our spokes."

"I see." Michael shook his head. "That doesn't help us." He pursed his lips as he studied the situation. "Perhaps, after you two scout around, we'll have a better idea." He held his head in his hands to stop the throbbing.

"We should never have brought you on this trip, Michael. You haven't recovered enough." Mr. MacDonald frowned. "I've been mentally kicking myself for allowing you to come." He sighed heavily. "We'll have to be careful. Walking in this heat and over this terrain will sap your strength. I know, it would be worse sitting somewhere waiting, but this relapse..." Mr. MacDonald shook his head. "If I had known how sick you were I would never have agreed to you coming with us."

"I figured that." Michael grinned sheepishly. "Where would you be if the shoe were on the other foot, Pappy? If it were you and Mom?"

"All right, I'll stop chastening you. But I am concerned. I don't want to lose you, Anna and Ruth," he scolded. "You need to make sure that you drink enough liquids and eat something more often. Jack has slipped off already to do some scouting."

Michael dutifully began eating a peanut butter and cheese cracker and drinking some watered-down juice. Mr. MacDonald grasped Michael's shoulder. "I'm going to talk to Oscar and Alfonso."

Michael closed his eyes and rested for a few minutes. Opening his eyes again, he gazed out the windows. The colors were so vivid, it almost made his head hurt. He surveyed the lush scenery, the colorful flashes of birds, and he listened, noticing how quiet everything had grown.

He looked over at where his father sat. Oscar was dozing, and Alfonso was sulking. Since his father's conversation with Alfonso didn't look to be going well, Michael caught his father's eye and motioned for him.

"What do you hear, Dad?" he asked in a low voice. They sauntered to the other end of the dining area, looking out the windows at nothing in particular.

"I see all sorts of things, Michael, but I don't hear anything." Mr. MacDonald gazed uncomfortably out the window as there was the hoot of an owl. "What a blessing." He nudged Michael and pointed to the two sleeping men. "Just maybe. I'll wait here for a minute while you move the packs to the kitchen. We can slip out from there." Mr. MacDonald shifted away toward a different window, while Michael quietly picked up both packs and moved softly around the corner into the kitchen.

At the second sound of an owl, Oscar moved and opened his eyes slightly. Reassured to see the tall older man standing by the window, his eyes closed again. Mr. MacDonald moved quickly, following Michael into the kitchen and out the back window. Gliding noiselessly through the shadows of the trees to where they last heard the owl, they paused beside a tree.

"Glad you could make it. I was afraid you wouldn't hear or couldn't get away. Let's go," Jack urged. "I found a trail, and those two are about to have company."

"Lead on. We're right behind you." Mr. MacDonald checked Michael's pack and adjusted his own load.

"How do you hurry in this terrain?" Michael felt the weight of his burden. *How easy it is just to blunder along a path, and how difficult it is to walk carefully.*

Not long after they started, Jack held up a hand, and they stopped. "Look." He parted some foliage and they stepped several feet off the trail they had been following. The trees and foliage had been disturbed but replaced.

Without speaking, Mr. MacDonald stooped and felt the ground in a certain spot. "Someone rested here for a few hours not long ago. Maybe daybreak."

"Several someones." Jack mouthed the words.

"Shh." Mr. MacDonald held up his hand for silence.

CHAPTER—29—

A noise like a soft breeze whispering through the leaves moved along the trail. Except for a discordant sound that accompanied it, the sound was imperceptible. They stood unmoving as the noise continued down the road. Jack came snaking back through the undergrowth about the time Michael realized he had disappeared.

"Six men." Jack signed. "With rifles and two prisoners. Moving down this trail. Let's give them a few seconds then follow."

Mr. MacDonald nodded and gave Jack a thumbs up. He was thankful that Jack, an able tracker and affable companion, had accompanied them. Even though Michael had overestimated his recovery, both of the older men understood that Michael could not sit idly by while Ruth and his sister were in danger.

The three men moved out silently with Jack still leading. Half an hour later, Jack came to a halt bordering a clearing with a group of pathetic, unkempt huts. There were several animals contained in rickety pens as well as several wide-eyed children huddled at the foot of the shelters. Unfriendly voices droned from inside a hut.

"I will work myself around to that side." Mr. MacDonald pointed and whispered. "And see if I can get an idea of what is going on in there."

"We'll wait... unless you signal," Jack said.

Michael and Jack melted into the foliage surrounding the village, waiting and listening to the angry voices inside the huts. *Frightened children,* Jack thought, *"Always it's the children that suffer most."*

"There are only women and children here—at the moment." Mr. MacDonald materialized out of the bush. "There are five military men here. The other man must have taken the prisoners somewhere else. These men are threatening the women—they believe the women know where the Americans are, but won't tell them."

"Which Americans? The ones we are looking for—or us?" Jack asked.

"Don't know. Apparently, the women don't know either." Mr. MacDonald shrugged.

"Any sign of the girls?" Michael asked.

"No. No sign of civilization either. This place is very primitive. I'm wondering where their men are?" Mr. MacDonald's brows furrowed. "We can't leave these women to be bullied and threatened by those men…So, what to do? They have weapons: we have no physical weapons. There are five in there and three out here. Pretty good odds I would say." He grinned at his companions.

"As my pappy would say—" Michael chuckled. "First things first. Let's pray."

"Right, then you lead, partner." Jack nodded at Michael, and they bowed their heads.

"Well, it's in the Lord's hands…" Mr. MacDonald put a hand up when they heard twigs crackle and snap, and men's voices wafted to them. Mac crept out and returned shortly with a man from the village. "The men were in the town doing some business and have just returned bringing some supplies. They haven't seen any other outsiders."

"How many men are there?" Michael squinted as if in thought.

"Five, and two young boys," Mr. MacDonald answered.

"Since those fellas in the huts are looking for Americans, I guess we can oblige them." Jack pushed his hat back on his head.

"Well, let's hear your plan." Mr. MacDonald rubbed his chin.

With pantomime and rudimentary English, Jack shared his idea with the men and boys from the village. A short time later, two boys could be heard running down the path toward the huts. They spoke in their native language—"Mama, Mama! Americans! Americans! Come see, quick!"

The man in the hut harassing the women grabbed the oldest boy roughly by the shoulder. "Where?" he growled.

"Come, follow us." They beckoned eagerly.

"You two stay here and guard the women." He singled out two of the men. "The rest of us will go." Shouldering their rifles, the three marched off following the young boys.

The boys followed the instructions they had rehearsed perfectly, and taking the men to the place where they had left the three Americans, they stopped.

"Here, here." They waved their arms, even though there was no one to be seen.

"Do you joke?" The man scowled and picked the nearest boy up by his shirt front. "This is not..." His voice rose threateningly.

Someone tapped him on the shoulder. "Hey...over here."

JOHN'S WEEK HAD NOT gone well. He was accustomed to the climate of his natural country, but that did not make it any cooler, nor the problems he had faced that day any lighter. A short, stocky man deeply tanned and polished by the elements, he was naturally cynical, for life had not been easy for him.

Caught at the beginning of his rant, he turned and looked up—then up some more, and finally, he looked up into the face of what appeared to him to be the face of a spirit. Yes, he had seen tall, blue-eyed Caucasians with auburn hair but—what he had expected to see was the brown eyes of his comrade who had followed him. However, not only was his comrade missing but he was replaced by this work of God. An incredible spirit with blazing eyes and flaming hair standing so close to him he could have reached out and touched it. His heart leaped into his throat and an unearthly fear paralyzed his mind. Believing he was in the presence of either God himself, or a holy angel, he fell to his knees and began confessing his sins.

The only thing that came to Jack's mind was the dumb cliché, "I must speak to your leader." So that's what he said.

"Yes, yes...I will take you. Come, come quickly." He babbled as they left the two boys and everything else behind. John and his angel traveled back along a new path toward a new destination.

Mr. MacDonald moved quickly and silently, although the brush and trees greatly hindered their progress as they kept Jack in sight.

"Dad, you can follow faster without me." Michael was tiring from the exertion. "Go on alone."

"No, my son. I won't leave you to get lost in this jungle." Mr. MacDonald was shocked Michael would suggest such a thing.

"But I'm slowing you down, and you must keep up with them," Michael insisted. "Look, they're turning off the main track into the bush."

"Be that as it may, the answer is no. I can easily follow the Path Jack is leaving. God has brought us safe thus far, and he is still in control." Mr. MacDonald scratched his head.

"Then you must set the pace, and I will follow no matter what." Michael gritted his teeth.

"I tell you what—" Mac compromised. "I will pick up the pace—slightly. We shouldn't have to be quite so careful now. But we won't be able to follow as fast as you would like." He sighed.

JACK DETERMINED TO leave a goodly trail for them to follow when the bandit turned into the bush and took an unmarked path. Jack O'Brien chuckled at the response of the man. He wondered, where was this going to end? *I must speak to your leader* wasn't quite as sappy as when he was a kid and they'd use the phrase, *take me to your leader*...but it was pretty close. He shook his head in wonder at his words.

Mr. MacDonald and his family were genuinely good-hearted, upright, and moral people. Ruth had encouraged Jack to come to church, to pray, to study his Bible, to obey God's Word. He wasn't set against it, but he wanted it to be his idea. He grimaced. Would he ever be anything except stubborn and willful? Hadn't that mindset caused him enough trouble? It was time to grow up.

Well, God, I confess I'm stubborn— self-willed, but I'm not self-sufficient, and I need your help. There's much more to bringing the girls...and their people...home safe than being a good tracker. Whatever happens, Lord, guide us, protect all of us and bring us home safe. In Jesus's name, amen, he added, remembering the recent prayers. Even though he was still not in the right relationship with God, he knew that the Master understood. And Jack determined he would make good on his promise as soon as the opportunity was available, and not a moment later.

Suddenly he felt a sense of peace. He knew he did not deserve mercy, but he put his trust in the hands of the Almighty.

The bandit and Jack reached a crude camp. The guard beside the door to a large tent challenged them with heated words as John insisted on an audience with someone inside the tent. At last, the guard disappeared, only to return quickly and hold the door for them to enter.

Jack remembered the story his mother had told of Daniel in the lions' den. The hair on the back of his neck prickled as a wiry man with piercing black eyes rose and stalked around him, looking him over intently with a no-nonsense appraisal.

"Bah!" He exclaimed in contempt. "This is no angel! This is a man...an American man, but where are the other Americans?"

Well, there you go. I've been demoted. I've gone from an angel back to a plain undeniably human man. Jack had an inward chuckle and sigh. *And so fast.*

He listened as the leader berated the poor bandit. Jack sympathized with the underdog. *Lord, just a small miracle to shut the mouth of the lion, so to speak?* After the leader finished spitting out his oaths, Jack was marched to a tent and put under guard.

Michael and his father were hunkered down close enough to the camp to observe Jack being escorted to the second tent and the guard set in place. They continued to watch from their cover as several groups of soldiers came to the camp from activities.

Oscar and Alphonso were brought in, and a sudden ruckus erupted as five angry men with much shouting half shoved and half dragged a third captive through the camp and threw him into the enclosure with the first three occupants. Everything quieted down for a short time before someone of importance arrived with a sudden burst of activity.

"Michael—" Mr. MacDonald frowned then whispered to his son, "—I'm moving to the other side of the camp. I'll either come back, or I'll signal. The signal is to let you know where I am. One hoot means, stay where you are. Two hoots, come to where I am."

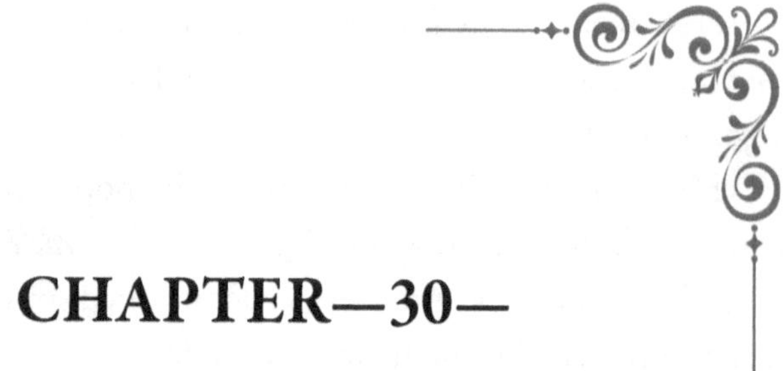

CHAPTER—30—

They moved along quietly. There wasn't anything to be said. Davis led the way, whacking a path with his machete. Ruth walked behind Kathy and Anna, listening, but unable to hear anything except the extraordinary throb of the jungle around her. They kept the creek on their right and continued following it faithfully.

"We've been walking a good hour." Davis stopped for a rest. "I would have thought that by now, Crowl and Spears would have caught up. We'll take a few minutes' break and get back to walking." He removed his hat, wiped his forehead with a sleeve, and slapped the hat back on.

"Oh no!" Kathy opened her pack. "Back yonder, I picked up the wrong pack. This one's Dan's." She frowned with a perplexed look.

"By now, most of what's left is water and some food. Right?" Ruth asked.

"These packs are considerably lighter than they were two weeks ago when we were brought in here." Kathy looked through the pack. "For a doctor, he doesn't have the healthiest food—" She pulled out a snack cake. "—But he has medicines... and what's this?"

Davis glanced over then did a double-take. "Let me see that—if we can get out of this jungle canopy..." His eyes narrowed and he examined the walkie talkie. "Drink your water and eat your snack cake and let's go." He smiled, but with urgency. "On second thought." He took a drink of water. "I'm going to run on ahead and do a bit of

276

scouting. You three finish up quickly and follow the path I leave. I won't go too far before I turn back. Don't dally though."

CUTTING A PATH AS HE ran, he still couldn't move as fast as he wanted, but it was faster than with the group. Something wasn't right. If Crowl and Spears hadn't caught up with them, it was likely that something had caught up with Crowl and Spears—and should have caught up with his group as well.

Where were they? Of course, he was at a disadvantage not knowing the area. Maybe there was a main road? Davis didn't want to get down the trail, so to speak, only to find a welcome committee waiting for them. After a few minutes, he slowed down, and then stood listening to the jungle sounds. He began a curious pattern of casting about in the direction they were heading, looking for any common animal paths that would show their coming and going to or from water. He was about to turn around when he heard voices. He peered out, and indeed there was the main pathway and several men from a local village speaking a local language, but they were going in the opposite direction from where he was going. *Okay, Scout, you need to get back to the girls.*

He could hear the girls coming even though they weren't talking and he had already made their trail when he went before them. He stopped and waited until they caught up.

Anna stopped when she got even with him. "What did you find? Anything useful?"

"I hope so. I found the main trail. It looks well used and should be easier and faster for our travel. We'll need to be quieter and listen carefully. It's only a few more minutes up this way." He turned and led the way.

ONCE THEY TURNED ONTO the well-traveled road, Ruth noticed Davis gently continued to increase their speed. She was concerned for Kathy and Anna. Anna's arm needed better care—and soon. Kathy was holding up well, all things considered, but for how long remained to be seen. They had been moving steadily for the most part since dawn. She stifled a yelp as she almost tripped over a tree root, catching herself just in time.

"We'll take a short rest." Davis held up a hand. Sweeping off a tree root with his machete he checked before the girls sat down.

"You must be made of steel or something. You just keep on going." Kathy smiled up at him. "I appreciate that."

"We all do." Anna wiped her sleeve across her forehead. "Too often we don't tell people thank you enough."

Ruth took a drink of her water and closed her eyes. "Now the question is, what do you think is at the end of our rainbow here? Will we find our way back to civilization soon?"

"This main trail points to a settlement somewhere, and probably close. Maybe a day's walking distance, probably less...but from where to where I don't know. And we only have maybe an hour left of daylight. Remember, when the sunsets at the equator, it sets."

"Davis—?" Ruth held up a hand. "I keep hearing... something."

"I do too." Kathy's brows drew together in a frown.

Each person strained to comprehend what it was they heard. "It's like a soft shushing sound." Ruth put a name to it.

Davis held up a hand for silence, and everyone froze in place while he silently moved toward the noise. Suddenly there was a soft shriek and a machete on metal rang out. The sound was followed by rustling in the bushes as a troupe of nine children came from out of the trees.

"What is going on here?" Ruth's face blanched. "God, help us. I only have a couple of bottles of water, and it'll take more than a snack cake for these poor little people—"

"I don't know what these children were being held for, but now that we have them, we need to be moving faster. I can guarantee we will be in for—let's just get going." Davis didn't say more. He didn't need to.

"Well, Scout, we're in this together." Kathy sighed.

"I don't know if God is trying to tell me something here or what, but the next time my friend Don Simon says to me, 'You should come with me, it'll be fun,' I'll tell him to find someone else, thank you." Davis raked his hand through his hair, and slapped his hat back on.

"God doesn't put us in the wrong places. What would we do without you?" Tears streamed down Kathy's cheeks.

"And I was a Boy Scout and... we are prepared. The three older children are carrying three younger children, so anyone grab an extra body and let's go." He swung a small girl on his back piggyback. He and Ruth helped Anna get a child situated on her back avoiding her bad arm, and then they positioned the remaining child for Ruth.

"Hopefully somewhere down the trail, these poor children will be less traumatized and be able to tell us what happened." Ruth sighed wearily.

WHAT A HORRIBLE THING to say. I don't know where that came from. Davis's face became a sober mask. *True, this has been one frustrating happening after another, but Kathy is right. I can see that plain as ketchup on your white tie dinner shirt.* Hitting his stride, he began a dog-trot pace. *Not the best when so many are so over-burdened, but the best we can do. God, help us get through this next hour.*

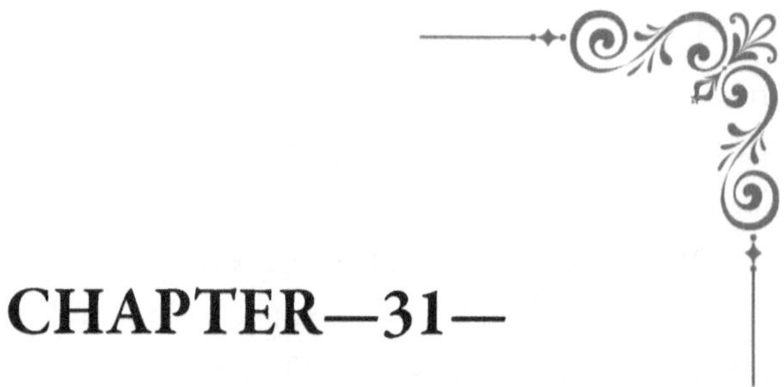

CHAPTER—31—

Michael was tempted almost beyond his control. The heat seemed to drip from the trees. Not a breeze moved a leaf. The insects buzzed, bit, and crawled intolerably. The perspiration streamed down his face and ran in rivulets down his body. He could have wrung the sweat out of his clothing. Time stood still. Today he was Joshua and the Israelites and God had caused the sun to stand still upon Gibeon. But instead of the enemies being the Amorites, they were the host of buzzing insects.

The enemies were outside and inside. These last few years had been an agony to his soul, waiting, always waiting, yet not knowing what he was waiting for. Here he waited again. He restrained himself by focusing on the blessing that had encouraged him through so many of his difficulties. Ruth's patient smile, kind eyes, and gentle touch, her peaceful presence and calm, accepting faith. He focused on these things, and he saw her face before him. The sweat dripped in his eyes and stung and burned. He shut his eyes.

People spoke of hallucinating when they were lost in the wilderness. They told stories about seeing people, hearing them talk, and the many strange tricks that the mind can play. Michael never dreamed that it could happen to him. His eyes opened slowly and he sighed.

Hallucinations always disappear at some point.

"Well, Michael, we do know where Jack is." Mr. MacDonald materialized beside him. "Where he is, isn't the problem. The question is what's the best way to get him out?"

"Two heads are better than one. What do you have in mind?" Michael asked.

USING A WOODEN BOX as a make-shift seat in the sweltering military tent, Jack wiped the sweat from his brow with his sleeve and scooped up the last of his beans and rice. It was good to know that it was okay for angels to eat. He heard the activity in the camp increase shortly before Alfonso and Oscar were pushed through the tent flap by an irate guard.

"*Hola, amigo.*" Oscar grinned affably. Alfonso looked as if he had just drunk a dose of cod liver oil.

"This neighborhood is getting—" Jack stopped as someone shouted in Spanish, "*Burro! Burro! Burro! Tu americano....!*"

"Hey! Hey! Watch who you're calling names!" Someone shouted just as loudly in English. "And watch the shirt!"

"Well, what in the—Whoa!" Jack jumped up off the crate in surprise as another addition rolled through the tent flap and stopped at his feet.

"I don't know why he had to get so personal." The new addition frowned indignantly and examined his torn shirt. Nathaniel looked up in astonishment from where he lay on the ground at Jack's feet. "Mr. O'Brien, what are you doing here? It's been a couple of days since Michael's barn shindig—three years ago." In confusion, he rolled over, sat up, and inspected his surroundings.

"On a mission to find and rescue you folks. Let me introduce Oscar and Alfonso." Jack waved at the two other men.

"*Buenos tardes, señores.*" Nathaniel dipped his head in recognition.

"*Hablas Espanol?*" Oscar's face lit up. Alfonso just scowled.

"*No mucho, lo siento.*" Nathaniel shrugged. "So, are you by yourself?" Nathaniel looked around the tent.

"No, no, Mac—and Michael are out there somewhere. Oscar and Alfonso are supplied by someone Mac knew." Jack pursed his lips.

"I see." Nathaniel raised an eyebrow. There was a pause. "So how'd you become a prisoner here? And where are the others?"

"I'm not technically a prisoner—I'm an angel." Jack shook his head.

"If you're not a prisoner and you're an angel, let's just leave." Nathaniel stood to leave.

"I'm not, but you are, and..." Jack lounged back against a cot. "We have to wait."

Nathaniel continued to gaze around the medium-sized tent. "We could probably make a run for it, but those fellas out there with rifles might have a different idea. What are you—we waiting for?"

"I'm not sure, but I will know when it comes. What made you such a favorite burro out there? That was some entrance you made." Jack frowned. "Are you by yourself or where are the others in your group?"

"I don't know what the game plan is. All six of us escaped together this morning about two o'clock. We laid low until daybreak and were heading down river when we were followed and attacked."

"Attacked? By whom?" Jack lowered his voice.

"There are two factions out here. Apparently. We patched up the one group after they had a shoot-out. This has been a real holiday, let me tell you. The group we patched up is mixed—you have at least English and Spanish languages, and sometimes a different language as well." Nathaniel tried to keep his voice low, speaking only to Jack. "We were attacked by the other group, but where we are now is back with the group we treated."

"You say there's a second group?"

"Yes. The other group was the one that caught up with us down by the river. The girls slid out of the way and Dan Spears, myself, and Scout—Davis Brown cleaned up the attackers, but they were mean as fire. A real different attitude. Dan was dazed in the fight and having trouble getting his bearings. We split up then, and Scout took the girls on downriver while I tried to get Dan up and going. Dan and I got separated when these guys caught up with me."

"How are the girls doing, and who's this Scout?" Jack's eyes narrowed.

"The girls, Anna and Ruth, and Kathy—" Nathaniel looked down at the tent floor, then back at Jack. "Anna has a flesh wound on her upper right arm. There were some stray shots, and a bullet grazed her arm. It needs better care. Kathy has battled low blood sugar since the beginning and is too delicate to be out here trying to fight her way out. Ruth? You never know the metal of a person until they're under fire. And Scout? I don't know where he's come from, but I don't know of anyone I'd rather have on my side. I've been taking martial arts forever and he's got me beat hands down... and smart? He's a real Boy Scout, always prepared." Nathaniel chuckled.

"Thank you for sharing that." Jack sobered. "Regrets." He shook his head. "The morning Ruth left home to catch her flight out, I wanted to put a protective bubble around her. I wish I knew where she is and if she's safe. Is my life always going to be a life of *might have been?*" He sighed.

"*Might have been*—you know, things are always changing." Nathaniel sighed. "Working around Ruth and Anna has been an experience. They act different, like actual ladies. One time a friend pointed to a woman, and said, 'The kids belong to that lady over there.' The woman in question was dressed slovenly, her hair not combed, and a cigarette hung from her mouth. That was a woman. She was not a lady. Anna and Ruth are ladies. They always dressed and acted like ladies. I haven't ever seen them look or act in any other way. Not when I was a guest in the MacDonald home, nor on this trip. As we treated the wounded patients, the men called them the beautiful angels of mercy." After a pause, Nathaniel added, "But we need to find them before that other faction does."

"Credit for my lovely daughter goes to God and good genes." Jack fished in the pocket of his dungarees and handed Nathaniel a locket dangling on a chain resembling a pocket watch fob. "Here's a picture of my mother, and the picture on the other side is my wife, Diana."

Nathaniel studied the two pictures carefully. "That's what I'm talking about— beauty of spirit. A quality of... something else that Ruth has also."

"Yes, Ruth is much like them." Jack massaged the back of his neck.

"Ah, dees are beautiful ladies." Oscar peered at the pictures close-ly. "But your daughter, she looks like you, no?"

"She has the O'Brien stamp." Jack stretched his long legs lazily and massaged his shoulder. "I'm getting too old for this." He guarded his expression carefully.

MR. MACDONALD SIGHED. The last few weeks had been a dif-ficult test of faith, even for the faithful. First the team's disappear-ance, and then... He shuddered as he remembered the shock when he first saw Michael's hollow cheeks and dark circled eyes. *Please, re-turn home. This journey will be long and hard.*

"Dad, if it was you and Mother—" Michael had paused to rest. *"—if our places were reversed... you could not do what you are asking me to do. I must go."*

Now, after the long day, walking the rough terrain, the jungle heat, added to the previous days of heart and nerve strain, Lewis

MacDonald felt tiredness in his bones. *God give us strength to finish our task here. To Your glory and honor, in Jesus' name, amen.*

Mr. MacDonald saw the hand of the Lord everywhere in this escapade. Now, as he slipped into the main tent, he again praised God that the tent stood unguarded at this moment.

Peace and strength flooded his soul as he stood quietly perusing the inside of the tent. This was a temporary structure that could be moved quickly and efficiently. In this section stood a collapsible desk and chair, and a bookshelf consisting of a box turned on its side holding a few books and some papers. The second section, partitioned off into a separate room by a large flap of canvas hanging from ceiling to floor, probably contained sleeping quarters for the leader and his aide. The tent was neat, orderly... and empty.

Suddenly, the heavy canvas section quivered and with a flourish, an immaculately dressed figure stepped into the outer section and found himself facing the American. The man never flinched or showed alarm. He never showed any change in his face or manner.

"Mr. MacDonald, you are an embarrassment." His voice contained a note of exasperation. "I don't know how you found us so quickly and lost the help we left with you so easily. Neither you... nor your comrades... are angels." He pursed his lips, and his heavy dark brows drew together appraisingly. "Some of my men, however, are convinced that you are supernatural." He spoke slowly, thoughtfully. "My mother has always held you and your family in high regard. I believe she would agree with my men. So, what to do with you?" He frowned and sat down to consider the options.

"Help me find the missionary team and send us home." Mr. MacDonald ruffled a hand through his hair. "That's the decent thing to do, as well as the wise thing to do."

"And what do I tell Felix?" His coal-black eyes became pensive as he toyed with the idea, and his frown deepened.

"How about, 'I'm getting out of this business?'" Mr. MacDonald rubbed his chin.

"That's a thought." Armando smiled a humorless smile and mechanically twiddled a yellow pencil. "If I got out, what would my life be worth? What will I do... if I survive?"

"Armando, each person born has a capacity for good, but they also have the same capacity for evil. What you fill your life with determines which it will be. Did you know that Felix once considered going into the ministry? He considered becoming an evangelist for the Lord. That was many years ago. Apparently, he chose... another path."

"I can't imagine my brother in that capacity." Armando continued his humorless smile. "Admittedly with his own family, he is the exact opposite of what he is out here. His daughters—all five of them—have him wrapped up and tied with a ribbon. They are what you would call spoiled. The best is not too good for his girls." Armando smiled and raised an eyebrow. His fingers continued to mindlessly fiddle with papers. "Good versus evil. Right against wrong. I don't know. I know which my mother would have me choose. My brother's hand would be the one against me if I chose..." He shrugged and ran a hand across his forehead. "But what life have I now? I've never taken a wife, never had a family of my own... and just for this very reason." He tapped the desk with a finger to emphasize each word. "At least if I die, I die alone. No one else will suffer."

"Oh, Mando—" Mr. MacDonald sighed. "No! No! No! My friend!" He reached a strong, work-worn hand toward the man. "Of course, someone will suffer." His simple words touched a lonely spot in the other man's heart.

"Would you remember? Would you care?" Armando looked at the other man and arched his eyebrows cynically. Try as he might, his thoughts were like sheep, scattered on the hills and uncapturable.

What is it about those blue eyes? Armando frowned and questioned in his mind.

"Surely I would." Mr. MacDonald smiled, pulled a picture out of his wallet, and handed it to him.

Armando held the old photograph gingerly with reverence. "You have kept the picture of you and I all these years?" He examined the picture of himself as a baby sitting on Mr. MacDonald's knee and looking up into his face.

"Yes, I cherish this picture. People, Armando…John three sixteen—for God so loved the world. Can you finish that verse?"

"For God so loved the world that He gave His only begotten Son that whosoever believeth on Him should not perish." Armando quoted without blinking.

"That isn't the ground we stand on, son." Mr. MacDonald gestured toward the ground. "That isn't the globe that turns around and around." He rotated his finger. "The world in that verse means you, Armando." Again he reached his strong hand toward the other man. "It means Felix. It means every last soul that lives and breathes and has its being on this planet. If the ruler and creator of this universe cared that much, how dare I care any less? Yes, my son, I care. And I remember." His blue eyes blazed with an inner fire.

Armando could see the earnestness in his face, the passion in his soul. Looking into those eyes and that face, he understood his mother's near worship of this man. He compared the man in the picture with the one standing before him. Yes, he was older, but the picture did not even do half credit to the real man. He understood the feeling that Lewis MacDonald was somehow beyond this world, as it were an angel clothed with mortal flesh. More than the eyes, Armando could feel the very heart and soul of the man reach out to him. The rays of the sun seemed to pierce the tent, and a glow surrounded the man of God. It wasn't possible, of course. There was no earthly explanation for what happened. It was not logical. Nor for that matter, was it even possible. Nevertheless, it happened, and Armando himself witnessed it.

"I'll do you one better than help you find the people from the team. I'll do better than to let your people go home free." His eyes narrowed in thought. Armando declared resolutely, tapping his pencil on the make-shift desk for emphasis, "I'll help you find them, I'll help you transport them to safety, and ..." He stopped and savored the moment as a connoisseur would savor a flavorful old wine, gazing at it in the goblet, then rolling it over his palate. "You are an evangelist. Is that not correct?"

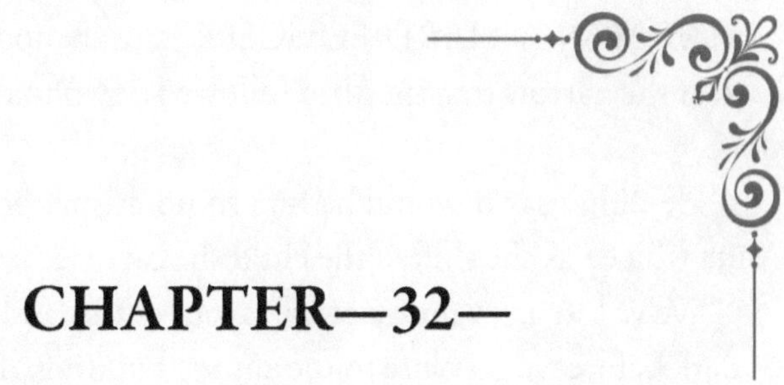

CHAPTER —32—

"Well, there it is." Davis looked through his binoculars at a small village below. He handed them to Ruth.

"Only a few rickety houses, but there's a two-story church building." Ruth passed them to Anna, who gazed over the town.

"But can we get there in the remaining daylight?" Kathy looked at the sky with a worried glance.

Davis turned to the oldest boy. "Young man, do you know this village?" The children had not spoken since their addition to the group. Their big eyes were a testimony to some of the tragedies they had seen. The two older girls, one of ten and the other eleven years of age, had carried the younger two girls long enough for it to be second nature. The two boys were only seven and eight but were already used to carrying burdens. Davis, in the gentlest voice possible, repeated his question to the older boy. "Do you know this village? Can you help us get to the church building? It will soon be dark."

The young boy nodded his head yes, but no one was sure what he meant—yes, he knew the town, yes, he could help them get to the church building, or yes to one part or all. Davis sighed. "There isn't anyone straight road or path here, and there looks to be a pattern of canals or waterways we must work through. I don't understand this...but let's press forward. As Kathy has said, daylight's running out." With a kind expression, he took the youngster by the shoulder. "Come on, kid, let's go."

"THAT WAS A HARD-FOUGHT half an hour." Ruth looked back at the narrow trail they had followed down to the bottom of the slope.

"He didn't say it would be fun, so no misplaced advertisement." Anna winced as she shifted the child she carried.

"We've lost any vantage of the layout of the land here. And it will be dark before we get close to the church building." Ruth just wanted to rest somewhere safe, away from the unfamiliar sounds.

"So far the kid has done a good job here." Davis encouraged his little charge, who had taken his new responsibility to heart. "Can you get us through to the church building, kid?"

Again, he shook his head yes, but hadn't committed anything to words, even as the shadows gathered.

"Okay, follow on." Davis pulled out his flashlight. Following close behind the kid, they found a street, then another hard-fought half an hour later they stood outside the church building. "You all stay put back there. I'll go next door and see who I can find. Staying out of sight might be a good thing until we know where we are."

"Come on then." Ruth put a finger to her lips as she led Kathy, Anna, and the children toward the back of the building. They found a clear spot to sit down out of sight of the roadway. "I don't know what's left in here." She opened her backpack and searched for any type of food.

"I have a big box of peanut butter snack crackers," Anna whispered. Opening the box, she helped the children open the individual packages.

"And I do have a few small juice packages to go with Doctor Dan's snack cakes." Kathy smiled. "That should be good for the kids."

"Here's a power bar for you, Kathy, and an undesignated fruit bar for Anna...*shh*." Ruth held up a hand as several dogs began barking. "What?"

The backdoor beside where they sat opened slightly. "*Psst,* in here, quiet."

Picking up their stuff, the girls herded the children in through the door. Once inside, the backdoor latched shut. "Follow me." The person began moving away.

Instead of obeying, Ruth stood between the person leading, and the group. "No," she whispered to Kathy and Anna. Trying to communicate in the dark didn't work well. "Go left. Kids to the left..." She hand-signaled. "Hide." Her face furrowed into a frown. "That wasn't a familiar voice. It could have been anyone, and I know it wasn't Davis."

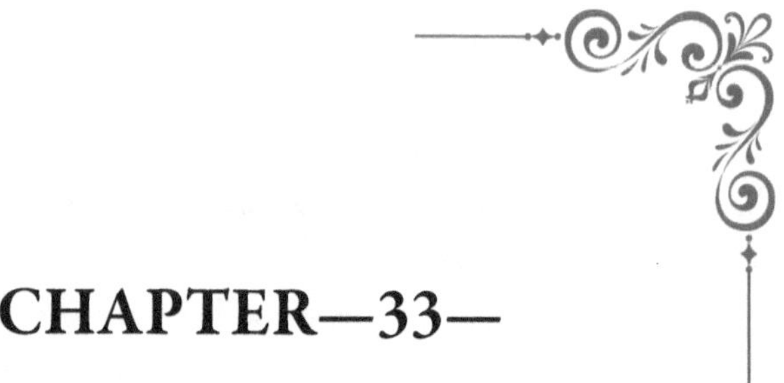

CHAPTER—33—

"Yes, I'm an evangelist." Mr. MacDonald raised an eyebrow. "There are a lot of men in this camp who have never heard that Word. Men who are dying physically as well as spiritually. Speak to them. Speak to them, Brother MacDonald. I will give you that opportunity."

The whole camp sat listening, to witness the gospel sermon. Few were old men. Most were young men made old by their profession. Mr. MacDonald looked into the impassive faces clustered there as if to memorize them. He remembered preaching other gospel messages where most of the listeners cradled rifles, yet in all this, God had promised him boldness in the face of adversity. Jack and Nathaniel were situated in the middle ring, on further still Michael sat listening, and who beyond that, he did not know.

"Since I have a mixed audience—" Mr. MacDonald explained first in English, then in Spanish. "—I will speak in Spanish and interpret in English... unless there is one who would be willing to do the interpretation for me?" He asked hopefully, but only silence answered.

"I will do the honors then." Mac paused to gather strength. "Thank you for this opportunity to speak the soul-saving message of the Word of God—"

A man in dirty, torn clothing emerged from the fringe of trees and limped toward the speaker, threading his way through the clumps of men to the front.

"I will do the honors for you."

"Thank you..." Mr. MacDonald peered closely and recognized him as one of the missing team members. "Is it Daniel? Doctor Dan?" he asked.

"Yes, that's correct." Dan nodded, forming his words with effort.

"Thank you, Doctor." Lewis MacDonald wondered at what ordeal this man must have been through. "As I look around the group assembled here—" He studied the group slowly and solemnly. "I wonder just where to begin." He paused giving his interpreter time to speak. "Do we begin with the love of God? The severity of God? Perhaps we should consider the justice of God?" Again he paused. "I suggest we open the Word of God and begin with all three."

DAVIS SCOUTED AROUND the exterior of the building searching for his lost comrades. He was sure the girls had followed his advice when he left them. Now, there was no sign of them or the children...except as he came to the back door of the church, he found on the ground the last cracker in a package of snack crackers and a half-finished bottle of juice—and a locked door.

The whole village seemed to be locked down. Nothing except the few dogs moved or yapped, and all was now silent. Davis squatted down and fished in his pack for what Kathy gave him from Doctor Dan's pack. There weren't any lights, and he wasn't real keen to shine the only light in town. Finally, he felt the object he was groping for. Trying to set a shield against being observed, he sighed. *At least we're out of the dense jungle canopy.* He set up the transmitter and began tapping Morse code: 'SOS Please send help...SOS Please send help'. This may be a long night. I don't know where we are. I don't know where the receivers are. I don't know who's out there, or if anyone is out there. Davis checked his watch. I'll send it again in half an hour.

He'd had lots of practice with all-nighters. His gut instinct told him to set a watch here.

RUTH NOW UNDERSTOOD why the children had kept quiet the whole trip. She was now aware and incredibly in awe of the power of silence. How the young girls had trained the little children to remain quiet throughout such an ordeal was beyond her comprehension.

Anna and Kathy had filed in, ushering the children to the left as Ruth had directed. There were two rows of barrels lined up with just enough room for them to scoot behind as a barrier.

"I know they came in." Two people were speaking at the end of the room away from them.

"Maybe they don't know that they are safe?" The second voice said. "Everyone—you're safe here. Come on out." The second voice called a bit louder.

Ruth shook her head at Anna. Trying to remember her sign language—*no light, no safe.* She spelled. At this rate, it would be a long night even inside a building. An hour later she was jolted out of a gentle doze by the first voice speaking a bit louder and maybe not quite as friendly.

"We know you're in here. Please make your selves known. You are safe here. We have food and water. Do not be afraid." There was a slight insistence to the words.

Ruth longed to stretch her cramped muscles. Still, she cradled the baby in her arms, holding her close. And the baby clung to Ruth as if her life depended on it. Where was Davis? Where was anyone? *It's so easy sitting at home in relative safety to trust and pray, or pray and trust, but what about where she sat now? Oh, my God, hear our prayers. I will still believe no matter what.*

And so the night wore on. Every so often the people behind the voices would try to persuade the group to step out into the open, and the small group continued to hunker down.

"We have had a power outage and there are no lights…"

Anna signed to Ruth, "?"

"Why wait till now to tell us that?" Ruth signed back, her stubborn streak kicking in. "They want us out there."

"I FEEL COMPELLED TO congratulate you, Jack, on your obedience to the gospel tonight." Mr. MacDonald shook Jack's hand.

"Words don't express how I feel, Mac. I've been nothing short of stubborn for so long and it's caused me nothing but heartache."

"That is the way of doing things our own way." Mr. MacDonald took a drink of water. "Armando made a commitment today also. The first part of the deal was he allowed me to preach the sermon. Next step—Just before dawn, we'll fly out…"

"What are you talking about? Fly out at dawn? Where from and where to?" Jack rubbed a hand over his tired eyes.

"That was part of my deal with Armando— He allowed me to speak to the men, and he's going to help us find our team members. His people will pick us up in the helicopter. This'll be a brush up on your rescue training. I don't know what we'll find."

"I haven't—holy saints and angels— rescue training… You mean special ops?" Jack's jaw dropped almost to his shirt collar. "I haven't done none of that for twenty plus years, Mac."

"Jack, I distinctly remember last year when you were helping us put up hay. When Lonnie passed out up in the hay mow and how you maneuvered on that hay rope and got him down and outside and revived. I'd say you haven't forgotten your training."

"I don't know, Mac. I can't think that's the same." Jack scratched his head.

"That's where we're going, Jack. Armando says they've been tailing this rogue group and they've followed them to a certain village. Dan and Nathaniel believe that's where the group was heading. Unbeknownst to the group, they may have just walked into a trap. And I suppose if you have to call on a cloud of witnesses, holy saints and angels would be a better alternative than cows, guacamole, or—" Mr. MacDonald rubbed his chin in thought. "Dan, Nathaniel, and Michael will go downriver by boat, and we'll take the helicopter."

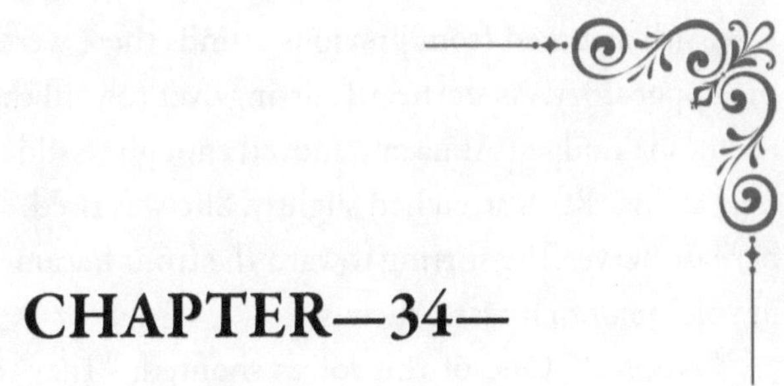

CHAPTER —34—

It's always darkest just before dawn. Davis checked his watch and sent out another Morse message. He perused the night sky, thinking how different the stars were this close to the equator. A few months before when he obeyed the Gospel, he thought he had put his past behind him. How many times in his soldier of fortune days had he believed he was doomed to die in some Caribbean dive as a nobody with no name? And now as a Christian, where was he? But he did have a name—a good name given to him by a Savior. So far, everything was silent inside the building, but it might be time to change things up—

SEVERAL TIMES DURING the night Ruth had been jolted awake by the people trying to shake her resolve and force them to come out into what they claimed would be safety. She wondered at the children's ability to be silent and still for so long. It had to be something they learned in their few short years. At times the older girls would make a shushing sound that seemed to soothe the little ones, yet other than that, their large, silent eyes burned into her memory.

It had to be close to dawn at her reckoning by the number of times they'd been awakened, and each time had been more urgent. Someone was behind all of this but—who? And why?

Ruth assumed from previous sounds there were stairs leading to the upper story. As she heard stirring over toward the stair side of the room, she nudged Anna and moved enough to slide her child charge over to her. Ruth stretched slightly. She was tired, sore, and tried to her last nerve. The stirring toward the front became louder, growing in volume until it was a ruckus.

"No, no!" One of the voices shouted. "They're here, we know they're—"

"Now! I want them now!" Roared an angry voice. "The kids are mine. I want them and those people who stole them from me. I want them too." It was more of a primeval growl. And the movement continued approaching across the room. "I will have them. We will move out of here before daybreak."

A beam from a flashlight waved briefly around the room. The four-foot barrel Ruth was hiding behind was picked up and spun across the room.

Ruth stood up. "You will not touch these innocents." Her eyes narrowed, and she repeated, "You will not touch them."

There was a momentary blaze of unbelief that hovered on the man's face. "This is what has been standing between me and—"

There is a sound that might not raise the dead, but it will give the living pause. It wasn't for nothing that Jack O'Brien had taught his son and daughter self-defense for the last fifteen years.

"Ruthie," Jack O'Brien had stressed, "You're not very big, but you do have a couple of things in your favor. The element of surprise, and the O'Brien lung capacity. Make the most of them, daughter."

DAVIS HAD SENT HIS message every fifteen minutes since midnight, and had just now moved to the front of the church building. He ran a weary hand over the stubble on his face and chin. What a person would give for a long leisurely shower and shave? He heard a chopper coming in. *Oh, God could it be?* He could only pray.

—He was jolted out of his thoughts by the most hideous scream. *What in the name of eternity was that horrible noise?* He barely heard the light contact as bodies slid from the helicopter rope onto the roof. Scrabbling across the pitched roof to an open window, they swung inside.

All Davis could think was what ghastly torture was happening inside that building. There was no door going to stand between him and his goal. He dismantled the door and entered in time to engage several of the soldiers stationed upstairs holding a handful of local civilians hostage, and he prevented any help from those soldiers to the fracas below. But he couldn't determine who the person sliding down the stairs was.

RUTH HIT HIM WHILE she had the element of surprise. She hit him, and he went down. Orvil was not one to be beaten by a woman. Especially one so young. He stood up slightly woozy, and she hit him again. He didn't like the taste of blood in his mouth. He spit it out and grimaced. After the third round, he stood and shook his head. This would never do. He hadn't gotten to the leader he was to let a mere child beat him. He let out a roar, put his head down, and barreled at her, not stopping this time.

"Out, Ruth, roll out. I got this!" Jack covered twenty feet and twenty years in two seconds.

CHAPTER—35—

"Well, Cyndi, what do you have to say now?" Ada gave her sister a sideways glance. She layered the pea salad as they prepared for the potluck that evening. "They have returned as good as new, and what were your plans for when that took place?" The younger sister arched her eyebrows looking down her nose at her sibling.

"Oh, for—" Cyndi snorted pretending to be annoyed at Ada. "If it weren't such a wonderful occasion—" She smiled. "—I would tweak your nose like I used to do when you were little. Besides, Anna did suffer a gunshot wound to her arm."

"But that is healing quite well. Thanks, of course, to the attention of her good doctor." Ada added a serving spoon to the bag. "There will always be a scar, but it should eventually be barely noticeable."

"We are all packed up and ready to head on over to the potluck." Cyndi examined their cache of goodies stowed in their trunk. "I am anxious to meet everyone. I've seen their pictures in the papers, but pictures just aren't the same as the real, in-the-flesh article." She sighed.

Ada and Cyndi scanned the crowd as they stepped out of their vehicle. The usual gathering was present. Even Cyndi could pick out the different members and put names to them by now. She anxiously looked for the members from the team who had been held hostage—not too hard to find when the others were eliminated. Anna's arm was out of the sling now, and that good-looking fella with her must be the doctor that everyone called 'her doctor' in that special way. Of course, the other woman would be the Kathy of the group, and there was Nathaniel and a Davis Brown—all nice enough looking folks, but they were ordinary... nothing that would set any of the team members apart from normal people.

"Come on up to the tables." Donna MacDonald ushered Ada and Cyndi forward.

Ada hesitated. The last two weeks since the team had been home recuperating, there had been something different. Ruth had always been quiet and introverted, but there was a new layer of untouchableness. How would Ada follow through on her resolve to ask both Michael and Ruth for their forgiveness? Mustering her courage, she approached the pair, but neither one saw her as she drew near. She turned to flee.

"Ada?" Mac gently put an arm around her as Ruth turned from a conversation with one of the other women.

"Ruth—" Ada's face turned crimson. "—I'm so glad you're home... so glad you're back. I want to tell you..." She stammered. "I'm so sorry."

"Ada, I'm glad to be back, and safely." Ruth moved over and patted the seat beside her. "Come...sit down."

"I prayed you would be able to forgive me. But—" Ada felt her way, unsure of what to say.

"Ada." Ruth's vivid blue eyes searched Ada's face, then looked deeply into her eyes. "Sometimes evil comes softly. It worms its way into our lives, and we don't see it. We don't see it coming. We don't even see it sitting there. It just happens. If it were to appear suddenly as full-blown evil, we would reject it, but it comes wrapped as something else."

"Ruth. I'm so very glad you're home." Ada wiped at the tears on her cheeks.

"Time doesn't heal all wounds and certainly not immediately, but many things will heal if given time. Give yourself time." Ruth touched Ada's hand and sighed.

"GOODNIGHT." MR. AND Mrs. Rudd said their farewells as the potluck wound down. "We're not as spry as we used to be, and after eight o'clock we turn into pumpkins." Mr. Rudd laughed at his joke. "I'm sure we've picked up all our dishes, and we'll see you Sunday."

"How pleasant it is to be able to kick off our shoes and just sit together." Mrs. MacDonald finished picking up some disposable tableware and tossed it into the garbage sack. She sat down and smiled up at Mac.

"I continually feel the need to pinch myself to make sure we're home and everyone is safe." Ruth slid her paper plate into the trash sack as well. She looked around at the group, mostly the MacDonald family, but the six-team members were guests as well.

"I'd like to thank you ladies for the professional way you handled the situation." Dan Spears changed the subject.

"What do you mean?" Kathy asked.

"You three women conducted yourselves in an exemplary manner. It made it much easier." He shook his head.

"You acted like ladies, and you did what needed to be done quietly in a Christian manner." Nathaniel took up where Dan left off.

"You men did your work well." Kathy arched her eyebrows.

"Yes, but your Christian example helped to lighten our fears and our burdens in a very difficult situation. The men of the camp took to calling them 'the beautiful angels of mercy,'" Dan explained to the group.

"It wasn't about us, though." Ruth twisted a napkin in her hands. "Whether we liked it or not, there were some of those men who would have died if we hadn't been brought in."

"That's true. Even Felix himself was in bad shape when we went in. I find it unbelievable how someone can operate on both sides of the law. I know it's done, but it's kind of like not letting your right hand know what the left hand is doing—or something." Dan rubbed a hand over his chin.

"And those dear children. I don't even want to think of what would have happened to them." Kathy twirled a lock of her hair.

"Have you and Scout finalized any plans?" Nathaniel asked.

"We have a supporting congregation who is funding our new work there. Kathy and I are planning on getting married and beginning an orphanage in Guyana." Davis smiled at Kathy.

"So this makes how many weddings for the future?" Seth gave a one-eyed look.

"Yeah, Michael, when is it you and Ruth are planning yours?"

"I think we are going to split the difference—Dad and Mom were married the first of May. Ruth's grandparents were married in the middle of June." Michael took a drink of pop.

"We thought the first of June. But that may all change yet." Ruth eyed Gwen, trying to remember when her baby was due.

"No double wedding with Anna and Dan?" Gwen poked at her sleeping Zoë.

"I think they're on their own. But like I said, who knows?" Ruth smiled at Anna.

"Well, I kind of feel like Mr. Rudd. I turned into a pumpkin a long time ago and need to be rolling on home." Mr. MacDonald stood with a stretch and a yawn. "Ahmanda, are you staying here or coming with me?" He smiled fondly down at his wife.

"You know, Mac, I think I'll come with you," She answered.

"Good night, y'all." The couple turned up the path toward their house amid the chorus of *"Goodnight," and "Goodnight Mom and Dad."*

"These last few weeks have been tough for them. Dad is beginning to show his age." Joshua ruffled a hand through his hair.

Michael emptied his cup and threw it away. "He outdid me on our trip. As we scouted through jungle paths—Dad and Jack both were unbelievable. I'm much younger, and they went slow for my sake."

"I believe it is time for us to take up our hats and wish y'all a good night. I need to get these ladies home and to bed. Gwen is supposed to take it easy, and look at baby Zoë—" Seth burst out with a laugh. "I love watching her sleep. That baby sleeps with abandon. Come to think of it, she does everything with the same strength of purpose." He sobered ruefully.

Little Zoë was lying across her Grandmother Alice's lap like a limp rag doll, one plump little arm thrown across her face. Her eyes were closed, the lashes dark against her pink baby cheeks even in the firelight shadows. The cinnamon-colored hair was just like her mother's, except it curled naturally into ringlets. She had worn herself out playing and eating, and the latter had left telltale signs on her little rosy cheeks and lips.

"Yep." Several other voices agreed. "Time to trundle off to bed." And there was a general flurry of people picking up their belongings. Some left for home, and some headed for their beds.

"WHERE TO FROM HERE?" Michael mused as he and Ruth followed slowly the same path that his parents had trod half an hour before.

"Michael, I'm tired. I just want some rest and peace."

"Like preparing for our wedding?" He frowned. "After all we've been through, I feel like we took the long way around—like we've been a long time getting here."

"Michael, I'm so sorry." Ruth began to weep. "I'm so sorry."

"Go ahead and cry, Ruth." He put his arms around her, knowing there was more to her words. "You've got some tears stored up. Cry it out."

After a time, Ruth stepped back and blew her nose on the paper napkin she had carried with her. "That night we had heard someone unlock our doors as the bandits left that night. They cleared out and left us to our fate. Doctor Dan came to our room and we were leaving when we were cut off by the new group coming in. As Anna, Kathy, and I hid in the supply closet, we heard the shooting and the shouting—" She shivered, reliving the nightmare. "My regret was I wouldn't ever see you again. I wouldn't be able to tell you I'm sorry."

"Sorry? Sorry for what?" Michael's brow wrinkled.

"I don't know exactly. Right after Joshua brought the case to a close the first year, I was still in shock. All the emotions were still raw, and I wasn't ready to commit to marriage—and you weren't ready either. And I felt a need to finish something."

"Then Junko got sick—"

"Yes, Junko got sick and... I'm just tired. I've put everything first and—I'm done. Do you think maybe we've waited too long now?" She held tightly to his arm as they continued to stroll homeward.

"June does seem a long time to wait, not that I'm not willing, but..." He could feel her tiredness. "This last year has been hard on all of us."

"I love this time of year." Ruth sat down on a nearby bench and inhaled deeply of the autumn aroma.

"You are changing the subject." Michael sat beside her. "Do you or don't you want to wait till June?" he demanded.

"I do not." Her eyes narrowed, and she sighed. "Reuben and Becky will be getting married in April." She picked at a spot on his jacket. "Reuben only has six months left then he has a job offer in Colorado."

"They won't be living around here?" He looked around the arbor.

"Not for a couple of years anyway. Maybe after they start their family." She leaned her head against him.

"Okay, Ruth Kathleen—" Michael took a deep breath and raised his eyebrows.

"Well, I have my Grandmother O'Brien's wedding dress. It just needs a few slight alterations. Nothing major. I would like to have the ceremony in Grandpa's big house. That can be accomplished in a short time with some elbow grease and lots of help. I don't want anything elaborate, just you and me and a few friends." Her eyes were deep pools of fathomless blue.

"Anything else? Where do you want to live? I have money saved, and I'll help Juan until I'm completely recovered. Dad and Mom wouldn't counsel a hasty marriage, but in our case, no one could call our marriage hasty." He smiled down at her.

"If you aren't opposed, I would like to fix up our old house. Make it home like in my grandmother's day before all the sad times came." Ruth looked down at her hands.

"Are you sure the memories might not be too painful, my lady?"

"I always loved that old house. There were a lot of happy memories there. Even if they weren't all happy, I believe I would be content—if you could be?"

"RUTH AND I DISCUSSED this with Dad and Mom this morning for a long time." Michael sat talking to his brothers the next afternoon. "We—Ruth and I—have decided to have an autumn wedding."

"No double wedding after all?" Joshua took a sip of his coffee.

"No. Ruth and I both need some downtime, and Dad and Mom suggested a nice little cabin..."

"I remember that little cabin. We spent the first nine years of our life up there. Uncle Hugh still owns that land, doesn't he?" Lewis Junior pulled at his earlobe. "It should be a beautiful time of year."

"That's what Dad and Mom said. Laura stopped by this morning and she volunteered Juanita to help with the few alterations on Ruth's dress. Those are so slight that they will only take a few hours. Ruth asked her grandfather if we can have the wedding there at his house. Alice is going to take care of the wedding buffet as well as the decorations..."

"Oh, ho, so the plot is widening. I'm sure Gwen has her oar in there somewhere." Seth laughed. "Well, Joshua and I have already done part of our share. We did the siding and roofing a few weeks ago on Mr. O'Brien's house."

"Funny you should mention it. Someone did say this will give Gwen something to occupy her thoughts before she has to be cooped up. It will take the whole bunch of them to spruce up the old bachelors' abode and prepare it for company." Michael smiled a wry, quiet smile.

"After the cabin experience, where is the blessed couple going to live happily ever after?" Seth raised an eyebrow.

"At Pat and Priscilla's first house, the one where Ruth grew up." Michael ruffled his hair.

Lewis Junior whistled. "Do you think that's wise? There have been some..."

"Yeah, but it was her idea. Actually, it is her wish." Michael's hand shook slightly as he took a drink of coffee.

"Two weeks. We can make a dent. And how long will you be at the cabin?" Joshua noticed how pale and shaky Michael still looked.

Peter emptied his cup. "—We better get busy, boys. We can't let the girls get ahead of us. They'll have the whole O'Brien house papered and painted while we're sitting talking. Take your cups to the kitchen, and let's go." He encouraged as they all laughed at the old challenge.

"ADA, HONEY, ARE YOU sure you're gonna be all right?" Cyndi brushed the hair off her sister's forehead and began pinning it into a pleasing style. "You know, baby, you have gone the extra mile in helping to prepare for this wedding. And on such short notice." She clucked. Standing back, she critically scrutinized her younger sister through narrowed eyes.

Cyndi grudgingly admitted Ada had certainly changed in the last year, and it was a charming change. She no longer had that gaudy, tawdry look, but in its place was a quiet, honest appearance. Cyndi looked at the bridesmaid's dress hanging on the door. The satin rose-colored dress trimmed with dark lace and tiny vivid flowers of autumn hues brought out the color and natural beauty of her beloved sister. Her abundant platinum blonde hair curled and braided was also accented with complimentary matching tiny flowers. "You know, baby—" Her sister repeated her favorite phrase. "I don't think I'm gonna let you go."

"What?" Ada's eyes grew large in alarm. "What are you talking about?" She pulled away looking at Cyndi with a worried frown.

"You were right all along. I thought you were crazy, but you were right." Cyndi nodded. "You look absolutely stunning. If I let you go, some guy will snap you up, and then who will I have to torment?" Cyndi was only half-joking.

"Oh, is that all?" Ada's breathing returned to normal. "I was afraid something awful was about to happen. If we're ready, let's go. I don't want to be late, especially since I'm one of the bride's maids. Do you think I'll catch the bouquet?" She smiled at Cyndi hopefully.

"It would be my luck," Cyndi muttered. "Come on then."

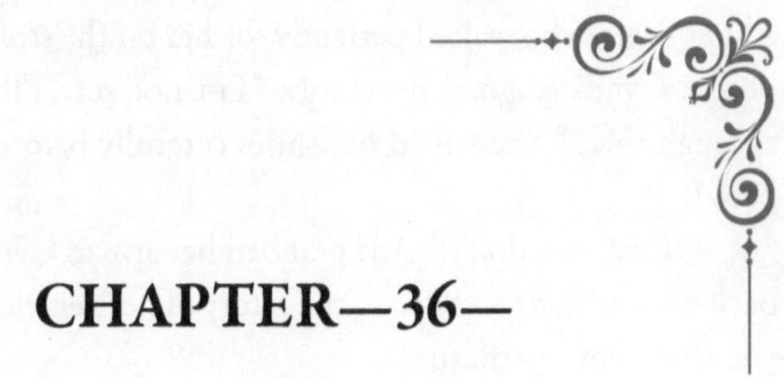

CHAPTER—36—

Cyndi had passed the old O'Brien farmhouse many times during her life. However, huge old oak trees surrounded it on the south side and massive pine trees on the north side. The view had always been limited. Today as she slowly pulled into the drive and as close to the sidewalk as she could, she felt her heart quake. "Oh, Ada, baby, this place is… massive." She gulped and breathed fearfully.

Ada opened the car door. "I'll wait for you on the porch." She smiled to reassure her sister then slid out. Opening the back door of the car, she carefully lifted out her plastic-wrapped dress and slammed the door shut. "Bring the rest of my stuff, will ya, Cyndi?" She walked to the house.

Cyndi parked in the shade of two sugar maple trees… as far away from the crowd as she dared. The season had been perfect fall weather, and the outside colors were vibrant. Cyndi breathed deeply of the autumn aroma and tried to quiet the pounding of her heart. She paused, appreciating the beauty of the yellow-gold sugar maples, the foliage of the scarlet maple, purple ash, red oak, and several other brilliant-leafed trees and bushes against the vivid autumn sky. The Victorian-style house sat primly at the end of the red tile Pathway, its new white siding sparkling like a bride with all the frosting worked in scrolls around the porch, here and there under the eaves, and in odd little places to add charm.

"Ada, you look just like a gorgeous autumn flower… or better yet, a sparkling jewel. Honey, you blend in so-o-o well." She complimented her sister, who waited patiently for her on the streamer-festooned porch. Cyndi laughed nervously. "I'm not sure I'll be able to live through this..." She wiped her shoes carefully before entering. "Oh, baby!"

"Oh no, you don't!" Ada grabbed her arm as Cyndi was about to back out the door and flee to the safety of her vehicle. "Just where do you think you are off to?"

Cyndi's mouth opened then closed, then opened again before words would squeak out. "Ada—I...I, well, this is just like a fairy... Ada... I don't think I belong here." She shook her head. She gazed up at the high ceilings emphasized by dark mahogany beams. The fresh paint smell had been replaced by the odors of simmering potpourri, fresh flowers, and sumptuous food.

Cyndi stood looking around. The autumn colors were reflected in the decorations throughout the house, and everything sparkled from the windowpanes to the antique chandeliers. The lace curtains were like frosting on the cake, which complimented the house full of antiques.

"Cyndi?" Ada came back into the room on an errand. "What are you still standing here for?"

"Weddings always make me cry, baby." Cyndi dabbed her eyes and sniffled softly. "This is so wonderful. I just can't..."

"Well, come on up and see the bride." Ada grabbed her hand, and they dodged around the bustling activity downstairs. "This is only the setting. What's upstairs is even more unbelievable." Ada pulled her along.

"Careful, Ada, these heels...It can't be any better than...oh my—" She gasped as she stood in the doorway. "How wonderful! I... oh, Ada, baby..." Cyndi was overcome as she stared at Ruth, who was seated at a vanity with a long mirror flanked by two large, elaborate dressing tables that stood a little higher than the knee. The contents of the half-opened vanity drawers spilled every sort of thing a woman could desire in dressing for this event. Ruth sat wrapped in silk and lace as Laura and Donna worked to pull the sides of her auburn hair into a soft roll secured on each side of her head. Then they accentuated the rolls with tiny flowers.

"Here, here, now," Ada encouraged Lewis and Donna's twins, Naomi and Johanna, to sit still.

"Let me help." Cyndi began to tuck in a few pins to hold the wild black mane in place.

"These two are the flower girls." Ada bent her head toward Cyndi. "However, they are just the right age that they have ideas about what that means—and they aren't afraid to express those ideas." She winked at Cyndi, and then spoke to the little pair. "I'll hold the mirror and you two watch as Aunt Cyndi puts some pretty flowers in your hair. Just sit carefully," she cautioned as she held the mirror just so while the girls with little round mouths peered intently enthralled at their reflections.

Cyndi snickered while watching Ada's knack for encouraging the little imps into proper behavior. With her powers of persuasion, they sat just long enough for Cyndi to bring a semblance of order to their black curls. Their big, brown eyes so like their mother's were accentuated by floral headbands of vivid autumn colors.

Mrs. MacDonald resembled a mother cat watching her kittens at play. There were two rooms with a common door. From where she sat, she could oversee the activities of both rooms. Ruth and Amanda smiled at each other in the mirror as the well-wishers continued their work, and the orderly uproar continued throughout the rooms.

PAT O'BRIEN WAITED to be seated, watching from close to the entry door as others were shown to their places. It wouldn't be a huge gathering, but his large party room would be full of the important people from Ruth's life. From Laura and Lewis's oldest children to their youngest, every child in the family had a part in the wedding. Pat chuckled as he watched Donna, Lewis' wife, giving her twins last-minute instructions. The twins appeared to understand the solemnity of the ceremony, and they, in turn, instructed Laura's son, Noah, just how to proceed as ring bearer.

He sighed noticing Mai, dressed in traditional Japanese clothing, looking like a miniature doll standing at the bottom of the stairs by her cousin David, both of them ready to lift Ruth's long lace train off the floor.

"Well, here goes." He smiled at one of Lewis' boys. Mark ushered Pat slowly down the aisle between the rows of chairs, showing him to the second row to his seat of honor.

The guests hushed as Michael's brother, Peter, began singing in his beautiful tenor voice then Anna joined him. Mr. MacDonald as the officiant, led Michael and his best man, followed by the grooms-men, out of the small room on the right of the altar. Noah, the little ring bearer, brought the pillow with the rings solemnly down the aisle, trailed by the two flower girls showering the carpet with petals.

The singing continued as Ruth, a lovely vision in satin and lace, descended the huge, ornate staircase. So many memories flooded Pat O'Brien's mind as his granddaughter crossed to where the portrait of his beloved Priscilla hung. Ruth placed a small bouquet under the portrait.

He sighed, remembering the day his beautiful bride had worn that same gown. Why was it women were allowed to weep at weddings and not men also? He knew, however, he could not have chosen a more perfect ambassador to tie the past to the future. Just a few steps to Ruth's left on the other side of the door hung a portrait of her mother, and she placed a bouquet under that portrait as well.

Her small tokens of remembrance accomplished, she turned ever so carefully, smiled, and bent to place a gentle kiss on Mai's cheek. David handed Ruth the large bouquet that she would carry, and then he carefully picked up the other corner of the train to help Mai support it.

Jack O'Brien watched the graceful form of his daughter, who was so like him and yet so like her mother and grandmother. His face reflected his joy and pride at what a beautiful young lady she was. Genuinely pure and good on the inside where God looked.

When Ruth in her gown and veil moved along to his side, he held out his arm, and she lightly placed her gloved hand in its crook. They both stood a moment looking to the past and how far they had traveled to arrive at this moment.

Ruth looked up at his dear, familiar face that was tanned by the sun and wind with its laugh lines. *When had he grown older? His hair is beginning to turn white at the temples.*

As he returned her gaze, she smiled softly. "Thanks, Dad." They began the journey down the aisle where he would give her hand to another.

Michael sympathized with Jacob who loved Rachel so intensely he agreed to serve seven years for her hand in marriage. As Ruth and her father came ever closer, his emotions wildly assaulted his senses. That first attempt at asking Ruth to marry him felt like a lifetime ago. Now here he stood on the brink of becoming the man of his own household, with his own wife to care for and somewhere in the future, God willing, children to provide for. Yes, it had been a long time coming.

The measured steps of the bride and her escort seemed to calm the thumping of his heart. He watched them continue their slow steps to where the assembled group awaited them in front of the flowers that formed the altar where the bride and groom would exchange their vows.

Mr. MacDonald gazed at the lovely bride in her gown and veil of lace, and Michael standing tall in his white tuxedo. The attendants arrayed in vivid colors were like jewels adorning pearls. Even the children performed their duties in a solemn, dignified manner. Mr. Mac-Donald knew life was not finished with the pair before him. Prayerfully, the rocky road would smooth out.

Michael and Ruth expectantly waited and watched, knowing that this was the second most important decision they would ever make in their lives. This was a beginning and an end.

"Who gives this young woman in marriage?" Mr. MacDonald asked.

"Her mother and I," came Jack's steady reply. With a brief smile at his daughter, he quietly slipped into his place as the father of the bride.

THE DAY HAD GONE TOO fast and too slow. Michael was living in a dream as they exchanged their vows and went through the ceremony. He watched entranced as she removed one dainty lace glove so that he was able to slip the matching wedding band next to her engagement ring. He had always admired her long, slender fingers, so feminine and graceful. As the rings came together, he raised her hand to his lips. Their eyes met through the veil as they waited for the final formalities to be spoken.

"I now introduce to you Mr. and Mrs. Michael MacDonald. You may kiss the bride." Mr. MacDonald turned the pair toward the assembled group.

After all they had been through, Michael wanted to hold Ruth next to his heart to protect her from any evil. Jack and Mr. MacDonald had gone in first for the rescue those few weeks ago in Guyana, but the memory of the fight against the enemy combatants was still firmly front and center in his mind. Lifting the veil gently and looking into her deep blue eyes, he noticed the hint of a blush as he bent and touched her soft lips with his.

At last. Ada sighed. *That's how it should be.*

They moved through the recessional, and after the photography session, the chairs were moved in the party room and tables were added for the luncheon. Guests were treated to a tour of the new paths and landscaping as the musicians began playing first on the porch. They all returned inside after the tables were set up and the room was made ready for guests to eat their meal.

Ada was only slightly disappointed when Ruth threw her bouquet and Anna was the one to catch it.

Pat O'Brien called for quiet. "An occasion like this calls for a toast," he declared.

"I propose a toast to a long life, a happy marriage, and may these young people be blessed with many little folks to sit at their table." Raising his glass in the direction of the newlyweds, he drank the punch in one motion then threw his glass on the hearth so that it shattered into many pieces.

"May your happiness be like the pieces of this glass—" Pat O'Brien continued his blessing. "—Some in large pieces, some in small, but impossible in a lifetime to gather them all." And there was a hearty cry of "Amen."

"Say, pardner, when will you be ridin' off into the sunset?" Seth asked Michael.

"Dad has made arrangements with Uncle Hugh." Michael looked at his watch. "We're heading out as soon as Ruth changes into a traveling outfit. We'll drive a few hours to our hotel and stay the night. And drive on east to the cabin. We're supposed to stay there a couple of weeks, but I don't know. —There's no place like home. There's just no place like home."

"That's exactly right." Joshua sighed and turned.

The group chorused, "Here she comes! Here she comes!"

As Ruth swept down the steps in her traveling attire, the line of well-wishers formed beside the route to Michael's silver bullet that awaited the couple. Michael grasped Ruth's arm as they hurried to her side of the car through the shower of flower petals. After helping her in and closing the door, he scuttled to his side, and with a general wave, slipped into his seat. As the tin cans and shoes clamored behind them, the silver car slid out of the driveway and sped off toward the setting sun.

"Isn't that just like in the movies?" Seth elbowed Joshua.

"What's that, kid?"

"The cowboy always gets the girl, and they ride off into the sunset."

"But it was sure a long time coming."

"Sure was. Say, let's go help clean up. I bet there's still food in there, Jo."

"And there's always tomorrow, kid." Joshua gently hugged Mai then took her hand and flung the other arm over Seth's shoulder. They turned to walk back into the brightly lit house, which sparkled against the silhouette of the pine trees.

"Yeah, always tomorrow, Jo," Seth repeated with a sigh.

List of Characters for All My Tomorrows

Lewis MacDonald (aka Lewis, Mr. M., Mac, Mr. MacDonald): Patriarch of the MacDonald clan

Amanda MacDonald (aka Ahmanda, Mrs. M., Mrs. MacDonald): Matriarch of the MacDonald clan

John O'Brien (aka Jack O'Brien/Jack (wife Diana, deceased)): Ruth & Rueben's father, son of Pat

Pat O'Brien: aka Grandpa O'Brien (wife Priscilla/Prissy, deceased): Ruth & Rueben's grandpa

Ruth O'Brien: neighbor of the MacDonalds who comes to live with them after her mother dies.

Reuben O'Brien: Ruth O'Brien's brother

<u>MacDonald children</u>:

Laura, husband **Juan Alvarez-Gonzales** – children: **Beth, Richard, Aaron, Lydia, Noah** (first husband **Lyle**-deceased)

Lewis Jr., wife **Donn**a – children: **Mark, David, Nathaniel,** twins **Naomi/Johanna**

James (deceased) wife **Lily**

Sara, husband-**Bob** – children: **Margaret, Emily, Annabel**

Peter, wife **Judith** – daughter: **Mary**

Rachael, husband **Lance** – children: **Debra, Rebecca, Adam, Neil**

Joshua, wife **Junko** – daughter: **Mai** (**Saiko** is Junko's brother)

Seth, wife **Gwen** – daughter: **Zoe-Junko** (**Alice O'Rourke**, Gwen's mother)

Anna, not married

Michael, not married

<u>Other Characters</u>

Charlie Anderson (son **Chuck**): friend and cohort to **Pat O'Brien**, friend and neighbor of the O'Briens

Becky: waitress from Mom and Pop's – friend to Ruth and Reuben

Nathaniel Crowl: Michael's college friend and later one of the missionary team members

Edwardo and Juanita: Juan's loyal 'hired' help from his family's estate, like family

Brother Matthew Wilson: worked with the congregation in summer visits on occasion (wife Maria, daughter Hannah, son Daniel)

Ralph: groundskeeper from Gwen's eastern estate;

Gerald: Gwen's butler from same estate

Ada Christianson (snag in stream of life) & her sister **Cyndi** (just wants her little sister to be happy): farm neighbors

Maria Gohmer: Mr. MacDonald's friend and beneficiary from long ago.

Felix and Armando: sons of Maria Gohmer

John: compadre of Felix and Armando

Missionary Team

Doctor Dan Spears, Eileen Williams, Raymond and Mary Sewart, Davis Brown, Don Simons, Doctor Kenneth Grunn and wife Doctor Margo Grunn, Robin Beech, Kathleen Atkins, Nathaniel Crowl

Don't miss out!

Visit the website below and you can sign up to receive emails whenever Donevy Westphal publishes a new book. There's no charge and no obligation.

https://books2read.com/r/B-A-TENK-CXXYB

BOOKS2READ

Connecting independent readers to independent writers.

www.ingramcontent.com/pod-product-compliance
Lightning Source LLC
Chambersburg PA
CBHW061554190726
48288CB00007B/2030